DEDICATION

For the generous friends who read my stories,
especially Margaret, Harriet and Anne Marie..

Marheh of the Silberay No.7

Mentor on the Water Road

Book 1: Darkness over Deerford

by

Rosalind Kentwell

L'Optimisme

Melbourne, Australia

Marheh of the Silberay Series

ACKNOWLEDGMENTS

It is high time that I acknowledged the kindness and generosity of the canal community at Braunston Marina who shared their knowledge and experience with me and enabled me to fulfill my dream of living and traveling on a canal boat, not to mention writing authentically about the life on the "water road".

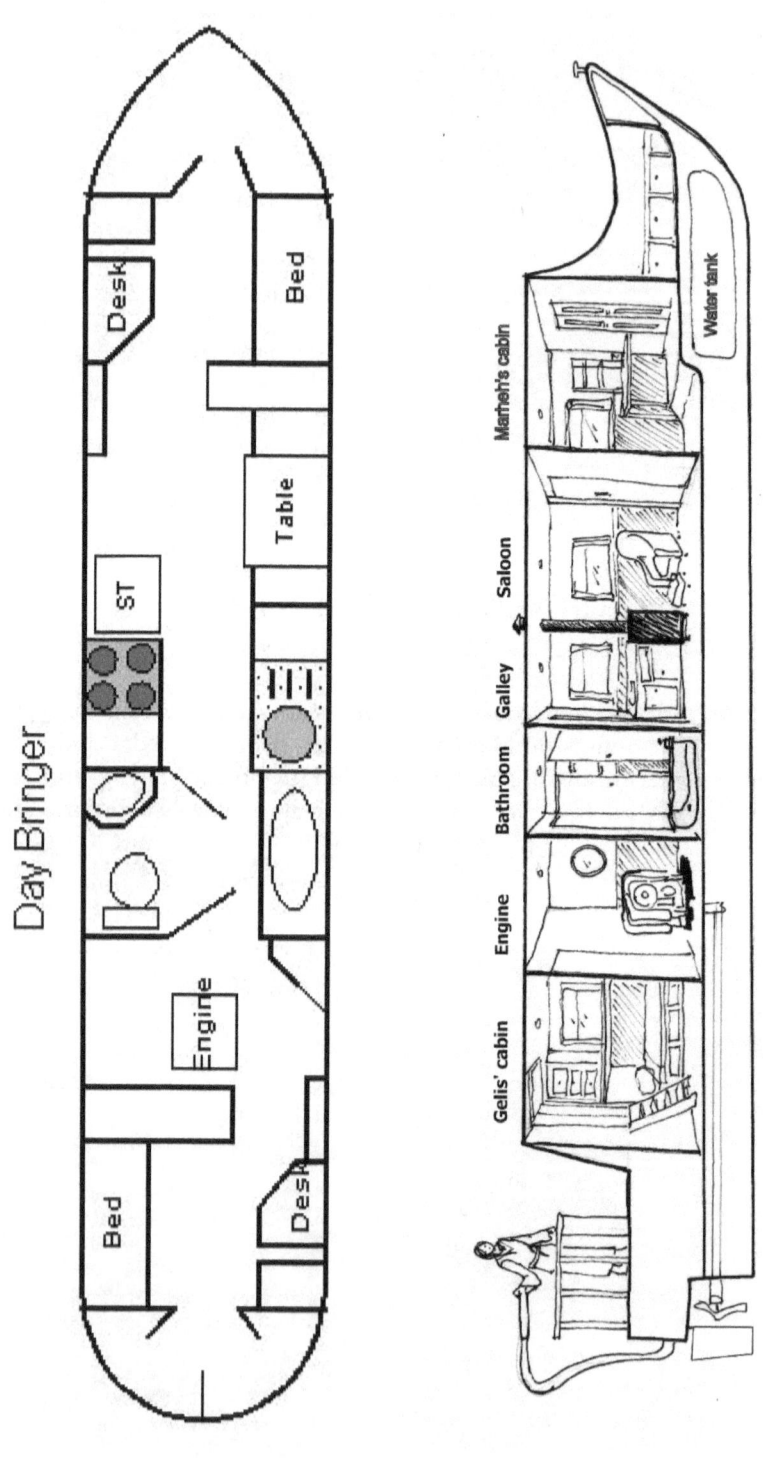

Day Bringer

Mail

PROLOGUE

There were three letters in Marheh's lap. She had just collected them from the post office in Market Mondborough. Now she sat in the well deck of her boat, *Day Bringer*, turning them over, postponing the moment when she would open them.

One she knew by the writing. Her sister-in-law, Fali, was her chief correspondent. Almost always, when she called at whatever post office she had designated, she would find a friendly note telling her about the family, her brothers, her nephews, nieces and now, great nieces.

It had always been her mother who kept her in touch, but Greya died two years ago and Fali had taken over the role. She was the wife of Tep, the youngest of Marheh's three brothers and the one who had taken over the family pottery after Marheh's father died.

Fali's letters were always cheerful and positive and Marheh was grateful for the thoughtfulness that prompted them though she still found it hard to think of the pottery without her parents. She would leave Fali's letter until last, she decided, secure in the knowledge that whatever the other two letters held, Fali's would hold love and comfort.

The second letter was from her Uncle Jik, retired now, well over ninety and living at the Harbour. He was Silberay and her first teacher, when, as a small child, she had demonstrated that she could see the water road. He loved her and knew her very well. Sometimes both the love and the knowledge combined to challenge her out of what was comfortable.

The third letter was from the Harbour Master, at least, so she assumed, since that was on the return address. That was the one she was reluctant to open. Letters from the Harbour Master never, in her experience, held good news. What was being asked of her that could not wait until the next Gathering, only three months hence?

There was not much point in procrastinating. She eased open the envelope and pulled out the single, folded sheet.

Dear Marheh, she read,

We have an applicant who wishes to become apprenticed to the Silberay and, since you will be seventy next Gathering, I am suggesting that you become her mentor. She came for an interview and I found her pleasant and well informed. Her name is Gelis (that is G as in guest). I believe you will be well suited.

Congratulations on reaching this next step in your life as Silberay

Warm regards

Yarla.

"But I don't want an apprentice," Marheh said aloud, as firmly as if her words could reach the Harbour.

Becoming a mentor was a responsibility she didn't want. It would mean changing her whole way of life. Surely there was someone else who could take a pleasant young woman called Gelis and be happy to have the opportunity. They had not been overrun with applicants in recent years. She wasn't seventy yet anyway and she didn't feel seventy. She felt much too young to be a mentor. She would write and refuse.

She tore open Jik's letter, wanting something else to think about.

Dear Niece, he wrote. His hand writing was very shaky now and she felt a small sadness at the sight. His words were not shaky however and a minute later she wanted to screw up the letter and throw it into the fire.

Yarla tells me she has written to offer you the opportunity to become a mentor. Knowing you as I do, I can imagine you wanting to refuse this challenge. Please think very carefully before you make any decision. You have a great deal to offer any apprentice, and the opportunity is not likely to be given you again. I am well aware that taking an apprentice will change the way you live now, but you have never, to my knowledge, refused a challenge, and I will be sad and a bit disappointed if you refuse this one.

Your loving uncle,

Jik.

She put the letter down with deliberate care and drew a deep breath. What would he know? she thought at first, but of course he did know. He had been a mentor. She wasn't like him, not loving or understanding, not patient. She would be no good at it and she didn't want to have to try. It was too hard and she didn't want to think about it now.

She opened Fali's letter, wanting something ordinary to take her thoughts.

Dear Marheh, she read,

Congratulations. I heard from Jik that you are to be a mentor. What a lucky girl your apprentice will be.

Silver in the moonlight,
Ribbon of water laid out before me
Enticing
Enhancing
Life.

Gelis

CHAPTER ONE

Today I, Gelis, joined the Silberay – the water road.

I have chosen and there is no going back. Despite the solitude, hardship even perhaps, I can only look to the beauty and the active pursuit of good that draws me toward the life of the Silberay. There was no fanfare as I commenced my apprenticeship, only the brief ceremony of commitment to the Silberay, and to my mentor and teacher Marheh. That too is a life commitment. For as long as Marheh lives, she will guide and teach me and I will perform those tasks that her increasing age and frailty find a burden.

Gelis sat back and looked at what she had written then picked up her pen again.

That's the theory, but right now age seems irrelevant when I look at her. Yes, she has grey hair. It hangs in a thick plait down her back, almost to her waist. I suppose her face has a few wrinkles, but what you notice are her amazing dark eyes. I think she is beautiful, though it seems odd to say that about a woman of seventy. We don't know each other very well yet, of course, and although she is kind she sometimes seems a bit remote. I think there is something worrying her actually, something to do with the small numbers at the Gathering. I must admit I was surprised. At my interview with the Harbour Master I was told there were about sixty boats, but less than thirty arrived for the Gathering.

She put her pen down again and looked up at the sound of footsteps on the dock and the feel of the boat moving as someone boarded. Then the doors from the back deck swung open. Marheh was silhouetted against the sky for a moment or two then she came swiftly down the steps and into the cabin.

"I'm sorry to burst in on you," she said, rather abruptly. "I'm not used to the new arrangement yet and this cabin is always a bit of a thoroughfare when we are under way."

"Are we...?" Gelis began.

"Yes, as soon as the water tank has filled. About five minutes. Can you be ready?"

Gelis nodded.

"I'll explain a bit more once we are moving, but for now, perhaps you could watch the water while I do the engine checks. Come and I'll show you."

Marheh took the steps two at a time and was out on the dock heading for the well deck almost before Gelis had extricated herself from the little desk where she sat.

"We have to come here to the loading dock for water now. There used to be taps on the gantries but the pipes froze in winter and the maintenance was too expensive to continue," she explained when Gelis reached her. "Just turn off the tap when you see the water then put the cap back on and coil up the hose. Try to keep the end of the hose clean so it doesn't contaminate our water supply. Can you manage that?"

Gelis nodded.

"Yes, I think so."

Marheh turned to go but stopped as Gelis called to her.

"The hose, is it yours or does it stay here?"

"Good question," Marheh said and Gelis saw her take a breath and change gear. "I'm sorry, I'm going too fast and it isn't fair on you. The hose is ours and lives in the locker in the well deck."

She came back to show Gelis which of the lockers she meant.

"Just as well you asked. We would have been in trouble if we'd left it behind."

Five minutes was all it took. Gelis heard the engine start up as she was coiling the hose and by the time she had stowed it in the appropriate locker Marheh was back to show her what to do with the front line. She felt a bit clumsy and awkward beside her, but when she had completed her task and made her way along the gunnel to the back deck Marheh smiled and thanked her.

"We wouldn't normally be setting out so late in the day, but things have been a bit unusual this Gathering. Go down and grab a coat if you're cold. When I've negotiated the bridge out of the Harbour I'll explain if I can."

"I'm not cold," Gelis said, wanting to watch how Marheh navigated through the Harbour and angled *Day Bringer* to make it easier for her to make the turn under the bridge and out onto the water road. Steering was a bit of a mystery to her although Marheh made it look so easy.

5

There were a few minutes of silence even once they had left the Harbour. Gelis looked around curiously seeing the back of houses on one side and fields on the other. They were heading north and the late afternoon sun was casting long shadows from the houses and catching the tops of trees and chimneys. It did seem rather late to be starting a journey and although the spring day had been fine and sunny it was beginning to get chilly now. She looked at Marheh and caught a moment of sadness before the smile that lit her face and welcomed Gelis into her world.

"You must be wondering what's going on," she said. "I don't know what Yarla told you at your interview, or what you expected of your first Gathering, but it isn't normally like this."

"I did think there would be more boats," Gelis said. "And Yarla said the Gathering was three weeks, with classes and celebrations."

Marheh nodded.

"And instead there have been no celebrations, few classes and less than two weeks for us to get used to each other."

She paused to smile at Gelis.

"It isn't fair on you really, but we couldn't celebrate with more than half our number missing. Except for me, most of the boats that had a northern route have not returned. I came in early so *Day Bringer* could be modified for me to take an apprentice so you've done me a good turn already. Now it is my job, our job, to go looking for them." She turned to look at Gelis. "And that is not fair to you either because there are likely to be difficulties you have not had time to learn about. I'll try not to go too fast."

She paused, moved the tiller to take a gentle curve in the water road then looked back at Gelis.

"And Gelis," she said. "I will do my very best not to take you into danger, but I can't even promise that."

A moment of solemnity for Gelis to take this in then she changed key again to become matter of fact and practical.

"We will have enough daylight to keep going for about two hours. If you like to stay up here with me I will try to answer any questions and tell you what I know about our job, but you are welcome to go below if you are cold or need to unpack."

"I will go down for my coat," Gelis said. "But I'd like to come back just to look at the landscape and listen to whatever you can tell me, if that is alright."

"Of course it's alright. That's what I'm here for."

The two hours seemed to fly past. They reached the entrance to the section of the water road called the Western Edgerington and Gracedale, or the WEG for short, just on dusk.

"We'll moor here," Marheh explained. "Part of me wants to keep going, but if there was ever a time for rushing, that time is past now. Better we act sensibly and think and plan."

She steered into the bank and stepped off with her centre line. Gelis followed her.

"Here, you can hold this while I look after the mooring pins. Tomorrow I'll show you how to help."

It was good to be down in the warm even if she did feel a bit useless. Marheh had everything done while she was still taking it all in, but she seemed to understand. Supper was a big pot of soup that had been keeping warm on the edge of *Day Bringer*'s fire. There was bread and cheese too, and Marheh showed her where to find cutlery and plates and suggested she set the table which made her feel better.

"You'll soon get used to things," Marheh said when they were sitting at the table with their soup. "Just tell me to slow down if I go too fast."

Gelis looked up and managed a little grin at that. Marheh laughed.

"I see, you won't will you?"

It was not until they had finished eating that she spoke again of the journey ahead.

"My mentor would never let me speak of problems while we were eating," she explained. "And I think that is probably a good rule. We'll make space at meal time to get to know each other and share the good things."

She fell silent for a few moments. Gelis wondered what she was thinking. The look of sadness appeared again then she seemed to gather herself and return to practicalities.

"I'd like to give you some regular jobs," she said. "Things that will help us on our way, and I'll teach you about mooring and locks as we come to them. Perhaps you can think about what might suit you to take on. Once you get used to the stove we might share some of the cooking. I've never been much good at that."

She gave Gelis a smile that held a hint of self mockery but quickly sobered again.

7

"The important thing now though is to start you on the soul song. Did anyone speak of that in the classes you did have?"

"Someone called Briz spoke to us about the disciplines, but I didn't understand all of it. It was in a group with three other apprentices who were all ahead of me. He apologised to me afterwards and said that you would teach me more than he ever could. Yarla gave me a copy of *A Brief History of the Silberay* and that helped a bit."

Marheh nodded thoughtfully.

"So really we need to start from the beginning."

"I think that would be best, but it doesn't have to be now if you are tired."

Marheh laughed at that.

"I know I must seem very old to you but I'm not decrepit yet."

Gelis blushed.

"I didn't mean…"

"I know you didn't. You were just being thoughtful and I shouldn't have laughed."

She reached across the table and covered one of Gelis' hands with one of hers.

"For me the soul song, the discipline of the soul, is our most important work and especially important now when we are likely to be facing some challenges. It is first a safeguard and a guide for what is best in us and ultimately a way of healing and helping the landscape and the people in the landscape to be true to themselves. When we sing the music unsettles our enemies and those of ill intent and makes space for light and nurture. Even the beginning stages when you don't think you will ever find the way of it, even the work of trying acts beneficently."

Gelis nodded to show she was listening and Marheh smiled at her earnest face.

"To begin with you need to find your portal. It's different for each of us. Perhaps I should have said it needs to find you, but you need to make space for it and the best way of doing that is to hold in your mind things that are especially beautiful for you, or especially full of meaning. Gradually the one particular thing will emerge. Shall we try?"

Gelis nodded again.

"Don't try too hard, let it happen," Marheh said, and closed her eyes to reach for her own portal.

She would not enter, not now, but hover beside Gelis as she made her first attempts. Although it had been easy and natural for her, she was aware that some struggled to identify their portal. Nemle, her mentor, had been able to guide her, but she didn't feel she knew Gelis well enough for that. She remembered Jik telling her that his apprentice, Dom, had struggled for more than a year until Jik had encouraged him to think of the work he loved and he had found that contemplating the work of the yeast in his baking had allowed him to enter.

Dom was one of those who had not returned for the Gathering, along with so many of the others; Bixa and her apprentice, Whin and his, Tippa, Pon, Lidy and, more important to her than all the others, her soul friend Kel and his apprentice.

Best not think of them now when she was supposed to be concentrating on her apprentice and her approach to the soul song. Resolutely she took her worry and fear for her friends, acknowledged it and lifted the candle flame that was her portal. This singing was for them as well as for Gelis. But she couldn't spend herself in singing, not yet, for the moment she must stay near her apprentice.

For a while she nurtured and encouraged the faltering attempts that she sensed beside her but gently drew the lesson to a close when she recognised the beginnings of weariness. There was no point in pushing, not in these beginning stages.

A smile and a few words of encouragement, the opportunity for Gelis to comment or ask a question and then she suggested bed.

"Such a lot of new things to think about. You'll be feeling a bit tired I expect."

"Not really," Gelis said, then yawned widely.

Marheh laughed.

"Not?"

"Only a bit." She grinned. "I could at least do the dishes first."

"Not tonight," Marheh said. "There will be plenty of other opportunities. I'd like to get away early tomorrow, alright?"

When she had gone, shutting the door between the galley and the bathroom behind her, Marheh stood for a minute looking around, collecting herself. Not much more than a month ago the cabin that now belonged to Gelis had been hers, the space in the bow had been her work area with shelves, bins for her clay and a solid work bench. All that was gone now, replaced by the new cabin that felt so strange and unhomelike. How could the years

9

have gone so fast? She didn't feel like an old woman, but others would see her like that. She shrugged and began to gather the few dishes from the table. Her song was not old. She would wash up then sing for the missing Silberay. They would be singing. Nothing would prevent that no matter what had happened to them. If she could join their song it would help her to understand, show her where to begin looking.

She spun her golden thread of sound pushing her melody further and further searching for other singers, harmonies to play upon, melodies to complement hers, but found only emptiness.

Disheartened she put herself reluctantly to bed in her new cabin, trying not to look back regretfully, not yet able to welcome the changes and needing to struggle not to resent them. Once under the covers she sent her mind searching for the communication she had so often shared with Kel, but her mind had no more success than her soul. It had been so long now, nearly a month since they had practised together, sharing themselves mind to mind, testing and honing their abilities in the discipline of the mind. Normally they connected nearly every other day. Where had he been that last time? Had he shared anything that would give her a direction? She buried her face in her pillow trying not to give in to the tears that threatened, the sense of desolation that seemed intent on undermining her, but it was a long time before she slept.

Next morning they were up at first light and away after a breakfast of porridge and toast. This time Marheh accepted Gelis' offer to wash up, but spent a few minutes first showing her how she could help their departure by taking responsibility for the front line. She could tackle the dishes once they were on their way. Yesterday's spring sunshine had disappeared and the morning was cold and cloudy with rain threatening.

Her half hour alone at the tiller had provided consolation of a sort and thinking time, so that when Gelis came out to join her Marheh was able to welcome her with a smile.

"Thank you for doing that. It's a great help if everything is put away when we are under way." She paused and smiled again. "Or even if we're not. In my first week as an apprentice I managed to break rather a lot of our crockery because I left it to drain instead of drying it and putting it away. It was an accident, but Nemle, my mentor was not impressed."

"I don't mind doing it. It's good to feel useful."

Marheh nodded.

"It is, isn't it?"

She paused to concentrate on her approach to a bridge hole. The wind had got up a bit, pushing the bow sideways. Gelis watched silently until they were through.

"Does the wind make steering more difficult?" she asked then.

Marheh nodded.

"Just a bit. You have to compensate and steer into it. Not the best day to learn. I'll let you try on the next calm day though. I promise."

Gelis beamed.

"I'd like that."

For as long as the rain held off Gelis kept Marheh company on the back deck. Marheh pointed out landmarks they passed and named some of the creatures, the water vole, the kingfisher, the grebe and the heron. However, when the rain came down in earnest Marheh sent her below.

"No point in both of us getting wet."

"But what about you?"

"I won't melt."

"Can't you stop?"

"I'll have a break at lunch time. I'll let you know in time for you to help moor up."

"Can I do anything towards lunch?"

"I thought we could finish off the soup. Is that all right for you?"

"Yes, of course."

"Go, go on."

Looking back, obviously a bit reluctant, Gelis let herself into her cabin and closed the doors behind her. Marheh looked up at the sky, felt the rain on her face and gave herself to the landscape and the solitude.

Two hours later it was still raining. Lunch ought perhaps be a priority now, although if she had really been alone she would probably have kept on going. If she went in and dried off it would be harder to give herself again to the rain but it would be a good five hours before they reached the place she planned for the night's mooring and foolish to think she could continue so long. Worry for Kel must be kept separate and not permitted to make her behave irrationally when what she needed was to be focussed, to plan and be sensible.

The sky was looking a little lighter and the rain seemed to be easing so she called Gelis and explained how she could help, smiling a little at her eagerness. When she was standing ready at the prow, the front line in one hand, a mooring pin in the other and the mallet tucked into her belt Marheh eased *Day Bringer* towards the bank.

"Wait until you feel the boat touch," she said, and she could see Gelis almost quivering with anticipation as she stood poised.

Her enthusiastic leap landed her squarely on the bank, but served to push the prow out again. Marheh eased back the throttle and stepped off with the centre line as the stern touched. It would have been so easy to do it all herself as she had for the past thirty years and more, but she managed to restrain herself and wait as Gelis hammered in her mooring pin, wound her line around it and took it back to the prow, finishing with the knot she had been taught at the Gathering. She looked anxiously at Marheh then.

"Well done. Would you like to tackle the stern now?"

When mooring was complete Marheh coiled the centre line and put it back on the roof before inspecting the work.

"You probably don't need to tie up quite so tightly. Sometimes a bit of give is helpful, but you've done well. Let's go in and have lunch. If we're lucky the sun might even come out while we're eating."

It didn't, but at least the rain eased until it was no more than a heavy mist. After she had done the lunch dishes Gelis came out in her water proof coat and stood beside Marheh who would really have preferred to be alone. She would not let her suspect that however but welcomed her with a smile and told her about the Rook Tree, where she planned to moor for the night and answered her tentative questions patiently. The question she couldn't answer, for herself any more than for Gelis, was the one that asked where they were going. North, was all the answer she could give, and to herself she added, north until I find him.

They reached the Rook Tree by tea time and Gelis had a second chance to practise tying up. Then Marheh showed her how to remove the tiller arm and where to stow it and explained the function of the stern tube greaser. After tea there was time for another try at the discipline of the soul then a demonstration of the best way of damping down the fire so it would stay in all night.

Gelis was an eager and intelligent learner but by the time they parted for the evening Marheh thought she had never felt so tired in her life.

Next day was much the same, damp and dreary with a chilly wind. Gelis began to relax a bit with the front line and also in the galley where she spent the afternoon preparing a casserole for their supper. Marheh had suggested it, knowing the meat would not keep much longer. She had set a target for the day's journey but the weather was hindering their progress and dusk came before she expected it. She would perhaps have continued as long as she could see ahead but suddenly as they rounded a bend, she almost ran into a tree lying across the water road. A quick burst of reverse slowed *Day Bringer* enough to keep her from any damage although the prow was buried in foliage.

Gelis felt the change in *Day Bringer*'s forward motion and popped up from her cabin to see what was happening.

"It's too dark to tackle this tonight," Marheh said, pointing out the obstacle. "I'll back up a bit and we'll moor. Will you take the front line?"

Gelis sidled along the gunnel as Marheh reversed *Day Bringer* out of the mass of foliage and back a dozen yards or so before angling in to the bank.

"Be careful," she called. "It will be slippery after all the rain. Wait until we touch."

Gelis waited as instructed then jumped off into the mud holding the line. It was slippery and muddy, very muddy. She began to hammer in her mooring pin but found herself sinking into the mud. She would need to find firmer ground, she thought, pulling out the pin and trying to take a step further onto the bank. Her left foot seemed to be held fast. Her right foot would not move either and now she was sinking. Don't be silly, she thought, trying again to extract her left foot from the gluey substance.

All that happened was the further subsidence of her right foot and suddenly she was trapped and sinking fast, past her knees, her thighs. In panic she called out to Marheh for help, twisting her torso around to look at her and beseech with her eyes.

Marheh stood on the back deck watching her, a dark, almost ominous figure in the gloom of the evening. Gelis whimpered, fear closing her to any communication. Still Marheh watched, her gaze focused and intense. Keep looking at me. Keep hold of the rope. Keep looking at me. Keep hold of the rope. The words repeated themselves in Gelis' mind until she heard them, then they changed. Keep looking at me. Keep hold of the rope. Step towards me.

"I can't," Gelis' voice was a sob.

"Look at me, believe me, you can."

The words might have been spoken aloud, or perhaps not.

"Look at me, keep looking at me, step towards me."

13

Longing to believe Gelis shuffled one foot forward. There was no resistance. Almost she looked down in surprise but heard again the sharp command. Keep looking at me. Step towards me. The other foot shuffled to turn her around to face *Day Bringer*. A step, then another step and she touched the hull, touched and clung. A moment later she had half climbed, half fallen into the well deck and Marheh was there to hold her as she sobbed her relief.

A few minutes in Marheh's comforting embrace and she began to recover.

"You're safe now, come into the warm."

"I'll make everything dirty."

"Will you?"

Marheh's question surprised her and she looked down at her legs to find her boots and trousers no different than they had been all day.

"But…"

Tears threatened again. Marheh gave her a little shake.

"It was an illusion. Come inside and I'll explain."

She pulled her to her feet, guided her through her cabin and pushed her gently into the armchair.

"Stay there while I look after *Day Bringer*. I won't be long."

Gelis had barely registered the sound of mallet on mooring pin followed by the cessation of engine noise when Marheh was back.

"Stay there," she said, when Gelis began to get out of the armchair. "I'll make sperit. I know how frightening a Yareblis illusion can be. Just relax."

The warmth and safety, the comfortable chair and Marheh's care of her worked to help her recover. Marheh moved quietly around her checking the casserole and setting the table for supper and she had time to think and wonder.

She had been so frightened, terrified, sinking into quick sand where she would suffocate, but here she was, clean and dry, as if it had never happened. What had Marheh done?

"I just helped you to see through the illusion," Marheh said, when Gelis asked her question.

She didn't think it could have been as easy as Marheh made it sound, since she looked drained and tired. She seemed to recover as they ate and *Day Bringer*'s warmth and comfort wrapped them in safety.

For the first part of the meal they ate in silence but the peace was healing. Gelis did not want to speak first and waited until Marheh laid down her fork and smiled across the table.

"Better?" she asked.

Gelis nodded.

"But I don't understand."

"How could you?" Marheh said. "You've probably never heard of the Yareblis, let alone experienced a Yareblis illusion."

Gelis shook her head.

"Will you clear the table and make sperit for us and I will try to marshal my thoughts for an explanation of sorts." She gave Gelis a grin. "How about that! I've made a little rhyme."

Gelis smiled back and stood up.

"I'll make sperit for us, without making a fuss."

Marheh laughed and shook her head.

"No more! Or I'll show you the door."

Gelis laughed too then gathered up their plates and took them to the galley. Marheh, watching her carefully, was pleased to see the traces of fear had gone from her face and set herself to preparing an explanation. She was very tired. It had been a long day and the effort of freeing Gelis from the illusion had drained her but Gelis was her responsibility and needed to understand.

Suddenly Gelis was setting a mug of sperit in front of her.

"I could wait until tomorrow if you're too tired," she said.

For a moment Marheh was tempted but recognised Gelis' polite concern for what it was and smiled and shook her head.

"I am tired, but not too tired, and I think it is important for you to understand."

She sipped from her mug then set it down.

"I'll start with the Yareblis. They were Silberay once and they can see the water road, but they broke away from us after the Great Debate. That happened before I was born, the year my mentor was apprenticed, one hundred years ago. The way she explained it was that the debate was about the way Silberay should use the disciplines. It seemed that some people were neglecting the discipline of the soul, thinking it was unimportant and over using the discipline of the mind in ways that went against Sila's guiding principles."

Gelis' puzzled face was enough for Marheh to stop and apologise and begin again.

"You know who Sila was?"

Gelis nodded.

"The Silberay were named for her. She was the founder. It was in the history. The Great Debate was in the history too, but I didn't really understand what it was about."

"It's the discipline of the mind that is fraught with problems," Marheh said. "The Yareblis use it to create illusions like the one that caught you and also to control people's minds. Silberay work with the discipline of the mind too, but never to control except against the Yareblis, or if our lives are threatened. We do use it to communicate between mentor and apprentice or between soul friends."

"Is that what you did, to help me?"

Marheh nodded.

"Ordinary talking wouldn't have helped because the illusion was too strong."

Gelis nodded. She had been terrified and no spoken words would have convinced her to believe she could move as Marheh had instructed.

"Will I...?" she began.

"It will be part of your learning," Marheh said. "But not yet. The discipline of the soul is first."

Again Gelis nodded. After a few minutes of silence when Marheh could almost see her processing what she had been told she looked up.

"Thank you for telling me. I'll do the dishes now, shall I?"

Obstacle

CHAPTER TWO

Next morning before they could continue they needed to tackle the obstacle across their path. Marheh was first up and attended to the fire before stepping off to examine the situation from the bank. She was just turning to go back to *Day Bringer* when she saw Gelis on the back deck, hovering anxiously.

"It's quite safe," she called. "You've beaten it once. The illusion is destroyed now. Don't let it control you."

A moment later she had gathered herself to step off and hurry towards Marheh.

"Well done. Come and look at the tree. Do you see? It has been cut deliberately to fall across the water. What better way to make sure the illusion would catch someone?"

Gelis bent to examine the cut trunk and then studied the small tree that blocked their way.

"Can we move it?"

She grasped a branch and tried to tug without much effect.

"Best to attack it from *Day Bringer* I think," Marheh said. "But we'll have breakfast first."

Worry for Kel could disable her if she let it so she was determinedly matter of fact and practical. She led the way on board and began breakfast preparation without further comment except to suggest that Gelis tidy her cabin and use the bathroom. She could have her turn while Gelis was washing up.

Twenty minutes later they were ready to move. Gelis went to the front line as she had been taught. Marheh thought the memory of the illusion still troubled her but she was dealing with it bravely and did not hesitate. She started the engine and dealt with the stern line then nodded to Gelis who had already placed the front line and mooring pin on board. She was still a bit tentative pushing out the prow but it was enough to set *Day Bringer* in the right direction. Marheh smiled at her as she edged carefully along the gunnel.

"It won't be long before it is second nature," she said.

Gelis grinned.

"You make it all seem so easy."

"I've been at it a good while."

She eased back the throttle as *Day Bringer* approached the obstacle and let the prow just nudge its way into the mass of foliage. When no further forward movement was possible she picked up the small saw she used for firewood and handed Gelis the clippers.

"I'll leave the throttle just engaged so *Day Bringer* won't drift back while we go and tackle the tree," she explained, setting off along the gunnel.

Gelis copied her on the other side and together they snipped and sawed, carving out a passage.

The tools they had were not ideal and it took quite some time before they had cleared enough away to allow *Day Bringer* to creep through. Marheh was anxious for the paint work and more anxious not to snag the propeller, but at last they were on their way again with nothing worse than a small, superficial scratch on *Day Bringer*'s hull.

"It is not always like this," Marheh said once they were clear and moving at the normal steady speed. "Usually travel is peaceful and uneventful and we can listen to the landscape as we go."

Gelis was looking at her, anxious to understand.

"The listening is linked to the singing. If we can put ourselves aside and focus on what is around us we can begin to recognise, to hear the health, the wellbeing or the pain of the places we pass through. Then we can sing, not just for our own wellbeing but to bring healing if it is needed."

It was too much, Marheh thought, seeing Gelis struggling to take in what she was hearing. She shouldn't have to care for the needs of an apprentice now when she needed all her energy for Kel and the others. It was not Gelis' fault though and her learning was important. Rushing was never helpful, certainly not now when all she knew was that the trouble was in the north. Listening was more important than ever really since that was her best hope of discovering the dark places.

Gelis was still looking at her with an anxious face and she pulled herself together to smile reassuringly.

"I know all this must be difficult for you. We'll stop for lunch in an hour or so and then we can practise singing again and try to make a plan that will give some shape to our days."

She paused, screwed up her face for a moment then continued.

"I'm learning too," she said. "So I hope you will forgive me if I get things wrong sometimes."

Gelis nodded.

"You saved me," she said.

She was very quiet for the next hour until they stopped and Marheh understood that she was thinking about what she had experienced and what she had been told.

After they had eaten she sat fiddling with her soup spoon.

"I thought it was real," she blurted out.

"It was real," Marheh said, knowing she was still worried about the illusion and her response to it. "Just a different kind of real."

"When we were going along I was remembering something that happened when I was still at school. It was sort of real and not real too."

Marheh stood and picked up their empty soup bowls to take to the sink.

"Why don't I put the kettle on for sperit and then you could tell me about it, if you want to that is."

Gelis nodded.

"I do want to. I think I might even begin to understand it if I do."

Marheh smiled at her.

"Good."

She began preparing their drinks, spooning the mixture of dried berries and spices they called sperit into their mugs ready for the boiling water. Gelis watched her, thinking about how best to tell her story.

"You said you were still at school," Marheh prompted when she seemed to be finding it difficult to begin.

"It was the start of my last year. They made us go to an adventure camp. It was supposed to be good for us and help us get motivated to study. At least, that's what they said. We had to do lots of things in teams, climbing ropes, getting over obstacles, as well as cooking and washing up. I didn't like it much."

"It wouldn't have been my sort of thing either."

Gelis flashed her a grateful smile.

"I didn't really fit at school," she explained. "It wasn't so bad when I could go home each day, but the camp was..." she hesitated. "Everyone else seemed to be enjoying themselves."

Marheh nodded sympathetically but said nothing.

"The second last day though, they gave us a map and a list of check points and we could go off in pairs or on our own. I remember waking up really early so I could go by myself."

Marheh saw her face change as she remembered.

"They'd given out the instructions and the lunch the night before so I got dressed really quietly and set off. It was a bit chilly and there was still dew on the grass but the sky was clear and I was so happy to be on my own doing something.

There was quite a steep hill through some woods first, but after about fifteen minutes I got to the top. There was a view from there, fields and trees and a few farmhouses. I had to find a stile. That was my first check point. I really like stiles. They always seem to invite you to climb over them."

Marheh laughed.

"They do too!"

Gelis grinned at her.

"Anyway, I found it and set off across a field. It was fun exploring and the check points helped me to be confident I was going the right way. I had to answer questions about some of them."

"Questions?"

"So they would know I had been there," she explained. "I remember I had to describe a drinking trough and count the windows in the front wall of a cottage. One was really sad. Near a tumble down cottage was a grave stone of a child who was only four." She paused a moment to pay tribute to the memory. "I was just getting hungry when I came to a river. It wasn't marked on the map, which surprised me, but I could see there was a bridge not too far along so I wasn't really worried. It was a nice view so I decided to stop and eat my lunch. I found a tree to lean against and put down my ground sheet although it wasn't damp any more. It wasn't very nice, the lunch, but I didn't care. It was just good to be there on my own enjoying the view. Then I heard voices. I kept very still because I didn't want anyone to see me. It was two boys from school and they didn't so much as glance in my direction. I expected them to turn and make for the bridge but instead they just kept walking. It was so weird. The shorter one disappeared altogether for a few moments and I could only see the top of the other one's head. They weren't swimming, just walking, and when they came out the other side they weren't even wet."

"It was the water road," Marheh said softly. "But you didn't know it then. You must have been very confused."

"I didn't know what to think. It was a bit scary really."

"It still feels strange, even when you know what you are seeing."

Marheh's quiet comments were encouraging. She understood because she saw the same way.

"I still had a way to go so I finished my lunch and set off for the bridge. I was walking along beside the river when a boat came through the bridge. I smiled at the woman steering and she smiled back. That made me feel better. She called out something about a lovely day and I laughed and agreed with her. I was still puzzled, but it didn't seem to matter as much then."

She stopped speaking to drink from her mug. Marheh wondered briefly who the boater had been.

"That evening at the camp the games and things were locked up and we had to get in a circle and talk about our day. I didn't really want to, I don't think anyone did at the start, but CB pushed a bit and people started saying things."

21

"CB?"

"For Camp Boss, he told us to call him that."

Marheh's face must have shown something of her concern for Gelis stopped to ask what bothered her.

"I'll explain later," she said. "You finish your story first."

"I didn't say anything until he asked me directly and then I said I had seen a river and a boat. The others laughed at me. One of the girls, Melanie, said I was lying to make myself interesting and I heard one of the others say there wasn't much hope of that."

"That must have hurt."

Gelis nodded.

"It was hard not to cry. I was glad there was not much light."

Marheh put a hand over one of hers and gave it a little squeeze.

"CB unlocked the games cupboard then and when they were all playing he came over to me. He said he had seen the river and the walk was a test and I was the only one who passed. He made me feel proud and a bit important but a bit uncomfortable as well."

She looked into her mug and found it empty.

"The next morning he made me have breakfast with him. There were pancakes with syrup and hot chocolate, not a bit what the others were having. I liked it, but it was very sweet and sticky and made me feel a bit sick after. He kept telling me I was special and I could have power and pay the others back for being unkind."

"Nothing much has changed then," Marheh said. "I'll tell you my experience later."

Gelis smiled.

"It is so good to tell someone who understands," she said. "I couldn't help thinking of Melanie and how she was always putting me down. The idea of having power to pay her back made me feel excited, but not in a nice way. He kept saying he could show me how to get even and part of me wanted to say yes, but part of me knew it would be wrong. I couldn't say no, even though I knew I should. I just thanked him for the breakfast and ran away."

Marheh was nodded thoughtfully.

"That was brave."

Gelis shook her head.

"It wasn't enough. Later, when we were doing timed circuits of the obstacle course he came up to me again. I'd already done my circuit so I was just watching, not very interested, while other people did theirs. Melanie was watching too and making unkind comments to her two friends. She was good at sporting things and really scorned people like me who weren't. I thought how good it would be if she just talked nonsense instead of making nasty comments, then suddenly that was what was happening. I thought at first it served her right and that I had every right to do it, but then she looked at me and I saw she was really frightened. It made me feel awful. I tried to say no, I didn't want it. I did say it and her babble stopped but then it was CB in my head. I knew it was him telling me off even though he wasn't speaking out loud."

Again Marheh reached out to touch her as she saw her struggle with the memory.

"I ran away. When everyone was watching one of the really athletic boys doing the circuit I kind of drifted until I could run without them seeing. I ran and ran and I was crying. Then I came to the river again and I didn't want that either. I fell on the ground running away from it. After a little bit there were footsteps and someone asked if I was alright. It was the woman who had been steering the boat and she said she had been looking for me. I didn't want to trust her at first but she was kind and just waited until I finished crying and sat with me where we could see the river and her boat and she told me about the Silberay. I thought I'd rather be like her than like the person CB wanted me to be."

"And here you are," Marheh said. "I'm glad you didn't want what CB offered. I think I'm lucky in my apprentice."

Gelis looked at her with glowing eyes.

"I'm lucky too," she said awkwardly, getting up to take their mugs to the sink.

Marheh waited to see whether she would speak again then got up too.

"Let's wash up, then we can practise the discipline of the soul. I think we've gone far enough today."

It was not until next morning when they were on their way again that Gelis reminded Marheh, rather shyly, that she had said she would tell her about her experience. It was not a very nice day, cloudy and cold with the occasional shower, and Marheh had offered her the choice of staying warm but understood her preference for being outside.

"If you're sure you're warm enough," she said smiling and shifting sideways a little so Gelis could prop herself beside her against the rail around the back deck.

There were a few moments of silence as Marheh arranged her thoughts for telling. Gelis waited, content to watch the landscape through which they were travelling. There was always something to see, a bird or a flower, a farmhouse, a horse in a field, the changing sky.

"I was like you," Marheh began. "A first year apprentice."

She went on to tell Gelis how she had pretended to be a younger girl and allowed herself to be taken to a farm where the Yareblis had established a school.

"I was very immature and much too sure of myself," she said. "But it seemed like a good idea at the time, and Nemle, my mentor, didn't try very hard to stop me. I think she knew I needed to learn the hard way."

She paused a moment to consider her approach to a bridge hole.

"Your Camp Boss, CB, reminded me straight away of the Yareblis. At the school it was SW, for Senior Woman, SM, Senior Man and SP, School Principal. The Yareblis try to avoid having names. It seems that they link knowledge of a name with having power over the person named. They don't use the soul names at all."

"Does that mean that CB was Yareblis?"

"I'm almost certain of it. He was perfectly placed to be doing a bit of recruiting and went about it in much the same way as SW did with me, indulging you with sweet food and individual attention and tempting you with the possibility of power."

She turned her head to smile warmly at Gelis.

"You did very well to resist, especially since you didn't really know what was happening."

Gelis glowed at Marheh's praise, pushed her hands deep into the pockets of her coat and looked along *Day Bringer*'s roof with determined concentration. Marheh glanced at her, smiling a little and thinking perhaps having an apprentice would not be as bad as she had feared.

"What was it like, the school?" Gelis asked. "Weren't you frightened?"

Marheh gave a short laugh.

"I didn't know enough to be frightened. Nemle tried to impress on me the need the for caution but it was not really until I got there that I began to understand what she meant. I was arrogant too and didn't want to admit to fear. I thought I knew everything and really I knew nothing."

Gelis' face showed she was sceptical of this admission and Marheh laughed again.

"What sort of apprentice do you think I was?"

"The best of course."

Marheh shook her head.

"I was nothing but trouble to poor Nemle, always thinking I knew best because my uncle was Silberay and I had grown up with family ties to the water road. I behaved so badly the first six weeks or so that one day, when I had been really rude, Nemle tucked me under her arm and spanked me."

Gelis' little gasp made her smile.

"I think Nemle hurt her hand more than she hurt my behind, but my pride was hurt. It made me think though and when I had given over crying and being angry I started to realise just how rude and childish I had been, so when she came to me and apologised and asked if we could start again I knew I had to apologise too."

Her face softened as she remembered the mentor who had loved and taught her.

"Nemle loved me through thick and thin," she said. "And I know there were times when I was a real trial to her."

"I'll try not to be a trial to you," Gelis said, looking at Marheh with more admiration than was comfortable to her.

"I expect we will both have some learning to do while we get to know each other," Marheh said. "No doubt there is good and bad in both of us. I know there is in me."

She smiled at Gelis.

"Very soon we will come to some locks. That's always fun and you will be able to help with them."

As they continued slowly along Marheh endeavoured to answer Gelis' eager questions about locks but finally told her, a bit sharply, that it would be easier to show her and that she did not have long to wait before they reached them. The hurt look Gelis tried to hide made Marheh feel guilty and she was glad to be able to point out the locks as they rounded the next bend.

"There are three, all going up, not too far apart," she explained. "We'll moor up when we get to the first one and do that together."

A few minutes later Gelis was ready to jump off with the front line. After they had moored she followed Marheh up to the big gates that held back the water. Marheh had given her a windlass and shown her how she had tucked her own into her belt so she would have both hands free.

"We can't open the gates until the lock is completely empty so the first thing we have to do is wind up the paddles that let the water out."

"But it's coming in from the other end," Gelis said, seeing the water leaking between the gates at the top of the lock.

"Not as fast as it will go out when the paddles are open."

Marheh showed Gelis how to fit her windlass onto the mechanism then walked across the closed gates to take up a similar position on the other side.

"Ready?" she said, beginning to turn her windlass.

She could make it look easy. Long experience meant that she had built up the necessary muscles as well as the knack of getting started but when she saw Gelis struggling she felt a bit ashamed of herself. Carefully locking into place the cogs that raised the paddles she crossed back to Gelis.

"It's tough isn't it? Don't jerk, try to pull smoothly, bend your knees as if you need to lift something heavy. Use your whole body not just your arms."

With these instructions Gelis soon had the paddle lifted. Marheh showed her how to place the locking mechanism then went back to the other side to watch the water disappear in bubbles of white foam. When it was all gone she leaned against the long beam that operated the gate. Gelis copied her and together they pushed so that the gates opened back into the lock.

"Now wind the paddle down again," Marheh called across the gap. "It has to be closed when we start to fill the lock."

Once she had done her side she made her way around the top of the lock and back to *Day Bringer*, telling Gelis to stay where she was. A few moments later she had undone the mooring lines, gathered up the pins and was steering *Day Bringer* into the lock. She took her carefully up to nudge the top gate. Once she was safely through Gelis closed the gate she was leaning on while Marheh climbed onto the roof and grabbed the centre line before hoisting herself onto the lock side to close the other gate. They met then at the top gate.

"This helps to keep her up to the gate," Marheh said, indicating the line she held. "Otherwise the water going in can push her back and bang her around a bit."

Gelis nodded to show she understood.

"You start opening the paddle," Marheh went on. "Just a little at first, watching *Day Bringer* all the time."

The lock began to fill, slowly at first, then faster as Gelis continued to wind.

As *Day Bringer* rose to her new level and the water settled around her Marheh wound the centre line and replaced it on the roof then joined Gelis so together they could push on the gate.

"The last step is to let these paddles down again and then close the gate behind *Day Bringer*. Why don't you do that while I move her out of the lock."

It was soon accomplished. Marheh throttled back and moved into the bank so Gelis could step on board.

"What do you think?" she asked as they set off for the next lock. "Could you do this one by yourself?"

"I think so." Gelis grinned at Marheh. "Open the paddles, open the gates, close the paddles, wait for you to come in, close the gates. Then do it all again only this time you will be going out."

"That sounds about right. I'll put you off when we're in sight of the next one and you can run ahead and get started."

It all went smoothly and soon they were through and on their way to the third one. Marheh congratulated Gelis and managed to hide her own sense of loss. She liked locks. She enjoyed doing them by herself and now it was a job she would have to share. She was being unfair. Gelis was a nice young woman and keen to help. She was lucky to have an apprentice.

Her thoughts were turned as they rounded a bend and came in sight of the next lock.

"Shall I go ahead?" Gelis asked eagerly.

"I'm not sure," Marheh said slowly. "I think we might have company."

She thought she could see figures around the lock, bits of bodies, heads, people who were not part of the water dimension moving beneath and through it.

"Does it matter, if they can't see us?" Gelis asked.

"I think there are too many of them for it to be accidental. The Yareblis know we are vulnerable at locks."

Gelis stared ahead. As they came closer she could see there were at least half a dozen young men roughhousing around the lock, disappearing beneath the water dimension then reappearing somewhere unexpected.

"But they aren't Yareblis are they? Not when they are in and out like that?"

Marheh shook her head.

"Not Yareblis, but not friends either and perhaps placed there by Yareblis influence. I think we will tackle this one a bit differently. It might not be safe for you to go ahead. Different perhaps if we were men."

Gelis thought about that comment as they went slowly towards the mouth of the lock. It would be different, although perhaps still a challenge.

"I want you to stay on board whatever happens," Marheh said.

She had throttled right back and let *Day Bringer*'s front fender just touch the closed gate, then she opened the throttle a little. *Day Bringer* pushed against the gate.

"She'll open the gates herself once the water has emptied," Marheh said.

She still had her windlass tucked into her belt and now she settled it more securely and climbed up onto the roof. Gelis watched as she strode along towards the prow. At the front edge she stopped and seemed to be assessing something. The lock mouth opened and curved out until it was the width of the water road, but where Marheh stood it was quite narrow and Gelis saw her launch herself across the gap and onto the grassy bank behind the lock wall. One of the youths shouted at the sight of her, but a moment later she was back in the water dimension and winding up the paddle next to her. She was watching the water carefully so as not to swamp *Day Bringer*, but she took a moment to grin at Gelis before slipping across the gate to start the other side.

While the water was slowly emptying Marheh perched on the lock beam and studied the youths who were hunting her, appearing and disappearing as she knew she had to them. The most vulnerable times would be running between the top and bottom gates. They would see her then, but if she was quick they would have no time to react before she disappeared again. *Day Bringer* was nudging the gates now and Marheh slid off the beam in order to push then dropped the paddle and waited until she was quite through so she could close the gate. Then, instead of going around and across via the top gate, she moved out onto the one she had closed, paused for a moment then stepped across to the sill of the other one. It was not a particularly dangerous move, but if she misjudged it was a long way to the water and uncomfortably close to *Day Bringer*'s propeller.

Gelis twisted around to watch as she closed the gate and dropped the paddle then she held her breath as Marheh darted towards the top gate. There was a triumphant shout as one of the youths spotted her, but she had chosen her moment well and reached the top gate unscathed. Very slowly she opened one of the top paddles. *Day Bringer* was nudging the gate and moving back again as the water moved in the lock. Timing was everything. Better to be slow and careful. *Day Bringer* was too important to be risked by undue haste.

She was rising nicely however and Marheh thought she would be safe to open the other paddle. The water dimension sometimes had thin places on the offside, but she had been hidden at the bottom gate and expected to be equally invisible here.

She slipped across on the sill of the top gate and stepped off to get to the paddle mechanism. Perhaps she had been over confident. As she was fitting her windlass to the winding gear there was another shout. She spun around and saw them gathered with arms raised.

"Stone the witch!" someone shouted.

She turned again to reach for the safety of the water dimension but not quite quickly enough. Some of the stones fell short, but three or four hit her so that she stumbled and fell forward into the lock.

She landed with a thump on *Day Bringer*'s roof. The boat had been rising in the lock and the roof was nearly level with the ground. Gelis stood frozen for a few moments. The youths were still prowling around and the water was still filling the lock and Marheh lay sprawled and unmoving on *Day Bringer*'s smooth green roof. What should she do? Was Marheh badly hurt? She scrambled up onto the roof and along to crouch down beside Marheh who lifted her head a little and made a face.

"Serves me right for showing off," she said.

Feel it, the wind
Its breath snatches mine.
Dashes away with it
Playing in ripples
Teasing the water and the grass in the field.

Gelis

CHAPTER THREE

"Are you alright?" Gelis asked anxiously. "Can I help you up."

It was a stupid question really, she thought, the minute she had finished speaking. Marheh was clearly not alright.

"Sorry, sorry," she muttered as Marheh did not reply. "What can I do?"

"Go and put the kettle on," Marheh said, her voice strengthening as she found the breath that had been knocked out of her. "I'll be down in a minute."

"You're sure?"

"Yes."

The response came more gruffly than Marheh intended and she felt a bit guilty as Gelis scuttled away. Then she put her head down again and tried to take stock. She hurt in quite a lot of places, but nothing she couldn't deal with. Stones had hit her back and in falling her hip had landed on one of *Day Bringer*'s small round ventilator caps. There would be bruises but nothing worse. She had been stupid to take the risks she had. If she was really honest with herself she would have to acknowledge that she had been trying to prove, to herself and to Gelis, that she was not old or incapable.

Perhaps she had also been driven by her anxiety for Kel. A few silent tears surprised her at this thought and she blinked them away angrily.

"I'm coming," she promised him, wanting her mind to reach him but knowing it had not.

It was cold on *Day Bringer*'s roof and a bit damp. She needed to move. She needed to reassure Gelis. Painfully aware of every separate ache she managed to raise herself to hands and knees and crawl along the roof towards the back deck. She felt a bit sick really but she was not going to give in to that. Turning around she reached with one foot for the little step on *Day Bringer*'s hull and let herself down until she was standing on the back deck, holding onto the roof to steady herself.

A minute or two more and she was making her way down the back steps and through to the saloon. Just to crawl away and lick her wounds alone would have been her preference, but Gelis was there, the kettle was boiling and sperit just poured. She made it to the armchair and sank into it, wincing a little as her bruised back made contact.

Gelis was beside her with a steaming mug a moment later. She wrapped her hands around it gratefully, surprised at how cold she felt.

"Can I get you a blanket?" Gelis asked.

"That would be nice," Marheh found herself saying.

"You're looking after me beautifully," she said when Gelis returned with a blanket from her own bed. "And I owe you an apology."

"What for?" Gelis asked, a bit surprised.

"Get yourself some sperit and come and sit with me."

Marheh gestured to the footstool beside her and waited until Gelis had complied with her suggestion.

"My mentor often said I was teaching her things and now I understand better than I did then." She paused. Gelis was looking attentively at her. "All my life I've been told that I'm arrogant and too independent and today I demonstrated both of those failings. I'm sorry."

Gelis frowned and shook her head.

"I didn't notice."

She studied the inside of her mug for a moment or two then looked back at Marheh.

"I thought you were amazing," she said, blushing a little.

Marheh gave a short laugh.

"Oh dear no! I was showing off. If I had been sensible we would have just sat in the lock mouth and waited for them to go." She smiled at Gelis. "You, on the other hand, did everything right. I'm grateful for my sperit and the blanket even if I thought I didn't want to be looked after."

She paused for a moment, longing for a few minutes alone, but not wanting to hurt this nice young woman who was her apprentice, who would be living with her for the next twenty years, who she must teach herself to love as Nemle had loved her.

"Have you something you could do in your cabin for a while," she said

31

at last. "I will have got myself together soon and then we can decide how best to proceed."

Gelis went off to her cabin with the idea of writing something in her journal. Writing always helped her to make sense of things, or just to come to terms with them. She had been very afraid for her mentor.

I thought she was dead. I really thought she was dead. I could not take it in. The gang of youths were shouting, running about. They had seen her fall. Marheb lay so still and seemed so small. She had blood on her cheek where a stone had hit her and she was very pale. Then she opened her eyes again. I know I had tears on my face, in my eyes, because I had to blink a few times before I could see properly.

She looked at me and immediately she was back to her proper size.

"Very clumsy," she said rather huskily. "Must be getting old."

I almost laughed at the relief. Events had all happened so quickly I had hardly realised the lock was still filling, but in spite of everything Marheb had not forgotten. She told me to put the engine to idle so that we would stay in the lock, otherwise Day Bringer would push her way out once it was full. She was still lying on the roof and her voice seemed a bit thin. I did not want to leave her, but of course I did what she asked. The lock was just about full. There were still two or three youths poking about including one who was obviously looking for Marheb under the water road because I only caught glimpses of him as he moved in and out. It was still disconcerting to see him appear and disappear and I understood what was happening. No wonder they had felt confused and threatened when Marheb came and went.

It was not hard to pull back the throttle and I knew I had been successful when Day Bringer seemed to relax into the water and the sound of her engine subsided to a gentle purr.

I didn't hurry back to Marheb. I wanted to, but it seemed to me that she didn't want to be observed as she took stock. When I did go back along the gunnel towards her she was on her hands and knees, her eyes closed, her face inward, shuttered as she concentrated on breathing, slow and deep. She must have sensed I was near her because she opened her eyes, turned her head. "Just bruises," she told me. "I'll be stiff tomorrow." Her voice sounded stronger, almost back to normal. I offered to bring a pillow and a blanket so she could have a rest where she was, but she gave a bit of a laugh and said she thought she could manage to get inside and I could make her some sperit.

Off I went to put the kettle on, which is what she wanted, so I didn't see her get off the roof and onto the gunnel. She was very pale when she came through to the galley though and I saw her wince once when she thought I wasn't looking. She seems so distant, but she was grateful for the sperit.

Marheh sat and thought of nothing for a few minutes then levered herself out of the armchair and stretched, awakening the many aches that had dulled while she sat but able now to contain them. She spent a moment folding the blanket and a few more minutes washing up the mugs and putting them on their hooks before going out through her cabin to the well deck. The lock was full and *Day Bringer* idling gently beneath her.

The youths seemed to have gone. They must have understood she had been hit and decided they had done enough. They had not been Yareblis, but, she thought, were Yareblis inspired. First the illusion, and now this in just a couple of days. It was more interference than she usually experienced in a matter of weeks, or even months. They must be feeling strong and confident.

What have they done to you Kel?

Again she sent her mind searching, again without success. There had been no contact now for so long. Time to get going again. Where was her windlass? Had she been holding it? Was it now at the bottom of the lock?

She turned to look along *Day Bringer*'s roof. It was not there, but then she saw it, still slotted over the winding gear of the paddle. That was a relief. She did have a spare, but the one she used had been given her fifty years ago when she was apprenticed and she would have been sorry to lose it. She stepped off to retrieve it and tuck in into its place in her belt then walked slowly down the length of the lock and onto the back deck.

Gelis put her head out through the door when she heard her arrive. Marheh smiled at her anxious face.

"Ready to set off again?" she asked.

It was not long before the lock was behind them and they were again travelling slowly through the countryside.

The weather had worsened. A strong wind had sprung up and the temperature seemed to have dropped several degrees. The sky was dark and turbulent, the clouds low and threatening. Marheh was holding *Day Bringer* steady with difficulty against the buffeting wind.

"We'll keep going as long as the rain holds off," she said to Gelis. "But you go in if you want."

"I'd rather stay here."

It was a sentiment Marheh understood. Battling the elements was exhilarating, a challenge that held no malice but made her feel alive.

They had travelled for nearly two hours before the heavens opened. Marheh steered for the bank and Gelis jumped off to help moor but they were both very wet by the time *Day Bringer* was secure. The wind was holding her against the bank at present, but Marheh was always meticulous in caring for her and winds could change direction.

Inside was snug and warm and it was not long before their wet coats were hanging in the engine room to dry and they were drinking sperit and eating bread and cheese in the saloon.

"It's ridiculously late to be eating lunch," Marheh said. "I'm sorry. You must be hungry."

"You gave me the chance to go in. I could have eaten if I'd wanted."

"True. Shall we heat up the soup and turn this into high tea then and just have a hot drink at bed time?"

Later they sat quietly together, having eaten and washed up and spent some time with the discipline of the soul. Gelis had not yet found the special thing that would become her portal, but Marheh assured her that this was not uncommon.

"I know of at least one case where it took a year of searching. The important thing is to continue to offer yourself. The portal will find you then."

She was sitting in the armchair with Gelis beside her on the footstool.

"I'll try not to be impatient," Gelis said.

She looked thoughtfully at the fire for a while then turned towards Marheh again.

"I was wondering," she began.

Marheh smiled encouragingly.

"Why is it just you?"

"What do you mean?"

"There were other Silberay at the Gathering, even if not as many as there should have been. Why aren't they helping to find the ones who weren't there?"

It was not an easy question and Marheh thought carefully before responding.

"I was the one who was called," she said at last.

Gelis continued to look at her, wanting more.

"I suppose there are two reasons really. Not all Silberay have the same skills. Those who made it to the Gathering this year were the people who are more comfortable staying close to the Harbour. They will be practising the discipline of the soul and that will help us in our task."

"But what did you mean, you were called?"

Marheh didn't answer at first and Gelis hastened to apologise.

"You don't have to tell me," she said.

Marheh smiled at her.

"I'm just trying to think of the best way to explain," she said. "The morning of the day we set out I heard the sound of a bell, deep and insistent. I knew it was a call for help. Already everyone was very anxious, but it was the Gathering and some people thought I should wait until it was over before answering. I had quite a job to persuade them that the Gathering was over before it had begun really because so few Silberay were there."

She stopped speaking, not wanting to confess that she had tried to leave Gelis behind at the Harbour, thinking she would be a distraction that she did not need.

"I haven't heard the call again so I only have a general idea of where to look. As we go north I'm aware of... of..."

She stopped speaking again. Gelis looked anxiously at her, hearing the pain in her voice.

"Part of me wishes we could go on and on through the night, but part of me believes that haste is not the answer. Proper preparation and time to gain knowledge of our enemies are more important."

Gelis did not really understand but she knew she could not press Marheh for any more. Instead she stood up and went to put the kettle on.

The explanation, inadequate though she felt it to be, had drawn Marheh's thoughts to fears she had tried to put aside. She drank the sperit Gelis made her and roused herself to be grateful and encouraging then suggested bed, longing to be alone.

She ached all over, but that seemed the least of her problems. The unfamiliar new cabin didn't fit her yet and she felt alien, exiled from the comfort of the back cabin which now belonged to Gelis. She paced to and fro in her own little space, two steps and turn, two steps and turn, unable to find the will to do any of the things she wanted to do or even just to undress for bed.

35

What are you running from?

The question came to her in Nemle's voice and she stopped in her tracks and sank onto her bed. Guilt. Guilt that she had not answered Kel's call the minute she heard it. Guilt that she had allowed other voices to waste time in argument.

"I'm sorry Kel," she whispered, tears spilling.

Angrily she rubbed her wet cheeks. Tears never helped anyone. If she had been wrong it was no good dwelling on it. Jik had counselled caution and he was wise. She was on her way. She spent a few minutes sending her mind searching for Kel's but without any real hope of success. Slowly and painfully she undressed and put herself to bed then she reached for her portal to the soul song.

She needed to sing. The need to remain with Gelis as she began the search for her portal had kept her close to her candle flame, hovering beside Gelis instead of soaring with the music. There had been no chance to use her song as she usually did, offering herself and her music in love to nourish the world around her. Now she put weariness aside. Her candle flame beckoned and she was through and singing. There were other voices, distant harmonies, but few near by.

Where she found herself was grey and opaque, like thick fog, hard for her song to penetrate. She persisted, pushing the fog away, letting the light of her music reach out. The distant voices came closer then one joined with her, a deep, supporting harmony that gave her melody new power. For a time they sang together and the fog retreated, became mist and disappeared.

As the song ended she realised the other singer had been Jik. There were things she had learned, she knew, but making sense of them was for tomorrow. Comforted, she slid into sleep.

Gelis had gone to her cabin not quite ready for sleep. Marheh had accepted her offer to wash up their mugs and let her deal with the fire which pleased her. She put on pyjamas and dressing gown and took out her journal.

I have so much to learn, she wrote then sat, pen in hand, thinking about the day. *Yesterday the illusion and today the attack at the locks. Marheh says it is unusual to have Yareblis' interventions (that's what she calls them) so close together. She is so amazing. I don't suppose I will ever really know her, but I feel really lucky to have her as my mentor. One of the other Silberay I met at the Gathering told me she is the most skilled of all the Silberay at something called the discipline of the mind.*

I haven't learnt about that yet. Marheh says the discipline of the soul has to come first. We've practised that together each day, but I know I haven't managed it yet. Marheh says not to worry, it will come in time. I have to keep practising, she says, and my portal will find me. It could be something quite unexpected. She told me she knows of one Silberay who took a year to find his portal and it turned out to be yeast as it works in the bread. She won't tell me what her portal is. She says it might influence my practice.

She put her pen down and looked at what she had written. There was rather a lot of "*Marheh says*". It made it sound as if Marheh was always telling her things, but she wasn't really. It was just that the things she did say were important, worth thinking about. She wasn't very tired, but if she went to bed she could practise emptying her mind and holding herself ready for her portal to find her. Of course, she might go to sleep.

The next three days passed uneventfully. The weather changed and although it was still cold, spring sunshine welcomed them each morning. Marheh kept her promise to teach Gelis to steer and even left her to do it alone, going below to start a loaf and a new pot of soup. There was another set of locks, going down this time and Gelis grew more confident with all the boating tasks she was learning.

For Marheh each new sharing was a bit of a wrench but she took herself to task and tried to do it gladly and take pleasure in Gelis' happiness in her developing skills.

On the third morning she got up before dawn. Restless and unable to banish her anxiety for Kel, she decided to begin the day's journey. Quietly she dressed and did the engine checks, hoping not to wake Gelis. She almost managed it, but the sound of the engine brought her out, still in her pyjamas, full of apologies.

"It's alright. You'll have your turn later. Why don't you go back to bed for a bit. Take your time getting up and then you can bring me some sperit. Be careful with the water though till we know whether we can fill up again."

But Gelis was thoroughly awake.

I didn't go back to bed exactly, though part of me would have enjoyed some extra sleep. Instead I pulled on some clothes and sat up with this journal. Marheh's injunction regarding the water had given me permission not to wash which seemed like an indulgence, though I did use a cold face washer to wake myself up a bit.

I don't quite understand myself at the moment. I don't mean that I regret my decision and I really enjoyed the last couple of days when things seemed calmer and Marheh encouraged me to steer and said I was doing well but ... There is a but, but I can't quite grasp it. I think it has to do with Marheh. I admire her so much and sometimes I feel really comfortable with her and I think she likes me, then other times I feel she just wants me to go away. How can I go away? I live here now.

That day at the locks she was just amazing, so courageous. She is so self-sufficient, perhaps that is part of it. She doesn't really need me, not yet, though she said she did. I'm glad she explained about being alone. I can see that after thirty years of solitude it would be a bit difficult to have someone around all the time. "Relax," she said. "There's plenty of time." Well, there is of course, twenty years. It's such a long time it doesn't even mean anything. It's my life all over again. She's made a commitment to me as well as me to her and I know she will keep it, but I want her to want me, and I don't believe she does.

Gelis sat and stared at her page for sometime after she had put her pen down. Marheh filled all her thoughts, but she was aware with part of herself, that this was not wise, that Marheh did not want her hero worship. She sighed, put away her writing and went to make sperit.

The pale, calm dawn had developed into a grey and gusty morning by the time Gelis reached Marheh with the sperit. Ribbons of cloud fled across the sky, trees tossed and waved, the fields rippled with the wind and *Day Bringer* seemed almost skittish as Marheh battled with the tiller to keep her on course.

"This will be a challenge for you," she said, smiling her thanks for the steaming drink.

"Me!"

"Why not?"

Gelis looked at the windblown landscape, at Marheh leaning in to the tiller, eyes narrowed against the wind, focused on what was ahead.

"What if I go aground or something?"

"What if..." said Marheh lightly. "This is the next step."

She moved away from the tiller, without letting go, so that Gelis could move in beside her.

"Feel the wind, steer into it a bit. You'll be fine."

She stepped away and went to lean her elbows on the roof and sip at her sperit.

Gelis grasped the tiller in both hands and looked determinedly ahead.

The wind seemed to be coming directly towards her. She had no choice. She had to steer into it. It did not seem too difficult, but there was a bend ahead. Marheh was still leaning on the roof sipping her sperit. Little tendrils of hair had escaped from the plait where they were customarily confined and blew about her head. She looked relaxed. Gelis took a deep breath and gripped the tiller harder as *Day Bringer*'s bow reached the bend. Cautiously she pushed the tiller across. *Day Bringer* began to take the bend in the usual, smooth curve. She was about half way round when the wind caught her. The smooth curve disintegrated. Broadside to the wind the whole boat was being pushed towards the bank. Gelis heaved at the tiller. *Day Bringer* lurched toward the opposite bank. Another heave, another lurch, another heave and gradually she steadied on her new course. Gelis began to understand what Marheh meant by steering into the wind, balancing *Day Bringer*'s forward movement against the sideways thrust of the wind. She let her breath out in a long sigh. Marheh turned to smile at her.

"You're doing fine." She took her empty mug and began to move inside. "Can you last an hour?"

It was quite exhilarating really, Gelis decided as she and *Day Bringer* battled on. To be out in the wind, listening to it, feeling its power, seeing its effect made her feel part of it. She was beginning to relax a little, feeling a little more confident, finding herself humming as she went. She had negotiated a couple of bridges without mishap although one had been very close to scraping *Day Bringer*'s paint work, and she had begun to learn to read the landscape watching for unexpected gusts.

It was a day for birds, not the very little ones, but the crows, ravens and sparrow hawks played in the currents of air. Gelis wished she knew more names and made a note to ask Marheh. She was watching a large bird of prey and wondering whether it might be an eagle when it happened. The combination of a bend, an extra strong gust and an aerial distraction was disastrous. Gelis took the bend late, panicked and pushed the tiller the wrong way, tried too late to go into reverse and watched helplessly as *Day Bringer*'s prow crunched into shallow water and shuddered to a stop.

For a moment she stood clasping the tiller and staring. The engine was still reversing helplessly, the propeller churning up mud and water. More reverse, she thought, and pushed the throttle as far as it would go. More muddy water bubbled around the stern but there was no movement. She eased the throttle back to neutral and waited for Marheh to come and rescue them.

She was only a minute or two, but it seemed an eternity to Gelis, waiting in the wind that now felt cold and unfriendly, for what she expected would be a reprimand. But Marheh when she arrived on deck was her usual calm, unruffled self.

"Oh dear," she said lightly, surveying Gelis' miserable face and *Day Bringer*'s unlikely position. "You did do a good job of it."

"I'm sorry ..."

"It happens to us all sometime or other." She smiled reminiscently. "My best effort took two and a half hours before we were clear. I was afraid Nemle would throw me overboard or beat me or something. She had a bit of a temper and she was trying so hard to control it I thought she was going to explode."

"You aren't angry?" Gelis ventured.

"You didn't do it on purpose. Come and take the tiller and I'll tell you what to try first."

Gelis backed away, but Marheh shook her head.

"I'll tell you what to do, but you'll do it. What have you to remember?"

"Push the tiller the way you want the back to go," Gelis replied.

"Right. And where do you want the back to go now?"

Gelis thought for a minute then shook her head.

"If you try to reverse now, so close to the bank, all that will happen is a lot of mud stirred up. You need the propeller to be in the channel where the water is deeper. To make that happen you need to continue forward and pivot on the stuck bit so the back moves away from the bank."

Gelis' face lightened and she pushed the tiller away from the bank, looking at Marheh questioningly.

Marheh smiled.

"You've got it. You won't need much throttle. Then, when the back is clear, a nice burst of reverse and we'll be on our way again."

It all happened just as Marheh had described.

"I was afraid you would be angry," Gelis admitted when she had got them back into the channel and settled to her steering again.

Marheh grinned.

"Oh, I was, dreadfully, and then I remembered my own errors."

"I don't believe there were any," Gelis said.

Marheh laughed.

"But you don't know me very well yet. One day I might tell you a few stories of my early days, but of course, at the moment, I want you to think me wise and omnipotent, a fount of knowledge and acme of perfection."

"Oh, I do," Gelis said giggling.

Marheh smiled.

"I will leave you to it for another hour, and next time a buzzard appears give him one eye only."

Enter the Clanning Branch

CHAPTER FOUR

On the morning of the fourth day they were both up early.

"We will be passing the entrance to the Clanning Branch today," Marheh said. "I haven't stopped there for years. We won't go far in, but two of us put more strain of the facilities and we can empty the toilet there and take on more water."

Gelis nodded, busy with her porridge.

"What do you want me to do?"

"The water probably, we'll see when we get there." She put down her spoon and stood up. "Will you clear up here and perhaps do a bit of brass polishing while I take us on."

Gelis nodded again and began to stand.

"Finish your breakfast first. Have some more toast if you want. I'll start a new loaf tonight."

Gelis watched as she disappeared into her cabin then she saw her feet in their sturdy, well worn boots, pass the window as she made her way along to the back deck. She felt *Day Bringer* move as she boarded and knew she was going to the engine room to do the checks that preceded every day's journey.

She would have some more toast. Marheh's bread was much nicer than shop bread. Marheh had been a bit disparaging when she said as much. Her bread was not nearly as nice as the bread her mentor had made, but it was convenient to make it since there was not always a shop handy, she had said.

Marheh was going to teach her to make bread too. There were so many things she was learning. She heard the engine begin to throb, saw Marheh pass again as she went to unfasten the front line, then a moment or two later, saw her return to the back. Marheh didn't really need her. She could do everything herself. She probably didn't want her either, Gelis thought in a moment of doubt. She had been kind and encouraging teaching her to steer and even letting her do it by herself. The day before yesterday after lunch she had stretched, grinned at Gelis and told her she was going to walk for a bit.

"I need to get rid of the kinks," she had said. "You can clear up here and catch up with me. I'll wait for you at a bridge hole."

She had not waited to hear Gelis' response, but disappeared into her cabin then out onto the towpath and away.

Gelis finished her toast and washed up still thinking about her mentor. She had a nasty bruise coming out on her cheek where a stone had caught her and there must have been other bruises, but she didn't complain. She never expected her to do anything she wouldn't do herself. She was really difficult to help. At least I can do a really thorough job on the brass, she thought, going through to collect the cleaning things from the engine room.

It was quite nice sitting on *Day Bringer*'s roof as they went along and rubbing at the ventilator caps with the brass polish was enough to keep her warm. There was satisfaction in getting them really shiny too. There were four of them, spread across the roof, and they really needed rubbing up each day. That could be her job. Marheh had confessed that she usually let a few days or even a week go by without doing it. She polished assiduously and dreamed about how else she could help.

Marheh, at the tiller, watched and smiled at her diligence, remembering how different these early days had been during her own apprenticeship. The brass cloth had never behaved in her hands the way Gelis was using it. How she had pestered Nemle to let her steer and Nemle had refused telling her she must learn humility first. Gelis was very different, eager to learn about everything, not just the boating tasks, and anxious to please. She was lucky in her apprentice really. Imagine if she had had one like she had been, or like Bixa's apprentice Beuda, who had been so brash and self confident. Bixa had set herself to love her and succeeded in giving her Silberay values and now that Bixa was old and close to retiring Beuda cared for her like a loving daughter. It should be so much easier for her to learn to love Gelis.

Love was a large idea that encompassed so many emotions. These days people seemed to think of it as something involuntary.

"I fell in love," they say, as if they had no control over it, and sometimes it did happen like that.

Her thoughts went briefly to Kel and his warm, steady, reliable love for her. He had loved her well before she knew she loved him and gone on loving her when she had been rude and dismissive. That was the challenge, to make a commitment to loving and stick to it. Nemle had. She had made a commitment to love an unknown young woman, to take her into her life and teach her by precept and example and she had done it. If she failed Gelis she would be failing Nemle too.

She eased her shoulders a little, sighed and committed herself all over again.

Gelis had finished her polishing and was coming towards her along the gunnel.

"You've done a splendid job on those," she said.

Gelis flushed and looked pleased.

"I was thinking," she began then hesitated.

Marheh smiled at her.

"Yes?"

"Well, *Day Bringer* is such a lovely boat and some of the other boats at the Harbour had flowers on the roof. They looked so pretty. I wondered, could we have some too?"

Marheh laughed.

"We could," she said. "But you'll have to look after them."

"I will, I want to."

"I'm an old grouch I know, but my mentor grew herbs and seedlings as part of our livelihood and I rather resented the demands they made on me. I got rid of them the minute she retired."

Gelis was silent for a minute or two.

"Would you rather not?" she asked, looking anxiously at Marheh.

"*Day Bringer* is ours now," Marheh said slowly. "Not just mine. If you want flowers and you do the work then flowers you shall have, but we might have to wait until after this job is over before we can purchase the wherewithal."

Over the next hour or so the weather began to deteriorate. A wind got up and the gusts were cold and brought spats of rain. Marheh suggested Gelis should go in, but she chose not to and Marheh didn't insist. Then came the entrance to the Clanning Branch. The water road opened out to permit the wide circle needed for *Day Bringer* to make the approach. Now the wind was broadside on and still coming in gusts. The bridge hole was narrow and the gusting wind made it more difficult to enter. Gelis, having now experienced the effect of wind for herself, was full of admiration for Marheh's ability. She saw how the brief protection from the bridge made emerging into the wind more difficult and was glad it was Marheh doing the steering.

The landscape changed once they were through the bridge. There were few trees, just wide, empty fields where some kind of crop was beginning to show and the wind, stronger now and tearing over the fields on their right, a north wind, cold and relentless. The water road too seemed to change. It was very narrow and overgrown with thick reed beds on either side.

"Nobody has been in here for a good while," Marheh said, thinking aloud. "We won't need to look for them in Clanning."

"Will we make it?" Gelis asked.

"Should do. Can you see the service area about one hundred yards ahead on the left? That's where we are aiming."

Day Bringer was wriggling carefully through the reeds, Marheh's hand, light on the tiller, sensitive to the smallest obstacle as well as the gusting wind.

They were still a good sixty yards from the service area when *Day Bringer*'s usual quiet throbbing became a sudden, shrill whine.

Instantly Marheh throttled back to neutral. *Day Bringer*'s forward movement continued briefly before the wind took her and pushed her into the reeds. Marheh muttered something under her breath and tried, very gently, to reverse. The whine came again immediately. Again she throttled back and this time stopped the engine altogether and removed the ignition key. The sudden silence and the feeling of helplessness were somehow shocking.

"What's happened?" Gelis asked into the silence.

"Something has snagged the propeller," Marheh said. "We'll need to

45

take up the deck boards and see if we can clear it through the inspection hatch."

She was tugging at the access handle as she spoke. Gelis stepped quickly out of the way.

"Can I help?"

Marheh slid the board she had lifted across to her.

"Put that down in your cabin," she said, lowering herself onto what remained of the deck.

When she had tucked the board away Gelis came back to kneel beside her and watch as she undid the hatch cover and lifted it out. Beneath was the water, muddy, opaque and cold.

"Never, ever do this with the engine running," Marheh said. "Not even in neutral."

She sat up, unfastened her belt and set it aside then pulled off her heavy over tunic and handed it to Gelis. Then she rolled up the sleeves of her undershirt. Her bare arms were lean and muscled, but there were still some yellow and purple bruises. She lay face down and reached one arm into the cold brown water, feeling for the propeller. Then she edged forward and reached in with the other arm also. She stayed silent and concentrating for some minutes, small movements of her arms indicating the work of her hands below the surface of the water.

"It's wire," she said at last, sitting up again, brown tracks streaking her arms, mud and green slime dripping off her fingers. "Can you find the pliers and a rag?"

Gelis hurried away. A minute later she was back with the tools. As she handed Marheh the pliers their hands touched.

Gelis gasped.

"You're so cold!"

"Yes."

Marheh mopped at her arms and the deck. Again she lay down and plunged her arms into the water. Bit by bit she cut away at the wire, passing up short pieces to Gelis as she knelt beside her. Sometimes she grunted with the effort. Once or twice she stopped and rested for a moment breathing deeply. At last she sat up, her arms, her face and neck and the front of her shirt were wet and filthy but she had lost none of her calm dignity.

"I can't clear it," she said. "Looks like I'm swimming."

"You can't!" Gelis protested. "Isn't there something else we can try?"

"We might try to pole her away from the reeds at least, they'll cut me to bits if I go in here."

Already there were thin lines of blood on her hands and forearms.

"Can we do that? With the pole?"

Marheh nodded, leaning down to replace the hatch cover and tighten the fastenings. Gelis went to get the deck board and soon it was slotted into place.

"Do you want your coat?" Gelis asked.

Marheh shook her head.

"I'm too dirty. The exercise will soon warm me up."

She went to lift the boat pole from its position on the roof.

"If we can move her at all we might as well try to get as far as the service area. Then at least there should be water to wash with when we've finished."

She handed the pole to Gelis and took the boat hook for herself.

"You go to the front and stand in the well deck. Given the direction of the wind it's probably best if you work from the port side."

Soon they were both in position. At Marheh's command Gelis leaned on her pole with all her weight. There was a moment of tension when it seemed as if nothing would happen then something seemed to give.

"Again!" called Marheh.

Gelis leaned once more and found that *Day Bringer* was sliding away from the reeds. She hauled up the pole and placed it again. Behind her she knew that Marheh was doing the same. A rhythm began to develop to Marheh's calls and surprisingly quickly the tree that marked the service area came closer. The poles were lifted and *Day Bringer* floated quietly on towards the mooring. There was a little bump as her bow touched and she swung outward again, but this brought the stern in and Marheh was able to step off with the centre line and use the bollards at the mooring to control her.

"That went better than I expected," Marheh said as they finished mooring. "Well done."

"I enjoyed it." Gelis looked anxiously at Marheh. "Do you really have to go into the water? Couldn't I do it?"

"I think it had better be me this time, but thanks for the offer." Marheh smiled. "I'm sure your turn will come."

"Can I help at all?" Gelis said hesitantly. "What if I leaned in through the hatch? I could hold things."

Marheh nodded thoughtfully.

"That could work. Anyway I'll have one more try through the hatch in case."

She looked at the muddy water beneath them and grimaced.

"It doesn't look terribly inviting in there."

So again they went through the process of removing the deck board and the hatch cover. Marheh spent a few minutes feeling the way the wire had worked itself around the propeller, planning her approach. Then Gelis reached down with one arm so that Marheh could explain what she would encounter and how she could help.

"We'll have about ten minutes," Marheh said. "It will be too cold to stay in any longer." She stood up. "I'll keep my clothes on. I don't know what I'll encounter in there and I'm very wet and dirty already."

She stepped onto the bank. Gelis watched her carefully as she sat down, edged forward and lowered herself carefully into the water. It was not deep, only just above waist height. Holding onto *Day Bringer* Marheh moved into position at the stern, crouched down until only her head was above water and reached under the counter to the propeller. She found Gelis' fingers and gave them a little squeeze then set to work. Once the cold numbed her hands and they lost feeling it would be inefficient, even dangerous to continue. Summoning all her ability to focus she closed her eyes and thought only of the propeller and what her hands were seeing.

Gradually she began to unravel the tangle, freeing the strands and offering them to Gelis and the pliers. She ached with cold, but a remote part of her welcomed the pain, knowing that as long as she could feel she was functioning. The minutes ticked by too fast, yet each one seemed an eternity. One cheek rested against *Day Bringer*'s hull as she worked. It felt comfortable, almost warm against her skin.

"Marheh!" Gelis' voice was high, shrill with anxiety.

Awareness returned. Marheh knew she was nearing the limit of her strength, but it was almost clear. She took a deep breath, ducked under the hull, brought her face close to the propeller and opened her eyes. There, through the murky water, she saw the barbed hooks that had kept the wire in place. Reaching out with both hands she grasped them, unhooked them and pushed herself away from the hull and up to the surface.

Gelis was on the bank ready to plunge in when she came up, gasping for breath, still clutching the hooks with the last, trailing strands of wire. She stood up, half blinded by the muddy water streaming down her face and staggered towards the bank. Gelis was there to help her out. It was a bit of a struggle, Marheh pushing up with arms and legs numb with cold and Gelis grabbing at any bit of her that would give leverage. She got one knee onto the edge and managed to roll onto the grass beside the mooring.

It would have been easy to let herself lie there, exhausted with the effort, but Gelis was hovering anxiously so she pushed herself to her feet. Her teeth were chattering and she was cold to the bone.

"I'd best get warm," she managed to say and began to fumble with the buttons on her shirt before giving up and just pulling it over her head. A few minutes later she had removed all her clothes and disappeared below.

Gelis stared after her then down at the pile of discarded garments. With anyone else she would have been shocked at their nakedness, but Marheh had made it seem merely practical. What had been shocking though were the bruises revealed, yellow and purple, where the stones had caught. She had an old scar too across her lower back. Never once had she complained of pain or wanted to be looked after. There were things she could do for her now though. She had been so cold. Her lips had been blue. The sound of the pump suggested that she was showering. If she put her dressing gown by the fire it would be nice and warm for her to put on.

She went in through Marheh's cabin, found her dressing gown hanging on the back of her door and put it by the fire then, still thinking of how she might help, went back out to the pile of wet clothes. They were very dirty with mud and weed. Grabbing their bucket from the locker in the well deck she put the clothes in it, filled it with water from the tap at the water point and left them to soak. Then she went back inside to put the kettle on. Surely Marheh would need a hot drink to help her get warm.

It had just boiled when the door from the bathroom opened and Marheh emerged, wrapped in a towel.

"I've put your dressing gown by the fire," Gelis said. "And the kettle has just boiled for sperit."

Marheh smiled at her.

"Sperit and a warm dressing gown, what more could I want?"

She put the dressing gown on and sat on the footstool by the fire rubbing her hair with the towel.

"Are you warm now?"

"More or less, sperit will complete the cure."

"You were in too long."

"Just a bit, but it had to be done."

Gelis poured the hot water over the spices and dried berries and carried the mug of sperit carefully to Marheh.

"I was frightened for you."

Marheh wrapped both hands around the mug and breathed in the steam.

"I was a bit frightened myself," she admitted. "But you were there. Getting out would have been very hard without you."

Gelis flushed with pleasure at this expression of need.

"I would have put the hatch cover back, but I wasn't sure how it fitted."

"It can be tricky," Marheh agreed. "I'll show you later, but I think we deserve some lunch first don't you?" She smiled at Gelis. "You might like a wash, or even a shower before we eat," she suggested.

Gelis looked down at herself and realised that she too was wet and muddy from their activities of the morning.

"A shower would be nice."

"We can fill the water tank here, so have one if you want."

When Gelis had disappeared into the bathroom Marheh pushed herself to her feet. She couldn't sit and snooze, much as she would like to. Into her cabin to dress and comb and plait her hair, then back out to the galley to cut bread for toast, grate some cheese and beat up a couple of eggs. It would be a good while before the evening meal if they were to continue as far as she had planned.

By the time Gelis had showered lunch was ready. They didn't linger over it, but Marheh was glad she had taken the trouble.

"We needed that I think, but I'm afraid we're going to be on short rations now for a while. We are obviously not going any further into the Clanning Branch, so no food shopping for a couple of days at least."

She let Gelis make them sperit to finish the meal then outlined her thinking about their next steps.

"We'll do the hatch cover and the deck boards together," she said. "Then I will look after emptying the loo while you fill the water tank."

"Shouldn't I do the toilet?" Gelis asked.

"Not this time." Marheh smiled at her. "But it's a good offer."

She drained her sperit and stood up.

"That wire was a trap and I don't want to risk getting tangled again so I want us to pole *Day Bringer* back out into the Great Northern. Are you up for that?"

She didn't wait for an answer, but went striding into the bathroom to deal with the toilet cassette.

Gelis put their plates and mugs into the sink and followed her out, remembering the bucket and Marheh's clothes soaking. The toilet cassette was obviously heavy. Marheh was lurching a bit to one side as she carried it. She would learn to do it so Marheh didn't have to.

She reached the bucket where she had left it by the tap and looked into it. The water was thick and murky. Obviously there had been more mud in the clothes than she thought. She picked up a stick and poked a bit, not wanting to put her clean hands into the murky water. She should have been able to feel the clothes with her stick but she just seemed to be stirring a gluey, porridge-like mess. Cautiously she picked up the bucket, moved off the narrow mooring deck and onto the grass beyond it and slowly poured out the contents.

The bucket held nothing but sludge and a few buttons.

"Marheh!"

Gelis' shout held a hint of desperation and caused Marheh to leave the half empty cassette and hurry out to where Gelis stood staring at the ground.

"What's the matter?"

She hoped she didn't sound impatient, but the interruption had not come at a good time.

"The water, it must have been the water."

"What?" Marheh snapped. "What about the water?"

"I put your clothes in the bucket to soak because they were so dirty, but they're gone. That's all that's left."

Marheh stared at her and then at the mess on the ground. She squatted

51

down to look closer and saw the buttons, small white buttons, the kind that had been on her shirt. She stood up again and looked at Gelis.

"You filled the bucket with water from the tap?"

Gelis nodded.

"I thought it would be helpful."

"Well, it's turned out to be more helpful than you could have imagined. If the water could do that to my clothes think what it could have done to *Day Bringer*'s water system."

"It might not have been very good for our insides either," Gelis commented.

Marheh seemed a bit surprised at this.

"But we can fight back," she said, dismissing the possibility. "*Day Bringer* can't."

She stood for a moment more studying the sludge and thinking.

"The best thing we can do is get out of here," she said briskly. "Can you give the bucket a good rinse in the water road and then fill it about a quarter full. We can't drink from the water road but it will be alright in the toilet. I'll finish emptying."

Ten minutes later it was done and they were both in position with their poles. This time they went backwards, Marheh watching out from the stern and taking care with every thrust. It seemed to Gelis that even *Day Bringer* breathed a sigh of relief when they had finally negotiated the bridge again and returned to the Great Northern.

Marheh still wanted to continue with the poles for another twenty yards or so, just to be safe, but at last she slid her boat hook onto the roof and motioned to Gelis to stow her pole beside it and come and join her.

The sound of *Day Bringer*'s engine seemed like music. Marheh cautiously engaged the throttle and they heard the normal steady pulse and saw the wake begin to spread out behind them.

"Well," Marheh said.

Gelis looked at her. The single word seemed to mean many things. Here we are again. That's that then. We got out of there. We're on our way. Perhaps she should interpret it as all is well.

After a long silence Marheh spoke again. This time her meaning was clear.

"We are going to need to be very careful with water. Those two showers will have almost emptied the tank I think since we were already low. There is a water point between here and Deerford, but I don't want to risk it. Can you bear not to wash for a few days?"

She didn't wait for Gelis' reply but continued to think aloud.

"If the Yareblis have contaminated the water supply that might be a reason why so many are missing. They won't have been able to get at the pottery's supply though. If it rains we can put out bowls, they can hardly have contaminated that."

She stopped speaking then and seemed to sense Gelis' puzzlement.

"I'm sorry," she said, looking at her. "I'm going too fast and talking of things you don't know about. Deerford is where my family live. They have a pottery and a mooring at the bottom of the garden. It will take us nearly a week to get there even travelling all day, but it will be safe water, and, I think, take us nearer to where we need to be."

Lunch

CHAPTER FIVE

A long afternoon of boating brought them to the entrance of the section of the water road that went through Deerford. It was usually referred to as the Eastern Reach, Marheh told Gelis, and promised to show her on the appropriate chart once they had moored for the night. Gelis could not help wondering when that would be. Marheh had not offered her the tiller all afternoon and now she was pushing them on into the twilit evening far longer than she usually did. At last, when it was almost too dark to see, she seemed to wake up to what she was doing. It was as if she had forgotten Gelis, for she eased *Day Bringer* into the bank and stepped off with the centre line as she had done for so many years. Only then did Gelis have the chance to help her.

Mooring did not take long. Marheh attended to the stern tube greaser as she went through the engine room and put the kettle on for sperit once she reached the galley.

"I'll do that," Gelis said. "Why don't you sit down?"

Marheh looked at her for a moment as if she didn't know who she was then sank into the armchair and closed her eyes. When she opened them again a few minutes later she seemed to have gained possession of herself.

"I haven't been very sensible this afternoon, have I?" she said. "Not at all a good example. I owe you an apology."

Gelis shook her head.

"I can tell you're worried."

"That's no excuse," Marheh said. "I'm very sorry I've been such an old grump and I owe you an enormous debt of gratitude. If you had not been so thoughtful and looked after my clothes, *Day Bringer*, you and I and the job we've been sent to do would all have been put at risk."

Gelis busied herself making the sperit. Marheh didn't need to apologise to her or thank her, but it was nice that she did. She carried the two full mugs carefully around to the saloon, handed one to Marheh and perched on the footstool beside her.

"I might not always be as grateful as I should be when you look after me," Marheh continued, the hint of a smile in her voice. "But if I'm too crabby you just say Clanning Branch and I'll grovel."

Gelis laughed.

"I think you must be a bit overtired." She made her voice exaggeratedly solicitous. "Dear Marheh, why don't I bring you your supper in bed?"

"Dear Gelis," Marheh responded in kind. "How thoughtful of you to suggest it. What supper?"

The change in tone of the last two words made Gelis laugh again.

"We still have rice and dried milk and I found some sultanas so I made a little rice pudding. I thought you'd need something."

"A domestic treasure too! How lucky I am."

They ate together in quiet accord then Gelis insisted that she could clear up.

"I'll leave the washing up water in the sink so we can use it again," she said. "There isn't much to do and you must be tired."

Marheh opened her mouth to protest then thought better of it. She was tired, more than tired and the idea of bed was very appealing.

"Very well," she said standing up from the table. "I shall set an example of obedience and have an early night."

Next morning was grey and overcast. Marheh dressed warmly, opened the doors to the well deck and stepped out to look at the sky. An ominous bank of dark clouds loomed on the horizon. She shivered a bit and closed the doors again. Best to get under way at once and get as far as they could before the storm hit. There was no need to wake Gelis. It was still early.

She did as much preparation as she could without entering the back cabin. However when it came time to start the engine she could not avoid it. The sound caused the bulge under the bedclothes to convulse and she grinned at the emergence of Gelis' startled face.

"There's no hurry. I can manage. Have a bit more sleep if you want."

She did not wait for an answer but stepped off to attend to the lines and begin the day's journey.

The weather quickly deteriorated and by the time Gelis had come out, dressed and carrying a mug of sperit for Marheh, the sky overhead was black and the wind howling.

Despite the gale Marheh looked as if she was enjoying the challenge. She grinned at Gelis and thanked her for the sperit.

"It looks as if we might be able to catch some rain quite soon. You might put some bowls out in the well deck. It's too windy for bowls on the roof."

Around them trees were thrashing and bending, birds spun in the air, shouted and dived for cover. A big gathering of crows wheeled overhead and raced away ahead of the wind.

"It makes you feel very small, doesn't it?" Marheh shouted over the noise.

Gelis nodded, wondering how she could be so cheerful when any minute, it seemed, an extra strong gust might carry her away. She didn't linger over her drink. Gelis waited to take the mug then disappeared below to find some suitable receptacles for the rain that would soon be upon them.

Marheh, happy to be alone again, held the tiller firmly with both hands, gave herself to the chaos around her and began to sing. It was not, this time, the struggle or the glory of the discipline of the soul, but a wild, wordless tune, merging and mingling with the gusting wind so she became one with the elements. No one could hear her above the noise so she had no need to confine the sounds she made to the civilized structure of rhythm or scale.

When the rain came, great sheets of water sweeping across the fields in front of the wind, she gasped at the shock of it then laughed and sang on. There had been times in the past when she had stripped and danced naked in the rain as if the storm had unlocked something wild and primitive, but now she was not quite so lost to the proprieties. Gelis' presence meant that freedom was lost to her and for a moment she grieved, but exaltation still held her and she sang on, moving her feet in a small pattern, stepping to a rhythm only she could hear.

Gelis' anxious face appearing from the back cabin brought her back to earth, but still she laughed.

"Go in!" she shouted. "I'm crazy but there is no need for you to be."

Gelis' eyes widened and her mouth opened, but the wind snatched her words. She disappeared, pulling the door closed behind her.

Marheh drove *Day Bringer* forward, no longer uplifted but determined to continue. Thunder rolled around the sky, but it was only when she saw distant lightening split the dark that she knew it would be folly to proceed.

Mooring was a challenge but she chose a place where the wind would hold *Day Bringer* against the bank and eased in to jump off with line and mooring pin. By the time she had secured the centre line Gelis was at the front line ready to help. She turned to smile and hold up her thumb in approval then made for the stern and the back line.

They were soon tied up and snug inside. Marheh had been extra careful with the mooring and put all *Day Bringer*'s fenders to use between the bank and the hull. She was wet to the skin despite her waterproof coat and even Gelis was damp from her few minutes of assistance. Outdoor things could hang in the engine room to dry. Marheh left her boots there too and padded through to her cabin in her socks.

"That's me showered," she said when Gelis commented on her wet clothes.

She disappeared into her cabin to change, then realised that the loss of a pair of trousers meant that she had only her best pair to change into. Instead she opted for dressing gown and slippers over her shirt and tunic. She would wring out her trousers and put them in the engine room too. If the storm passed and she had to go out again she would put them on damp rather than risk her best ones.

Back in the saloon with Gelis she suggested they practise the discipline of the soul. The noise of the storm made conversation difficult but *Day Bringer*'s feeling of safety and comfort was enhanced by the turmoil outside.

Gelis had been wondering whether the evening star might offer her a portal since she had been absorbed by its beauty and the way it seemed to beckon her into the unknown when she watched it gradually emerge as the sky around it darkened. Marheh encouraged her to make this a focus for her contemplation and she was eager to try.

They sat together, Marheh in the armchair and Gelis on the footstool leaning against the chair and just touching Marheh's legs. Marheh was carried back to the time of her own apprenticeship and the comfort and safety contact with Nemle had given her. Would Gelis find safety and comfort in her touch? It was a challenging thought. Would the need to provide safety and comfort change her song? That too was a challenging thought. She was used to soaring, spinning her song in threads of gold to the edges of the dark but for now it was her job to be the ground for Gelis' attempts at melody.

She reached for her candle flame. This was not the time for introspection. Now Gelis had to be her focus. Resting in her portal she waited, her song humming quietly, ready to reach and support. Time ceased to have meaning while she held herself still and focused outside herself. Then, for a few faltering notes, she encountered another song and gave herself to nurturing its baby steps.

By the time the song ended the storm had passed but the day had moved on and the effort had tired them both. They had not eaten either. Marheh decided there would be little advantage to be gained by continuing. It would be more useful to talk to Gelis about her experience of the soul song, to make a fresh loaf and take stock of their remaining provisions. The water they had collected could be poured into the kettle and a jug.

The lack of water was her most immediate concern, but as long as they had enough to drink they would get by. When Marheh explained her thinking to Gelis she asked if Marheh would teach her to make the bread, so the rest of the afternoon was spent in quiet instruction, not just the bread but, more importantly, Gelis' first steps into the soul song and what she had experienced there.

"Well," Marheh said, when Gelis finished telling her. "You're on your way now. I'm happy for you to practise alone if you want to, but not without telling me first please."

Gelis nodded. She thought she would do anything for Marheh. She kneaded the dough assiduously and thought about how Marheh had saved her, how she had taught her to steer and about locks, how she had told her about her own early experiences and listened sympathetically to Gelis' story and how she had led her into the soul song.

She was sitting relaxed in the armchair now, her feet up on the footstool. Gelis looked across at her and blushed as Marheh's eyes met hers. Marheh raised her eyebrows but did not comment.

"Could you tell me about Clanning please?" Gelis asked, still busy with the dough. "Why was it like that, all choked up?"

"I think you could put the dough to rise now," Marheh said. "When you've done that I'll tell you what I know."

"You know everything don't you?" Gelis dared to tease just a little.

"Sometimes I behave as if I think I do, but you're not to encourage me." She grinned. "Or I might need a spanking for arrogance."

Gelis laughed.

"But you're allowed to know everything when you're seventy," she said with heavy emphasis.

"Ouch!" Marheh said. "That was below the belt."

"Spankings usually are," said Gelis, straight faced.

Marheh looked at her for a moment then they both collapsed into laughter.

"And I thought you were a nice, humble, respectful young woman," Marheh said when she could speak.

"I am," said Gelis, pleased to have made her laugh. "That's why you are going to tell me all about Clanning."

So when she had put the dough to rise and seated herself on the footstool at Marheh's knee, Marheh began to tell her.

She explained how the Clanning Branch was the last bit of the water road to be made and told her of the challenge she and Nemle had met there when she was still an apprentice.

"For a little while after that we visited quite regularly. It was our assigned route and we were welcome although Nemle was never very comfortable there. We went back every year for about six years and there were people who made us welcome. We had friends in Ponder too, but the original reason for the water road being encouraged was gone with the coal that had been mined and carried by Silberay boats. Our route changed and lengthened. The decline in Silberay numbers meant that we were more and more stretched covering the whole of the water road. It was too easy for a short branch that led nowhere much to fall off the map. I think that is what happened. I know I've never paid it much attention and it hasn't been included in any route I've been given since those years with Nemle. Perhaps it should have been," she finished thoughtfully. It will be something to look into once we have found the others."

They ate sparingly that evening. Marheh was very conscious of their lack of provisions, not so much for herself, she and Nemle had been on short commons more than once, but for her apprentice. Gelis was observant and protested when Marheh tried to give her the lion's share. Once everything had been tidied away as well as it could be, given the condition of the washing up water, cold and a bit scummy in the sink, Marheh took herself off for a short walk in the twilit evening. Evidence of the storm lay around, leaves and small branches littered the ground, but the sound and fury had passed leaving a clear sky and the promise of a new and better day.

Back on *Day Bringer* she said as much to Gelis before bidding her goodnight and disappearing into her cabin. The fate of her friends still weighed heavily on her mind and for the moment the only help she could give them was her song. She put on her nightdress and dressing gown and opened the doors into the well deck. The air was cool and still and the night sky blazed with stars. She stood in the doorway for a few moments then took up her cloak and wrapped it around her before settling in the well deck. The slatted seat was hard. She would not go to sleep. Without the need to nurture Gelis' song she could give all of herself to reaching out, to spinning her golden threads of melody towards the darkness that lay in wait.

Much later she returned to herself, cold and stiff and disheartened. There had been music and other songs that sang with hers, but they were not the ones she sought. True, they had supported her and she was grateful. She needed their music to anchor her explorations. She thought she recognised Jik's song and guessed that others of the old ones at the Harbour had been singing with her, perhaps even those old ones who had gone beyond the Harbour.

Despite her late night, Marheh was up with the sun the next morning. She had already learned that Gelis was not an early riser, but at the moment that did not matter. She enjoyed a solitary hour at the tiller before breakfast and was happy to hand over to Gelis once she had breakfasted and to take time over her own breakfast, taking it out into the well deck to enjoy the sunshine that seemed anxious to make up for its recent absence by making everything sparkle.

She closed her eyes, the better to feel it on her face, then opened them again to see how it bounced off the water road and danced in the new spring green.

As she did every morning she sent her mind seeking Kel's but was not really surprised when she did not find him. The ache of sadness that lay dormant during the day's activity awoke then, but after acknowledging it briefly she put it resolutely aside. Indulging her feelings would not help Kel or anyone else.

A bit of tidying in her cabin, a check on the clothes that were still drying in the engine room and she made her way through to the back deck. Gelis' bed was made and her cabin tidy she was glad to see. She would have felt a hypocrite had it been necessary to offer a rebuke. Housework had never appealed, but somehow *Day Bringer* seemed to insist on tidiness.

Gelis smiled a greeting when Marheh appeared and indicated the tiller, offering it to her.

"You keep going a bit longer," Marheh said. "Unless you're tired."

Gelis shook her head.

"No, I love it."

She did look happy, Marheh thought, trying to come to terms with her casual attire. She wore shorts, quite short, bright pink shorts and a sleeveless top, also pink, and her feet were bare. Of course the Silberay uniform had become more of a ceremonial garment now. Most of the younger Silberay did not wear it every day as Marheh did, and knew she always would.

She smiled at Gelis.

"You look as if you are enjoying the sun."

Gelis grinned.

"It's lovely isn't it."

"It is, especially after the last few days."

She paused, knowing there was one thing she needed to say and wondering how best to say it.

"It's fine to wear what ever you're comfortable in," she said at last. "But when we are moving you must wear shoes. You can't respond quickly and safely with bare feet."

Gelis looked at her feet and blushed.

"I'm sorry, I didn't think."

"You didn't know," Marheh said. "But just pop down now and put them on."

She reached for the tiller and Gelis disappeared below. Marheh closed her eyes briefly, opened them again and sighed. She would not allow herself to become an old grouch, but really, pink shorts! What was the world coming to?

The next few days were full of sunshine and they made good progress. Steering was easy and Gelis gained in confidence so that Marheh felt comfortable leaving her to steer while she gave herself to the soul song.

When she took her own shifts at the tiller she often found Gelis remained outside with her. Sometimes she lay on her stomach on *Day Bringer*'s sun warmed roof and scribbled in her journal, but at other times she stood beside Marheh and asked for stories.

Although she had read the little pamphlet she had been given at the Gathering it had been first published before Marheh was born and never updated. She was fascinated by the links created by ownership of *Day Bringer*. It was a kind of genealogy really, right back to the founding of the water road. Marheh, apprenticed to Nemle, apprenticed to Hafa, apprenticed to Tala, apprenticed to Rinteh, one of Sila's friends, and now she, Gelis, was part of the chain.

Marheh smiled at her enthusiasm and racked her brain for things Nemle had told her. She was glad to be distracted from thoughts of Kel and recognised that the telling encouraged her towards optimism.

"Tell me about your mentor," she asked one morning.

"Nemle."

Marheh's face softened and her eyes turned to some distant remembering.

"Please," Gelis added quietly.

Marheh smiled at her and leaned more comfortably against the rail around the back deck.

"You realise that I didn't meet her until she was seventy, the same age as I am now."

Gelis nodded.

"She was born last century, part of a different age really. She didn't complain, but I understood from the little she said that her parents were strict and unloving. They wanted a son and the only use in a daughter was to work for them. They tried to prevent her from joining the Silberay. She said that for her life really began when she became apprenticed to Hafa. It was Hafa who encouraged her talent for healing and made sure she had the opportunity to learn about the medicinal use of plants."

"The ones you had on the roof?" Gelis asked as Marheh paused in her recital.

"The very same." Marheh smiled wryly. "I know she was disappointed when I didn't want to learn from her, but she was generous enough to understand. She was very disciplined, which was a good example for me, and she could be stern if I did something wrong. She reduced me to tears once or twice. Most importantly she loved me, even when I was not very lovable. She used to call me the daughter of her heart and I think, by the end of her life, she half believed I was her daughter."

Gelis heard the hint of a sigh as Marheh looked back, but her next words were brisk.

"No point in being sentimental. Nemle was never that. Now, how about you take the tiller while I go down and make us some sperit. We've still enough water for that."

She swung down the steps and through to the galley. They had decided that the easiest way of conserving their limited provisions was to go without lunch, but Marheh was conscious that this was easier for her than for Gelis. While she waited for the kettle to boil she had a little hunt for something she thought she remembered seeing in her back pack. It was still there, although it should have been thrown away weeks ago, a single, very tired looking, cracker biscuit.

Mother and Nemle would both have been ashamed of me, she thought, putting it carefully in the centre of a plate.

When the kettle boiled she took the two mugs in one hand and the plate in the other and made her way through to the back deck again. Putting the mugs down carefully on *Day Bringer*'s roof she turned to Gelis with the plate.

"Your lunch Madam," she said, presenting it ceremoniously.

Gelis grinned.

"I don't like to deprive you," she said in the grand manner.

"I insist."

Marheh continued to present the plate with mock deference. Gelis took the biscuit, broke it carefully and returned half to the plate, then had to make a grab for the tiller as *Day Bringer* decide to find her own path.

"I think we should share," she said, when control had been re-established.

Marheh nodded, studied the pathetic little object on the plate, crumbled it in one hand and fed it to the fish.

"I can't seem to fancy it somehow," she said.

Gelis laughed at her die away tone and did the same.

"Where did you find that?" she asked.

"Lurking in the bottom of my back pack. I'll never win any prizes for good housekeeping."

She turned around to pick up the mugs and hand one to Gelis.

"I have not managed very well so far, food and water both rationed. You could be forgiven for wanting to jump ship."

Gelis shook her head.

"Not likely." She was serious now. "Not unless you want to get rid of me."

"Not likely," Marheh said, a smile in her eyes. "And go back to doing all the work myself."

*****

"If all goes well today, we should reach Deerford tomorrow," Marheh told Gelis the next morning when she came out with sperit for her. "We should moor at the bottom of the locks tonight."

"Tell me about Deerford," Gelis said, handing over Marheh's mug.

The morning was quite chilly despite the sunshine and Marheh settled the tiller against the small of her back so she could warm both hands on the mug. Gelis looked at her in surprise.

"Not you, not yet," Marheh said. "And only on a calm day and a straight stretch."

Gelis nodded.

"I'll wait until you're not looking to try it," she said.

"Umm, that's what I would have done," Marheh said. "I'm obviously teaching you all the wrong things."

Gelis grinned.

"Tell me about Deerford," she said again.

"You're always making me work." Marheh pretended to grumble. "I thought the apprentice was the one who worked."

"That can't be right," Gelis said, all innocence. "The mentor is the one who teaches and that must be work."

"Cheeky," Marheh said, laughing. "You're right about that."

She resumed a more orthodox position at the tiller and drank from her mug.

"Deerford," Gelis said severely.

"Yes ma'am. Anything you say ma'am." She drained her sperit and handed Gelis the mug. "After you have put that carefully away in the galley."

Gelis laughed and did as she was asked. Marheh looked after her with a smile. The pink shorts were cheerful and Gelis seemed to be treating her more like a human now instead of some kind of higher being. It was good to have someone who laughed with her. There was no harm in forgetting her worries for Kel and the others for a bit. She was not going to lose sight of her purpose.

"Deerford," Gelis said, bounding up the steps from the back cabin.

Marheh laughed.

"You're not easily distracted are you?"

"It's one of my better qualities."

Gelis attempted to look modest and again Marheh laughed.

"Alright, Deerford it is. I told you my family live there. It's where I grew up. My family have a pottery. It's been in the family for four generations now. The water road runs along the bottom of the garden and there is a mooring there that was made when one of my great uncles joined the Silberay and used his boat to carry goods for the family firm."

"Great uncle, uncle and now you," Gelis said as she paused. "I bet there are not many Silberay who can say that."

Marheh smiled and shook her head.

"I've been scolded for boasting about it on more than one occasion. My youngest brother Tep and his wife Fali live there now and run the pottery with the help of my nephew Tith and his wife Kina. They have a little girl, Nicken, and my other great niece Lorac is apprenticed to Tep and she lives there too. That's where we're going. They'll look after us, feed us, let us fill the water tank, maybe even offer us baths."

She grinned and sniffed the air.

"In fact, definitely offer us baths."

Gelis giggled then sobered.

"They won't mind if I'm there?"

"Of course not. They'll be keen to meet you. They know I have an apprentice now."

"Is Deerford a nice village?"

"I've always thought so, but I'm a bit concerned about it at the moment. My singing has shown me some worrying signs."

She stopped speaking for so long Gelis felt forgotten.

"Worrying signs?" she prompted.

"We seem to be travelling into darkness," Marheh said. "It suggests to me that we are heading in the right direction for our task, but I'm worried for my family if Yareblis are at work there."

"I know the Yareblis are our enemies now, but I don't really understand what they do," Gelis said.

"They like power," Marheh said bluntly. "I think their ideal world would have them at the top and all the rest of us doing their bidding, never thinking for ourselves or questioning what they do. They choose to deny the soul and only practice the discipline of the mind in order to control people."

"I don't understand," Gelis said again.

Marheh looked at her.

A moment later she turned, descended the four steps into her cabin then hurried back out again to stand in front of Marheh.

"Did you make me do that?" Gelis asked uncertainly.

"Yes, I did," Marheh said. "I wanted you to understand."

She throttled back and took both hands off the tiller to put them gently on Gelis' shoulders so she would meet her eyes.

"If I was not your mentor I would have broken the law," she said. "And now I promise that I will never enter your mind again without your permission."

"But you will always have that," Gelis said, looking at her with awe.

Marheh shook her head then made a grab for the tiller as *Day Bringer* decided she had been neglected for long enough.

"When you are more confident with the discipline of the soul we will begin the discipline of the mind. For now it is the discipline of the soul that is important, critical really, because it is your defence against the Yareblis."

She opened the throttle a little then concentrated on her approach to the bridge that appeared as they rounded a bend.

"There will be Yareblis," she said when the bridge was safely behind them. "I wish I could say differently. There will be Yareblis and I think they are in Deerford. They want to stop us from countering their attempts to increase their power. In the past they have focused on individuals, but now I'm wondering whether they plan to destroy the water road itself."

Grey heron with spread wings
Slowly beating, slowly beating
Slowly
Rising
Grey spirit of the water's edge
Take me with you.

Gelis

CHAPTER SIX

Gelis had plenty to think about as she took her turn at the tiller and as she worked at polishing the brass. She wondered whether she should feel afraid, but she couldn't believe that Marheh would allow anything to harm her. They were passing through lovely and varied countryside that seemed benign as well as beautiful and the sunny day encouraged optimism.

The brass didn't take much time if you rubbed it up every day, she thought, stretching out on *Day Bringer*'s nice smooth roof and enjoying the sun on her bare arms and legs. When they were able to get a trough she would plant pansies, she decided, picturing their cheerful faces and maybe some lobelia if Marheh was happy with her choice.

Tonight, in her journal, she was going to make another poem. She hadn't felt the urge since the one she had written at the Gathering. Well, probably poem was too big a word, but the rhyme she had written then had satisfied her. Now she wanted to catch something of the contrasts; the lovely landscape and the darkness Marheh spoke of, happiness and the undercurrent of Marheh's sadness. Rhythm would be more important than rhyme, some words that danced and some that paced solemnly. Perhaps instead she might write something called *Marheh in My Mind*.

Marheh, at the tiller, watched her, wondering what she was thinking and hoping she had not said too much or too little about her fears. If the Yareblis managed to stop the Silberay from travelling, the water road would die, as the Clanning Branch appeared to have done. Where were the missing ones? Was she right in thinking that Deerford was at risk? Gelis seemed so innocent with her pink shorts, cheerful smile and crop of brown curls. Perhaps she could be persuaded to stay with the family while she tackled the Yareblis.

They would be getting to the locks before dark. She thought she would have Gelis steer into them in the morning. *Day Bringer* would keep her safe if there were Yareblis waiting for them and she could tell her that it was part of her learning.

All this country held so many memories. Her friends Gul and Sybi at Willow Rise had been a special part of her life for twenty or more years. Gul had been dead now for at least six years and Sybi for four, but she always remembered them when she travelled past. Usually she stopped to sing at the mooring for Willow Rise and always the song seemed to hold something of their music. No stopping today, but she could still hold them briefly in her mind with love and gratitude.

"Bridge," she called to Gelis.

It was not safe for her on the roof, even lying down. Some bridges were lower than others and sometimes the water level varied.

Gelis slid down to the gunnel and made her way along to Marheh.

"Is it my turn?"

"Would you like it to be?"

Gelis nodded.

"After the bridge then," Marheh said.

She steered them expertly through and relinquished the tiller to Gelis.

"Call me when you've had enough," she said.

They made good progress through the spring sunshine and nothing hindered them from reaching the locks by suppertime. The long twilight evening tempted Marheh to continue but she knew it would be foolish. She had been attacked at these locks in the past. Instead she worked with Gelis as she practised the discipline of the soul and suggested an early night after they had eaten the last of their remaining supplies.

Although she was not sleepy Gelis was quite happy to go to her cabin to wrestle with the words and ideas she had been playing with as she steered. Prose was enough to describe Marheh's appearance but it needed something more to capture her mentor's essential quality.

She was uneasily aware that Marheh would not really want the kind of tribute she wanted to write, but since she was not planning to show it to her that seemed not to matter. In the end she only managed four lines that almost conveyed what she felt, a quiet, rather sad beginning, with a crescendo towards the end.

Depth and stillness, Remote as a distant mountain.

69

> *Wisdom's quiet working*
> *Until a candle flares. A smile telescopes distance.*
> *Light welcomes warmth.*

She studied it critically and frowned at the page in her journal. Maybe she would come back to it later. She went to bed still thinking of words and images and found sleep elusive.

Marheh woke with the dawn. She always opened her curtains before she slept and last night she had opened the doors to the well deck as well. Her cabin was flooded with light. It was not warm. She couldn't expect that, not so early in spring, but the bright freshness beckoned. She got out of bed and hurried into her clothes before stepping out into the well deck to sniff the air. Whatever the day ahead might hold, this beginning was filled with promise.

Into the saloon to waken the fire and put the kettle on for sperit. Sometimes she missed the old stove that she had struggled with as an apprentice but the gas stove she had had for the last half dozen years did mean she didn't need to wait for the fire before she could have a hot drink. Briefly she wondered what Gelis would have made of the tasks that had been hers. Normally it didn't matter that she slept late, but this morning the locks awaited them. She made sperit for them both and carried Gelis' mug through to the back cabin.

The curtains were still closed but there was enough light for Marheh to see the tangle of bed clothes that suggested a disturbed night.

"Gelis," she said softly and turned to put her mug down on the little desk so she could open the curtains.

Gelis' open journal still lay there. It was not possible to avoid seeing her name and she was glad the book was upside down so it was difficult to make out anything more in the single, almost involuntary, glance she gave it. What Gelis chose to write was none of her business.

She turned back to the bunk and saw that Gelis was struggling to wake.

"Time to get up," she said briskly. "Locks this morning."

Gelis pushed back the bed clothes and swung her legs out.

"It's cold!"

"It is," Marheh agreed. "But it promises to be a nice day. There's sperit for you on your desk. Don't be long."

She took herself back to the galley to start the porridge with the meagre handful of oats that was all that was left. Gelis' journal might be none of her business, but it was difficult to keep from wondering. She remembered, with a little stab of guilt, how she had once drawn a cruel caricature of Nemle in her journal and left it open on the table in the saloon, wanting her to see it. She had been busy hating Nemle then. She didn't think Gelis was hating her. She stirred the porridge once more then turned off the gas. Locks and Deerford, that was where she needed to fix her mind.

Gelis came through wearing the pink shorts, but with a jumper over her skimpy top. Marheh thought she looked a bit uncomfortable and her greeting seemed a bit awkward.

"There you are," she said, putting a dollop of porridge into a bowl and passing it to her. "It's a rather penitential breakfast I'm afraid but better than nothing."

"I'm sorry I overslept."

Gelis slid into a seat at the table without looking at her.

"And I'm sorry I had to wake you, but the locks need us both today." Marheh sat in the seat opposite. "I want you to take the tiller. Your steering is coming on nicely so it will be a good challenge."

Gelis' face brightened.

"Really?"

"Yes really."

Marheh laughed as Gelis demolished her porridge in two big spoonfuls and got to her feet.

"I'll just go and tidy my cabin and put my shoes on."

Twenty minutes later they were on their way. Marheh had watched while Gelis did the engine checks and stayed to help loosen the mooring lines before jogging up the steep slope to the lock side to empty the lock.

While the water was running away she looked out over the landscape, listening with her heart. Beyond the path were wide, empty fields with just a hint of spring green tinting the red brown earth. This landscape had changed very little in all the years. The other side was hilly. There was land for grazing and a few cows standing about but on the horizon she could see chimneys and roof tops that had grown there during the last ten years or so.

The lock empty, she pushed open the gate where she was then walked around the top to get to the other side. No need for crossing the gap today. *Day Bringer* was close now and she smiled at Gelis' concentrating face. She took *Day Bringer* into the lock neatly with just a tiny bump on one side.

"Well done."

Marheh had dropped the paddles. Now she pushed the gate closed and went around for the other side. Gelis had throttled back and was looking anxiously up at her.

"Just keep her nose up to the gate. You're doing fine."

Water in, gate open, *Day Bringer* out, gate closed, Marheh completed the familiar tasks automatically, keeping most of her mind alert and listening to the landscape, but although there was darkness and a degree of pain she could detect no immediate threat. Between the locks she walked, enjoying the exercise, while Gelis took *Day Bringer* slowly on.

It was not very long before all three locks were behind them. Marheh congratulated Gelis as she stepped back on board and took over the tiller.

"You did very well, and I'm beautifully warm from the exercise," she said. "Now an easy hour and we'll reach Deerford."

They travelled on, each with their own thoughts, Marheh at the tiller, Gelis standing with her folded arms resting on *Day Bringer*'s roof. It was perhaps a half hour later when a grey heron spread its wings and took off just ahead of them.

Gelis made a small sound then turned to look at Marheh.

"It's so beautiful."

Marheh smiled.

"We'll meet him again before long. He'll see us through his territory."

Gelis looked eagerly ahead and, sure enough, a few minutes later she saw him, poised and still at the water's edge. Then as they approached, the great wings stretched and lifted so that he flew gracefully away in front of them before disappearing below the tree line.

Day Bringer moved slowly onwards. They rounded a bend and there he was again, an elegant statue posed at the entrance to a bridge. *Day Bringer*'s patient throbbing continued to carry them forward and, as before, the heron stretched his wings and flew, but not, this time, ahead of them. Instead he made a wide, sweeping circle, as if to bid them farewell, then disappeared behind them. A moment of silence held them. Then Marheh spoke quietly.

"Beyond the bridge is Deerford."

The bridge was so narrow and low that Marheh had Gelis take the chimney down and lay it on the roof before coming to join her on the stern deck. Gelis watched and shivered suddenly as the shadow of the bridge fell over *Day Bringer*'s prow. Marheh's quiet words had held a depth of meaning. What awaited them in Deerford? The shadow came closer. Inevitably it would cover them. It had never mattered before at the many bridges they had encountered but this time Gelis wanted to turn, like the heron, and avoid the darkness. She glanced back to Marheh and took comfort from the steady, concentrated gaze of her mentor. Then, as the shadow passed over them, she looked ahead and saw *Day Bringer*'s prow again in sunlight before she had to duck.

Day Bringer had almost to find her own way the last few feet, as Marheh had to duck too, though she kept one hand on the tiller. Gelis wondered whether she would ever be able to steer with such skill and sensitivity as if she and *Day Bringer* were one. They were only a moment crouched in the darkness but it seemed to take forever before they emerged. The sun was still shining in Deerford, as it had been on the other side of the bridge, but it seemed as if the clear, bright light they had travelled by had become more lurid and somehow oppressive.

"Just made it," said Marheh as they came out of the bridge hole. "I've never known it such a tight fit, as if the water has risen." She looked at Gelis. "You could put the chimney up again please. The fire goes better then."

Gelis was glad of the activity. She was not quite sure what she had expected of Deerford, but it wasn't this blankness.

They were travelling between high walls, too high to see over from the stern, though when Gelis climbed up and stood on the roof, she could see slate roofs and chimney pots and catch a glimpse of an occasional tree.

"It's eerie," she said. "I feel as if I'm invisible."

"You are in a way. What's that saying? None so blind as those that won't see."

Gelis came back to the stern and sat on the roof again.

"This is the expensive end of the village. They've turned their backs, literally, on anything that reminds them that there are alternatives. Once these houses had gardens running down to the water road."

They travelled slowly onward.

"It gets better," Marheh said. "Around that bend the walls finish and the view opens out a bit. There's a pond and the green."

Marheh pushed the tiller ready for the long curve ahead. Gelis watched eagerly, looking forward to seeing something of the village. Suddenly *Day*

Bringer's prow swung in towards the bank. Marheh muttered and struggled with the tiller, trying to get her back on course.

Gelis watched in surprise for a moment then forgot everything as they rounded the bend. The water road seemed to divide. The narrow way that was their route was dwarfed into insignificance by the entrance to a large pond. As they approached the junction, decorative wrought iron gates swung open. *Day Bringer* seemed to be drawn towards them despite Marheh's struggles. She was reversing now, using all the power of *Day Bringer's* engine to move them back, out of the current that drew them off course.

"Let's go there," shouted Gelis. "I want to go that way."

"No." Marheh jerked the words out, her attention on *Day Bringer*. "Not that way." She looked at Gelis, just for a moment, focusing on her. "Practise," she said. "Practise now."

Gelis blinked. "Practise?"

Marheh had managed to get *Day Bringer* back into the straight walled section they had just travelled.

"Practise the soul song," she said. "That's your armour."

She reached forward, touched Gelis' shoulder and looked again into her eyes. "Ready?" she asked.

It was not really a question. They had no option but to go on, this time knowing what awaited them. Marheh pushed the throttle forward and headed *Day Bringer* not for the narrow channel of the water road, but for the outside bank. *Day Bringer* surged forward. Marheh was murmuring to her, almost as if she were alive, no long, easy curve this time, instead a fierce thrust of power.

The water surged white behind them as they pushed forward against the current. Despite Marheh's preparation and clever steering they were still drawn towards the pond entrance, but this time Marheh was ready and *Day Bringer* seemed to leap to her command. For a moment it seemed as if they would miss the channel of the water road and ram the bank, but the current suddenly let go of them and they were through.

Immediately Marheh throttled back. It was as if they had entered a tunnel, the way was so narrow and over grown. Overhanging trees drooped on either side, sweeping the cabin roof. The chimney was knocked over and pushed back along the roof towards Gelis who still sat there almost as if entranced.

"Watch out!" Marheh's voice was sharp with anxiety. *Day Bringer* was too heavy to stop quickly and Gelis seemed unaware of her danger.

"Gelis!" she shouted.

Gelis blinked as if waking and tried to scramble off the roof. The branches caught her before she had done more than twist around, feeling for the gunnel with her feet.

Marheh let go of the tiller and grabbed at her as the branches swept over them. The chimney hit the water with a splash and *Day Bringer* rocked as Marheh attempted to steady Gelis. A moment later they were through. Gelis was scratched and her shirt was torn, but she was safely on the stern and Marheh was back with the tiller and throttle easing *Day Bringer*'s passage.

"That was unexpected." Marheh spoke lightly. "It looks as if that was the worst of it though." The trees were beginning to thin and stretched taller on either side, so that instead of a tunnel, they seemed to pass through a leafy chasm. "At least we can see the sky now."

Gelis was silent. She licked the back of her hand where a long scratch grew small bubbles of blood.

"Are you still in one piece?" Marheh's voice was still light, expressionless. "Do you need to put something on that?"

Gelis shook her head, staring determinedly in front of them.

Marheh fell silent, her attention given to *Day Bringer* and the water road. They travelled slowly onward. Nothing about them moved. There were no birds. *Day Bringer*'s quiet pulse seemed loud and intrusive, drawing attention they would rather not have.

"We need to moor," Marheh said at last.

Gelis looked around. The trees came almost to the water's edge, the bank looked overgrown on both sides. Marheh throttled back until *Day Bringer* was barely moving.

"There is a place," she said, answering Gelis' questioning glance. "It is shallow and overgrown and it's a long time since I've used it, but it used to be possible."

She was scanning the bank as she spoke, then she throttled back still further and turned *Day Bringer*'s bow towards the edge.

"Will you go forward," she said to Gelis. "I won't be able to get the back in. Jump off when we touch and tie the front line, around a tree will do. We'll worry about the back later."

A few moments later the bow scrunched into the mud by the bank. Gelis flung herself across the narrow strip of water and landed safely on all fours, the rope clutched in one hand. Once she had secured it Marheh tossed her the stern line and had her tie that loosely so the stern was still in deep water. Only then did Gelis wonder how she would get back on board.

Marheh saw her consternation.

"Don't worry," she called softly. "I won't leave you there."

She walked along the gunnel towards the bow, grabbing the gang plank from the roof as she went. Between them they manoeuvred it into place and Gelis was able to walk carefully back on board.

"Well done," Marheh said. "It isn't ideal, but we will be able to stay here overnight at least. I don't want to moor at the pottery until I know what kind of attention that might draw to them."

They went together through Marheh's cabin and into the saloon.

"What about supplies?" Gelis asked as Marheh went to put the kettle on for sperit.

"We'll have to hope that my family can help us," Marheh said. "I think we might throw ourselves on their mercy for a wash and our evening meal. Fali, my sister-in-law, always provides generously."

Gelis looked anxious. "Perhaps you had better go without me. Two might be too many."

She went to get their mugs.

"Even the sperit is running low now," she said, spooning some into each mug, ready for the boiling water.

"I won't go alone," Marheh said. "I'd be in big trouble if I left you behind."

She poured the water into their mugs.

"Now," she said gently. "Come and sit down and tell me what is really worrying you."

Gelis looked at her, then down to the mug she held in both hands.

"I wanted to go there," she said. "It looked so pretty. There was a flock of white boats floating, proud and graceful, like swans." She paused. "I don't understand. I really wanted us to go there."

"Of course you did," Marheh said. "That was the intention and you haven't the experience to arm yourself yet."

She touched Gelis' hand lightly.

"I'm sorry I couldn't protect you properly, but I needed all my concentration to keep us out of there."

Gelis was silent for some moments then she looked again at Marheh with troubled eyes.

"But part of me still wants to go there," she said at last. "Even now that I know it is a Yareblis place."

Marheh touched her again.

"Drink up your sperit and stop worrying. None of this is your fault. You've only been with me ten days and already you've coped with more than some apprentices do in their first couple of years. When you've finished your drink we will sing together and that will help you get your thoughts sorted out."

A short time later they had found the place of stillness. Then Marheh gave Gelis some salve to put on her scratches and sent her off to rest for an hour or so. Marheh too was weary from the exertions of the last few days. Even the need to think of Gelis was tiring, used as she was to a solitary life. She stretched and sighed and settled herself to quietness, to wait, listen and think.

A couple of hours later they set off together to visit Marheh's family, each with a towel and a change of clothes in their day packs. Although the place they were moored was lonely and seemed remote from the village, Marheh was worried about leaving *Day Bringer* and spent sometime fixing the moorings. In the end she decided to drop the anchor from the off side where it was less likely to be seen. Then they took the boat hook and picked up the gangplank and hid them both. Although the villagers were not likely to even see them, the Yareblis would have been alerted to their passing by the action of the gate. Before they left Marheh blessed the lines, touching each gently and speaking low.

"Be strong in purpose, hold fast," she said, turning to explain this traditional blessing to Gelis before leading her along the path through the trees.

It was not much of a path and in places they had to scramble over fallen branches or duck beneath overhanging shrubs. Conversation was not possible walking one behind the other, but occasionally Marheh would stop and wait for Gelis so she could indicate some landmark or point of interest. Gelis found herself thinking of Marheh as a child, playing here, running along beside the water road, waving and calling out to the boats as they passed.

"Where are the houses?" she asked as they stopped to look around. "Where do people live?"

Marheh gestured to the bank of shrubbery that blocked their view. "Behind there are houses and a road that turns and goes over the tunnel and into the village centre, but these have turned their backs on the water road too."

"Why?" Gelis said, almost to herself. "What has gone wrong?"

Marheh turned to smile at her. "We'll be able to spend hours on that one," she said. "But not now."

Soon the trees thinned and they were able to move faster across the clearer ground. It was not long before they reached the high brick wall that enclosed the pottery. There was a gate, quite close to where the wall met the water road, but when Marheh tried to open it she found it immovable.

"But it's never locked," she said, pushing at it.

Gelis said nothing. Obviously it was locked now.

"We'll have to go around the front," Marheh said, accepting that this entrance was closed to them.

She led the way along a thread of a path beside the wall, Gelis following. When they reached the road she turned, still following the wall, and made her way towards another gate set in a pretty archway with a canopy of green growing over it. There were buds just beginning to open, roses, Gelis thought. This gate opened smoothly and Marheh led the way into a walled garden, neat and pretty. The flowers of early spring bloomed in beds around the walls and behind them was the promise of later blossoms and summer flowers. There was a side gate and Gelis thought they were going that way until Marheh looked at her and grinned.

"Let's pretend to be visitors," she said making for the front door.

A moment later she was pressing the door bell.

A light went on and the door opened a cautious inch before being flung wide to greet them. A man was silhouetted against the light. He swept Marheh into a hug then released her to turn to greet Gelis. She went hesitantly towards him, feeling a bit shy, and was about to speak when an inner door opened and a small girl appeared.

"Marheh!" she shouted and came running down the hall towards them.

Marheh held out her arms and the little girl was scooped up and held.

"I'm Tep, Marheh's youngest brother," the man said to Gelis, smiling at the rapturous greeting. "And this is Nicken, my youngest granddaughter."

"Hello Nicken, it's nice to meet you. I'm Gelis, Marheh's apprentice."

Nicken smiled, bright brown eyes beaming.

"Hello Gelis, are you coming to supper?"

Gelis looked at Marheh.

"Of course she is," Marheh said, smiling at her.

Tep closed the front door and slid a chain into place.

"That's new," Marheh said a question in her voice.

"Yes," said Tep, ushering them along the hallway. "Into the kitchen with you. I had a feeling you might be on your way and Fali has been cooking extra these last three days. What kept you?"

"This and that," Marheh said. "Nothing special."

She looked at Fali.

"We badly need a bath," she said. "Both of us. We ran short of water."

Fali, Tep's wife, was small and sturdy with the same bright eyes as Nicken.

"Of course, she said. "Gelis, you go up first. Nicken will show you. Supper will keep till you're ready."

By the time baths were over all the family had gathered in the big, warm kitchen. Gelis sat quietly enjoying the good smells and trying to work out who they all were. She had been allotted the bathroom first, so she was already clean and dry when Marheh appeared. There were more greetings then. Marheh was obviously someone special. She crossed the room to hug her older niece Lorac and greet Nicken's parents. Fali tut-tutted as she passed, her hair in its long thick plait was wet against her back.

"Look at you," Fali scolded. "Just sit down here and let someone look after you for a change. Nicken, run and get a towel and a comb."

"Gelis looks after me very nicely," Marheh said, smiling at her.

"I'm sure she does." Fali had pushed Marheh into a chair and was already undoing the plait. "When you let her."

She seized the towel Nicken had brought and took possession of Marheh's head, rubbing energetically, spreading the long strands across the towel then rubbing some more. Gelis smiled to herself at the sight.

"Your hair is amazing," she said, when Fali had laid a dry towel over Marheh's shoulders and was combing her hair over it. "Have you ever cut it?"

She looked around, surprised, as the others began to laugh. Marheh hid her face in the end of the towel for a moment then looked up, her eyes dancing.

"Only once," she said. "And they've never let me live it down."

"Marheh got the cane," Nicken chanted, jumping up and down. "Marheh got the cane."

"Alright scrap, you tell Gelis."

"No, Papa Tep should tell it," Nicken said. "Papa Tep was there," she told Gelis.

Tep smiled at her and looked affectionately at Marheh.

"She was ten," he said. "With three young brothers she had been told to look after. We were all in the kitchen waiting for her so we could start tea. In she came, head up, back very straight, a sort of don't-even-think-of-asking look on her face. She did look a sight. Her hair was dark then, nearly black, and she used to wear it in two plaits, one each side. She'd chopped them off close to her head, but not quite evenly and bits stuck out all round at odd angles and different lengths. Our mother gave a sort of gasp as if she didn't know whether to laugh or cry. The three of us boys ducked for cover and our father looked at her for a moment before he asked rather ferociously what she was up to.

"She put on her best Marheh the Great look and told him she had decided she would rather be a boy, because boys didn't have to look after their little brothers. 'I see,' said our father, with the sort of look that would have had me ready to burst into tears. 'In that case you won't mind if I punish you like a boy.' There was an awful pause and I think all three of us boys shivered. '- and give you the cane,' he finished.

"Marheh's lip trembled and I remember I thought for a moment she was going to cry. I had never seen Marheh cry. But she just stuck up her chin and gave him another look and said 'If you wish Father.' 'Go and wait for me in my study,' he told her, and off she went. A queen going to her execution couldn't have done it better.

"Father gave us all a bit of a telling off for being the kind of little brothers that Marheh did not want to look after, then off he went to the study. As soon as the door shut behind him the three of us scooted into the hall to hear what was happening. At first the rumble of his voice, then ten loud smacking noises, then nothing.

"It seemed forever before she came out of the study, still wearing her Marheh the Great look, so that none of us dared to ask her what had happened."

Marheh had buried her face in the towel by the conclusion of this narrative. Now she looked up at Gelis.

"Never, ever, be a big sister," she said, laughing. "It's a wonder I can still hold my head up."

Nicken ran to give her a hug.

"Poor Marheh, but you didn't really get the cane, did you?"

Marheh shook her head.

"I don't think I quite knew what getting the cane was, except that some of the quite big boys cried after they got it at school. I was so frightened those few minutes I waited in the study. I was shivering and tears were running down my face. Then father came in. He took one look at me and scooped me up in a big hug. He told me I was a silly girl, tousled my hair and said he thought that would be punishment enough. Then he put me across his knee, but instead of spanking me he clapped his hands together ten times. Then he let me off his knee, mopped up my tears, gave me another hug and whispered 'Our secret.'"

"What a spoilt brat you were," Fali said affectionately, giving Marheh's hair a little tug as she divided it carefully into three strands and began to plait.

"I was too," Marheh said. "Father thought I would be teased at school over my hair, but one of the boys told his class that I had had the cane, which seemed to give me a certain status, since girls weren't normally caned."

She grinned at Gelis.

"Of course I couldn't give father away."

Gelis laughed. Fali finished off the plait and flipped it over Marheh's shoulder.

"That's better," she said. "Now we'll have supper."

Soon they were all sitting round the table eating a rich savoury stew and Fali's home baked bread. There was plenty of conversation and Gelis listened with interest looking from one to the other and trying to sort out each one's place in the family. Nicken and Lorac were cousins, not sisters as

Gelis had initially assumed. Nicken's parents, Tith and Kina, lived with Tep and Fali and worked in the pottery. Lorac was apprenticed to Tep. Gelis went round the table again, trying to fix the names in her mind.

Lorac smiled as their eyes met.

"Feeling confused?" she asked.

"Just a bit."

"Don't worry, we'll all fall into place before long."

Lorac stood up and began to gather up the plates and cutlery.

"Let me help."

"There's no need," Fali said, putting one hand on Gelis' arm.

Gelis turned to look at her.

"Please I'd like to."

Fali smiled and nodded. Gelis stood up and followed Lorac to the sink, carefully carrying a load of crockery.

"Shall I wash?" she asked. "Then you can put things away."

She put down her pile of dishes beside Lorac's.

"I think these dishes are just beautiful," she said, taking the soap and the dish cloth Lorac handed her.

"They are aren't they."

Lorac carefully placed the last pile beside Gelis.

"My great grandfather Sef, Tep and Marheh's father, made them for his master work. They only come out on special occasions."

Gelis poured hot water into the sink.

"The colours are so clear and bright and the shapes are so simple and graceful."

Lorac nodded.

"We still make tableware, but nothing as fine as this."

Carefully Gelis lifted a stack of plates into the water.

"Is this the kind of work you do?" she asked.

"I wish!"

Lorac was polishing plates carefully.

"I'm making nothing but mugs at the moment, sets of six, matching," she grimaced. "It's good training though – getting the size right every time."

"How long have you been apprenticed?" Gelis asked.

"Four years, since I was seventeen."

"You must be just a year older than me – but I've only just started."

"But that's different. You don't know enough to choose your kind of life at seventeen."

"Marheh knew."

"Marheh's special and even she was not apprenticed to the Silberay until she was twenty."

Lorac stretched to put a pile of plates in a cupboard.

"She could have been a potter if she'd wanted and her signature pieces are still sought after. She hasn't done one yet this year though."

The dishes were soon finished and Lorac put the kettle on to make sperit for them all. She was just setting out the mugs when there was a tap on the kitchen window and a moment later a tall, thin young man opened the kitchen door. Lorac beamed and set out an extra mug.

"This is Ved," she told Gelis.

Gelis saw a rather scruffy, skinny young man with red hair, but she also saw a light come on in Lorac and sensed that he cared for her also.

They sat round the table for some time after the washing up was finished, talking and drinking sperit. Tep added a drop of vodka for each of the adults and Gelis wondered whether it was that which encouraged her to produce a little sperit rhyme.

> *"Sperit*
> *Nice spice*
> *Merry berry*
> *Warms the tum*
> *Yum, yum*
> *Sperit,"* she said, lifting her mug in salute.

Marheh laughed with the others. Gelis had never seen her so relaxed, seemingly untroubled. When Nicken begged her for a story Marheh offered to tell it to her when she was in bed, but there was a chorus of protest from the others so she pushed back her chair and embarked on a traditional Silberay tale.

"Once upon a time," she began. "The Silberay Lor visited the village of

Nuttindene, alone on his boat *Tempest*. He moored by the village green and watched the villagers passing, crossing the green on their way to shop or visit the pub or a neighbour and he saw they were angry and unhappy," Marheh said.

Gelis found herself wondering how much Marheh identified Deerford with Nuttindene.

"Some of the younger villagers yelled insults at each other and even threw stones across the green."

Gelis knew she was remembering their own episode of stone throwing and was not surprised to see Nicken hanging on every word. Tep and Fali were watching and listening with amused affection, Tith and Kina had relaxed, happy in the knowledge that Nicken was enjoying her treat and Lorac and Ved held hands under the table as they sat together.

"After a while Lor stepped off *Tempest* and onto the green. He strolled across the grass, his hands in his pockets. For a few moments the villagers were taken by surprise then some of the bolder individuals began to approach him with new insults and threatening gestures. 'Go back where you came from!' 'We don't want your sort here!' But Lor paid them no attention, just stepped quietly over the grass and went to sit on a bench at the edge of the green."

Marheh leaned back in her chair, stretched out her legs and surveyed her audience.

"He smiled benevolently at the people approaching him," she went on, "And spent his energy picturing them with contented, purposeful faces."

She paused, suiting action to words.

"'Nothing to do? Nothing will do for you,' said Lor. 'What are you on about?' cried a young and angry voice. 'No one to be? No one will be for thee,' replied Lor. 'You're crazy!' 'You're not talking sense.' Then Lor said quietly 'It's a puzzle. Tell me about Nuttindene.'"

Marheh's eyes flashed and her face changed with the villager's anger, then she was Lor again, calm and quiet, promising to be angry along with the villagers if theirs was good anger.

"Be angry about injustice, ugliness, corruption," Marheh said. "That's good anger."

It seemed she spoke for herself as well as Lor.

"'We've got all of those here,' a young girl called, and suddenly there was a babble of sound as the villagers crowded around, all trying to tell Lor about workers being exploited, public gardens being shut and common land enclosed.''

Marheh paused to draw breath, leaving the babble of voices filling the silence.

"'This is your village,'" she went on. "'What are you going to do about it?' 'Fight! Take action! Expose!'" She held up her hands to calm the crowd. "'But first you must arm yourselves with something beautiful, or in touching corruption you might become corrupt.' Lor looked from one to the other then his eyes rested on a small, stout school boy, right at the back of the group.''

Nicken giggled as Marheh seemed to become the shy, plump child. She pushed her hands into her pockets and tried to bring them out holding onto something.

"I've got something beautiful," she said huskily, struggling with the contents of her pockets. Then she cupped her hands and held them out.

"Do you see?" she said. "His pockets were full of marbles, each one swirled with colour and pattern, each one lovingly polished. Lor held up first one and then another, turning them so the pattern danced and the light shone through the colours. The boy whispered something and blushed. Lor looked at him with love. 'Are you sure?' he asked.

"The boy nodded. Lor put a hand on his shoulder. 'Mit offers you each one of his treasures,' he said. 'Something beautiful to think on.'"

"So the group lined up to select a marble from Mit's cupped hands. Some saw only the pretty colours, but a few saw the loving sacrifice. When they had all taken a marble Lor spoke again. He suggested some possible actions for them and promised to meet with them each afternoon to listen and encourage. 'Hold on to your beautiful marble and think about how it came to you,' he said. 'And then decide what action to take.'

"Then he moved away, through the group and back to *Tempest*.

"Next day when he met the villagers they told him about how they had gone quietly to sit in the garden that was no longer theirs and think about something beautiful. Lor smiled and encouraged them.

"Each day for a week they met him on the village green and each day they stood straighter and smiled more often with their neighbour and no one stood and threw insults or stones, so Lor knew it was time for him to move on.''

After the story Tith and Kina took Nicken upstairs to bed and Lorac disappeared with Ved. Then the shadows returned.

"So why did you come to the front door?" Tep asked. "Where's *Day Bringer?*"

"Yes," Fali said. "I was so pleased to see you I didn't think about where you came from."

Marheh looked from one to the other.

"I didn't want to draw attention to the pottery. I've moored down by Archer's Wood, what is left of it. We were attacked as we came through the village, back by the village pond, or what used to be the village pond."

"You didn't need to do that," Tep said. "You bring *Day Bringer* here and moor at the bottom of the garden like you usually do."

Marheh smiled gratefully at him but shook her head.

"Maybe tomorrow."

She paused, covered her face with her hands for a moment, then looked up.

"Tell me what's wrong here. The back gate is locked, there's a chain on the front door, that's never been needed before."

She paused again. Her eyes were troubled and Gelis was suddenly aware of a weight of sadness.

"The Silberay are under attack as never before. There are nearly thirty boats missing. *Storm Cloud* is one of them."

"Kel's boat?" Fali asked quietly, aware of how much Kel meant to Marheh.

She nodded and looked away for a moment to hide her sudden tears.

"I was called. The closer we've come to Deerford the more convinced I am that the heart of the trouble, the darkness, is here."

There was a long silence when she finished speaking.

"There have been ... changes in the village," Fali said slowly, her quiet words barely breaking the silence. "People are not neighbourly now. You rarely get a smile if you pass someone in the street. Tep put the bolt on the back gate after a couple of young men came in and tried to paint a slogan on the side of the kiln."

"It's a bit like your story," Tep said. "There's anger and unkindness. The Local Council has lost its way, or perhaps been usurped by incomers with a different agenda. You said you were attacked by the village pond, but it isn't the village pond any more. The council have apparently given the land to some club to use, adding to the amenities of the village they call it," he finished bitterly.

"What about Yareblis?" Marheh asked.

"I've no doubt they are behind some of it, but no one actually believes they exist."

"Which gives them more power," Marheh said.

"They don't believe in the Silberay either," Fali said. "Tep and I are just old fashioned fools."

"With a poor misguided sister no doubt," Marheh said with a smile and a hint of challenge in her voice.

Fali took her hand and squeezed it.

"It's wicked. Our Lorac is suffering too. Ved's mother doesn't approve of us."

Marheh stood up and turned to Gelis.

"We had better go, it's getting late."

She walked around the table to hug Tep and Fali.

"Thank you for feeding us. You've given me plenty to think about too, and I must confess I'm a bit worried about *Day Bringer*."

"We'll expect you at the pottery mooring in the morning," Tep said.

"Perhaps," Marheh said.

Gelis stood up and began to thank Tep and Fali, who smiled and hugged her.

"You're welcome any time."

Tep put a hand on her shoulder.

"You'll look after my big sister, won't you," he said, smiling at her.

Gelis laughed and nodded.

"But she doesn't really like it when I try."

Marheh tossed her head.

"I hear you."

Tep laughed.

"Don't you let Marheh the Great intimidate you," he said. "Sometimes she needs looking after." He paused. "Other times it's probably a spanking she needs."

Gelis giggled as Marheh put on her best Marheh the Great is displeased face.

"Enough of this nonsense," she said with mock severity. "You are undermining my authority."

Tep raised his eyebrows and Fali laughed.

"Come on then," Tep said. "I'll show you out the back way."

He went with them to the gate and would have accompanied them further, but Marheh assured him they could find their way. He let them through and closed the gate behind them and they heard the sound of the bolts sliding home.

King's Vegetables

CHAPTER SEVEN

The night was dark. If there was a moon it was hidden and a scattering of cloud blotted out many of the stars. Marheh seemed to be able to see. She was forging ahead, but Gelis was struggling to keep up. At least there was a little light reflected in the water road so she could follow that if Marheh disappeared. However, at the place where the trees began, she stopped and looked back.

"Are you alright?" she called softly.

Gelis did her best to hurry towards her, stumbling a little in her haste.

"I'm sorry," Marheh said as she reached her. "I forgot you don't know the path. It might get a bit tricky in the trees."

"I'll manage."

They set off again, quietly, side by side.

It was a happy evening," Gelis said. "Your family made me very welcome."

"Of course." Marheh's voice sounded as if she was smiling. "They were happy to meet you."

They walked on a little.

"They spoil me rather," she said. "It isn't good for me. Was I showing off?"

"They love you," Gelis said, glad of the darkness to say what she thought.

"Yes I know. I'm very lucky."

"I loved the story, especially you being a plump little boy." Gelis giggled. "And the story about your hair."

"How much vodka did Tep put in your sperit?"

"Marheh got the cane," Gelis chanted as Nicken had done.

"Too much obviously."

Marheh stood still so that Gelis bumped into her and giggled again.

"I think you had better hang on to my belt or I might lose you."

She grasped Gelis' hand and wrapped her fingers around the heavy belt she always wore.

"It is getting too narrow now to go side-by-side."

"I'm alright really," Gelis said, but she enjoyed the reassurance of Marheh's closeness and the security of her apparent ability to see in the dark.

Her own night vision seemed to be improving as they went and once Marheh had shown her how to look she found she could pick out the reflected brightness in the eyes of small night creatures. She had not been paying attention to where they were, so she was taken by surprise when Marheh stopped suddenly. She managed to pull up without bumping into her, but she was close enough to hear Marheh's sharply indrawn breath. Then Marheh began to run.

Gelis lost her grip on the belt, staggered and tried to run after her. Then she tripped on a tree root and fell headlong. It took a minute or two of floundering before she was back on her feet and had located Marheh standing quite still on the bank of the water road. She went carefully to stand beside her and watch what she was watching. *Day Bringer* was no longer lying quietly moored beneath the trees. Instead she was caught in some kind of current that was trying to draw her back towards the bridge and the Yareblis pond. Her anchor chain was fully extended and even in the darkness the water was visible, breaking around her bow.

They were silent for a few moments then Marheh said apologetically "I'm sorry. I thought she had gone. Did you hurt yourself?"

Gelis stood close to her.

"Thank goodness you thought to put the anchor out."

They contemplated the scene a bit longer. Then Gelis said, as firmly as she could, "Well, if anyone has to get wet, it should be me – it's my turn."

She felt, rather than saw, Marheh's smile as she thanked her

"We had best see if we can find out what has happened to the lines before we rush into anything."

She went cautiously along the bank to the clump of bushes where she had so carefully tied the front line. There, undisturbed, was her knot and the neat coil of rope.

"Cut," Marheh said. "Poor *Day Bringer.*"

She untied the knot and gathered up the rope.

"This could be useful however. I don't like the look of that current."

"It looks really powerful," Gelis agreed. "But the water won't be very deep will it?"

She stood on the bank and gazed at the dark water then tossed a small, pale twig as far out as she could and strained to see where it was swirled away and sucked under by the current.

Marheh went to look for the stern line and Gelis remembered the boat hook. She turned slowly, trying to pick the place where they had hidden it, took a couple of tentative steps towards a likely looking clump of foliage then suddenly identified the spot, found the boat hook and carried it triumphantly to Marheh. *Day Bringer* seemed to be dragging her anchor slowly away from them and it was clear that they were not going to be able to reach her with the boat hook, nor draw her in with it if they could.

Marheh looked at Gelis.

"Are you sure you want to get wet?"

"Not want to exactly, but one of us has to, and I do want to be the one."

Marheh nodded.

"Alright – if you're sure. I'm worried about the current. It is so strong it might have deepened the channel."

Gelis continued to study the water road, watching intently as the occasional piece of flotsam bobbed quickly by.

"What is causing it do you think? It wasn't like this when we left it, obviously."

Marheh shook her head.

"I don't know. Some sort of contrivance of the Yareblis perhaps. It seems to have been created with intent."

"Is there any point in trying to find out and stop it at the source?"

"I don't think we have time. The anchor is barely holding it seems to me."

Gelis nodded.

"I'd better get out there then."

She began to take off her coat, but Marheh stopped her.

"Not yet, a bit more planning first. The important thing is for you to be safe."

Soon enough however Gelis had stripped to her underclothes and stood, shivering with cold and excitement, while Marheh tied the cut rope around her waist. Then she handed her the boat hook.

"That might help steady you against the current."

"What if I lose it?"

"If it helps you that won't matter. You know where to find the spare key?"

Gelis nodded.

"Take your time with the engine once you get on board. You know what to do really."

Gelis nodded again.

Marheh gave her a quick hug.

"You're sure?" she asked again.

"I'm sure."

Using the boat hook like a staff she stepped into the fast flowing water. It was not much past her knees this first step, but she knew it would be much deeper in the channel where the current was strongest. She had not been prepared for how cold it was either. Clasping the boat hook in both hands she prodded the bed of the water road where she would step next. Already it went down further so that, with another couple of steps, she was up to her arm pits and fighting to stand against the current. The rope around her waist gave her confidence but if she fell Marheh might have quite a job to pull her back.

Another couple of steps and she might be able to reach the anchor chain, but the boat hook went down and down as she felt for the bottom and she knew she would have to swim for it. If she could push across the current enough it would carry her to *Day Bringer* since she had gone in up stream. She took up the boat hook and reached out with it. Another foot and the hook might catch the anchor chain.

Marheh had been paying out the rope very carefully, keeping it just firm and she was grateful for the sense of security it gave her. Now she needed it to be loose. She was going to risk everything on a plunge towards the chain that strained away from *Day Bringer*'s prow. As if Marheh had read her mind, and perhaps she had, she felt the rope slacken. Holding tight to the end of the boat hook she took a deep breath and lunged, letting the momentum take her with it. The hook caught in the chain, but now her feet were off the ground the current took her and swept her back against *Day Bringer*'s hull. She clung to the boat hook with all her strength and gradually pulled herself, hand over hand, towards the anchor chain.

At last she could touch it and cling to it. Almost wrapping herself around the chain she carefully unhooked the boat hook and pushed it up and over into the well deck. *Day Bringer*'s prow looked horribly high above her. For a moment she despaired of being able to hoist herself up enough. The anchor chain helped and she found the cut end of the front line which helped even more. Then, when she had both hands gripping the edge of the well deck, she found the current helped as she strained to get a leg up onto the gunnel. A last big effort and she rolled into the well deck and lay for a moment catching her breath.

She heard a faint cheer from the bank and knelt up to wave to Marheh. Then she untied the rope from around her waist and made it fast on the front stud, glad she had practised the few knots she had been taught during the Gathering. She saw Marheh's shadowy figure move with the end she held and realised that she was tying it to a tree. That would take some of the strain off the anchor and give her time to go slowly over the next important steps.

The cold was getting to her now the glow from the initial exertion had faded. She reached into the locker and fumbled for the spare key, held on a magnet against *Day Bringer*'s hull. A few moments more and she had the door to Marheh's cabin open. Warm air greeted her as she stepped inside and she realised gratefully that the fire was still in, despite the loss of the chimney. The warmth in the saloon wrapped itself around her like a soft blanket and she stopped there to strip off her wet clothes and luxuriate for a minute or two as her damp skin began to dry. There was more to do however and Marheh was waiting, cold and anxious on the bank, so she went through to her cabin for dry clothes then back to the engine room. This was where she needed to be careful and deliberate. Marheh was always up first so she was the one to do the engine checks and start the engine. Gelis had only done it once before, but now it was critical. She rehearsed the steps in her head before acting and felt a surge of relief when she finally turned the ignition key and heard *Day Bringer*'s engine begin its usual steady throbbing.

After that it was not as difficult and she even had time to remember the cut stern line and pull in the end so it would not foul the propeller. She could just make out Marheh's waiting presence in the dim light. That was where she would aim. She gripped the tiller in one hand and pushed the throttle forward with the other. At first, although she heard the engine sound change, it seemed to make little difference to *Day Bringer*. She pushed the throttle further forward and sensed rather than saw a release of tension. On the bank Marheh was leaning against the rope and Gelis realised that *Day Bringer* was moving. She increased the throttle still further. There was a surge of power and suddenly the current seemed to release its hold. *Day Bringer* leapt forward and a moment later her bow was nestled up to the bank, not far from where they had left her, only a few hours earlier.

She eased back the throttle then a wave of exhaustion washed over her and she stood, staring at nothing, only dimly aware that Marheh had tightened the front line then found the gangplank and placed it so she could board. A few moments later she was on the back deck, hugging Gelis and congratulating her.

"That was a mighty effort. Come on down into the warm."

She led Gelis down to the saloon and pushed her gently into the armchair.

"You must be exhausted. Just sit there and I'll make sperit."

She wanted to protest. She should be looking after Marheh, not Marheh looking after her, but somehow she didn't have the energy. She closed her eyes. Next thing she knew Marheh had perched on the footstool beside her. She touched her gently and held out a mug of sperit.

"Better wait for bed before you sleep," she said.

Gelis nodded and took the mug in both hands, then looked at Marheh over the top of it. There was something she needed to say but words were too difficult.

Marheh smiled at her.

"It's my turn to look after you. Come on, drink up."

Gelis sipped obediently and found she was grateful for the warmth.

"You might be a bit stiff in the morning. Getting into the well deck was difficult I could see."

"I was scared I wouldn't make it," Gelis said with a little shiver as she remembered the dark, rushing water and *Day Bringer*'s prow far above her.

"Then we will spend a few minutes making sure you don't have nightmares before you go off to bed."

Marheh waited quietly while she finished her drink then took both her hands and led her into the discipline of the soul to a place of peace and beauty.

She had not been singing, not really, she thought, in the moment before she slept, but Marheh's had been the song that held her.

Once she had seen Gelis into bed Marheh turned her attention to *Day Bringer*. The engine was still throbbing gently and although she was now on the edge of the current Marheh was uneasy. She went out to the well deck to pull in the gangplank and check that the line was holding. Then she shortened the anchor chain. The back line was now too short to be of any use in this situation and she had, in fact, left the cut end on the bank in her anxiety to get on board. It was too late to get it now but she would pick it up in the morning and try to splice it together. It would do then until she could replace it.

She was standing in the well deck thinking about what else needed to be done when she saw the moment that the current ceased. One minute something pale was rushing towards her then suddenly it seemed to pause and even in the darkness she saw a release of tension before it sailed gently onwards, moving more and more slowly as she watched.

It seemed like a sign. She went through and stopped the engine, turned the stern tube greaser and made a few additional checks. Gelis did not stir. No wonder she was tired. She had had a real battle with the water and then a struggle to heave herself on board. Marheh had been anxious for her. Now she was reluctantly realising that she might not have had the necessary physical strength to have accomplished it herself. She returned slowly through the boat to her cabin, turning off the lamps and banking the fire before undressing and putting herself to bed, though not immediately to sleep. There was too much on her mind for sleep to come easily.

Next morning, however, she was still first to get up and had wakened the fire and boiled the kettle before Gelis emerged.

"No bad dreams I hope?"

Gelis shook her head.

"I don't remember if I did."

"No aches and pains?"

"My shoulders are a bit stiff, that's all."

Marheh passed her a mug of sperit.

"We'll be off as soon as you've drunk that and wait for breakfast until we get to the pottery."

It did not take long to get ready. Marheh had remembered to collect the piece of rope from the bank and promised Gelis she would teach her to splice once they were at their new mooring.

"I'd like you to stand in the well deck and watch out for problems as we go," she said.

There was a bit of juggling in the well deck with the anchor, the gangplank and the front line and then they were away. The water road was grey and still, reflecting the sky above it, with no sign of the turbulence of the previous day.

The short journey was accomplished in not much more than fifteen minutes, but even that little space with her hand on the tiller and her heart listening to the landscape was a renewal of sorts and once at the pottery mooring she was home. Mooring was easy, even with the shortened lines, since the little dock had a row of nicely spaced bollards for them to tie up to.

They had not got as far as turning the engine off when family appeared from everywhere. Nicken was first, running ahead of everyone and begging to be allowed to go on the boat. Tep was not far behind her and Gelis saw a look pass between him and Marheh.

"It's in the family," he said. "We shouldn't be surprised really."

Marheh smiled at Nicken.

"Wait until Gelis tells you and then step very carefully."

Once Nicken had gone happily onboard with Gelis, Marheh led Tep onto the back deck so he could join them.

"I think you could almost manage without me," she said as they followed Gelis and Nicken through the boat.

"Almost perhaps," Tep said. "But almost is not quite good enough is it?"

Marheh grinned at him.

"Do you have anything for us to fire?" he went on.

"Not as much as usual. I couldn't seem to work while they were refitting *Day Bringer* even though I had plenty of space in the annex, and now my time is not as much my own."

"You've earned retirement if that is what you want."

Marheh shook her head.

"I'm not truly myself if I can't work my clay. There is nothing suitable for a new signature piece but there's a new doll for Fali and a couple of boxes of small things."

Leaving Nicken happily exploring with Gelis they went back out to greet Fali, Kina and Tith, who were standing together on the dock waiting for Marheh to emerge from the water dimension. There were hugs all round before Kina presented her with a big box of vegetables and Fali bent to attach the garden hose to a nearby tap. The warmth and affection seemed to dissolve some of her worries. She carried the vegetables onboard and returned with a box of her work to give to Tith.

"There's more," she said. "I'll come up with you. Gelis can do the water."

She was not away long, but by the time she returned water was flowing into the tank and the vegetables were packed neatly away in the galley.

"I helped," Nicken said proudly.

"Well done." Marheh hugged her. "Now do you think you could do something else for me?"

She nodded.

"Will you take Gelis and show her the pottery? I know she would like to see it."

"Would you Gelis?" Nicken asked.

"I'd love to."

"Come on then."

Gelis smiled her thanks to Marheh before following Nicken.

"Will Lorac be working," she asked as they walked up the neat, brick path.

Nicken nodded. "We'll go and see her first. Maybe she can come with us. She can explain things better than me."

"I'd like to say hello to Lorac, but I'm sure you will explain things very well."

Nicken beamed and slipped a confiding hand into Gelis'.

"Alright, we'll just say hello."

The first building they entered was the studio. It was not a large room, but very well lit and thoughtfully equipped with three potter's wheels in the centre and shelves, benches, troughs, bins and cupboards all around. Lorac was working at one of the wheels. Gelis watched, fascinated by the speed and skill used to fashion a tall, graceful mug. Lorac did not look up until she had taken a wire and carefully drawn it under the base of the mug, removing it from the surface of the wheel.

"Now there is just the handle, but I'll use slip to fix that on when this is a bit firmer."

"It's a lovely shape."

Lorac smiled. "A mug, is a mug .. but thank you, I try. Are you having a guided tour?"

"That's right. Nicken is showing me around."

"May I come too Nicken? I'd really like to see Marheh's pieces. They've just been unpacked in the drying room."

Nicken beamed. "That would be good, wouldn't it Gelis? Then you can help when I don't know things."

They walked together through a door leading outside into a small, enclosed courtyard.

"The kiln and the drying rooms are here," said Nicken. "They are a bit separate because of fires and things."

Gelis nodded.

"That makes sense."

"The kiln takes three days to heat up and cool down," Nicken sighed. "It's a long time to wait to see if your pot has come out alright."

"I didn't know you were a potter too."

"I'm not really," Nicken said. "But Tep lets me make things sometimes."

The drying room was filled with shelves and the shelves were filled with drying pots. Lorac's mugs were clustered together alongside rows of bowls and plates.

Lorac led the way to where Marheh's sculptures were ranged, filling three shelves with wild creatures, closely observed and lovingly represented, as well as small figures resting or completing some action. Another shelf held pieces that had been fired once already. These were decorated and glazed, but they needed the fire to melt the glaze and bring out the detail.

"She is a real artist," said Lorac wistfully.

"You are too!"

Nicken squeezed Lorac's hand, responding to something in her tone.

"Perhaps one day if I work."

"I'd love to see a finished piece sometime."

Gelis looked again at the sculptures.

"I've got one. You can come up to the house and I'll show you."

Gelis smiled at Nicken.

"I'd better not. I think Marheh wants to be away quickly, but perhaps next time we come."

"You can't go yet." Nicken was definite. "Grandma Fali is expecting you to eat breakfast. Even Marheh has to do what she wants."

They went out of the drying room and walked around the outside of the kiln. The bricks were warm to touch although the kiln was in its cooling phase.

"Is everything fired in there?" Gelis asked curiously.

Lorac shook her head. "There is a small kiln in a corner of the drying room. It can be regulated more exactly. Marheh's pieces will probably go in there. Sculptures are more tricky than crockery because of the different thicknesses."

They began to walk back towards *Day Bringer*.

"Gelis showed me all around the boat and I helped to put the hose for the water," Nicken told Lorac.

Lorac looked curiously at her. "Can you see the boat and the water?" she asked.

Nicken looked puzzled. "Of course, it's just there, at the bottom of the garden."

Lorac looked down the gentle slope to where *Day Bringer* floated quietly. Marheh was standing on the bank talking to Tep and Fali. Tith and Kina were walking up the path towards them.

"I know it's there if I don't look right at it," Lorac said. "But I wish I could see it properly."

"Of course you can see it." Nicken was definite. "It's beautiful. Dark green, shiny and polished, and it has golden lines and shiny bright round things on top .. and the name, *Day Bringer*, painted in lovely big letters, white and yellow, and there is a picture on the side near the back, sunrise, with pink clouds and water and two little ducks peeping."

"I'm sure it is there, just like that, but I can only see a shadow." Lorac sighed. "Father can't see the water road at all. I think that's why he moved away. Silberay have always been linked to the pottery and it was too hard when almost everyone else could see."

Tith and Kina met them then.

"Your daughter has just been describing *Day Bringer* to me," Lorac said. "I'm very envious."

"She obviously sees further than either of us, but I'd say it's a mixed blessing."

Kina gave Nicken a hug.

"Come on daughter, let's go and set the table for Marheh and Gelis to have breakfast. Grandma Fali has made pancakes for them and if you're lucky there might even be one for you."

"Thank you for showing me around," Gelis said as the possibility of a pancake sent Nicken scooting towards the kitchen.

"I'd best get back to work," Lorac said. "Enjoy your breakfast. Fali's pancakes are something special."

They were too, Gelis thought, pushing back from her empty plate with a sigh of satisfaction.

"That was delicious," she said as Fali looked at her across the table.

"Would you like another one," Fali asked. "There's more mixture."

"I'm full," Gelis said regretfully.

Marheh also declined.

"It was a lovely treat, but we've already been here too long."

"Tell me again why you can't stay like you usually do," Fali said.

"Just being here will draw Yareblis attention to you. I know you and Tep are prepared for that but Lorac and Nicken are vulnerable."

She reached out a hand and placed it over Fali's as it rested on the table.

"I'm coming to believe that the trouble we've been sent to address is centred hereabouts, but I can't pinpoint the source. Moving on will help to clarify things I think."

Gelis, watching and listening, saw the look of sadness return to her face.

"I can't find them, none of them, however hard I try, not even Kel."

A moment later she was all business.

"Fali thank you for breakfast and for listening," she said standing up. "Will you forgive us if we don't help with the dishes?"

Fali walked around to give Marheh a hug.

"Look after yourself and don't hesitate to come back here if you need to. Between us we will look after Lorac and Nicken."

She hugged Gelis too then.

"I'm glad Marheh has someone to care about her. She forgets to care about herself sometimes."

She came with them down to the mooring and stood watching as Marheh and Gelis busied themselves with the lines.

"There are times when I almost see," she said as they stepped off for a final hug. "Go well and come back safely."

Marheh was already steering towards the tunnel mouth but Gelis looked back and saw her wave uncertainly then turn away. A few moments more to see her straighten and move purposefully towards the house and then the tunnel was upon them.

Terror strikes
A winged predator.
Paralysis, blindness
And death
Result.

Gelis

CHAPTER EIGHT

It was not a particularly long tunnel they entered, but long enough to be dark and damp. Gelis hurried along the gunnel after coiling the front line and stood beside Marheh.

"I don't suppose you would consider going below?" Marheh asked.

Gelis' face fell.

"Do I have to?"

"Stay with me if you want to," Marheh said, considering. "I'm probably worrying about nothing."

Shadow covered *Day Bringer*'s prow. Marheh switched on the headlamp and light glinted off the damp, curved walls that surrounded them.

"There can't be anything untoward this end," Marheh said, as if she was thinking aloud. "The pottery is so close they couldn't get near it."

"It's very narrow," Gelis said.

The roof was close enough to touch in places and the curve of the walls only inches from *Day Bringer*'s hull.

"Mm, and damp too I expect, once we get further in. At least this one is straight. It's horrid when you can't see the end."

"It must be awful."

They were travelling slowly and the sound of *Day Bringer*'s engine echoed in the confined space. Their voices were distorted too as they raised them in order to be heard. The headlamp picked out the dampness around them. The steady drips from above were caught in the light before they splattered onto *Day Bringer*'s roof, or onto Gelis and Marheh if they could not dodge in time.

"Do you wish you'd gone inside?" Marheh asked, after a particularly extravagant water spout had splashed over them both."

"Of course not!"

There were white arrows painted at intervals on the walls. At first these pointed back the way they had come.

"Watch the way they point," Marheh told Gelis. "When we are going in the same direction as the arrows then we've passed the half way mark."

They were perhaps two boat lengths from the exit and Marheh was beginning to relax her guard when suddenly Gelis gave a yell and started to scramble over the rail around the back deck. Marheh let go the tiller, wrapped both arms around her and managed to haul her back, but Gelis continued to fight her as if she was desperate to escape. Marheh did not dare let her go even for the moment it would take to pull back the throttle and stop the propeller. *Day Bringer* was jolting from side to side against the walls, but at least she was continuing forward toward the tunnel exit. Marheh concentrated on holding Gelis, finally sprawling on top of her on the deck, hugging her with both arms and using all her strength of mind to wrap her in light and warmth. Just let them get through this, then she would worry about the cause.

Day Bringer continued her halting progress. Marheh continued to hold Gelis with all her strength. Gradually her struggles lessened, her efforts to escape weakened until they were no more than spasms of violent shivering. Still Marheh did not release her hold, pouring all the warmth and comfort she could into the clasp of her arms and the strength and skill of her mind.

At last *Day Bringer* carried them out into the sunshine. Once Marheh felt its warmth augmenting her own she began to ease her hold on Gelis though without withdrawing the comfort she offered. She reached up to pull back the throttle so that *Day Bringer* drifted gently whilst she sat on the deck with Gelis still quivering in her arms.

Peace and warmth enveloped them. A light breeze moved *Day Bringer* gently against the bank and held her there. Marheh neither spoke nor moved, but held Gelis for long minutes until her shivering ceased and she drew in a long sighing breath. She looked up at Marheh, her face white and streaked with tears then she leaned her head against Marheh's chest and began to cry, deep shuddering sobs.

For a while Marheh continued to hold her while she struggled to get control of herself. Next time Gelis looked up Marheh spoke to her gently.

"As bad as that?"

Gelis shivered again and Marheh's arms tightened.

"Can you tell me?"

Gelis shook her head and Marheh did not press her, but a few minutes later she began to speak, falteringly, with long pauses between stammered sentences as she forced herself to remember.

"A bird," she said. "Huge and dark, with eyes of fire and a long sharp beak. I knew it would drill its beak into my head, just where my neck joins. Then when I couldn't move it would pick out my eyes. I couldn't get away and it was coming for me." She shivered again. "It was my nightmare when I was a child," she finished softly.

Marheh nodded as if she understood something, then gently relinquished her hold on Gelis, got up and suggested they go below.

It was perhaps an hour later, after they had eaten something and Gelis had more or less regained her equilibrium that Marheh made her suggestion.

"I'm going to go back to get rid of the trap that has been set in the tunnel," she said. "Will you come with me?"

Gelis wanted to protest, opened her mouth to refuse, but no sound came out.

"You don't have to," Marheh went on. "I'll put you ashore if you choose, or you can stay below, but there comes a time when we have to deal with our nightmares."

There was a long silence.

"You'll help me?" Gelis asked at last.

"Of course I will."

"I'll come."

They stood together on the back deck. Gelis took the tiller, but Marheh held it too, her arms around Gelis so she could be both guide and comfort. Marheh had faced her own nightmares over the years and the trap had no power over her. Now, with Gelis' permission, she was hovering in the back of her mind, watchful, supportive, ready if she was needed to teach or defend. Just moving *Day Bringer* backwards was a challenge for Gelis, but with Marheh's guidance she managed to get her going slowly in the direction she wanted.

As the shadow of the tunnel mouth touched them, Marheh felt Gelis stiffen, saw from within her mind the shape of her nightmare. Once they had entered the tunnel Marheh reached out to ease back the throttle, allowing *Day Bringer* to drift backwards without any need for her attention. Gelis was holding herself rigid and staring at her monster. Marheh could feel her fear. From within Gelis' mind she too looked at the great bird, claws and beak and fiery eyes. It was a fearful thing.

"Light can dispel the darkness," she prompted Gelis, allowing a spark to gleam from her own mind through Gelis'.

Tentatively Gelis tried to copy her, willing her mind to shine and illuminate the object of her fear. The fiery eyes were not so very bright now, the pointed beak not so very different from that of the heron she loved. This success encouraged her. Marheh felt her new confidence. She drew back a little, allowing Gelis to step out alone with her light. Her last sight as she finally slipped out of Gelis' mind, was of a small chirruping creature, blue black feathers shining, yellow beak open in song.

Gelis felt her leave, but she was no longer afraid. She spent a few moments more alone with what was left of her nightmare then she turned and smiled joyfully at Marheh.

"We can go now," she said.

Marheh stepped back from the tiller.

"She's all yours."

Proudly Gelis took control of helm and throttle and steered *Day Bringer* back out into the sunshine.

Within an hour they had moored up in the quiet countryside beyond Deerford. It was not really very far from the village, but the place seemed to Gelis to be a haven of peace and beauty. She was still uplifted by her success in the tunnel and was quite content to sit on the roof with Marheh and a tin of brass polish helping to attend to *Day Bringer* and sharing Marheh's quiet companionship. She rubbed industriously at a stubborn spot then sat back to survey the effect.

"I haven't forgotten about the pots," she said, a hint of challenge in her voice.

"I didn't think you would."

Marheh took a moment to survey the results of her own industry.

"And you shall have them, I promise."

Gelis sighed and looked into some imagined future.

105

"We could have fresh herbs and maybe even some pots with tomatoes and strawberries."

Marheh laughed.

"I'll have to starve you more often if it gives you ideas like that."

Gelis went off into a daydream of beautiful pots and offering the first fruits to Marheh to enjoy. Marheh watched her affectionately, wanting her to have space and peace to recover from her experience in the tunnel.

Soon enough the brass was all shining and they were lazing on the roof watching the twilight settle the landscape comfortably, preparing it for the night ahead.

"You must be wondering what is going on," Marheh said, breaking what had been a long, contented silence.

"I know you're looking for them, the missing ones," Gelis said. "But not, not how you're looking."

"I'm not sure I know that myself," Marheh said. "I think that is part of the problem. I can't seem to marshal my thoughts and focus properly."

She paused, wondering how much she should say, how much of herself she wanted to reveal.

"I told you I was called," she went on. "And that I just reacted to the call without really thinking."

Gelis nodded to show she was listening.

"The call came from one person, my particular friend, and it hasn't come again, so I'm worried about him and that has not helped. I've been struggling to put that worry aside and focus on all the missing ones. I'm sure now that the danger is in Deerford and that we need to go back, but perhaps not openly in *Day Bringer*. We've seen no boats since we left the Harbour. Normally we would have met two or three at least. Fali said she thought she had caught a glimpse of one. It is almost as if Deerford has swallowed them up."

"Like it tried to swallow us," Gelis said, nodding her understanding.

As the light faded they got off the roof and Marheh showed Gelis how to splice a loop at the end of the cut ropes. Her's was not as neat as Marheh's, but strong and serviceable. She was quite proud of herself as she looped it over the T-stud at the prow and used it to moor up again, instead of the old and scruffy bit of rope that Marheh had dug out from a locker.

For supper they enjoyed some of Kina's vegetables and a big wedge of cheese she had tucked in with them. Gelis had been quiet and thoughtful during the meal and its preparation but now, as they washed up together, she suggested tentatively that she might walk back to Deerford the next day.

"I could get a few things from the shop," she suggested. "And perhaps people would talk in front of me, or I might see something useful."

Marheh scrubbed thoughtfully at the inside of a mug.

"We certainly need provisions," she said. "In spite of Kina's generosity, but I'm not sure I like the idea of you going alone."

"What could happen?" Gelis asked, dropping forks into the cutlery drawer as she dried them. "Surely I'll be just another visitor, a student with a daypack out walking."

"But it's my job to keep you safe. I don't feel as if I've done very well so far."

"Marheh!"

"Yes, alright, perhaps that was a silly thing to say. I think what I really feel is that I should be the one to do dangerous things."

"If it is dangerous, it would be much more dangerous for you because everyone knows you and you wear traditional dress so you can't hide. I've done heaps of walks. Why should this be any different?"

"Why should it?"

Marheh spent several concentrated minutes on the saucepan in her hands.

"Alright," she said at last. "But promise me you'll look and listen only – no leaping into action."

"I promise."

Gelis took the saucepan from Marheh's hands, shook it and held it up.

"I don't believe I've ever seen it so clean," she said, grinning.

She went to bed early in preparation for an early start next morning, but she found sleep was slow in coming. Despite her words to Marheh, she could not help feeling nervous about what might lie ahead. The events of the last few days had been disturbing enough. Her narrow bunk had never seemed so hard or so confined. She tossed and turned, then put the light on and sat up. Her journal was close at hand and writing things down sometimes helped to clarify them. She was still scribbling some twenty minutes later when there was a soft scratching at her door and Marheh's voice calling her name.

"What is it?"

All kinds of emergencies leapt into her mind.

Marheh opened the door and came in carrying a lighted candle. She set it down by Gelis' bed.

"You go to sleep, or you don't go," she said, removing Gelis' journal and pen and putting them aside.

She waited until Gelis had snuggled down under the covers then switched off the light.

"Bad as my mother," Gelis muttered.

"Concentrate on your breathing," Marheh said. "Long, slow breaths."

Obediently Gelis closed her eyes and breathed deeply. Her last conscious image was of Marheh sitting straight and slim on the step beside her bunk. The last sound she heard was Marheh's deep, quiet voice directing her long slow breaths into sleep.

Once she knew that Gelis slept Marheh made her way back to the saloon. This whole mentoring thing was taking her back to her own apprenticeship. There had been many times when she had tried to persuade Nemle to let her be the one to act. She understood now why Nemle had often been reluctant to allow it. Gelis was much more amenable to reason that she had been. She could trust her to be sensible but, even so, she, the mentor, was responsible for the safety of her apprentice. What had Gelis said, 'Bad as my mother'? She had never wanted to be anyone's mother. She had not wanted to be anyone's mentor either, but it had worked out much better than she had feared. The hardest part had been that first private commitment to loving. Now the growing affection she felt for her apprentice made that easy.

She spent a few minutes tidying the saloon and damping the fire. As she did every night she sent her mind seeking Kel's but without success. Then she entered the soul song. Her music struggled against an emptiness that tried to suck the gold she spun into a vortex of darkness. Continuing for any length of time was not an option, not when she would need to be strong for Gelis in the morning. Reluctantly she withdrew. She would be sensible and sleep if she could. Her fear for Kel and her own fear of what might be ahead must be acknowledged and put aside. Nothing must be permitted to take her attention or weaken her focus or the emptiness could consume her before she could engage with her task.

The morning came soon enough, a nice bright day, just right for walking. Gelis was soon ready to go. Not the shorts today, Marheh was glad to see, but well worn blue jeans above her walking boots and a short sleeved cotton top.

"I've put a cardigan in my pack, just in case," she said. "But walking should keep me warm enough once the sun gets up a bit."

Marheh nodded.

"Breakfast first though, and I'll come with you for the first section, just to see you find the path."

"That would be good. I was a bit worried about that."

They settled to their breakfast without need for further speech. Marheh could see that Gelis was pleased about the possibility of adventure, but saw too, that she was much more sensible than the young Marheh had been. The kind of admonitions that Nemle had been wont to give would not be needed.

"Don't worry about the dishes," she said when their porridge plates were empty. "I'll look after those when I've seen you on your way."

Five minutes later they were walking beside the water road, Marheh in front. Another five minutes and she had stopped beside a well defined track leading across a field. Gelis could see a stile where the track met the hedge that bounded the field.

"You can't miss it," Marheh said. "There are stiles where you need them and then the road."

Gelis nodded. She had taken a last look at *Day Bringer*'s chart of the area before they left and kept the picture in her mind. Marheh looked at her and put her hands on Gelis' arms wanting her attention.

"The important thing to remember is that you can't see the water road," she said.

Gelis nodded again.

"Off you go then." Marheh gave her a hug. "I'll be thinking of you."

Gelis returned the hug and set off along the path. When she reached the stile she turned to look back and saw Marheh still watching from beside the water road. She waved and felt a moment of warmth, like Marheh's smile, before turning again to tackle the stile.

It was true, she couldn't miss the way. Each stile was sturdy and well maintained and she could see from one to the next. She reached the road before she expected it and stepped out along the verge enjoying the view and the day. The road ran above the water road and below her were neat fields, a few with cows or sheep grazing, a few showing signs of a crop. There were trees lining the side furthest from the water road, a small wood with a glimpse of bluebells beneath and then, after the wood thinned, she had a glimpse of buildings, houses she thought, tucked in below the brow of the hill.

After about ten minutes of walking, the little road she was on gave onto a bigger one. She had expected it and knew her way, but found the walking much less pleasant as every few minutes a car zoomed past making her jump and scattering dust and small stones. She began to feel grubby and hot.

The water road had disappeared some time ago, but now, as she followed the road up a small, steep rise, she glimpsed it again beneath her and realised that she was walking over the tunnel. The village would not be far now. She looked to her left and saw, beyond the houses alongside the road, the tall chimney of the kiln at the pottery. The memory of Marheh's family who had made her so welcome, gave her a sense of safety and companionship.

After another five minutes of walking she reached the market square that was the centre of Deerford. It might once have been the village green, she thought, pausing to look around, but now it was mostly a car park, paved with bumpy, greyish black stuff pretending to be cobble stones. There were not many people about although quite a lot of cars. A toot behind her made her jump and a car whizzed past her and slotted into a space opposite the village store. A sleek, plastic coated woman got out, hobbled across the stones on spiked heels and disappeared into the shop oblivious of the elderly man who was walking a small dog slowly around the edges of the square. Gelis smiled as the dog barked, just once, as if to say 'Mind out, I'm here.'

A small, sturdy woman with grey hair wheeled a shopping trolley towards Gelis. As she passed, Gelis tried a tentative smile of greeting. The woman looked surprised for a moment, then she beamed.

"Hello dear. You visiting then?"

Gelis nodded and smiled again.

"On a walking tour? Don't get many coming on foot nowadays."

Gelis smiled again, more broadly.

"Not many who smile either."

"Don't people smile in Deerford?"

"Only the neighbours, and not always them." The women looked at Gelis. "Too many newcomers, with too much money," she said. "But it doesn't make them happy or friendly... no time for anything."

They stood and watched an altercation between two motor cars vying for the same space. A shiny blue one, like a large blue beetle, won the day and the red beetle scuttled away to look for territory of its own.

"See," said the woman. "Too much hurry."

Gelis laughed. "But we have time to stand and talk and watch the world go by."

"That's the way of it," said the woman. She prepared to move on. "You have a nice holiday dear."

"Thank you."

Cheered by the encounter, Gelis walked slowly towards the Post Office and General Store, feeling in her pocket for her shopping list.

The Post Office section was at the back of the store and there was a queue. Gelis joined the end of it, feeling that it gave her a perfect excuse to linger and knowing she could always use some stamps for letters home. As she waited she looked around the shop. The women from the cars mostly seemed to want milk or cigarettes, although there was also one waiting ahead of her. It was very quiet. The only conversation seemed to concern the business transactions that were taking place at the counter where she waited, or at the cash register at the front of the shop.

A woman came to join the queue behind Gelis. She looked well polished and thin, even gaunt. Gelis turned to smile at her, but received no answering smile or any acknowledgement of her presence at all. She was shocked at the emptiness in the eyes that looked determinedly through her. She turned back and stepped forward with the queue. Immediately she began to feel uneasy. She shifted from foot to foot, eased the straps of her pack and turned to look behind again. The empty eyes continued to look through her. Gelis nodded uncomfortably feeling she had been intrusive then turned away again wondering at her discomfort. She looked determinedly ahead, studying the pattern on the shirt in front, trying to read the various notices that adorned the wall around the post office window.

She was tempted to step out of the queue and not bother with her stamps, but she could not understand why. She was in no hurry, in fact she was carrying out the purpose of her visit. She took a deep breath, stepped forward again and stood firmly, resisting the temptation to leave before she was ready. She felt as if she was being thrust aside, ejected, but did not move. "What's going on?" She did not speak the words aloud, but to Marheh, who suddenly seemed very close. Gelis did not expect Marheh to respond, but perhaps she had in some way, for now the correct action seemed easy. She turned back again to the woman.

"Are you in a hurry?" she asked. "Would you like to go ahead of me?"

There was no change in expression, no acknowledgement of her offer, but a brisk step forward. It seemed to Gelis the woman would have stepped through her if she could. She fell back into line and was not surprised to discover that the uneasy feeling had gone. Still in line, she watched as the woman moved up the queue. Few seemed able to resist for long. Gelis wondered whether the trivial gain was worth the effort or whether the satisfaction was in the exercise of power. She had no doubt she was in the presence of Yareblis.

The queue moved on, and soon enough she was asking for six stamps and sliding her money beneath the plastic shield in front of the woman serving.

"Thank you," she said, picking up her change. "Could you tell me please, when is the last collection?"

The woman jerked her head towards a printed notice to one side of the window and looked past her to the next customer.

No friendly smile, not even 'Will that be all?'. Gelis moved away and stood in an aisle putting away her stamps and her wallet and getting out the shopping list she and Marheh had made. There was only a couple of items on it but looking for them gave her a chance to linger and listen. Marheh had talked about listening with her heart. She didn't think she was doing that, but the sounds in the shop and the absence of other sounds made her feel uncomfortable.

There was no friendly interaction at the till either, when she took her few purchases there to pay for them.

Outside the shop she stood under the awning to put the things into her pack. She had learnt that Deerford was not a friendly place, but was that enough to justify her journey. She looked again around the square and decided to take a bit of a walk. Three roads entered the square as well as the one she had come from. Perhaps she could find the pond and the white boats. There must be something to be seen from the village and she could tell Marheh.

Reality evaporates
Footsteps falter
Comfort and safety fade
I am alone with myself.

Gelis

CHAPTER NINE

Once she had seen Gelis disappear across the fields Marheh made her way back to *Day Bringer*. There was no need to hurry so she took time to enjoy the day and to think about what might be ahead. It would be important to hold Gelis in her mind so as to offer help and protection should it be needed, but it would take her a while to reach Deerford, and she was unlikely to attract attention much before then.

She kept wishing she could talk to Nemle about being a mentor. She wanted to apologise too. Nemle had given her so much and relinquished so much because of her and she had not understood until now.

"I took from you so often, without thinking," she said aloud to the water road beside her and the little breeze that played in the reeds and grasses. "I'm sorry Nemle."

Gelis was more mature and thoughtful than she had been, but even so she could not avoid taking from her and she had to be willing to give, not just the cabin that had been hers, but a half share in *Day Bringer* and a place in all the things she loved. She had to give Gelis all the opportunities to learn that Nemle had given her and if that meant stepping back sometimes she had to be prepared for that too.

Reaching *Day Bringer* she opened the doors to the well deck and then took some clay from the box under her bed. She had not touched it since the Gathering. It made the loss of her work space too raw and immediate but, after all, she had not had a work space while she was an apprentice. She could learn again to manage without.

The day felt comfortable, familiar. She put a board on her lap, took up a couple of tools and began to work, not with any particular plan, just letting her fingers respond to her thoughts.

Since most of her mind was walking with Gelis now, it was hardly surprising that what began to emerge was the figure of a girl with a mop of curls, lying on her stomach studying an open book, wearing shorts and a skimpy top. Marheh looked at it and smiled before crushing it back into a ball. She was lucky really. Already she had grown fond of her apprentice. She put the clay away and settled herself to turn inwards. It was time to give her more active support.

Gelis took time to look around the square for something that might point to a direction for her walk. Marheh had spoken of listening with her heart. She didn't really understand that, but if she tried to be open to what Deerford was saying would it guide her? Probably not, she decided, and marched across the square towards the pub on the opposite corner. That was an obvious thing for a walker to do. She stopped to study the menu chalked on a black board propped against the wall. The food seemed expensive and over elaborate for a pub, no fish and chips or sausages and mash.

A little lane ran away along one side. Gelis started down. It was narrow and quite dark, with a tiny ironmongers spilling untidily onto the pavement between two empty shops. Then there was a row of cottages, red brick, with front doors opening onto the footpath. As she continued though, the cottages became larger, with little neat front gardens and on the corner where there was an intersecting street, she came to a very grand looking house. She chose to turn to her right, where the way led down hill. It was not far before the road swung round and began to climb back up towards the square, but on the outside of the bend a short drive branched off the road and led to a pair of enormous white, wrought iron gates.

Gelis stood and stared. The gates reminded her of the ones that had opened so invitingly when *Day Bringer* went past two days ago. She went a little closer, feeling apprehensive, would she somehow be drawn in if she got too close. She thought of Marheh and was strengthened. She stepped into the road, then hastily back again as a little car swung round the bend. Once it had gone she crossed and walked towards the gates. They were closed, but through the decorative ironwork she could see the fleet of proud, white boats she had seen from the water road. There was a road leading from the gates to an enormous white building, shiny with glass and bright with flags flying. A formidable sign at each side of the gates declared that access was for members only.

"And very choosey they are too," said a voice behind her.

Gelis jumped and turned around. It was the elderly man she had seen in the square, still walking his dog.

She smiled tentatively.

"Are they?" she asked. "Exclusive?"

"Only newcomers," he said gruffly.

He had not quite smiled, but Gelis thought he might be trying to.

"What do they do there" she asked. "Is it a club?"

She was suddenly conscious that she had no idea what he would see through the gates if he did not see the water and the boats. She bent to greet the little dog, who looked at her with bright brown eyes peering through a straggly fringe.

"Funny sort of club that doesn't want members," he said. "All very secretive too – security!" He invested the last word with a degree of scorn. "Locks and cameras."

"Truly?" asked Gelis.

"So they say."

They stood together in silence, staring through the gates. As she watched, Gelis saw one of the white boats detach itself from the fleet and sail slowly out of sight. She wondered whether it would be going on to the water road and thought for a moment of Marheh and *Day Bringer*, moored and vulnerable.

"Used to be I could walk the dog there," her companion said. "Nice garden, no fences. Now look at it."

Gelis turned to offer her sympathy, but he did not look at her, just jerked the lead and walked heavily away. She continued to look through the gates, but could see no more movement. The hill and the white building blocked her view of part of the area. She was about to turn away when she heard the gates creak and saw them shiver into movement. She backed hastily to one side as they slowly opened and watched as a shiny blue car, like the one she had seen in the square, swept around the corner and through the gates, which closed slowly behind it. The blue car continued imperiously along the drive and disappeared behind the white building. Gelis sighed and began to walk slowly back towards the square. She doubted she could learn any more without going through the gates herself, and she was not ready to try that yet. She would go back to the shop and complete her purchases, then head for home.

Marheh closed her eyes and created the image of Gelis, walking steadily as she had last seen her, then she placed herself a few steps behind and kept pace with her in her mind. It was concentrated work, and Marheh was soon entirely immersed. The quiet landscape still surrounded her, but she was largely oblivious of it, focused as she was on providing some kind of protection for Gelis. Time, too, lost its meaning. Every moment was the present. The gentle shifting of *Day Bringer* cradled her physical self, helped her relax, so that all her energy could be spent within the mind and spirit.

She was deeply involved, entirely alongside Gelis, when the steady calm of their walk seemed to falter. A hint of darkness, snagged the edges of consciousness. She began to arm against it, placing a curtain of light between Gelis and the encroaching dark. For a while the darkness seemed to withdraw, the curtain was steady, glowing softly. Then, imperceptibly the light began to dim and the curtain to shift fitfully as if in a breeze.

Marheh stretched herself to hold it firm against the dark. *Day Bringer* moved uneasily beneath her. The image of Gelis came and went as if a mist swirled about her, though she continued to walk serenely onward, untouched by the darkness Marheh held at bay. Almost fearfully, Marheh stretched herself still further, testing her ability, the wisdom and power she had built in faith over so many years, until she felt like a fine gold wire, taut, extended, or a sharply focused beam of light, bright, cutting. Gelis' image seemed scarcely to matter as she struggled simply to maintain the light.

Suddenly the darkness threatened to overwhelm her. *Day Bringer*'s gentle rocking became more like violent tossing and Marheh realised that the danger was not threatening Gelis, but was hers and about to burst through the barrier she had set around herself.

Gelis went back to the shop and took a shopping basket. She did not feel as if she had accomplished very much by her visit to Deerford so she decided to load herself up with provisions as a way of justifying her morning. Rice, flour, butter, cheese and sugar went into the basket and she was just studying the different types of tinned vegetables when suddenly she felt as if the earth had moved and a chasm had opened at her feet. It felt like an unexpected jolt into a new reality. She put the basket down and stood still, breathing hard, yet when she managed to look around her again, nothing had changed.

She grabbed a few tins, almost at random and managed to make her way to the front of the shop, hand over her money and stow her purchases away in her backpack. She was the only customer and the woman at the till was not the same person who had served her earlier, but she seemed totally disinterested in Gelis and she could not believe that anything the woman was doing could be affecting her to such an extent.

116

Outside the shop the feeling persisted. All she wanted was to leave Deerford and be stepping out along the road home. Marheh and *Day Bringer* spelled security and she wanted to be there with them. It seemed strange to her that when she had been walking into Deerford, into the unknown, she had not been afraid, but fear and a sense of urgency accompanied her every step of the way out of Deerford, past the small, ramshackle dwellings and over the tunnel.

She eased the shoulder straps of her pack and paused for a moment, glad to be off the gravel road and walking on grass. Soon, she thought, she would reach the section where there was a view, where she could see the distant hills and catch a glimpse of the water road. The loaded pack was heavy and tiring and she was hot and hungry, but the fear that had come upon her in the shop still lingered and pushed her onwards faster than she might otherwise have walked.

Soon the walking had built up its own rhythm and that rhythm eased her anxiety and encouraged reflection. She thought back over her day. Two things seemed to stand out, three if she counted the sudden fear that came over her. The woman in the queue was the first. Gelis saw again the blank, empty eyes. Had she been the cause of her uneasiness as she stood in the queue, or was it just coincidence, she wondered. The large clubhouse and the fleet of boats were next in importance. Gelis thought Marheh would be interested in that information.

She could look out across the fields now. She made a mental note to ask Marheh what people saw if they did not see the water road. Not much further and she reached the pathway leading back. She was relieved to have recognised it, and paused a moment before starting down. She had only taken a few steps when a sound like a great clap of thunder reached her. Surprised, she looked up from the path. There were no clouds in the sky, no hint of a storm in the spring landscape. Then, fleeting away along the water road, she saw a white boat, heading for Deerford.

When Marheh realised she was under attack, she had only moments to redirect her focus. She was aware that Gelis would feel her sudden withdrawal, but she had no choice. She needed all her energy for defence. For a moment she faltered. The hours of protection she had given to Gelis had drained her. The threatening darkness came closer in stealthy fingers, an emptiness like a chasm of ice, waited for her to fall headlong. The dark fingers were poised, ready to push. Then somewhere she found the energy to resist. As the darkness closed around her, she clothed herself in light, as the cold drew her to it, the light became warmth until she seemed to be living within a candle flame. Then she laughed, a clear melodious peal of joy for the beauty that enclosed her and the power that protected.

She had no idea how long she remained poised within the candlelight, but gradually she became conscious that the dark fingers were scrabbling helplessly and the icy emptiness was melting in her warmth. Again she laughed, not to mock the enemy whose defeat was now inevitable, but to celebrate the light and warmth that enabled her. A little longer she lived in the flame and then came the howl of frustration and anger that signalled the departure of her enemy. Slowly she relinquished the flame and the light and returned to the sunshine and *Day Bringer*'s gentle cradling. As she looked around her, she caught a glimpse of a white boat, heading swiftly away, back towards Deerford.

Weary, but filled with contentment, Marheh turned her thoughts again to Gelis, but found she no longer had strength for the concentration and energy needed to shield her. She had no sense that Gelis was in any danger though so she stretched out on the roof of *Day Bringer* and let herself relax while she waited for her return.

Perhaps she dozed in the afternoon sunshine, or perhaps time was suspended, but it did not seem long before she heard Gelis approaching, singing quietly as she walked. A smile of greeting and no real need for words underlined the growth of companionship. Gelis began to empty her pack into the storage cupboards whilst Marheh put the kettle on and made them both a sandwich.

It seemed to Gelis like coming home. It was the first time she had been away from *Day Bringer* since she joined Marheh and she was surprised at how right it felt to be coming back. Her pack emptied she sat down at the table with a little sigh and eased her shoulders, the pack had been very heavy. Marheh slid a plate with a sandwich on it across the table then sat down opposite with her own. She looked tired too, Gelis thought, but relaxed and satisfied, as if she had accomplished something difficult.

"You shouldn't have waited for me," Gelis said. "You must be hungry."

"And you're not?" Marheh raised her eyebrows and smiled. "Unless of course you had an icecream in Deerford."

"I was going to and then the world fell in and I forgot." Gelis explained what had happened while she was in the shop. "After that I just wanted to get home."

"I'm sorry you didn't get your icecream," Marheh said apologetically. "I think that might have been my fault. I had to bring myself back here in rather a hurry. I was afraid you might feel it."

Gelis looked at her, puzzled.

"I was trying to keep you safe," she said. "Then I found I had left myself a bit vulnerable."

She took a bite of her sandwich and chewed reflectively.

"There is so much I don't understand," Gelis said after she had taken the edge off her own hunger. "No wonder it takes twenty years … sometimes it feels as if even that won't be long enough."

Marheh laughed a little at that. "It isn't of course. You go on learning all your life."

As they ate, Gelis began to tell Marheh about her day in Deerford. Marheh listened intently, nodding occasionally when something seemed important to her. She confirmed Gelis' opinion that the woman in the queue had been Yareblis.

"Just practising, I expect," Marheh said. "Not really with any serious intent."

"Practising?"

"They want to keep up their skills, just like we do. It's probably just as well you didn't stand up to her too long, that would have drawn attention to you."

"It seemed as if you told me what to do," Gelis said, rather hesitantly.

"Good," Marheh said.

She was silent and thoughtful for some time. Gelis sat quietly with her finishing her sandwich and trying to relax after her long walk. At last Marheh stood up and picked up the two plates.

"What about another sandwich?" she suggested. "And some fruit? We're so late already that we could make this tea."

"Let me."

Gelis went to get up, but Marheh stopped her.

"You've done enough. You must be tired after that walk."

"But you're tired too."

"We are both tired. Does that mean we should each get our own, or both starve?"

"You've been looking after me all day."

"It's my job."

"I don't see why you had to look after me anyway. I can take care of myself."

Marheh took a deep breath.

"Gelis just sit there and be quiet. In a minute we'll both say something we'll regret."

There was silence then while Marheh put together a couple more sandwiches and put them and the fruit bowl onto the table. Gelis muttered something that might have been thanks without lifting her eyes from her plate. Marheh sat down heavily and looked at her.

"What an old grouch she turned out to be," she said reflectively to no one in particular.

Gelis looked up and gave a little giggle as Marheh put on the face of an old grouch.

"That's better," she said. "Am I forgiven?"

"If I am," Gelis said, reddening.

Marheh reached across the table to clasp her hand for a moment and there was no need for words.

When they had finished their meal and tidied up the few dishes Marheh suggested they go out and sit on the roof to enjoy the sunset. Soon they were comfortably settled, Marheh lying on her back gazing at the pale, clear sky above them, Gelis sitting cross-legged beside her watching the horizon where pale pinks and oranges coloured the landscape.

They were silent for some time before Gelis said hesitatingly. "I don't understand how you could protect me when you weren't there."

"But I was there," Marheh said. "Part of me. I couldn't protect you physically, but my mind went with you."

"But you didn't need to," Gelis said.

"Not as it turned out, but it was better to be safe."

Gelis sighed. There was another long silence. Marheh gazed at the sky and waited. She knew Gelis had more questions.

"I'm not a child," she said at last. "I was only going shopping. Why did you need to be there at all?"

Marheh thought carefully before she spoke.

"I know you're not a child," she said at last. "But at the moment you are more vulnerable than an ordinary person because you have the mind of a Silberay without the knowledge."

She rolled onto one hip, propped herself up on her elbow and looked at Gelis.

"If the wrong people know you are Silberay they will want to take over your mind, and we know there are Yareblis in Deerford."

"But you can't baby sit me for the rest of my life!"

"Of course not." Marheh's matter-of-fact tones calmed Gelis. "You'll learn to defend yourself. If you're not too tired we'll have your first lesson now, but it's a lot of learning. It won't happen overnight."

Gelis looked at her sharply.

"What sort of lesson?"

"I'll try to enter your mind and you'll try to stop me."

"How can I stop you when you're in my mind before I know it?"

Marheh put a hand out to touch Gelis.

"Don't be cross. I know it's confusing."

Gelis looked for a moment as if she would burst into tears. Then she took a deep breath.

"What do I have to do?"

"Try to imagine a shield of some kind, build it in your mind against me when you feel me try to enter."

"But you can enter my mind without even trying."

"This time I'll make some noise so you know I'm coming." Marheh sat up and looked at her. "Ready?"

Gelis nodded. Then she looked surprised, then she began to giggle.

"Stop it!" she gasped. "You're tickling me!"

Marheh grinned.

"Come on. You can stop me. Concentrate."

Gelis writhed and gasped.

"Oh stop! Stop!"

"Make me," Marheh teased. "Come on."

Suddenly Gelis realised Marheh had not spoken aloud. The tickling was no more than a feather touch now and in her mind Gelis could hear Marheh tease.

121

"Come on, stop me. You can do it. Concentrate."

Laboriously she tried to focus, blocking out the persistent tickle by concentrating on putting a wall between herself and Marheh. It was a wall of glass and so fragile that Marheh's feather could dust it away, but it was there in patches. She began to feel a sense of excitement. Perhaps she could make her wall thicker.

Marheh was still teasing, encouraging her to concentrate. How could she possibly concentrate when she was being tickled? She needed to be rid of the irritation. Marheh's feather seemed to be everywhere. She could build a wall to keep it out, but it wasn't happening well enough. There were too many gaps. What else could stop a feather? Concentrating on the problem seemed to be part of the resistance, but Marheh was still there, still teasing and tickling. It was too much!

"Go away!" she shouted, but her shout was from her mind and poured out over Marheh's feather like a cold douche.

There was a sense of surprised withdrawal then something crept back to give her a little pat of approval before leaving her. She waited a moment, basking in the approval then took herself back to *Day Bringer*'s roof.

Marheh was laughing at her.

"That was very well done," she said. "You really gave me what for."

Gelis grinned.

"I didn't mean to."

"Oh yes you did. You couldn't have done it if you hadn't meant it."

"It kind of came together all of a sudden."

"I could tell," Marheh said, still sounding amused. "Ouch!"

"I didn't hurt you?"

Marheh shook her head.

"Just tipped a bucket of cold water over me."

"You deserved it."

"I did," Marheh agreed.

Around them the light was nearly gone and one or two stars were beginning to emerge. They waited while a thin sliver of moon crept over the trees on the eastern horizon, watching in companionable silence. Then Marheh yawned and stretched and slid towards the edge of the roof.

"I think I need my bed," she said, lowering herself onto the gunnel. "I'll see you in the morning. Sleep well."

● * * *

Lorac was alone in the pottery. She had finished the last of the sets of mugs that morning and Tep had suggested she might use the rest of the day to try some ideas for her masterwork. In her mind was a shadowy image she was trying to capture. She had sketched three wide, shallow bowls, balanced on long stems, and was wondering how she would give them the brilliant colours she envisaged. With the sketch propped in front of her she leaned over her wheel, her concentration complete as she experimented with shape and form.

She had been working for several hours when Ved slipped into the studio. He stood for a moment watching her, admiring the way her dark hair curved forward round her jaw line and parted softly over her slim, white neck as she bent over her work.

He sighed, and at the small sound Lorac looked up, swinging round to see him and smile.

"Ved," she said unnecessarily, savouring the sound of his name.

He went towards her.

"I'm playing with ideas for my masterwork," she explained. "What do you think?"

"Beautiful," he said, but he was not looking at the shape she had built or at her sketch.

"I want to make three pieces, all the same shape but different sizes and with complementary designs in brilliant colours." She sighed. "But it is a challenge and I still don't know if I can do it."

"Of course you can."

Ved had no doubts. He held out his hand. She showed him that hers was covered in clay, but he took it anyway and swept her into a hug. She responded for a moment then wriggled away from him.

"I'll just put this into the drying room," she said. "And wash my hands." She took a wire and carefully detached her piece from the wheel. "It isn't quite what I want, but it will be useful to see how it fires."

While she carried it carefully away, Ved began the job of cleaning her tools so that when she returned all that was left for her to do was scrub down the surface of the wheel.

123

"Sperit?" she asked, when the work was done. "And there is cake too, I think."

They went together to the kitchen, filled with late afternoon sunshine, but otherwise empty. Lorac grabbed the kettle, filled it and put it on the stove to boil.

"I don't suppose we'll be the only ones who want a drink," she said, taking down half a dozen mugs from their hooks in the cupboard.

"Quite right," said Fali, emerging from the pantry. "I was just thinking it was afternoon tea time."

She flashed a smile at Ved and went back into the pantry for the cake.

"How are you getting on with your idea?" she asked Lorac.

"I suppose it wouldn't be a masterwork if it wasn't difficult." Lorac sighed. "I can see it more clearly now, but I'm not sure I'll achieve what I want."

"Probably not." Fali sounded sympathetic. "But then we never do, if we set our sights high enough." She put the cake on the bench beside the mugs and turned to Ved. "What do you think?"

"It looked pretty good to me, even in its unfinished state, but I don't really know enough to judge." He turned to Fali. "I just wish I had something to make that would add beauty or usefulness. We seem to be making nothing but twisted rods at the moment, and there is virtually nothing for me to do except watch the machine."

Lorac put her hand over his where it rested on the table.

"I knew you weren't happy." She pushed him into a chair and sat down beside him. "It isn't just work, is it?"

Ved looked at the two women, grandmother and granddaughter. "You two," he said fondly. "You make everything better."

Fali laughed.

"How can we make it better? We don't know what it is yet."

She placed a large wedge of cake on a plate beside him. Lorac got up again to pour hot water and place three steaming mugs of sperit on the table.

"Come on, what is it?" she said.

Fali sat opposite, facing them.

"You know we'll listen, even if we can't help any other way."

He nodded.

"I know."

He wrapped both hands around his mug and sat looking gloomily into its depths.

"It's my mother," he said at last. "She's taken against Lorac even more lately, ever since she was invited to dine at that new club in the village."

Lorac and Fali looked at each other.

"She has never really approved of our family," said Fali. "And she hates our connection with the Silberay. I remember her as a girl, mocking Tith because his aunt Marheh was so stupid."

"A lot of nonsense, she calls it," Ved said. "And just closes her eyes to anything she can't see or touch."

He looked at Lorac, then at Fali.

"She won't even call me Ved any more, says she doesn't believe in soul names and calls me David as if I'm just an acquaintance."

"So what happened at the club? Did she say? Asked Fali.

"She hasn't even been yet, the invitation is for next Tuesday. The executive of the Women's Union has been invited to dine at the club and hold their regular meeting there. She is full of it, how exclusive it is, the beautiful grounds, the dining room and how rich the members are."

Ved put his head in his hands.

"It's like she's a different person," he said.

Fali stood up and went around the table to give him a hug.

"She loves you though. You need to hang on to that and keep loving her even if you don't care for her ideas."

He smiled ruefully.

"I do keep loving her," he said. "That's why it hurts so much – what she's doing."

There were a few moments of silence while the warmth of the sunshine and the warmth of affection grew in the quiet room. Then Tep and Tith came in calling for cake and the warmth turned to laughter.

* * * *

Next morning after breakfast, Marheh and Gelis were preparing to go boating. They had discussed the events of the previous day, trying to understand the significance of the white boat in particular and decided that the sensible thing would be to continue to a place where they could turn the boat around, then at least they would be pointing in the right direction if it seemed that they should return to Deerford.

"And you can have some more steering practice," Marheh said, as if that clinched the matter.

Gelis grinned.

"Well I'm sure I need it," she said. "It certainly isn't second nature yet."

They set off into the morning sunshine, Gelis at the tiller, Marheh standing on the deck beside her. The water road made its slow passage between folded hills, green and gold, punctuated by clutches of farm buildings, underlined by thick, dark hedges. It wound around, following the contours of the land, and Gelis felt she was getting some good experience as she negotiated the tight bends, careful to keep in the middle.

"I still have to think though," she told Marheh. "Most of the time I'm saying to myself, push the tiller the way you want the back to go."

Marheh smiled.

"Well, that's alright. It will probably be a few months of cruising before it becomes second nature, and even then you might have to stop and think if you come to a tricky situation."

"But the cruising is just the surface really, isn't it?"

Marheh nodded.

"Yes, but it is important, keeping the water road alive is part of our job. It doesn't matter that many don't see it." She paused, looking for words. "It has a beneficent influence."

There was a short silence while Gelis negotiated a narrow bridge, then Marheh continued.

"You've had to cope with more than your share since you've been with me. Normally we could have expected some gentle summer cruising so that you could focus on one thing at a time. Instead you've had to try to pick up bits and pieces of all sorts."

Gelis looked at Marheh.

"You've made me feel as if I have contributed, and you're always encouraging," she said, then had to thrust the tiller hard over as her brief glance away had them heading for the bank.

They laughed together and continued quietly onwards.

It was only a bit over an hour to the turning place and Gelis learnt how to nose into the bank and use the throttle and tiller to push the stern around. She was glad of Marheh's quiet instructions and her brief "well done" warmed her. Then she negotiated the return journey feeling as if she was beginning to understand what she was doing, at least when it came to steering.

They moored up again and went inside. Gelis felt restless and found she could not settle to anything, even her journal had no appeal. The brass was already shining and the cabin sides gleamed. She had made her bed, put her clothes away and re-arranged her cupboards. She wandered into the galley and stopped short. Marheh was sitting at the little table. There was a piece of clay under her hands and she was kneading it absently. Her eyes were closed and her face blank. She looked up as Gelis turned to go.

"Come and help me Gelis," she said quietly, and for a moment Gelis understood that she was suffering. "I feel as if time is running out, but I can't find the way to proceed."

Gelis came slowly towards her.

"How can I help?" she asked.

"Lend me your strength, listen with me for a while."

Gelis sat down opposite her. They were silent together for long enough that time ceased to have meaning. Gelis felt her way towards something beautiful and offered it, in her mind, to Marheh.

"We'll have to go back," Marheh said, breaking the silence at last. The words seemed dragged out of her. "We'll have to go back," she said again. "But I'm afraid for *Day Bringer*."

Because I see, it is not virtue in me.
Virtue is what I do with what I see.
Because I know, it is my work to grow.
By growing I keep faith with what I know.
Because I live, I try to learn to give.
Giving is how I spend the life I live

Gelis

CHAPTER TEN

Gelis looked at Marheh, wondering whether she had heard aright. Did Marheh really say she was afraid? Saying she was afraid for *Day Bringer* was not quite the same as saying she was afraid, but it still seemed to Gelis an over-reaction. Nothing that had happened so far had been seriously frightening, she thought, conveniently forgetting the terror she had experienced sinking in the mud and the nightmare in the tunnel. For the first time as she studied the quiet figure opposite, she saw the weathered skin, the grey hair, the lack of elasticity, the age. She looked away, almost embarrassed by her discovery.

Marheh was old.

She reached across the table to touch the hands that still worked the clay, shaping it so that it seemed as if some beautiful form was about to emerge, then folding and kneading again when the beauty was scarcely glimpsed.

Poor Marheh, she thought.

"Why don't I put the kettle on?" she said gently.

Marheh did not move for a moment then she lifted her head slowly and deliberately and looked at Gelis. It was not a hard, or unkind look, there was even a suggestion of amusement lurking somewhere, but Gelis felt herself blushing.

"That would be very kind," Marheh said quietly.

Hastily Gelis scrambled to her feet, anxious to escape that penetrating gaze and busied herself with the kettle.

Marheh said nothing while Gelis hovered around the stove, fussed with mugs and sperit and finally placed a steaming drink on the table in front of her. Gelis had thought perhaps she might take her own drink outside, but Marheh made it very clear she was to sit with her at the table.

"Poor old Marheh," Marheh said.

A small smile hovered about her lips and lurked in her eyes.

"That's what you thought, isn't it?"

Gelis looked away for a moment then back at Marheh.

"Well I am old, of course and my body is not as flexible as it once was and I don't heal as quickly, but those things are not really important. I'm not important even though I still like to play at being Marheh the Great, but *Day Bringer* is the past and the future as well as the present, your future as well as mine. Without *Day Bringer* we are not Silberay and if we are not Silberay the water road dies."

Gelis looked up.

"I don't understand why you're afraid. What could happen to *Day Bringer*?"

She tried not to sound defiant, but she felt as if Marheh had put her in the wrong.

"You keep talking about danger, you baby sit me when I walk into Deerford, you even say you're afraid. I'm not afraid, why are you? What are you afraid of?"

She stopped suddenly aghast at her outspokenness.

"What am I afraid of?" Marheh repeated.

She looked at Gelis and now the hint of a smile was gone and her eyes were sad.

"I'm afraid I won't have the skill, or perhaps the strength to keep us safe, all three of us, but afraid or not there is no turning back so all three of us will have to take our chances."

"Why should you have to do it all?" Gelis said. "You said Nemle wouldn't let you touch the tiller for six months. Aren't you doing the same kind of thing to me if you won't let me help?"

"But you do help," Marheh said, reaching out to her. "Haven't you just been giving me something beautiful?

"It doesn't feel like helping. You're still afraid."

Marheh stood up and walked around the table to kneel beside Gelis and take both her hands in hers. She waited, looking steadily upwards, while

Gelis searched her face for something, reassurance perhaps, understanding.

"You were afraid," Marheh said at last. "But you went back to the tunnel and the nightmare."

"Because you were there," Gelis said slowly, trying to work something out. "You weren't afraid then. Does it help you that I'm not afraid now?"

"Yes," Marheh said.

"But you weren't afraid then because you knew you were stronger. I'm not afraid now because I don't know anything. I feel as if you're keeping things from me, as if I was a child."

"You do know," Marheh said. "You're not thinking. You were caught by the mud and the nightmare."

"Yes but they weren't real," Gelis said.

"Weren't they?" Marheh paused. "What if you had been alone?"

Gelis' eyes widened as she thought back.

"But they were just in my mind."

"And what is more important, your mind or your body?" Marheh looked at her sympathetically. "It's difficult isn't it?"

She waited a moment then gave a little grin.

"Now I think I've knelt at your feet long enough. Help your poor old mentor get up and I'll tell you a story."

She laughed with Gelis as she allowed herself to be hoisted to her feet and went to sit in the comfortable chair. Gelis stood back, looking down at her. The laughter died from her face and she held out a hand to her.

"Come, bring the footstool and sit near me," she said. "I don't think this will be easy to tell, but perhaps it will help you understand."

Silently Gelis obeyed her. When she was comfortably settled, leaning against the armchair, Marheh began.

"This is something that happened to me about halfway through my apprenticeship," she said.

Gelis turned to look at her, surprised. She had expected a story from Silberay history.

"It was late afternoon and we'd moored at a new place – new to me anyway and Nemle had not visited during the twelve years I had been with her. We had run out of milk and I offered to take a can and see if there was a shop or a farm that could sell us some.

"It didn't always come in bottles back then. It was a very ordinary thing for me to do, especially in the summer when the milk didn't keep very long. Nemle enjoyed a milk drink at bedtime. Occasionally I would meet someone who didn't like Silberay, but usually it was enough just to ignore them. If not I had developed enough skill to defend myself by turning their mind to something else."

Gelis caught her breath and looked at Marheh, remembering how she had walked her across the deck.

"This particular day I had reached a farm on the outskirts of a village when I met a gang of youngish men, eight of them."

Marheh's voice faltered as she remembered.

"They began by calling insults and then spread themselves out to block my way. Eight together were quite a lot to deal with, but I made one of them start a fight with another and I was just thinking that would be enough to distract them when a mind began to attack mine."

The quiet voice stopped, then continued expressionlessly.

"I had to choose. I could not defend my mind and my body. The attack on my mind was sudden and aggressive. I understood later it had been planned that way so I would have nothing left to keep the men away. If it had succeeded my mind would have been destroyed, as it didn't they could imprison my body."

She paused again then continued, keeping her voice even and expressionless.

"They took me into a barn and stripped off my clothes and began to hurt me. The mind that was attacking mine had planned it that way hoping I would try to protect my physical self so he could possess my mind. It didn't work though, because the struggle to keep him out of my mind distracted me from what else was happening enough so I could put the pain aside."

She stopped speaking abruptly. Gelis reached out to grasp the hand nearest her.

"Nemle rescued me, and Kel and his mentor. It seems I had called very loudly."

She squeezed Gelis' hand.

"It's a long time ago now. Perhaps I shouldn't have told you, but you see why I couldn't leave you to walk unprotected."

131

Gelis looked at her with troubled eyes, full of questions. Marheh leaned forward and suddenly they were holding each other in an untidy, awkward, comforting hug.

At last Marheh leaned back.

"All this emotion," she said lightly. "This mentoring business is a bit exhausting. I wonder if I'll last the distance."

Gelis sniffed, rubbed her sleeve across her face and tried to smile back.

"I'll keep you up to the mark," she said and pushed herself to her feet. "Stay there and I'll make some dinner."

She moved quietly around the galley area preparing vegetables, putting rice to boil. Every so often she looked over to the saloon to Marheh and was happy to see that she had her feet up and her eyes closed. Marheh's story had shocked her and she had many questions, but just now it was good to do ordinary things and to be caring for Marheh in a small way. The meal of curried vegetables and rice did not take long to prepare. She divided it into two big bowls, added a fork to each and carried them into the saloon. Marheh opened her eyes and smiled as she approached.

"I'll come to the table," she said, swinging her feet off the footstool and standing up with her usual efficiency and grace.

Gelis laughed.

"Poor *old* Marheh," she said. "What a fool I am!"

"Only sometimes," Marheh said, grinning as she slid in behind the table. "That smells good. I'm hungry."

It was not until they had finished their meal, eating for the most part in companionable silence, that Marheh spoke again of future planning.

"So," she said, pushing her bowl to one side and leaning her elbows on the table. "We plan to return to Deerford."

She smiled at Gelis.

"We might think about going back tonight instead of waiting until morning."

Gelis waited in silence while Marheh thought aloud.

"It would mean making the journey in the darkness, including the tunnel, but we might get back without alerting them. We would just appear, moored up, in the morning, for those who could see us."

She paused.

"And I think it might be best if you are not seen to be associated with me. I can't hide once I leave *Day Bringer*, I've been in Deerford too often, but you could."

Their eyes met across the table. Marheh's glance was almost mischievous.

"Shall we?" she asked.

Gelis smiled.

"Why not?" she said, excited by the idea of a night journey and apprehensive about the possibility of danger to come.

They decided to wait until dark before setting out and agreed they should try to get some sleep. Gelis went to her cabin and lay down, sure she would not actually fall asleep. Marheh, she thought, would probably be practising the soul song and perhaps she should too. She closed her eyes.

Marheh's light tap on her cabin door woke her a couple of hours later. She scrambled off the bed and went to help. Although night had fallen it was not completely dark. There was a slim, curving scallop of moon and the stars blazed brightly. They put no light on in the boat in order to preserve their night vision and the soft glow from their heating stove was reflected from the dark windows.

Gelis made them each a mug of sperit while Marheh checked the engine then they were off, *Day Bringer*'s deep, slow pulse sounding unusually loud in the still landscape. Once she had tidied up the front line, Gelis took her mug and went to perch on the roof near to Marheh in her usual spot. It was a beautiful night. The hills around them were shadowy and soft. Dark corners ran out into hedgerows across the fields. Beside and beneath them the water chuckled quietly and silver-edged ripples traced their path. Nothing else moved.

They were travelling slowly, watching the way ahead carefully. There was no need to speak. Gelis wrapped both hands around her mug, glad of the warmth, and let the night soak into her.

It took nearly two hours to complete the short journey to the tunnel mouth. Here Marheh slowed *Day Bringer* still further. Unwilling to put the headlight on, she sent Gelis to put the lights on in the galley and open the curtains so that some light spilled onto the rough, dripping walls that surrounded them. Ahead the water road seemed unfathomably dark, with only a grey half circle in the distance promising the possibility of an end.

They edged their way onwards, the grey arch ahead growing gradually larger, until at last they were through and out into a night that seemed even brighter than before.

They were scarcely out of the tunnel when they reached the moorings at the pottery. Carefully and quietly they drew in, the engine barely ticking over as they nosed up to the neat, stone-edged wharf. They tied up, turned off the engine and went to bed.

Next morning it was Nicken who alerted the household to their presence. She was down at the boat before Gelis and Marheh had done more than yawn and stretch, knocking on the roof to be let in. Marheh sent her back to tell Kina or Tith where she was and put an extra egg in the saucepan and an extra piece of bread on the grill.

After breakfast they all went together up the path to the house. Only Tep and Fali were in the big kitchen when they arrived, though there was a sense of morning activity about the place, light quick footsteps on the stairs, a door opening and closing with a click. Fali came to welcome them with a smile and a hug. Tep called a greeting from the sink where he was just finishing washing the breakfast dishes.

Marheh looked from one to the other.

"I'm sorry," she said. "But I think we have to be here. We can't act effectively from outside the village."

Fali and Tep looked at each other.

"We were thinking that," said Fali. "And after all this is our struggle too."

Marheh smiled with relief.

"I was hoping you would say that, because we are going to need your help – not just with mooring."

"I'll help you."

Nicken slipped her hand into Marheh's.

Kina came into the kitchen with Nicken's school bag in time to hear this offer. Marheh looked across at her then back to Nicken.

"Just now, the best way to help is to keep us secret," she said. "So we have time to make plans and think what is best to do."

Nicken looked important.

"I can do that," she said, then looked at Kina. "Do I have to go to school?"

For answer Kina held up the packed school bag. Nicken sighed deeply and reached for the strap.

"But you'll still be here when I get home?" she asked and went off with Kina when Marheh nodded.

When they had gone, the others sat down around the kitchen table.

"I think it's that club," Marheh began. "That's the centre of the trouble. What can you tell us about the club?"

* * * *

In the pottery Tith and Lorac were preparing to make a mould from a special piece of Marheh's. They were studying it silently, working out just where each piece of the mould would fit. Suddenly the door swung open and Ved came running in. He stood in front of them, panting. Lorac touched him lightly.

"What's wrong?" she asked as he struggled to get his breath.

"They want the pottery," he gasped. "That club, they want the pottery."

Tith and Lorac looked at each other in alarm.

"What do you mean?" Tith asked carefully.

"That club where mother went last night," Ved said, more calmly. "They want the pottery."

Lorac took the damp cloth that had covered Marheh's sculpture and wrapped it up again.

She looked at Tith.

"I think we had better go up to the house."

He nodded.

"Yes, Tep and Fali need to hear this, and Marheh."

He looked at Ved.

"You'll come?"

Ved nodded.

"Of course."

Together they put away their work and hurried across to the house. The others were still sitting around the kitchen table discussing the activities of the club. They all looked up as Lorac pushed open the door and held it for

135

Ved and Tith.

"What's wrong?" Fali asked anxiously, as they gathered around the table.

Ved looked at her.

"My mother went to that club last night. This morning she told me they are planning to acquire the pottery."

He looked at Lorac.

"She was hoping to turn me away from you. She was gloating."

There was a moment of silence. Fali looked suddenly old, drawn. Tep's face hardened. Marheh reached out to Fali across the table and squeezed her hand. She smiled at Ved.

"You'd better sit down and tell us all you know."

Tith was already drawing up a couple more chairs. Everyone looked at Ved as he sat down next to Lorac. She smiled at him and put one hand lightly over his where it rested on the table.

"I told you she was invited with the office bearers of the Women's Union," he began slowly.

The others nodded.

"It was last night."

He hesitated, choosing his words.

"I was in bed by the time she came home, but this morning she talked and talked."

Lorac smiled at him encouragingly.

"They really feted them," he said. "Gave them a four course dinner, wine, tour of the club house and told them what important people they were and how much the village valued what they did. The club president and a couple of other officials ate with them and it sounds like they just kept buttering them up. From what mother said I got the impression that Elizabeth Entally saw through them."

He looked at Fali.

"I think she is the treasurer?"

Fali nodded.

"Any way, mother said she was rude to them, or abrupt at least, and not prepared to go along with the others in accepting all they were offered."

He paused.

"It seems as if mother just thinks they are wonderful and is falling over herself to keep in with them."

He looked around.

"She thinks she is going to be invited to join the club, apparently it was hinted at. They call it YRTHA – Your Right to Happiness Association."

"But what about the pottery?" Fali asked, as he paused again.

"They talked about buying it, mother said, but they knew enough to know you wouldn't willingly sell. I don't quite know why, but I got the impression that the invitation to join the club was contingent on her support for compulsory acquisition."

He put his head in his hands.

"I guess she wasn't prepared to acknowledge that – even to herself."

There was a moment of silence while the group around him tried to absorb his words.

"Compulsory acquisition," whispered Lorac. "Can they do that?"

"No," Tep said gloomily. "But the Local Council can."

"But the Local Council wouldn't do it without a reason," Fali protested. "And there are some conscientious people on it."

"I expect they're trying to influence all sorts of people," Marheh said. "Do you know anyone on the Local Council you could talk to? Maybe they have had the wining and dining treatment too."

Tep nodded.

"I ought to know one or two of them, but I've rather dropped out of village affairs."

"Actually I think Elizabeth Entally might be a member," Fali said slowly. "I know she goes to the meetings."

Fali was beginning to recover from the initial shock.

"What I don't understand is why. What have we got that they want so badly?"

Marheh spoke slowly.

"I've been wondering about that," she said. "And I think what they want is control of the tunnel. They already control the bridge. If they controlled the tunnel too they could keep Silberay out of Deerford and the

137

water road through the village would die."

"And if that happened Deerford would die too," Fali said sadly. "It is already wounded and hurting."

There was silence while each one absorbed the truth of her words.

"But it hasn't happened yet."

Marheh looked around the table.

"And it's our job to stop it."

"I wish we knew more about what they're planning," Tep said. "I can't quite grasp the truth of it. Our family has been here, working the pottery, trying to live honestly for close on 150 years. How can they even contemplate closing us down?"

Fali took his hand.

"Maybe we have closed our eyes too long. Did we try to do anything when we started to see what was happening in the village?"

"What could we have done?" Tith asked. "Except mind our own business and try to keep honest?"

Fali shook her head.

"I don't know what we could have done, but we didn't even try."

Marheh looked from one to the other.

"We will try now. All of us."

She smiled at Ved.

"Is there anything else you can tell us?"

He shook his head slowly.

"I don't think so."

Lorac squeezed his hand.

"We'll fight," she said. "This is my life."

They were all talking to each other, trying to grasp what the threat might mean to them, when the bell at the front door rang loudly, as if from a vigorous tug. The echoes had scarcely died away when it rang again.

"It's the front door," Fali said. "No one who knows us comes to the front door."

Tep pushed back his chair and stood up slowly.

"So it will be someone who doesn't know us," he said, then added as the bell rang again, "Someone impatient."

They watched as he left the room, closing the door behind him.

"What if it's them?" Lorac asked anxiously.

She stood up and went to the door Tep had just closed.

"We need to be sure he's not in danger," she said, opening it a crack.

"I will go and stand with him," Fali said.

She stood up.

"Tith, Lorac," she said. "You must come too."

She tucked her arm into Tith's and took Lorac's hand.

"If this is the visit we fear, then we are all involved."

They went out leaving Gelis, Marheh and Ved looking anxiously at the closed door.

As Fali, Tith and Lorac moved from the kitchen to the small entrance hall, Tep was opening the front door, not far, so they could not see who was outside, but they could hear the rumble of voices and see Tep shaking his head. Detaching herself from Tith and Lorac, Fali went up to him, slid her arm under his and looked out at the visitors. There were two men standing there. One she recognised as a representative of the Local Council, the other, standing behind him, she had never seen before. She put on a polite smile and greeted the men.

"These gentlemen are asking to come in and discuss a proposition they have," Tep told her.

"What kind of proposition?"

Fali looked from one to the other.

"Do you want some pieces to sell for fundraising?"

The council representative reddened.

"You've always been very generous in the past," he said.

He was short and plump. His chubby fingers held a crisp white envelope, which he shifted from one small, carefully manicured hand to the other.

"This is for the good of the community too," he said. "But it is a bit more than a donation. In fact we are anxious to pay you."

Fali smiled politely.

"What can we do for you?"

"It would be easier to speak about it if we could come in."

The other spoke smoothly and gave Fali a charming smile that did not quite reach his very blue eyes.

Fali looked at Tep.

"Perhaps we could go into the office," she suggested, giving him a little nudge to remind him that they should not reveal that they knew what was coming.

Tep opened the door wider.

"Come this way gentlemen," he said.

Fali could hear his struggle for politeness.

"But I don't have very long," he added. "This is a working day."

The two men entered and walked across the entrance hall to the room Tep indicated. Fali slipped ahead and opened the door. Lorac and Tith stood silent, nodding briefly as the men passed them and went into Tep's small office. Fali looked at them and winked as she closed the door and turned to face their guests.

"I represent the YRTH Association," the plump man began when they were all seated.

"What's that?" asked Tep. "Never heard of it."

"We have the club in the village."

The plump councillor folded his hands on his stomach, the white envelope still between his fingers, standing up like a small flag.

"My colleague is the Club Treasurer," he added reverently.

Fali thought she could hear the capital letters in his voice. Tep and Fali remained silent, so that he cleared his throat and continued.

"We want to make you an offer for the pottery," he said.

Tep and Fali looked at each other. It was actually happening as Ved had told them.

"We are not interested in selling," Tep said at last.

140

"It is a very generous offer."

The Club Treasurer spoke, again with the charming smile colouring his voice, but not touching his eyes.

"Doesn't matter," Tep said bluntly. "I'm not after money."

The man raised a quizzical eyebrow.

"Not?"

Tep looked at him. The polish was so shiny it was hard to see below the surface. He shrugged.

"Perhaps you would not understand," he said. "The pottery has been in our family for 150 years, my son and grand-daughter work here. It is not a commodity, it's a way of life."

"With our offer you could set up somewhere else," the local councillor said.

"Why?" Fali said. "You said it was for the good of the community. Is it good that we leave Deerford?"

"You wouldn't have to leave Deerford," the local councillor said. "You could set up somewhere else in the village."

"Why?" Fali said again, her clear brown eyes studying the two men, waiting for their answer.

"The Club."

The local councillor was not happy in his explanation.

"The Club is prepared to be extremely generous, to you and to the village."

He began to convince himself.

"Your Right to Happiness is for everyone. The village will benefit significantly."

"Why?" Fali repeated.

The Club Treasurer extracted the envelope from the local councillor's fingers and offered it to Tep. His smile was not in evidence.

"Our offer is explained in this letter," he said. "We'll give you some time to think about it."

He nodded to Fali and turned towards the door.

"You're wasting your time," Tep said as Fali opened the door to usher

141

them out.

The Club Treasurer stopped and looked back.

"I don't think so," he said, his very blue eyes hard and sharp. "I don't think so."

He turned again and brushed past Fali leaving the local councillor to flounder in his wake. Tith held the front door for them and they passed through without an acknowledgement. For a moment Tith and Lorac watched their departure, then Tith closed the door firmly and turned back to the others.

"So it's true," he said. "They do want us out."

They stood together in the little entrance hall, Tep still held the white envelope, unopened. After a moment of silence, Fali squared her shoulders and put her arm under Tep's.

"We're not beaten yet, she said. "Let's take that envelope and go into the kitchen with the others."

Marheh, Ved and Gelis were still sitting around the table.

Gelis jumped up was soon as they entered.

"I've put the kettle on," she said. "I thought you might need a hot drink."

Fali smiled at her.

"Thank you, I'm sure we could all do with one."

Lorac went across to get down the mugs and help prepare the sperit. When they were all sitting again Tep held up the envelope.

"Let's see just what they consider to be a generous offer," he said.

Slowly he prised open the flap and took out the single folded sheet. He read it silently, his face expressionless, then laid it on the table.

"The sting is in the tail," he said, and read slowly. "Should we have the expense of a law suit to acquire the property, the compensation would necessarily be reduced."

He passed the letter to Fali and then it went around the table.

"It shows they are serious about it, but doesn't explain why."

"We can keep saying no, but what if that isn't enough?"

"Where's Kina? She should be here too."

"Is it a generous offer?"

The letter went back to Tep.

"No, no and no," he said and crumpled it tightly in one strong, potter's hand.

Marheh took it from him gently, carefully smoothed it again and gave it to Fali.

"I think we should keep this. Of course we will keep saying no, but we need to take action of our own."

"I was thinking," Gelis said tentatively. "Maybe I can help, because they don't know me."

"Why should you help?" Tith asked, then reddened. "Sorry, I didn't mean that the way it sounded. It was good of you to offer."

"I think it is part of my job," Gelis said, and felt warmed by Marheh's quick smile at her words.

"Did you have any ideas about how?" Marheh asked.

"I just thought it might be easier for me to get near them," she said. "If they serve food in their club, perhaps they need someone in the kitchen."

"Go and work for them," Lorac gasped. "You can't. What if they find out?"

"What's to find out?" Gelis said. "I'm a student on holiday, wanting a job to keep myself for a bit."

Marheh looked at her.

"Have you really thought about this? Are you sure?"

"I'm really the only one who can," Gelis said. "Aren't I?"

Warmth of smiles, and red glowing bricks
Warmth of sperit and welcoming eyes
A bulwark
A shield
A defence.

Warmth to remember and hold in my heart
Warmth to cherish and build up with care
A choice
A challenge
A task.

Gelis

CHAPTER ELEVEN

Marheh and Gelis followed Fali up steep narrow stairs to a small attic bedroom. Gelis carried her day pack and Marheh a small bag.

"The room is very tiny," Fali said as she opened the door.

"I know."

Marheh smiled.

"It was my bedroom for about sixteen years," she said to Gelis.

Fali laughed.

"Tep and Nicken still call it *The Palace of Marheh the Great.* Nicken comes up here to play occasionally."

"It's lovely."

Gelis stood in the doorway looking at the small, neat space, the sloping ceiling and slanting walls, the deep padded seat under the window.

"You'll be out of the way here," Marheh said, putting the bag she carried on the end of the bed.

"I wish I could stay on *Day Bringer* with you, but I can see it's best I don't."

Gelis swung her day pack into a corner and went to kneel on the window seat.

"It's lovely to be so high up. I can see right over the tree tops and out into the country."

Marheh came to stand beside her.

"Behind those hills is Corestone," she said. "You can't see the water road from here though. It's on the other side of the house."

"It's lovely," Gelis said again and turned around to smile at Fali.

"There are a couple of empty drawers in that little dresser if you want to unpack," Fali said, moving to the doorway. "I'll leave you to come down when you're ready."

When she had gone Marheh helped Gelis to put her things away then sat with her on the window seat.

"Are you sure about this?" she asked Gelis as she had done in the kitchen.

"I'm sure," she said steadily, looking at Marheh. Then she looked away and added quietly "But I'm pretty scared."

"Of course you are," Marheh said. "You'd be silly not to be."

She put her arms around Gelis and held her for a moment.

"But I'll make sure you're well prepared and give you as much protection as I can."

"You won't tell the others?"

Marheh shook her head.

"And you'll help me … get my story straight."

She gave Marheh a little grin.

"That sounds like I'm an undercover agent."

"You are."

Gelis looked startled.

"I suppose I am in a way."

Marheh leaned back against the window frame.

"So let's think about who you are."

Together they prepared a story for Gelis. Her idea of being a student on

145

holidays would need to be modified a little because it was not holiday time. Marheh suggested she might be a creative writing student taking some time off to earn and also to have some experiences. It seemed a good idea to Gelis who had considered writing of some kind as a way of earning her living. She was quite keen to begin the task Marheh suggested and make a writer's journal or notebook with dates covering the last couple of months.

"It shouldn't be too difficult," she told Marheh. "I'll just have to go back to the time before I started preparing to be your apprentice."

"Not very long at all really," Marheh said.

"It seems a long time though," Gelis said then glanced sideways at Marheh. "My mentor is such a hard taskmaster."

Marheh nodded.

"Makes you do all the dirty work and beats you if you complain."

Gelis laughed a little, then turned her head suddenly away. Marheh waited, watching her anxiously.

"Tell me Gelis," she said at last. "What is it?"

"What if somebody wanted my mind?" she said, a catch in her voice. "I wouldn't be able to do what you did."

Marheh leaned forward to hug her for a moment then leaned back and took her hands.

"I can't promise it won't happen," she said. "But it's very unlikely. Nobody knows you are Silberay and even if they find out, you have not learned much yet. No one will want to damage your mind if they think it can be used by them."

Gelis traced Marheh's fingers with one of her own.

"Why you?" she asked. "Why would anyone do that to you?"

"Even before I began my apprenticeship people knew who I was," Marheh said. "Because of my Uncle Jik who was Silberay and my family being who they are. And I turned out to be very good at the mind stuff. It seems the Yareblis were watching me. You're much more of a dark horse. Only the Silberay at the Gathering know I have an apprentice."

Gelis nodded.

"They were afraid of you," she said. "Or of what you might become. They won't be afraid of me."

Marheh smiled.

"Not yet any way."

She stood up and went to the head of the bed.

"I wonder," she said, reaching behind the bed head.

She seemed to struggle with something for a moment then smiled and stood up holding a shell and a pebble.

"Treasures from childhood," she said, showing them to Gelis. "Let's think of something beautiful."

When they had spent some time in the soul song Marheh led the way downstairs again.

"Everything alright?"

Fali smiled at them as they came into the kitchen.

"The others will be coming in for lunch any minute. You'll stay won't you?"

"You know me," Marheh said. "Always ready for a free lunch."

Fali took hold of her wrist as she passed and gave her a little smack on the back of her hand.

"Ouch," said Marheh. "What was that for?"

"Behave yourself," Fali said with mock severity. "Or you'll stand in the corner and watch while we eat."

Gelis laughed. Marheh was full of surprises and her family seemed to bring out the clown in her.

"You don't treat me with sufficient respect," Marheh grumbled. "I'll never be able to boss Gelis at this rate."

"And neither you should… boss Gelis indeed."

Fali's scolding voice was full of affection and suppressed laughter.

"Gelis is wondering whether she has wandered into the mad house by mistake," said Tep from the doorway.

"Are you Gelis?" asked Marheh with such a look of innocent inquiry that Gelis laughed again.

The others came in then, Tith and Lorac from the pottery and Kina from the garden. Fali shooed them all to the table and Gelis helped her carry around bowls of soup.

"Teacher's pet," Marheh said wickedly as Gelis put a bowl in front of her.

Gelis spluttered and slopped the bowl as she put it down.

"Marheh!" Fali said warningly. "Just wait until your father gets home."

Marheh buried her face in her crossed arms.

"Marheh can be very silly sometimes," Tep said to Gelis amidst the general laughter. "I think it must be reaction to always being the big sister."

"I like that!" Marheh said. "Fali is just as bad."

Fali leaned across the table with a cloth and mopped up the spilt soup.

"What was that you said?" she asked, the wet cloth held poised.

Marheh leaned back hastily.

"Nothing Fali. I'll be good. Promise."

Gelis put a couple of big plates of bread and butter on the table and sat down next to Lorac. Fali brought the last two bowls of soup and sat down next to Marheh, to keep her in order, she said.

Lorac looked at Gelis.

"Do you love being her apprentice?" she asked.

Gelis nodded.

"But she isn't like this when it's just us. She's so funny."

Lorac looked across the table to where Tep, Fali and Marheh were absorbed in conversation.

"We don't see her very much, but there is something special about her."

"I know. I feel really lucky to be with her, even when she gets cross."

"Does she?"

"Not really, but she makes me feel as if I've done the wrong thing sometimes and then apologises – to me."

"She's worried isn't she? About what you're going to do? Grandpa Tep says she fools about when she is worried."

"Mm, she is I think."

Gelis turned to Lorac.

"You could help me," she said. "It's important no one knows I'm Silberay, but I don't know what people see who don't see the water."

148

"Well I can certainly tell you what I see, but I wish I could see the water."

"It's funny isn't it?" Gelis said. "I don't see anything else."

Lorac smiled at her.

"It's actually quite pretty, especially just now. At the bottom of the garden is a green sloping bank with wildflowers just coming out, cowslips and buttercups mostly, then over where the hill begins, where Marheh says there is a tunnel there are brambles and hawthorn."

"It sounds lovely."

"It is, but not special, like the water."

"Is it all like that?"

"I don't really know where the water road is, except places Marheh has told me. I know there is a bit that's near the village pond, because Marheh used to moor there and go to the shop. It used to be quite nice, but there is lots of rubbish there now and just weeds mostly. Do you really not see it?

"Do you really not see the water?"

They looked at each other and smiled.

"I'll need to be really careful," Gelis said. "Best to try to say nothing I guess."

"Are you scared?" Lorac asked. "I would be."

"I am a bit," Gelis confessed. "But Marheh's helping me."

Lorac nodded.

"She won't let anything happen to you."

Lunch over the others went back to their various tasks while Gelis went upstairs again to work with Marheh and begin to concoct her writer's notebook. Ved came to see Lorac after supper and mentioned to Gelis that his mother sometimes took paying guests. Since she could not go back and forth from the pottery it seemed a good option and she resolved to try there for accommodation once she really started her adventure. By the time she went to bed that night plans seemed to be taking shape.

Next morning she woke early. Her little room seemed full of light and she could not stay in bed. Quickly she dressed and went to the window to look out at the morning landscape before descending, quietly and carefully to the floor below and then to the kitchen, which seemed to her to be the core of the house and Fali its warmth and life.

Although it was so early the stove already bore a steaming kettle and Fali was moving quietly about preparing for the day. She smiled at Gelis and welcomed her.

"What would you like for breakfast?" she asked.

"Whatever is going," Gelis answered. "Can I help?"

Soon she was busy cutting bread for toast while Fali made porridge. It was peaceful and ordinary and Gelis relished it, thinking that peace and order were likely to be missing from her life in the near future.

Light, running feet sounded from the stairs and next minute Lorac arrived. She kissed Fali and began to set out crockery and cutlery for breakfast. Soon everyone was gathered, even Marheh had come up from *Day Bringer* to share the meal. The kitchen was filled with good smells, good food and good company. There was not much talk, everyone was preparing for the day ahead, but the feeling was of warmth, good humour and a sense of common purpose.

Within an hour everyone had gone again. Tith had taken Nicken to school and the others were at work in the pottery. Only Marheh and Fali remained with Gelis in the kitchen. The three women began to clear away the dishes and tidy up. It seemed to Gelis that they were moving in some ageless pattern, like a slow dance, where each one had a part to play. There was no need to speak and the silence was part of the ease and grace that upheld them.

When all was done they hugged each other warmly, sat down together and smiled.

"Thank you," Fali said, looking from one to the other. "Both of you."

"Your kitchen is special," Marheh said.

Gelis nodded her agreement.

"And so are you Fali."

Fali shook her head and reached out to pat Gelis' hand.

Marheh looked at her.

"May we stay here with you and let in the darkness – just a little – to help arm Gelis against it?"

The three of them moved a little closer together. Marheh's words seemed to harden the soft, warm, shadowy corners into something dark and cold that hovered just out of reach.

Perhaps two hours had gone by, perhaps longer, and they were just emerging from the place Marheh had taken them when there was a knock on the back door. They looked at each other. Marheh smiled at them both.

"Are you alright?" she asked.

Fali smiled back and Gelis nodded.

"I'll just go upstairs and have a think about everything," she said. "And stay out of the way of your visitor."

Marheh looked at her again. Gelis felt the warmth of her concern and took it with her out of the kitchen and away to her hideaway under the roof. Fali went to the door and opened it for her visitor. Ved's mother stood on the doorstep, hand raised to knock again.

"You took your time in coming," she said crossly. "I'd begun to think I had a wasted journey."

Fali raised her eyebrows.

"Hello Evelyn, did you want to come in?"

"Well of course. I'd hardly come all this way to stand on the doorstep."

She bustled in, heels clicking, tight grey curls bobbing.

"Hello Mary," she said to Marheh. "What are you doing here?"

"Visiting my family," Marheh said quietly. "How are you Ehvah?"

The woman bristled.

"Evelyn is my name," she said – and added with heavy emphasis. "Thank you *Mary*. I've come to see *Felicity*."

"Do sit down," Fali said. "What can I do for you? Would you like a mug of sperit?"

Evelyn shuddered dramatically.

"I'll have a cup of tea, if you have one."

She looked at Marheh again.

"Have you decided to grow up, or are you still pretending to live on a boat and save the world?"

151

Marheh laughed.

"I doubt whether I'm capable of saving the world."

"Well it's time you woke up to yourself and started doing a proper job and living in the real world."

She plumped herself down on the chair Gelis had vacated and looked around.

"I could have sworn there were three of you in here when I looked through the window."

Fali placed a pretty cup and saucer in front of their visitor.

"Milk and sugar?" she asked.

"Yes thank you, and I'll have a biscuit too, since I'm sure you've been baking with Mary visiting."

Fali raised her eyebrows and a smile flickered in Marheh's eyes, but the tea and biscuits were produced politely and they all sat down together. Marheh and Fali drank their sperit quietly, comfortable with silence. Evelyn ate three biscuits in quick succession, sipped her tea with conscious restraint and carefully rearranged her cup on its saucer several times.

"Say something!" she snapped at last. "Don't you want to know why I'm here?"

Fali smiled gently.

"I expect you will tell us when you are ready."

Evelyn put her teacup down noisily.

"First of all I want you to tell that girl to stay away from my David."

Fali sat straighter and looked at Evelyn.

"My grand-daughter has a name, which you know. She is a fine young woman and your Ved loves her."

"His name is David and he can aim higher than a has-been potter family, who still believe in fairy tales."

"Evelyn," Marheh said carefully. "Since that is what you prefer, don't you think Ved should be able to choose for himself?"

"His name is David."

Evelyn's voice was almost a shriek.

"David!"

She turned to look directly at Marheh, her face contorted with hatred.

"As for you – you're just a deluded layabout, battening on the credulity of the masses."

Marheh stared at her in surprise. Clearly there was no point in trying to defend herself.

"Those are not your words," she said instead. "Someone has been feeding you poison."

"You are the poison! You and your kind and those who support you."

Evelyn seemed scarcely rational.

"You pretend to be so virtuous, but you are living a lie and trying to persuade the world that it is true."

She paused to draw breath.

"Well I'm not fooled, and I'll not let David be drawn into your lies."

Marheh and Fali looked at each other.

"Evelyn," Fali said carefully. "Even if Marheh's life is a delusion, how does it harm you? Why are you so angry?"

"I'll not have my David's mind twisted by your nonsense."

She drew breath and a triumphant smirk replaced the hatred.

"Anyway," she said. "We'll not have to worry about you much longer. YRTHA want the pottery and they'll get it too."

She paused and looked from one to the other.

"I'll be supporting compulsory acquisition if you won't accept their offer to buy."

"You really dislike us so much?" Fali said sadly. "I'm surprised you would risk eating my biscuits, drinking my tea."

She reached across the table and picked up the empty cup, cleared the saucer and the remaining biscuits.

"We won't be selling the pottery," she said quietly. "Please pass that message to your new friends."

"That's your look out."

Evelyn pushed back her chair and stood up.

"We will get it anyway, one way or the other and then we'll be rid of you."

She glared at Marheh.

"And then you will have nowhere to hide."

She marched to the back door. Fali was there before her to open it and let her out.

"Goodbye Ehvah," Marheh said gently as Fali closed the door quietly and firmly behind her.

"Oh Marheh, don't."

Fali turned back, suddenly old.

"I'm sure she heard you. She went purple."

She reached out blindly. There were tears streaming down her cheeks. Marheh was beside her in a moment, arms around her.

"Oh Fali, I'm sorry. I meant it as a blessing, not to provoke."

She paused.

"Well not much anyway," she added, trying to be scrupulously honest.

Fali wiped her eyes and smiled, returning Marheh's hug.

"It's just the enmity," she said unsteadily. "It must be eating her up – and I'm afraid – how can we fight them all?"

"We have to," Marheh said firmly. "For her sake, and sake of all the minds they have twisted as well as for us and the pottery."

* * * *

Upstairs in her little room Gelis was planning the journal she would create in the book Fali had given her. It maybe that no one would ever see it, but it had to be convincing and she must make no mistakes. She must forget the month spent at the Harbour learning and testing her vocation and the time with Marheh and go back to her life with her parents. She scribbled diligently. As a writing student she would, of course, be jotting down her observations of the world and the people around her, as well as the things she did day by day. She created dates for her entries, not writing every day and varying the length so that some days contained thoughts, jottings and descriptions, some a few sentences about what she had done, and one read simply "*What a lousy day!*". She was rather pleased with that one and underlined it ferociously, trying to capture the mood.

When Marheh came up to visit her, she had filled about a third of the little book, and was just completing a carefully edited account of her visit to Deerford, nothing about boats or cold, empty eyes, so she gave her best effort to a character study of the elderly dog walker.

She welcomed Marheh and waved the book at her.

"I've basically finished. You'll check it for me won't you?"

Marheh smiled.

"Of course."

She tucked it carefully into her pocket.

"Have you got everything else you need?"

They went over the contents of Gelis' pack.

"What have you been doing for accommodation since you set out?" Marheh asked.

"I thought a bed and breakfast one or two nights, then a couple of nights with friends and perhaps a youth hostel. I've been in one before."

Marheh nodded.

"Let's go down and see if Fali has a map and perhaps she will help us plan a route for you. You'll need to be able to field any questions without contradicting yourself."

They went down stairs together. Fali produced a map and together they poured over it, working out where Gelis might have stayed, the paths she might have followed, the place she caught a bus. At last she looked at them.

"I don't think I can remember any more," she said. "My head is spinning."

Marheh touched her apologetically.

"We want to take care of you, but of course we can't really, so we are over-loading you with information."

Gelis smiled.

"You are taking care of me. I know it is important to have my story consistent and logical and I couldn't have worked it out without you."

She paused and looked at Marheh.

"The hardest thing is knowing so little of what to expect of the Yareblis."

Marheh nodded.

"And I cannot help very much. What I do know is that your best

155

protection is to be unrecognised."

Gelis took this in, then asked hesitantly "And if I am recognised?"

Marheh spoke slowly.

"I think they will try to enter your mind, to try to turn you or perhaps to enslave you."

Fali reached out to give Gelis a quick hug.

"You don't have to do this," she said.

Gelis squeezed her hand.

"Yes I do.. this is part of the job."

She looked to Marheh again.

"And my defence is to think of something beautiful?"

Marheh nodded.

"Hold onto it with all your heart and mind – make time to practice when you are alone if you possibly can."

Gelis reached across, a hand to each of them. She wanted to speak, to share her fear, to thank them, to express her affection, but she could not find words, so they sat in silence, hand-linked, while loving support built between them.

Next morning Gelis came downstairs to breakfast with her pack, ready to go. The previous evening Fali and Kina had prepared a special meal and they all toasted Gelis' undertaking with high solemnity and a great sense of occasion that soon relaxed into high spirits and hilarity. Breakfast this morning was businesslike and matter-of-fact. The household was focused on the day's work ahead. After she had eaten and said her goodbyes, Gelis climbed into the back of the little van used for local deliveries and Tith took her along with him to the next village. Corestone was only a couple of miles from Deerford, but it was not on the water road, so it was a useful starting point for her adventure.

At a suitably quiet and unobserved spot Tith decanted Gelis from the van, wished her well and drove away. She shouldered her pack, took a deep breath and looked about her. She stood on the verge of a paved road, dwarfed by a high stone wall. Although the day was sunny, she was cold in the shade of the wall, but she looked around carefully before making a move. Satisfied that she was alone, she crossed the road into the sunshine and walked purposefully towards the centre of the village.

There was a pub and a church, but no shops and few dwellings. It was still early and the golden morning lit the brown stone facades of the cottages. Long shadows threw into relief the headstones in the churchyard and striped chimneys across the cottages roofs. Gelis looked around carefully as she walked, tucking pictures away in her mind in case she would need to call on them later.

In only a few minutes she was through the village and heading back towards Deerford. It was the sort of day when walking was a pleasure, so she tried to put the future out of her mind and simply enjoy the moment. It was a pity she had to be on the road rather than a footpath through the fields, but there was not much traffic and she knew it may become important that a passing motorist had seen her walking between Corestone and Deerford.

There was no need for her to hurry and she was glad to be able to stand and watch a kestrel hovering on the breeze, and, as the road climbed a low hill, to pause and look back to where Corestone grew out of the surrounding fields. Then, from the top of the hill, she found she could see Deerford. She took it in slowly, the shadowed shapes of buildings clustered together, the silver ribbon of the water road, a few slow smudges of smoke rising, dark trees here and there. She shivered a little despite the sunshine, hitched up her pack and stepped out again.

After perhaps an hour of steady walking, she reached the village square and stood studying the window of the shop, where a few handwritten notices offered baby sitting services, home delivery of fresh vegetables and agistment for horses, and thinking about her next move. Accommodation first or job, she wondered. She decided to go in and ask about both. It seemed a logical place to start. It would be awkward if she was offered a job in the shop, but she decided there was not much chance of that.

She went inside and wandered along the aisles. She would need some lunch later so she selected some bits and pieces, a drink, a chocolate bar, cheese and fruit and took these to the counter. The woman serving did not look very approachable, but she handed Gelis a short, type-written list of possibilities for board and shook her head unsmilingly in response to the job question. No jobs and no suggestions seemed to be the message.

Gelis thanked her and picked up the bag containing her purchases. Where to now? She wondered. Was it too soon to go asking at the club? Perhaps she should try the pub first. There was not much point in looking for a room if she didn't get a job. She left the shop, crossed the square to the pub and stood looking at it for a few moments before deciding against going in. It was time to try her luck at the club, she couldn't put it off any longer.

Slowly she walked down the lane she remembered from her last visit and soon she was standing outside the big white gates wondering how she would get inside. There would have to be some way for ordinary people to enter, she thought. There would surely be deliveries and sometimes services like plumbers or electricians. She examined the surrounding gate posts and fence, looking for some means of communication, but could see nothing. Tentatively she pushed at one of the gates. To her surprise it swung open smoothly and quietly and the way was open before her. She stepped inside, spent a moment studying the white building at the end of the road, then started off, conscious of her heart beating faster as she drew nearer the huge shining clubhouse and her first meeting with the Yareblis.

Gravel crunched under her feet and she was tempted to move off the road and onto the grass so her approach would be quieter. Then she decided that it was more natural to use the road, hers was legitimate business after all.

As she drew closer to the clubhouse she saw that it was faced with white marble and was even larger and more splendid than it appeared from the gates. She had been approaching from the side, but as the road swung round she saw that the front spilled out onto a series of terraces, some paved and set with small tables and chairs, others bright with green lawns and flower gardens. She stopped to stare, hoping to see some sort of side entrance. There was no one about and the fleet of white boats were still. She looked for a moment at the picture they made, at rest against their narrow jetties, then reminded herself that she could not see them. Turning away she continued slowly towards the grand entrance doors, glad at least to be able to approach from the edge without having to cross the terraces. She expected any minute to hear a shout or be accosted by someone demanding her business.

At last she reached the entrance. Four ornate doorways stretched along the front face of the building. The doors themselves were made of darkened glass and gave her a sudden glimpse of her own reflection, looking white and startled. She walked along, touching the first and the second before the third swung inwards to admit her. At first she thought there was no one there. The space was lit sparingly, with pools of light. It had the effect of making the area look like a stage set awaiting actors to bring it to life. When a woman came towards her from behind a pool of light Gelis stepped back in surprise. Then it occurred to her that this was the effect the woman had intended.

"Yes?" said the woman, standing, cool and slim, looking at Gelis with unsmiling blue eyes.

"I'm looking for a job in the district," Gelis said, trying not to babble. "I was told you did food here, so I thought perhaps in the kitchen…"

Her voice tailed off as the woman's cold stare began to unnerve her. She thought for a moment of Marheh and Fali and stood straighter. Her brown eyes looked quietly at the woman for a few moments before she spoke again.

"I'm sorry to have bothered you."

She began to turn away.

"Wait!"

The voice was sharp and peremptory. Gelis looked at her again.

"I will send for someone to take you down to see the chef."

She took a few steps away then turned back.

"Name?"

"Gillian."

"Stay here."

The high heels clicked busily as the woman walked away. Gelis wondered why she had not heard her arrival since her departure was so emphatic. She took a deep breath and looked around her. The focal point of the space was an arched opening, elaborately decorated, carved and gilded and lit so that beyond it was only darkness. To her right was a pool of light enclosing a few comfortable looking, pale-coloured leather armchairs and a low table. Just beyond the light was another shadowy opening. On her left a staircase rose to a landing where a strange, metallic sculpture was highlighted, casting a pattern of black shapes onto the wall behind it. There were two pictures decorating the walls, one on each side of the further doorway. Lights were focused on each one, but they were too distant for Gelis to make out any detail, beyond the fact that they each depicted an individual and a white boat. She was tempted to go closer, but before she could take a step, a long decoratively woven curtain on her right was pushed aside and a strange figure appeared.

At first she thought he was a child as he was several inches shorter than she was, but when he came closer, she saw that his face was covered with a web of fine wrinkles and his eyes were ages old.

"You for the kitchen?" he said, and his voice was high and piping. "You for the kitchen," he said again, and Gelis suddenly saw herself being turned into food. She gulped and nodded.

"This way then."

He turned briskly and headed back towards the curtain. Gelis hurried to follow him.

Behind the curtain was a small landing and a staircase leading downwards. As they descended the light became brighter, but harsh and rather clinical. The staircase turned twice so it was not until they reached the last section that Gelis realised that she was about to enter an enormous kitchen.

At the foot of the stairs her guide stopped and gestured widely.

"The kingdom of cookery!" he proclaimed, bowing with exaggerated grandeur.

Then he turned and skipped nimbly back up the stairs, leaving Gelis to stand and stare. The big space was very clean looking, bright with shining metallic surfaces, two big sinks against one wall and several hobs and big ovens on another. There were no cooking smells and no one about. Cooking utensils hung from convenient hooks and shelves beneath the work surfaces were filled with pots and pans.

Gelis stepped further into the room. There were doors in each wall, but no windows, just a few large extractor fans set into the walls and the ceiling. Everything that was not metal was white; white tiles on the floor and about three quarters of the way up the walls, white paint everywhere else. She wondered in a moment of flippancy, whether the food produced here was also white. She took another couple of steps forward, feeling entirely out of place in her very ordinary, blue jeans and mustard coloured top. She wanted to giggle at the idea of white mustard and knew she was close to a kind of mild hysteria. Deliberately she took herself back to the warm, golden kitchen at the pottery and the affection of Marheh and Fali. So she was almost relaxed when a door opened and a tall, heavily built figure appeared.

The person, Gelis was not yet sure of the sex, was much taller than Gelis and though not fat, was heavily built, so that Gelis thought of giants or perhaps giantesses.

"Come here girl."

The command was issued in a voice that would have been high for a man.

Woman then, Gelis guessed as she went towards her. She stopped in front of her and looked up, taking in the white, tailored trousers and jacket, white shirt and white tie. The tie had a fine thread of silver, diagonally striping, and a single pearl in a silver setting holding it in place. The face above all this was pale also, large and strongly defined, in proportion with the big frame that supported it. Only the eyes seemed smaller than was natural, of a light blue grey, and hard as stone.

"They tell me you want a job in my kitchen."

Gelis nodded, opening and shutting her mouth a couple of times before managing to speak.

"Yes if there is work available."

"Always work in a kitchen. Can you cook?"

"Not really, but I can take orders."

The woman looked at her sharply.

"Do as you're told do you? That will be a change. References?"

Gelis shook her head.

"I was just on a walking holiday, but I'm running out of money."

There was a short silence while the woman looked at Gelis and seemed to be summing her up. Gelis found it hard to stand still under the scrutiny, and impossible to meet the woman's eyes.

"I dare say you'll do," the woman said at last. "Be here at four o'clock and we'll see."

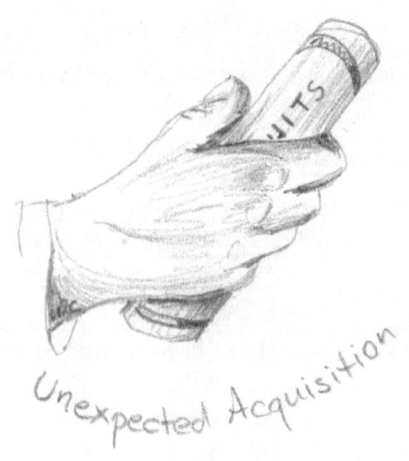

Unexpected Acquisition

CHAPTER TWELVE

Marheh breakfasted with Gelis and the others and gave her a hug to send her on her way. She could not help worrying that she was somehow failing her apprentice by allowing her to take action that could be dangerous. It helped a bit that she remembered how she had pushed Nemle to allow her to go into danger when she was still a first year apprentice. Gelis was much more sensible and mature than she had been. She sighed a little and picked up a tea towel to help Fali with the breakfast dishes.

Fali looked at her sympathetically.

"Are you worried about her?"

Marheh nodded.

"It would be so much easier if I could just take action myself."

Fali put a bowl in the drainer and then another.

"I didn't want an apprentice," Marheh went on. "Didn't want to think that I might be getting old, I suppose."

She dried a couple of plates and piled them on the bench.

"And didn't want the responsibility of another life either. You and Jik together made me see that I was being selfish."

Fali gave her a quick look.

"Not selfish, not really."

"Yes, selfish," Marheh said. "I didn't want my life to change, but now I can see that Gelis has been good for me. I've had to think about someone other than myself for a change."

Fali smiled at her.

"I think you are being a bit hard on yourself."

Marheh stared at her then began to pace, still clutching the tea towel around a breakfast bowl. Fali watched her for a few moments then went to step in front of her, taking the towel and bowl and stopping her in her tracks.

"Give yourself some space. You don't have to do anything just now. Gelis is old enough and sensible enough to go looking for a job without you. I know there is danger in what she is attempting, but she wants to do it and you have to let her because it is part of her learning."

"And mine," Marheh said, taking back the tea towel. "It would be easier to do it myself, only it is something I can't do, and Marheh the Great has never liked to acknowledge that there is anything she can't do."

Fali laughed and went back to the sink.

"Go away and play with some clay or polish some brass or do some of your singing. There will be plenty of things needing to be done that only you can do, I have no doubt, but right now you have to wait for Gelis."

Marheh nodded.

"I won't go until the dishes are done, but then I'll head back to *Day Bringer*. Singing will be the most useful thing I can do."

●   * * *

Very late that same evening Gelis sat with her journal, trying to keep up the fiction that she was a writing student and wanting to clarify her thoughts about the day's experiences.

It has been a very long day, she wrote. *Beginning with a walk from Corestone to Deerford after breakfast and ending with a walk from my new job to my new lodgings sometime after 10.00 pm. I've got a job in the kitchen of the big new club here in Deerford. It's a huge place and I felt really intimidated by it. Going up the drive I kept wanting to run away, but I really need the money and the experience will be useful so I'm glad I didn't.*

Once I had the possibility of a job I needed to find some accommodation and I was lucky enough to get a room at the first place I tried. My room is very small but there is a little table in the window where I can write and it is comfortable and clean. Evelyn, my landlady, only ever takes one lodger, she told me, but it is a quiet time of year and she has not had anyone for some weeks. She will give me breakfast and I will be given an evening meal at work.

I'm going to try to describe my time in the kitchen as a kind of writing exercise, to see if I can recreate the feelings I experienced. I had to take the long walk up the hill from the road, but fortunately I did not have to brave the front entrance again. Although the kitchen is mostly underground there are steps cut out and a door, which opens into a kind of scullery where I can hang my coat and where flowers are prepared for the tables and vases are washed and stored. From here another door leads directly into the main kitchen. Kitchen hands have a uniform, including slippers, so shoes are left in the scullery too, and there is a small wash room and changing room off to one side.

Everything is white unless it is stainless steel. It is quite overwhelming really, but I suppose it helps to make sure everything is clean. Of course my uniform is white too, with YRTHA embroidered in silver on the pocket. My first job after I had changed, was to peel and chop carrots, lots of them, but at least they were normal carrot colour. I made them into straws and left them ready in a big bowl. The menu each evening seems to be limited to one or two dishes, at least that is what I helped prepare, vegetables to go with a lamb dish and a pie of some kind.

There seems to be only one other kitchen hand, or perhaps he is a cook. Madam twists him round her little finger, praise one minute, abuse the next. I can see that abuse will mostly be my share. She has a good line in sarcasm that is really unpleasant. Madam is how I am to address her, but fortunately I don't often need to. Karl issues most of her orders when they are for me.

After the carrots there were potatoes and beans and then washing up. Dishwashers had to be stacked with crockery, which was bad enough, but all the pots had to be done by hand – yuk! I seemed to be standing at the sink for hours.

I wouldn't mind the work though if there was a bit of good humour to go with it, but the atmosphere is really tense. I think Karl is quite jealous of Madam's favours because he did try to put me in a bad light. He dropped a baking dish full of roast potatoes when he was taking it out of the oven. Luckily the floor is clean enough to eat off, because the ones that fell out just got put back. I was the one told to be more careful however.

I was given a good meal and half an hour to eat it, but otherwise it was rush, rush, rush – no time to do anything but work when one is at the bottom of the heap.

Gelis put down her pen and sighed. She felt very tired and suddenly very much alone. Her room was quiet and comfortable and Evelyn seemed friendly enough, especially since Gelis was able to confirm that she was working at YRTHA, but she missed the warmth and companionship of the pottery and the peace and sense of purpose she found on *Day Bringer*. Of course these were the things she could not say in this new journal. She stood up and stretched and went to her window. It was dark outside and late now. She had worked until 10.00 pm then walked to her new lodgings and written in her journal. It was probably close to midnight. The moon was up and its light came and went as clouds moved slowly past. There were one or two lighted windows, but mostly she saw only darkness and deeper darkness.

She drew the curtains and went to change into her pyjamas, then switched off the light and went back to open the curtains again. She liked to have the moonlight lay its shadow patterns around her as she slept and to wake with the sun. Without the dazzle of light in her room, the landscape seemed to brighten. She could see a faint gleam that might have been the water road and make out the dark silhouette of the church spire. In the middle distance she noticed a faint light moving steadily across her field of vision and wondered what it might be.

In the morning she must study the view from her window and try to understand what she was seeing. She yawned and turned away. She was too tired now. Something beautiful, she thought, getting into bed and pulling up the covers. For a moment she saw Marheh smile, then she fell asleep.

● * * *

Marheh had found the day difficult despite her resolve to spend it with the discipline of the soul. She was cross with herself for burdening Fali with her feelings and her jangling thoughts made it difficult to find the necessary focus. When she did there was no pleasure in it, only more struggle, even pain, as she pushed against a surrounding darkness that seemed to swallow her light and her song even as she made them.

After several hours of effort she emerged feeling tired, miserable and alone. No other songs had reached hers. The world was empty not just of Kel, but of all light. Where were Jik and the other old ones when she needed them? She wanted to shout and hit something but managed to keep herself from seeking the family knowing she would be liable to take out her bad mood on them. What was she doing here? What use was she to anyone? What use were all the years of practising the disciplines if her mood could still get in the way?

For a while she sat in the armchair staring at the fire and battling with herself.

Hard experience had given her some strategies for getting out of the doldrums but none seemed presently available to her. A long energetic walk would take her too far from Gelis and the family and she had commitments to each. Wedging some clay used to help, but now the idea just emphasised the loss of her workspace. Perhaps she should go up to the pottery and beg to be allowed to use a wheel, but she knew she could no longer throw a pot that would satisfy Tep's high standards. She had been away from wheel work for too long. She could still work with the clay she had she told herself fiercely and pushed herself out of the armchair and into her cabin to get it from the airtight container under her bed.

She should be keeping her mind on Gelis, she thought, working the clay into a usable consistency. Already the effort to begin had pulled her out of her dark mood.

"I'm sorry Nemle," she said, speaking aloud as she sometimes did to the mentor who had loved her. "I've been wallowing in self pity. I'm ashamed of myself and I've let you down."

Admitting it was another step towards the light. Nemle would forgive her and she could begin to forgive herself.

As her fingers shaped the clay she brought Gelis into her mind. Deliberately this time, the figure she was making was that of her apprentice. She would build it with love and listen while she did so. The love and the listening as well as the piece itself would be a gift and an apology.

When Nicken came running down to *Day Bringer* to tell her that tea was ready the figure was finished and she was in control of herself. Nicken's hug completed the cure and she found herself happy to be joining the family. The meal and the warmth of affection both nourished and strengthened her and when she returned to *Day Bringer* it was with new heart. Now she could put herself aside and hold Gelis in her mind without the morning's struggle.

●   * * *

Gelis would have liked a bit longer in bed the next morning after her late night, but she had been given to understand that breakfast time was scheduled to suit the son of whom Evelyn was so proud. When she sat down he was introduced to her as David and smiled and greeted her as Gillian. The breakfast table was in the kitchen, and Evelyn was busy with the frying pan so there was no opportunity for private conversation, instead Gelis asked Ved about himself. He worked for a small local factory, making finished goods from a range of metals.

"I did my apprenticeship with them," he said. "Finished last year. I quite enjoyed it then because we made a variety of things and I could use and develop my skills setting up tools for the different product runs."

"What sort of products?" Gelis asked, thinking she had not seen Ved as himself until now.

"Sometimes it was range of components for machines, engines especially, sometimes it was special fastenings, door handles, knobs, things like that. All small runs, pretty specialised."

He was neglecting his breakfast as he tried to explain.

"He was top apprentice," Evelyn said proudly, bringing more toast to the table and sitting down herself.

"Congratulations!" Gelis said.

"But it's all changed now."

Ved gathered his tea cup in both hands and stared gloomily into its depths.

"What happened?"

"The company was taken over. It all happened really quickly. All the management and about three quarters of the staff were sacked and now all we do is make metal rods, day after day, the same."

Gelis made a sympathetic face.

"Boring," she said.

"Not just boring, I'm losing my skills, because all I do is watch the machines work."

"But you're working," Evelyn said. "You're getting paid well."

Ved looked apologetically at Gelis.

"None of the others have got jobs locally. There is not much employment around here."

"I was lucky to get the job at the club then," Gelis said. "But of course it is unskilled, and I don't plan on doing it all my working life."

She was enjoying the bacon and fried eggs that Evelyn had put in front of her and turned her head towards her to tell her so. Evelyn flushed with pleasure at the fairly ordinary compliment and Gelis suddenly felt sorry for her.

She turned back to Ved and smiled.

"Perhaps you will come to the end of the rods soon. Surely there must be a limit to the number of metal rods people want."

Ved grimaced.

"I keep telling myself that, but we've done thousands now and no indication of any change."

"What would they be used for do you think?"

He shrugged.

"I wish I knew. I've made all sorts of guesses, but that's all they are – reinforcing rods perhaps, or a fence."

He took the last mouthful and put down his knife and fork.

"I'd better go – it doesn't do to be late."

He pushed back his chair and hurried away. Gelis stood up too.

"May I give you a hand with the dishes?" she asked Evelyn, taking his plate across to the sink along with hers as she spoke. "I don't have to be at work until 4.00 pm, so I'm in no hurry."

She picked up a tea towel and stood against the bench looking around the tiny kitchen. It was clean and very tidy, but had none of the warmth of the kitchen at the pottery, or the homeliness of the galley on *Day Bringer*. There was one window over the sink, but it looked out on a brick wall and let in no sun and little light. The ceiling light was on, but cast a rather cold and anaemic beam, which left the plain, painted cupboards and walls rather grey looking.

Gelis smiled at Evelyn.

"Do you have other family besides David?" she asked.

Evelyn plunged her hands into the sink and stared out at the brick wall.

"Just David," she said. "His father left us when he was still a baby."

She swished her hands aimlessly in the warm water.

"And good riddance," she said firmly.

"That must have been hard for you," Gelis said sympathetically, standing beside her with a tea towel.

"It was quite a struggle."

Evelyn gave a little wriggle that seemed to puff her up as if she was a bird with feathers to fluff.

"Not many realized it. I'm not one to whinge."

Gelis nodded and applied her tea towel to the first plate Evelyn placed in the drainer.

"David has always been a good son, helping me with his earnings as well as doing chores about the place."

Gelis nodded again, stacking the clean, dried plates carefully on the bench beside the sink.

"I just wish he hadn't got himself involved with that lot of day dreamers at the pottery."

Evelyn seemed almost to be thinking aloud.

"If it was up to them, Deerford would stay in the dark ages until it rots."

She put a handful of dripping cutlery into the drainer.

"But YRTHA are more than a match for them."

She nodded importantly.

"YRTHA have plans for this village, modern, practical plans that will make everyone happy. They'll not be able to stand in the way of progress."

Gelis went on drying the cutlery, keeping her mouth closed and wondering.

* * * *

In the kitchen at the pottery, Marheh put on her coat and held out her hand for Fali's shopping list.

"I must," she said to Fali. "I cannot stay hiding in here. They know I am in Deerford and they know I am their enemy. They mustn't know I am afraid of them."

Fali stared at her.

"You're afraid.. you!"

Marheh grinned.

"Yes me. It doesn't do to dwell on it, but they are very strong here and horribly persuasive."

She paused and her smile faded.

"And without conscience."

Fali watched as she slung a shopping bag over her shoulder and tucked the list into the back of her money pouch.

"Then I'll come with you," she said at last, but Marheh shook her head.

"Not this time. This time I have to go alone."

169

The two women hugged and Marheh let herself out of the kitchen door and into the yard. For a moment she paused, drawing strength from the familiar environment, then she set out towards the village centre. Her long, easy stride took her steadily along the road. She looked around her, carefully noting the changes since her last visit. The dwellings that lined the road as it rose over the tunnel seemed to have become shabbier and whereas they had previously been cheerfully ramshackle, now they seemed dilapidated and depressed.

The day was bright and clear, but a chill wind blew and Marheh was glad she had put on her warmest tunic. It had been an odd spring so far, very changeable and both hotter and colder than normal. Nobody else seemed to be walking, though one or two small vehicles passed her, one giving a raucous toot that echoed the driver's rude gesture. Marheh waved cheerfully. She would not let it bother her.

It was not long before she reached the village square. She stood for a moment, remembering how it had been when she was a child. At this time of year there would have been flower boxes and baskets full of spring blooms. The square would have been bright with colour and there would have been people – buyers and sellers, walkers, talkers, some who simply observed. Now there were cars, rubbish and synthetic greyish black pavers that tried to be cobblestones.

She sighed and walked on towards the shop. She was about to turn in through the door and was just feeling for the shopping list when she looked up to find the doorway blocked by a large man who perused her through narrowed eyes.

"Hello Kevin," she said, smiling at him. "I'm glad to see there are still some familiar faces in Deerford. There seems to have been quite a lot of changes since my last visit."

The man gazed at her without speaking or moving.

"You seem surprised to see me," Marheh said lightly. "Is everything alright with you?"

She was wearing the clothes traditionally associated with the Silberay, loose trousers and a coloured tunic over a plain shirt. It was a deliberate statement of who she was.

She continued to look at the man, seeing the small fat bully he had once been and beyond that to the unhappy child who had seldom experienced anything that resembled affection, let alone love.

He shifted uneasily and Marheh took the opportunity to slip past him into the shop.

"Thanks Kevin," she said, stepping away down one of the aisles to begin her shopping.

She walked slowly up and down, looking for the items on her list, but very conscious that she was being watched. There was a short queue for the Post Office, and she looked for any familiar faces as she walked past, but there were none, only a few incurious glances and one hostile stare.

She was just checking her list for omissions before going to join the queue at the service counter, when Kevin again stood before her, barring her way.

"We don't want your sort here," he said, reaching to grab her arm.

Unaccountably he misjudged and looked in surprise at the packet of biscuits clutched in one large fist.

Marheh smiled at him again, rather a sad smile.

"I'm sorry Kevin. I *am* here," she said, and moved past him to the end of the queue.

Behind her, the big man put the biscuits carefully back on the shelf, still feeling puzzled, then went back to guard the doorway.

Marheh could see him there as she waited to be served and knew he was waiting for her. She was not really afraid of him, despite his strength, but dealing with him was tiring and would distract her from any dealings with the real power in Deerford. She put her selection on the counter and smiled at the woman serving. In return she received a blank blue gaze and knew her identity had been noted. There was no other indication and her purchases were processed efficiently. Marheh put them in her bag and paid the sum owing. The woman did not acknowledge her polite thanks, nor look at Marheh again, but she was aware of a stab of bitter cold, gone in an instant, but a clear challenge nevertheless.

She moved towards the door and Kevin, standing scowling in her path. He did not move as she approached so she stopped perforce and waited quietly, looking at him without challenge, but insisting that he meet her gaze. He tried to stare her down, but could not face Marheh's steady appraisal for long. She knew he wanted to explode into violence and she was careful not to give him any excuse, but neither was she about to let him think she could be intimidated.

After a few moments she said quietly "Please may I pass Kevin."

A sneer appeared on his face.

"Ask me again," he said, a kind of triumph in his voice.

Marheh made sure she met his eyes then spoke again, quietly and firmly.

"Please may I pass Kevin."

"Again," he said, grinning with the pleasure of what he thought was power.

He leaned towards her, puffing himself up.

"No Kevin," Marheh said. "Twice is enough."

She looked at him again and stepped towards him confidently. He shifted back from her in surprise and she walked quietly past him with a soft word of thanks.

She had gone a couple of paces before he recovered enough to yell abuse after her, but she took no notice, just maintained her usual steady stride. She had thought perhaps she might have gone into the pub, but realised it would give him another opportunity to corner her, so she continued on down the hill past the ironmongers. Nobody seemed to be about and she wondered where the daily shoppers and the dog walkers were, the ones who enjoyed the regular contact with others as they picked up the bread and milk or exercised their pets.

Soon she reached the bottom of the hill and stood looking at the gates to the club, wondering how the Yareblis had managed to acquire this space that had once been wild and lovely common land. She was still standing sadly, remembering the place she had known as a child, when there was light touch on her arm.

As she turned a voice said "It is you! Thank goodness!"

"Beytha!"

Marheh's face brightened.

"I was just thinking back to playing here in the summers after school."

She looked at the woman who had greeted her.

"It is hard to believe that was sixty years ago."

"There were children playing here only two years ago," the woman said sadly. "But now we have lost their heritage."

"Not you."

Marheh smiled.

"I gather that Elizabeth Entally is not ready to go along with YRTHA."

She looked at the kind, intelligent, elderly face of her friend and her smile broadened.

"You know, I didn't realise it was you at first, when both Ehvah and Fali called you Elizabeth Entally."

"Not many use the soul name now and there are not too many you would want to share it with."

She paused and touched Marheh again, holding her at arm's length.

"It is good to see you. We need help so badly. You look so young too, not my generation at all any more."

Marheh laughed.

"That's nonsense. I am your generation. I wish I had come sooner though. Mostly when I've visited Deerford I've just called in on the family and left my bits of clay. They are rather isolated where they are and perhaps a bit insular."

"Self-sufficient more likely," Beytha said. "As things have got worse in the village the pottery has quietly retreated, but now YRTHA have their eye on them."

"How did they manage to get such a foothold," Marheh asked.

Beytha frowned.

"I'm not quite sure. Lies and promises I think. There are lots who are taken in by the name – *Your Right To Happiness Association!*" she finished scathingly. "Whose right? At whose expense?"

Marheh nodded.

"Is there somewhere we could talk? I need to know more and I've things to ask you. The pub doesn't look very inviting anymore."

"It's about all there is, unless you want to come on to my place. Do you have time? It isn't far."

Marheh hesitated.

"I've had a couple of fairly hostile encounters since I showed myself. I don't want to make things difficult for you."

Beytha gave a short laugh.

"I'm not exactly popular, you know. I've been pretty outspoken at times."

Marheh smiled.

"Thank goodness – it wouldn't be you if you weren't."

173

Beytha laughed.

"Come on then. I can even offer you sperit."

● * * *

At the pottery Tep, Tith and Lorac were doing their best to go about their normal daily routine. Tith managed best as the kiln was due for emptying and he could tackle a job that required strength, but not too much thought. Tep found he could not settle to anything and went backwards and forwards between the kitchen and the pottery drinking innumerable cups of sperit and muttering dark predictions under his breath.

After one such excursion he got back to the pottery to find Ved with Lorac.

"Shouldn't you be at work?"

He sounded out of temper and Ved looked at him in surprise.

"It's my lunch break and I've come to report," he said.

"And to interfere with my apprentice."

This time though the grumble was accompanied by a wink and a slow smile.

"Sorry Ved, I'm a bit on edge at the moment."

"Gelis is staying at Ved's house," Lorac said.

"And she has a job at the club," Ved added. "We were talking at breakfast, but she couldn't say much because Mother was there. I gather it is pretty hard work, chopping vegetables and washing up."

"Yuk!" Lorac grimaced. "Poor Gelis, I hope she thinks it will be worth it."

"Mother thinks it's wonderful that she is working for YRTHA, keeps asking her about everything, which is good in one way because it gives Gelis a chance to talk about it, only I'm not sure how much is altered to fit what Mother wants to hear."

"She is not likely to have anything significant to report quite as soon as this. Kitchen hands are pretty invisible, but she hasn't had time to become part of the furniture."

Lorac looked at Tep in surprise.

"How do you know about kitchen hands?" she asked.

Tep laughed and shook his head.

174

"Part of my misspent youth," he said.

"Grandfather!" Lorac protested, but he said no more only turned to Ved and thanked him for his message.

"You'd best be getting back, I expect," he finished. "Have you had time to eat something?"

Ved grimaced.

"I can eat while I'm watching the machines, which is all I seem to do these days."

He gave Lorac a quick hug and turned to go, but he had hardly moved away from her when Fali appeared in the doorway.

"Those men are back," she told Tep. "I said you were busy and that we were not interested in their offer, but they won't go without seeing you."

She looked at Tep and he suddenly saw that she was distressed.

"They came in as if they own the place already and would not leave when I asked them to."

Tep was by her side in a moment and the others were not far behind. Tep's face had darkened with anger and he was about to storm into the house when Fali touched him and whispered something. He looked at her and drew a long breath.

"You're right of course," he said. "I do need to be in control of myself – and I am now."

He looked from one to the other.

"Are we all coming?"

There was a murmur of support from them all.

Fali shook her head.

"Not Ved," she said, looking at him. "Better if you stay out of their way while Gelis is at your place."

She touched him lightly.

"We know you support us."

He nodded.

"It makes sense. I'll go out the back way and get back to work."

He looked from one to the other.

"Take care. Let me know what happens."

He went quickly and together the others turned towards the house.

Fali had left their visitors in the study where Tep had received them before. As they approached they heard the sound of a drawer closing and when he reached the doorway Tep saw the Club Treasurer standing behind his desk flicking through his address book.

He stood stock still in the doorway for a moment, so that the others had to stop behind him, then he strode across to his desk and wrenched the address book out of the Club Treasurer's hand.

"Out," he bellowed. "Get out now."

The Club Treasurer, urbane, undisturbed, remained where he was. Two large men in suits moved away from the wall and went to stand one each side of him. The Club Treasurer smiled, stretching his lips and crinkling the skin below his eyes.

"I haven't given you my message yet," he said.

Tep's rage was building like a head of steam, but he managed to hold it, simmering, so that he was still in control.

"You have nothing to say to me that I am prepared to listen to," he said, the words emerging one at a time as if powered by that same head of steam. "Unless it is an apology for invading my home and distressing my wife."

The Club Treasurer said nothing and for a moment no one moved. Tep was flanked by his family, Tith, Fali and Lorac, the Club Treasurer, by the two large men. Tep did not take his eyes from the Club Treasurer, though the contact became almost painful as the silence and stillness continued.

At last the Club Treasurer, still smiling coldly, reached into the breast pocket of his jacket and took out a long white envelope. He flicked it lightly onto Tep's desk.

"We have renewed our offer," he said. "For 24 hours only." He paused. "But whether you accept it or not, we will have the pottery."

* * * *

Marheh hugged Beytha as she said goodbye at the door of her small cottage. They had spent an hour together while Beytha talked of what she knew and Marheh listened and wondered. As she set off back to *Day Bringer*, she tried to make sense of what she had learned. Beytha said there were now four, what she called "new villagers" on the Local Council and somehow they had swayed the majority. The shop had changed hands six months ago and it was now owned by a new villager and there was a new villager managing the pub.

What was it about Deerford? Marheh wondered. Was there something special about the area, or did it just happen to fall into their hands. Beytha could not see the water road, but she knew the Silberay and had not seen anyone for longer than she could remember. That was the most worrying thing, no boats, nothing to suggest that any of her friends had ever been there, no clues to what might have happened to them, but somehow she felt certain that the answer was here in Deerford. She sighed, feeling the burden of responsibility weigh heavily. Then she tried to empty her mind and let the rhythm of the walk back to *Day Bringer* take her to the place where she would find strength and guidance for the action that must follow.

* * * *

The Club Treasurer gathered up his henchmen and left without saying anything more. Fali closed the front door after them and came back to where the others were still staring at the envelope. She picked it up and gave it to Tep. Lorac let out a long shuddering breath as he held it, turning it over and over in his hands. Fali took it gently from him again and opened it carefully. She gave him the folded paper it contained. He opened it, stared at it for a moment and held it out to them. It was a single, blank white sheet.

* * * *

Gelis said goodbye to Evelyn and hung the key she had given her around her neck. It was 3.30 and she was off to another day's work.

"Thank you for the key," she said to Evelyn, who stood nodding in the doorway. "I expect I'll be home about the same time as yesterday."

Then she set off without looking back.

Candle

CHAPTER THIRTEEN

The walk to work only took about fifteen minutes. As she went Gelis tried to let the rhythm of her steps steady her and take her to her portal to the soul song. She was not experienced enough to enter the song in such a short time, but Marheh had impressed upon her the importance, even of the attempt, in providing a safeguard for her.

After her first day of work she was no longer quite sure why she needed a safeguard. She had been so afraid yesterday when she approached the club, but today she pushed open the gates and started up the drive as if she had been doing it for weeks.

Since she was in good time she did not hurry, but walked slowly, looking around, reminding herself that she could not see the white boats that were gathered there. She even turned, as she climbed higher, to study the view behind her. There were some rooftops and attic windows to be seen, but she could not decide whether hers was one of them. It would be interesting to know if her view included part of the YRTHA grounds.

A moment more to enjoy the sunshine then she made her way to the kitchen entrance. Yesterday the work had been boring and innocuous and today would probably be more of the same. She needed to remember why she was doing it and keep alert.

A few minutes later she was inside, ready in her uniform and waiting for orders.

Karl put down a big bag of potatoes beside her with a grunt.

"Peel, cut and put in water for boiling," he said, glaring at her.

She thought he intended to be intimidating but just appeared foolish and grumpy.

"We must be expecting a crowd," she said lightly. "If we are to get through all that lot."

"None of your business. Just get on with it."

"Yes Sir!" Gelis said, and realised from his look of satisfaction that he didn't know she was mocking him.

Potatoes, potatoes and more potatoes. Peeling them was mindless enough that she could speculate as she worked. Karl came in and out on some mysterious project of his own. Once when he came to examine her work, she asked him to get her another saucepan. He stared at her and grunted, but she had already filled two pots and just went on peeling and cutting as if her request was entirely natural. A minute or two later a pot was thumped down beside her, then another. She turned to thank him.

"Get them yourself if you need any more," he said. "I'm not here to wait on you."

He stalked off across the room and left via a door she thought might lead to the dining room, since the waiter from last night had come and gone that way. When he had gone she put her peeler down for a moment and took a deep breath. He was never going to treat her any differently, but that didn't really matter. She had not expected this to be a congenial workplace. The kitchen seemed very large and empty when she was alone in it. From the size it seemed as if there should be an army of kitchen workers scurrying about under the direction of half a dozen chefs and under-chefs, not just her alone with a mountain of potatoes.

She kept on with her task, her thoughts drifting to Marheh and *Day Bringer* and her new friends at the pottery. She was doing this for them. Marheh had been encouraging, pleased that she had offered, but concerned for her as well. That was the hard part really, being away from Marheh. Thank goodness for Ved. At least he could provide a link.

About an hour had passed and she had nearly finished her task when the big door at the end of the room slid open and Madam entered with Karl trailing behind. She swept into the centre of the space and struck a pose as if the kitchen was filled with dozens of diligent workers all doing her bidding instead of just Gelis and half a dozen pots holding newly peeled and cut potatoes.

"There will be seven eating in the private dining room," she said. "And three tables booked in the restaurant."

She paused and looked severely at Karl.

"You will have to manage the restaurant meals. I won't be here."

Karl seemed to swell a little.

"I can do it," he said. "What have you chosen for the menu?"

Gelis, watching quietly, saw the moment when Madam decided to be pleased with his compliance.

"Nothing you can't manage," she said graciously. "Soup will be the leek and potatoes left over from yesterday. There is lasagne in the freezer and a chicken and mushroom casserole. They will do for mains with salad or veg. The girl can do those."

She paused and Karl nodded deferentially.

"I shall be eating at the strategy meeting in the private dining room and I shall take responsibility for that meal."

Again Karl nodded as she struck a pose.

"My special fish pie I think. Fish enhances brain power."

Karl looked suitably impressed and Gelis tried to make herself invisible in the hope that Madam would continue to speak.

"Is the strategy meeting important," Karl asked as Madam continued to look at him.

"Critical," she said. "There has been a Silly wondering around the village. It even went into the shop. This one must have got past our security somehow. We need to decide how to deal with it. Sillies can be dangerous."

The last two pieces of potato slipped from Gelis' fingers and made a small splash as they dropped into the pot of water. Madam looked at her.

"Teaspoon of salt in each pot and put them to boil for half an hour," she said. "Then you can get on with the carrots."

"Yes Madam," said Gelis, wondering what a dangerous Silly was and cursing her butter fingers.

As she went for the salt she saw Karl follow Madam into the large freezer and come out with a salmon and a big piece of smoked haddock.

The serious business had begun.

* * * *

Marheh walked back to the pottery thinking about her encounter with Kevin as well as her visit with Beytha. She had known both of them since school days. She and Beytha had been in the same class and friendly in a casual way but she understood now that the young Marheh had not been an easy person to know, full of passions and moods and as changeable as the weather in spring. Hopefully she understood herself better now and did not allow the moods and passions to rule her. Well, not usually, she thought, with a wry smile.

It was different with Kevin. Two years younger than she, he had been a big, slow, unhappy boy and she had found him bullying Tep one afternoon in the playground. Tep must have been about six at the time, which meant that she had been twelve. She had launched into attack without considering possible consequences which had been a bleeding nose for Kevin and an unpleasant interview with the headmaster for her.

It was not the first time she had been caught fighting and the headmaster had called her parents to the school. She could still remember her sense of outrage when she realised that her conviction that she had been right to fight had not impressed Sef and Greya and not only had she been sent supperless to bed, but she had also been expected to apologise to Kevin.

He had left her brothers alone after that though and avoided her as much as possible. She could not help wondering who, or what, had given him the courage to confront her now after all these years.

Reaching the pottery she let herself in through the kitchen and stopped to give Fali a hug of greeting before going down to the mooring. *Day Bringer* was where she belonged, she thought, stepping onto the back deck and pausing to contemplate her shining paintwork and gleaming brass. She did look nice. She had Gelis to thank for that. Gelis would be part of her life for the next twenty years. The solitude she had prized had to be relinquished. She had to accept it as part of her learning. Gelis was working for Deerford and the Silberay in a way she could not, but there was still work she could and should be doing.

Gathering herself, she opened the back door and stepped inside. This cabin at the stern that now belonged to Gelis had once been hers. She did not linger there, but moved through to the galley and from there to her own cabin. It was neat and plain. Peace lapped around her and she drew a deep sighing breath. Here she would have strength and concentration for the next step. She lit a candle and placed it beside her narrow bed, then she lay down, all her movements slow and deliberate.

Gelis did not need her just now so she could give all of herself to the soul song.

She reached for the candle flame that was her portal. This would not be the usual singing. She planned to stretch herself to the limit in an attempt to find some clue to where she might find the others. There were dangers in this. If she stretched herself too thinly she might lose the connection, the path back and if that happened there were no other singers here to guide her home. The real candle burning bravely beside her might help and she would try to be careful and sensible, but care and good sense would fall away if they became a handicap in her quest.

Gently, easily, she entered the song. This part was second nature now, fruit of her long years of disciplined practice. At first, even here, she moved within light, but she knew it was not in the light that she would find what she sought. Faint, distant harmonies encouraged and supported her as she established the pure line of melody that would run before her and between. High and sweet it carried her outward, sounding the space. She played with it, the music and the light entwined in a dance of delight, but she knew the light must fall away. Deliberately she stretched further, spinning herself into a fine thread of song that nudged at the shadowy places where she must go.

There had been times in the past when she had done similar work, but always there had been another song to anchor hers. Nemle or Kel had been there holding her safe so she could fling herself at the dark places. Now she must keep the connection herself if she were to return.

This stretching of herself was filled with pain and she needed all her strength of will to keep reaching outward into the dark. Aching loneliness pushed her on, seeking the song that would complete hers. Her golden thread of sound was so fine now, so vulnerable in the empty darkness, but she could not draw back, not yet, when all her effort had produced no result.

Then something changed. Her song seemed to falter then came back to her reflected from some obstacle. She poured herself into the music, pushing aside the pain of it, exploring, testing the obstacle. How could the darkness solidify? What was it?

Then, with a kind of wild hope, was there something, someone, on the other side of it?

Carefully, with feather touch, she set her song to explore the block. Note after note caressed the impervious presence and returned to her, a faint echo of the music she sent out. Then a note seemed to falter. Aching with effort she sent more melody to test the place, poured note after note to wriggle and sing into the tiny crack she had found.

After what seemed like an age of struggle, the effort eased and suddenly she heard her own song floating again, upheld by a harmonic chorus, slow and sorrowful. For a moment there was delight in the completion of the music and the sense of unity, but then the awareness of danger took over and the urgent need to communicate.

She had found Silberay, more than one, their spirits somehow imprisoned, and she understood that she had given them new hope by managing to reach them, but this way of communicating could not tell of detail that belonged to the world. Only the language of the soul spoke through the music and now she was being told to go, to withdraw from their prison before her own spirit was trapped far from her body.

"Follow me," her song beckoned, as she drew it carefully towards her through the narrow crack. She felt their consternation as she lingered for a moment between the confining walls. Then one, then another danced beside her, through the shadows and into the light. There was no way back for them and they risked being separated from their bodies forever, but they would be with her while she sought them and would strengthen her when she fought for them, as she knew she must.

Slowly she returned to herself, preparing the place where she could welcome and hold the accompanying spirits. This was not something she had ever heard of happening, but she had no doubt. If Kel could hold her mind, as he had on occasion, then it must be possible for her to hold the souls she had released. Such things usually had a cost in pain, but she had not been prepared for the flare of anguish and knew she had cried out as they crossed the threshold she had prepared for them, but they were all song and the music continued within her so that she was soothed and comforted. Exhausted with the effort she slept then, and in her sleep she smiled.

She woke some hours later, ravenously hungry. Her candle had burned out and the sun was low in the sky. There were so many questions , but she was not capable of considering them just now. Still feeling weary she made her way out and up the path to the kitchen. She had been absent a long time and Fali would perhaps be anxious. Fali would give her a hug and feed her without making demands and she yearned for that physical comfort.

The kitchen when she reached it was warm and full of the smells of cooking. Onions were there, and something a bit spicy as well as something rich and warm that made her think of her mother. She blinked back a couple of tears. Fali, looking around from the bench where she was working, saw her standing in the doorway a bit uncertainly. She was very pale and there were dark circles under her eyes. Leaving her work she went to her, hugged her, took her by the hand and led her to the table. A minute or two later she put a mug of sperit and a couple of griddle scones in front of her and waited to see her begin to eat. She did not really understand what it was that Marheh did, but she didn't need to be told how much it had drained her. She saw her take the first mouthful and went back to her cooking. Marheh would speak when she was ready.

It was more of a sigh than words when the scones were eaten and the sperit drunk.

"Thank you Fali."

"Another scone?"

"No I can wait for dinner now."

"You looked so tired. Was it worth it, what ever you did?"

Marheh nodded.

"I haven't had time to make sense of it yet but I do know that there are Silberay here. I found their spirits and joined their song for a moment or two, but they were so sad and somehow imprisoned. That's what I can't understand. The Yareblis deny the soul. How can they have imprisoned something they don't believe exists?"

"You'll find the answer. Give it time."

Fali came to sit beside her.

"No wonder Deerford is such an unhappy place. Do you think Gelis will be safe?"

"I don't think any of us are safe, whether we involve ourselves or not."

Fali nodded and stood up to return to her cooking. Marheh offered her help and was given carrots and potatoes to peel and slice. Together they worked to prepare dinner in quiet sympathy with each other.

About half an hour later, Lorac came in with Ved.

"Will there be enough for Ved to stay for dinner?" she asked, taking his hand and drawing him into the kitchen.

"Of course," Fali said. "You're welcome Ved."

"Thank you."

Ved stood awkwardly between the three women.

"Come in, sit down," Fali said.

"Sperit for everyone?" Lorac asked, getting out the mugs.

"What's wrong?" asked Marheh, sitting down with him at the table.

He sighed deeply.

"I want to resign," he said. "I really hate what I'm doing now. It's all changed since the new owners took over." He looked at Marheh. "And now I think I might be working for YRTHA."

Fali and Lorac stopped what they were doing and turned to look at him.

"What makes you think that?" Marheh asked.

"I was just checking the materials supply," he said. "That end of the process is near the offices and this afternoon there was a visitor. The manager was all over him. They went into his office and I forgot about it for a bit, but then they came and talked to me, asked questions. Can I speed up the process at all? Can anything be added to the raw materials at any point?"

He paused.

"I didn't like him much. He seemed really arrogant and he had the coldest, stoniest eyes I've ever seen, so I started to wonder who he was. Then I spotted it. His tie pin was made up of the letters. It was only small, and I only saw it because his coat swung open when he bent to look at something that I was explaining on the machine. When I was telling Lorac about it she said he sounded like the same man who came here with his threats."

He looked at Marheh, his eyes troubled.

"I don't want anything to do with them. I hate what I'm doing, but my mother depends on what I give her and I'm not likely to get another job."

Marheh put her hand over his.

"You won't stop them by leaving, but you might by staying," she said. "If you really are doing work for them, and it certainly sounds like it."

"What do you mean?" There was a hint of hopefulness in his voice. "I'll fight them if I can."

Marheh smiled.

"Not literally," she said. "And not without understanding what you are fighting."

"They're trying to steal the pottery," he said. "Isn't that enough?"

"Well perhaps," Marheh said. "But that makes them sound like petty criminals and that is to seriously under-estimate them."

Fali and Lorac had drawn closer to listen to the conversation, but now Lorac remembered the kettle. She poured the sperit and brought it to them, then sat by Ved. Fali sat by Marheh and they raised their mugs together.

Then Marheh spoke again.

"Ved," she asked. "What do you know about who I am? Who Gelis is?"

Ved spoke slowly.

"I know you live in boats on water I can't even see. You're called Silberay – or crazy."

He smiled apologetically.

"At least by people like my mother."

Marheh laughed.

"We've been called worse than crazy," she said. "But we don't just live in boats. Somehow we have been born with an ability to live in two worlds. Almost everyone has it to some degree and it can be developed, but obviously the more you start with the more developed it can become. Silberay have a tradition of actively trying to encourage goodness and beauty in this world and the other."

She looked around the table.

"I know we are not alone in that, but we formally dedicate ourselves to the life, and work to develop extra insight and understanding."

She paused.

"One of the really important things we try to do is give people power over their own lives, not just do things for them. What we don't speak of much is that some who could be Silberay chose to be opposite, to develop their abilities in order to enslave, to increase power for themselves."

"And that is what is happening here," Fali said softly in the silence that followed Marheh's explanation.

"Nicken can see the water road," Lorac said. "Does that mean she is Silberay?"

"She could choose to be," Marheh said. "It is a choice, though sometimes it feels more like a calling."

"I wish I could see it," Lorac said wistfully.

"Me too," said Ved.

Marheh smiled at them.

"I expect you can with a bit of help. Will you trust me to show you *Day Bringer*?"

"Of course." Lorac and Ved answered as one. "Fali too?" added Lorac.

"Fali too if she wants, but Fali can see already."

"We'll all go," said Fali, pushing back her chair and standing up. "I love going on board."

Together they followed Marheh out of the kitchen and down the path to the mooring. She stood with them there, looking at *Day Bringer*.

"What do you see?" she asked.

Lorac looked at her.

"I mostly see a grassy bank with wildflowers," she said. "But if I half close my eyes I can imagine I see ripples across the grass."

Marheh looked at Ved.

"Just the bank with the wildflowers," he said. "It's a pretty place."

Marheh smiled at him.

"Is it?" she said. "I'm glad. I have to trust you on that. I can only see the water and *Day Bringer*."

She took Lorac's hands.

"Close your eyes," she said. "I'm going to keep hold of you and lead you on board. Can you trust me enough to keep them closed."

"Of course," Lorac said, her eyes already shut.

"The gunnel is just in front of you, a little step up, maybe three inches."

Marheh stepped backwards onto the back deck, still holding Lorac's hands. Ved gave a little gasp as she disappeared but Lorac managed to keep her eyes closed and follow Marheh's instructions. Ved gave another little cry as she too disappeared but they heard Fali reassuring him.

"There are four steps now," Marheh said, standing behind Lorac, her hands on her shoulders to guide her. "Feel with your foot for the top one."

Once she was in the back cabin Marheh told her to open her eyes.

"This is Gelis' cabin," she said. "Why don't you sit here for a minute while I go back for Ved and Fali?"

Lorac gave her a big grin then flung her arms around her. Marheh laughed and returned the hug.

"I won't be long," she said, mounting the steps two at a time.

"I can hardly believe it," Ved said when she appeared beside him again. "I saw you disappear, but then Lorac went too. It's a bit confronting."

Fali gave his hand a quick squeeze.

"You get used to it," she said. "At least, maybe not used to it exactly, but it stops being extraordinary."

Marheh smiled at him.

"Will you come with me?"

She held out her hands and a few minutes later he had joined Lorac in the back cabin. Then it was Fali's turn. She hardly needed Marheh's help, but just the touch of her hand as she stepped on board.

"We are a bit like sardines in here," Marheh said watching the wondering faces of her two younger guests. "Come with me into the saloon. There's a bit more room there."

She led the way through the engine room, the bathroom and the galley. She gave Fali her armchair and sat Ved and Lorac at the little table then perched on the footstool and looked at them.

"You can explore by yourselves in a minute, just get used to it a bit first."

"It's so pretty," Lorac said. "And so cleverly put together."

Ved was taking in the neat fittings that made use of every inch of space.

"There is such an atmosphere of peace," Fali said. "A strong peace, built by work and prayer, not just the absence of noise."

Marheh's eyes thanked her.

"Just like your kitchen," she said.

They sat in companionable silence for a few moments, then Marheh took Ved off to the engine room and suggested to Fali and Lorac that they look around the rest of the boat.

"It isn't just things though," Ved said when they were together again. "It's what Fali said. It's bigger than just things."

He turned to Marheh.

"I want to help.. maybe we can make Deerford somewhere bigger than just things."

Lorac nodded her agreement.

Marheh smiled at them.

"We will," she said. "Together we will."

* * * *

Gelis looked wearily around the kitchen. Before she could go home it had to be as sterile and spotless as it was when she arrived. The restaurant was nearly empty now, just the last table of diners lingering over their coffee, but nothing had come down from the private dining room yet. Karl was in and out of the big freezer and she thought he was making some kind of check on the contents.

She had not seen what happened to the potatoes she had prepared. They had stood simmering on their hobs for an hour or so, until they were more like potato flavoured slush and then she had been given her meal. When she came back from the cloak room, where there was a small table for staff meals, the pots were empty and awaiting her ministrations with a dishcloth. She had ventured a question to Karl and been told it was none of her business, so she wondered the more.

She was just emptying the last load of plates and cutlery from the dishwasher when a buzzer sounded. Karl rushed out of the freezer and stood looking anxious.

"Was that a buzzer?" he asked Gelis at last, when he had listened for a minute or so.

"A buzzer did go," she said carefully. "Just before you came out."

"That will be Madam," he said. "The dishes are ready for collection."

He hesitated, then drew himself up.

"You will go for them. Dirty dishes are not my job."

"Yes Karl," she said, drying her hands and dropping her tea towel on the bench beside the dishwasher.

She was suddenly alert. It was her first chance to explore a little and perhaps learn something.

"Where do I go?" she asked politely.

Karl pointed to the door he and Madam had entered by earlier in the day. Gelis had not realised that behind it was a big lift.

"Up," Karl said, as she went towards it. "Up two floors, door opposite."

189

She entered the lift, which was another shiny, stainless steel space, large enough to contain food trolleys as well as people. She was interested to see that there was access to a floor below as well as three above. She pressed the button for her floor and the doors slid closed. It was very quick and quiet and moments later the doors were opening again.

Curiously she stepped out and looked around. There was not much to see, a small foyer with a door opposite and one to either side. Cautiously she went to try the door on her right. It was not locked. Taking a deep breath, primed with the excuse of collecting the plates, she pushed it open.

The room was empty.

It appeared to be a small lecture theatre as there was a speaker's lectern on a raised platform to her right and stacks of chairs against the wall to her left. There appeared to be another entrance in the wall opposite the speaker's lectern. She backed out of the doorway and pulled the door closed behind her. For a moment she stood in the foyer wondering whether to try the door on the left or to go about her legitimate business. Quietly she walked across and tried the handle carefully. It was locked. She knocked, waited, then knocked again, but there was no response. Finally she turned to the middle door, the one opposite the lift. This was where the dishes were to be collected. Should she knock, or just go in?

"I'm just doing what I was told," she encouraged herself. "They can hardly hold that against me."

Without giving herself time to think any further, she took hold of the door handle, turned it and walked in.

Throwing stones

CHAPTER FOURTEEN

I worked hard today. Potatoes, potatoes, potatoes to begin with and I've no idea what they were for. It is quite boring work. I hardly saw Madam, and Karl only appeared to give me more work, except for about an hour when the restaurant was a bit busy. He had to cook for the restaurant today as Madam was in the private dining room in some kind of meeting. He sent me up in the lift to collect the dirty dishes, but I think he got into trouble for it because Madam had told him to do it.

Gelis put her pen down and read over what she had written. It was a difficult balance, writing a false journal and perhaps it was unnecessary, but she had to be careful.

She thought back to the moment when she had entered the private dining room. The door had opened into a small kitchen, really more for keeping food hot, or cold and for serving than for actual cooking. In the centre of the room stood a trolley piled with dirty dishes, cutlery and serving pans. Obviously this was what she had come to collect, so she had walked quietly towards it, hoping she might be unobserved and so able to linger and perhaps even catch some meaning from the murmur of voices she could hear on the other side of the serving hatch.

She had taken hold of the trolley and edged with it closer and closer to the serving hatch, but although she could pick out voices and individual words here and there, she had not been able to get any sense of what was being discussed. Then Madam had come and shouted at her and she had had to scurry back to the kitchen with her trolley.

Now she tried to remember the few words she had picked up. "Silly" was one of them, and "sillies" and she remembered Madam saying "Sillies can be dangerous" and another half caught phrase which sounded like "terylot". She murmured it aloud, trying to get the rhythm she had heard. It seemed so close to something she understood, but she could not grasp it.

She felt very tired. Dealing with the trolley from the private dining room had meant she was still working until nearly 11.00 o'clock. Then there had been the walk home. As she walked down to the gate she had felt uneasy, as if an alien presence was about and once in the streets of Deerford she was conscious of footsteps echoing hers. Nothing had happened and she had seen no one, but she had been very glad to be safely inside her lodging.

She longed for Marheh and *Day Bringer* and the opportunity to talk over her experiences, but knew it was not possible. She was lucky at least to have Ved. Switching off her light, she went across to the window to open her curtains. For a few moments she stood gazing out while her eyes grew accustomed to the dark. Then, gradually, she was able to make out the dot of light. "Same time as last night," she thought. "Probably just someone going home." Nevertheless, in the morning she must see if she could pinpoint the location.

Yawning she turned away from the window and climbed into bed. "Terylot," she murmured sleepily. "Terylot., terylot.." and her eyes closed.

Next morning she woke with the daylight. She lay on her back looking at the ceiling enjoying the changing pattern of light and shade as the clouds passed across the sun and enjoying the luxury of a proper mattress and a wide bed. She closed her eyes again and let herself drift. She did not need to get up yet. Suddenly her eyes opened.

"That pottery lot," she said aloud.

She said it again, thoughtfully. That was what they had said, more than once. She would have to get Ved on his own this morning. They needed to know that the pottery was raised in the strategy meeting.

She sat up in bed, yawned and stretched. If she did not get up now she would miss Ved. He would be off to work soon. She sighed a little. Bed was very inviting, but, telling herself she could come back later for a nap, she pushed back the covers and got up. A sight of the time had her scrambling into her clothes and almost running down the stairs to breakfast.

"You were very late last night," Evelyn said, with a hint of disapproval in her voice.

"I know," Gelis said, sliding into her place at the breakfast table. "I had to stay and finish some washing up."

She smiled apologetically at Evelyn.

"I'm so sorry if I woke you."

There was a hint of a sniff as Evelyn put a bowl of porridge in front of her.

"I suppose if they wanted you."

She went back to the stove.

"But it's too late for a young girl to be walking home alone. Deerford is not what it was."

"Would it be a good idea for me to meet you?" Ved said. "I'd be happy to do that."

He had nearly finished his breakfast and was just lingering over his cup of tea.

"That's so kind of you! But you have to start work early, you can't be up late as well."

"When do you normally finish?" he asked.

"I'm supposed to finish at 10.00 pm, but I haven't been there long enough to know what's normal."

"10.00 o'clock would be fine, just a nice stroll before bed."

Evelyn nodded.

"That's very sensible David."

She came and stood behind him, a hand on his shoulder.

"A nice young girl like Gillian, working for YRTHA, we need to look after her."

Gelis smiled at them both.

"But if I'm kept late I won't be able to let you know."

"I shall march in and knock on the door," Ved said.

"Perhaps I should try to talk to them about getting home, tell them I'm being met. Maybe they will have some suggestions."

"Well I shall come for you this evening anyway." Ved smiled at her. "I'll see you at the gate at five past ten."

"That would be great. Thanks v.. David."

Evelyn's hand rested a moment longer on Ved's shoulder. She looked rather smug Gelis thought, and with reason. Ved was a son to be proud of if only she knew. Evelyn moved away to the stove and began cooking Gelis' eggs. While her back was turned Gelis made a face at Ved and tried to mouth her need to communicate. He shook his head slightly.

Gelis thought furiously.

"Have you got a bit of paper?" she asked him. "I'll just draw a little plan of where the kitchen entrance is, in case I'm kept late."

He nodded, stood up.

"I'll get some, just a minute."

A drawer in the sideboard yielded a pencil and a piece of scrap paper. He handed them to Gelis and stood behind her while she drew a few lines, then wrote quickly – "they are planning something to do with the pottery".

She frowned and muttered.

"That's no good, I'll try again."

Then she tore the strip of text off the bottom of the paper and drew a neat map. Ved leaned over her and she indicated the place on her drawing.

"That's the kitchen door … it's a bit hidden," she said, and handed him both pieces of paper.

"I'll find you," he said, putting the papers in his pocket and nodding to her.

"Thank you," she said again and let her breath out carefully, suddenly realising she had been holding it.

Evelyn came across with Gelis' eggs. Ved grabbed his coat from behind the door, gave his mother a quick kiss and hurried away. Gelis sighed, and smiled at Evelyn.

"After breakfast I might have another little sleep," she said, picking up her knife and fork.

● ***

Marheh too woke with the daylight. She had left the doors to the well deck open and felt the morning chill although her bed was warm and snug. She had not slept well despite her weariness. Although she had welcomed the two souls she had invited to share her body she had not understood what it would be like. She felt oddly invaded. She had never carried a child, but she wondered briefly whether an expectant mother would feel a similar sense of invasion.

More than once, in the past, she had escaped into Kel's mind when her own mind had been threatened beyond her strength. Kel would not have used her mind for escape though, not when he had an apprentice to protect.

This was different. It was souls she carried, come to her through the soul song, and nothing she knew or had heard of prepared her for the possibility, still less the reality.

For a little while she lay, half drowsing, half puzzling about her discoveries of the previous day and wondering whose souls she had released. One of the souls seemed so familiar she hoped it might be Kel's. What would that mean if she couldn't find and release his body? She still found it hard to credit the possibility that the Yareblis might have imprisoned souls they did not believe existed. Perhaps they had not realised. If they had imprisoned body and mind could the soul continue in freedom? Of course it could. She knew that really. It was why the soul song was a sure defence. But... ?

She sighed and stretched and turned her attention to the business of washing and dressing.

Fali's quiet presence at breakfast, Nicken's tempestuous hug as she went off to school, and the affectionate greetings from the rest of her family warmed and strengthened her. She was aware that she must return to the work of the soul song, but allowed herself a couple of hours in the studio playing with clay, centring herself. Then she returned to *Day Bringer* to lay her body aside for the time being and find again the place where she could communicate with her guests.

Carefully, as she had done before, she prepared *Day Bringer* and herself, using the candle's gentle light to take her out of herself. As she moved gradually towards the light, as her soul's song began to emerge, she lost the sense of invasion and felt only exultation as her song completed the harmony that defined the existence of the other two.

Like a dance they sent their songs weaving together, touching and separating, turning, skipping then treading solemnly together. Gradually Marheh began to distinguish the voices. Her own song was full of passion and longing like the sound of strings, then there was a pure, high, bitter-sweet tone, plaintive and calling and the third was deep, steady with a dark tone that spoke of pain and striving.

195

Reaching out to them, she tried to understand what they were telling her, who they were and what had happened to them.

"I am young," the high voice sang. "I have not lived. I have not begun the work I was created to do."

"I have struggled," sang the deeper voice. "I have worked and learned. I have not failed in courage but my strength was overcome."

"Together we will be strong," she sang back to them. "Together we will seek out the evil and turn it around."

On *Day Bringer*, within her still figure, the mind of Marheh was stretching to keep a link with the dance of the souls, to provide the more down to earth direction that would lead them to the place where they could act.

"Hand-in-hand into the darkness," she sang. "Come with me."

The fine thread of sound still held between her mind and soul and somewhere she recognised that her attendant souls had drawn closer. Between them they created a probe of light that began to test the darkness. The song was almost silenced now, only a faint humming bound them to each other and to Marheh's mind that guided and directed.

Soon they found again the darkness that imprisoned the Silberay souls. Now there was no tiny crack by which to enter and the darkness seemed thicker and stronger, not the quiet peace of a dark night, but a miasma so full of misery and pain that their bright probe could barely hold its own against it. For a timeless age they persevered, nibbling at the edges, burrowing, piercing, but there was no sense that they were progressing, or even engaging the enemy.

At last, exhausted, Marheh began to draw them back into herself. The thread of song that linked her mind and soul was now spun so finely she could scarcely maintain it, but the harmony of the other two souls lifted and supported her. Slowly they withdrew, yet as they went they seemed to draw the darkness with them. Then she heard it, a harsh shriek of anger and desire. With her last strength Marheh drew the others to her and turned back to the darkness, sending their song that was light and beauty towards the cry.

Again the cry came, but fainter, and around them the light grew. Marheh knew she did not have the strength to pursue, but together they sang and brightness built with the song. Then she returned to herself, welcoming again the two souls, drawing them through the pain to rest safely within.

●　＊＊＊

Ved had hoped to be able to get away from work and deliver Gelis' message in his lunch break. He was just putting on his coat when he saw the same YRTHA official who had come before, getting out of his car. Gelis' message did not appear urgent, so he decided to stay on site, hoping he might learn something for a report of his own. He took his lunch box and sat outside on a bench, not far from the manager's office.

At first he was optimistic, for he heard the manager greeting his visitor and the rumble of a reply, but then nothing. He gulped down his sandwiches and sauntered past the office, but it appeared to be empty. He hesitated then turned and strolled back towards the factory door, taking another look through the office window as he went. It was open at the top and Ved assumed that had enabled him to hear the greeting, but now there was no sign of anyone. In fact he had the impression that the office door was half open. If they were in the factory, he needed to be there, he thought, and hurried to return to his machines.

The two were examining the raw materials that waited in tidy piles ready for the mechanical arm to lift them into the furnace where the process began. When they caught sight of him, the YRTHA official asked him, as he had before, whether it would be possible to add anything to the raw materials.

"You could add things," Ved said. "But lots of things you might add would just vaporise in the furnace."

He looked at the man.

"What sort of thing were you wanting to do?" he asked, hoping the question sounded innocent.

The man did not answer him, but turned back with the manager and went into the office again. Ved sighed and continued with his work. Surely they must have expected him to ask, it was the logical question.

Even when he finished work, he could not go straight to the pottery with his news. He had promised Evelyn he would be home in daylight to do some chores around the garden and he knew she was cooking one of his favourite meals as a reward.

When he finally reached the pottery, Marheh had already gone down to *Day Bringer*, but the others welcomed him, studied Gelis' note and listened to the tale of his own experiences.

"We've had a quiet, ordinary day," Fali said. "Only nothing feels ordinary because we're waiting for the next thing to happen."

"And obviously it will," Tep added. "Judging by Gelis' note."

"It was a good idea to arrange to meet Gelis after work," Lorac said. "Do you think I could come too? I'd love to see her."

"Best not," Fali said, before Ved had time to answer. "We don't want them to associate Ved with us."

"I suppose not." Lorac looked a bit wistful. "I want to be doing something useful too."

"You are," Tep said, and his look included Tith and Kina too. "You're keeping the pottery going as normal. That's what is important."

"I suppose so." Lorac held her hand out to Ved. "Come and see how I'm progressing with my master work," she said.

"We'll say goodnight then," Kina smiled at them. "We're going up now. I need to check that Nicken has gone to bed."

Ved managed a general smile of farewell before Lorac hurried him outside and across the yard to the pottery studio. He kissed her lightly, then put his arms around her to make a more thorough job of the next kiss.

"Where's this master work then," he said at length, releasing her reluctantly.

"That was just an excuse," she said. "You don't really have to look at it."

"I'd like to though," he said. "I like to see what you're doing. Then I had better go, or I'll be late meeting Gelis."

●   ＊ ＊ ＊

Gelis thought she had never been so bored. She had spent a quiet day, which included quite a lot of sleeping, and a good hour studying the view from her window and trying to identify the various landmarks so she would know where the light she saw at night was coming from and going to. She even drew a little plan and thought she might discuss it with Ved on the way home from work.

It was not the day she found boring, but the job. She arrived to find a mountain of dirty pans awaiting her attention. Once Karl had given her her instructions he disappeared, and she saw no one for a couple of hours while she scrubbed and scoured. Most of the time she spent wondering who had managed to dirty so many pots between her departure last evening and her present arrival, and why. Perhaps a big YRTHA breakfast meeting, she decided, realising she still knew very little of what went on in the club upstairs.

When she had almost finished washing up and there was still no sign of anyone to instruct her in another task, she began to slow down. Looking for a home for her clean pots provided her with an excuse to do a bit of poking around, but apart from wondering at the large quantities of everything, she found nothing out of place. The time crawled by, and she wondered whether she would ever have the opportunity to learn anything worth while. It seemed as if the restaurant was the least part of the activities of the kitchen, although that was the ostensible reason for its existence.

She was given her meal in the early evening. Karl gave her a choice from the freezer and graciously allowed her to heat it up herself. Clearly the restaurant had no custom at all this evening.

It was not until 9.00 pm that Madam sailed in. Gelis and Karl stood to attention while her gaze swept the kitchen. Gelis saw herself multiplied into a hundred kitchen slaveys, like an army awaiting instruction.

"Tomorrow," she paused impressively. "Tomorrow we have a private booking. CT will be entertaining about twenty men to a late meal."

She looked at Gelis.

"You can begin cutting up meat before you go home. The menu is steak and kidney pie or sausages and mash."

Karl was instructed to bring the meat and gather the other ingredients that would be needed. She was almost out the door again before Gelis managed to get her attention.

"What?" she said imperiously. "What is it?"

Gelis tried to explain about the walk home and being met. Madam looked at her in some surprise.

"I suppose, if you must," she said. "If you're needed later in future I'll find you a bed here."

"Yes Madam," Gelis said. "Thank you Madam."

She looked at the floor in order to hide the spark of interest she felt at this possibility.

"Now get on with the job. There is no need to stay late tonight."

She swept out without waiting to see whether she was obeyed. Karl slapped a few big slabs of meat in front of her and a couple of kidneys and left her to get on with it while he went in and out of fridge and storeroom accumulating ingredients.

Gelis finished her task in good time, left the meat in a big covered bowl in the refrigerator and went off to meet Ved, feeling a bit more positive than she had earlier. She had no need to hurry as she walked down to the gate and she listened carefully for any sound of movement, but the sense of something alien was missing tonight. The stretch of grass and shrubs that bordered the drive seemed quiet and at peace under the stars. Ved was waiting when she reached the gate and she smiled gratefully at him.

"It's good to see you," she said. "Thanks for coming."

"It's a chance to talk," he said. "There is a lot you cannot say in front of Mother."

She nodded.

"There are things that are puzzling, but I can't say I've made any significant discoveries."

As they walked home together she told him about the YRTHA planning meeting, about the kitchen and the various incidents and oddities she had experienced whilst doing her job. She told him too about the light she had seen, crossing the landscape each night, and asked him if he could pinpoint the location.

Ved listened with interest, storing up all she said in order to be able to repeat it accurately at the pottery next day. They paused beside the shop to look at Gelis' little plan by the light coming through the window. It did seem as if the night wanderer was walking in the YRTHA grounds. She told him too of Madam's suggestion that she sleep at the club if she had to be late again and he tried to impress on her that she should not consider exploring outside in the dark even if the possibility arose.

They were still arguing amiably about this when they reached home, parting at the foot of the stairs, Gelis to go up to her room and Ved to the kitchen to say goodnight to Evelyn.

Next day passed uneventfully. Gelis slept late and spent most of the morning in her room. Ved got up early and went to the pottery to report before going to work. Marheh was especially glad to have his news of Gelis as well as the information he brought. She listened with interest to all he said and asked him to repeat Gelis' description of the kitchen and the work she did there as far as possible in Gelis' own words.

The normal work of the pottery continued and again Marheh allowed herself the respite of a little sculpting, sitting in the studio with the others and allowing the clay to dictate what she produced.

Over the evening meal the family tried to act as normal. There had been no further approach from YRTHA despite Gelis' message, but no one felt optimistic that the trouble would evaporate. There was a heaviness and a sense of anxious anticipation that seemed to dampen attempts at conversation. Only Marheh seemed unmoved by it, calm, steady and at peace with herself and only Marheh knew how much it cost her to maintain that peace.

There seemed to be a reluctance to leave the warmth and company of the kitchen despite the lack of conversation. Lorac and Tith did the washing up, glad of a purposeful activity. Kina was attempting to reason with Nicken, who did not want to go to bed. Tep and Fali just sat. Tep's hand rested on the table with Fali's over it. Everything seemed as normal, yet nothing was.

It was almost a relief when the first rock hit the roof.

"What was that?" Tep looked up at the sound.

"Something banged onto the roof." Fali was listening intently. "I hope it hasn't broken the slates."

She had scarcely finished speaking when there was another crash and then another.

"What's happening?"

Lorac paused by the cupboard where she was putting away a pile of dishes.

"Someone's throwing stones," Marheh said quietly. "I'm going upstairs to see if I can see anything."

She went quickly out and up the stairs, Tep close behind her. There was a small window on the top landing that looked out over the front of the house. Together they approached it, one on each side. Although it was already dark, they had been careful not to put a light on so they would not be seen by anyone outside. Several more crashes had jarred the roof.

"What do they think they're doing?" Tep muttered, staring from the window. "What harm have we done them?"

Marheh put a hand on his arm.

"Go carefully little brother," she said lightly, standing beside him and looking out intently.

There seemed to be a small army outside. They were making no attempt at concealment, but standing in the road in two lines, each with a small pile of stones beside them. As they watched two more crashes sounded from the roof. It looked as if someone was directing the proceedings because there was no frenzy of hate, just a coldly deliberate attack, carefully orchestrated.

Stones fell again, more this time, but smaller. Then the chant began.

"Out, out, out!" softly at first, but building up, each group of three louder than the one before, until the loudest shout ended with a hail of stones. Then it began all over again.

"Out, out, out!" soft and menacing, "Out, out, out."

Tep and Marheh looked at each other.

"Can we do anything?" Tep asked. "Or do we just sit and let them get on with it?"

Marheh shook her head.

"It's very controlled. Those are men from the village out there. I doubt they would hurt us personally, but could we stop them? I just don't know."

The chant rose and fell again and Marheh made up her mind.

"We could at least try to get a glimpse of who is controlling them," she said. "They won't see us if we go out the back."

Tep nodded.

"No need for you to go," he said.

"Got to look after my little brother," Marheh teased, and led the way downstairs again.

In the kitchen the others were all gathered around the table. None of the windows looked out to the front of the house, but Fali had carefully drawn all the blinds so that there was a feeling of enclosure. She looked anxious when Tep and Marheh explained what they had in mind, but did not protest, only suggested that Marheh put a dark coat over her light coloured clothes. Marheh gave her a quick hug before following her advice, then she and Tep slipped out through the back door and into the pottery yard.

From outside the noise and chanting sounded more intense, more menacing. In the moonlight they could see that bits of rock and broken slate had fallen into the yard. As they stood watching another small rock slid down the pitch of the roof and fell beside them. Tep's face was white and strained. Marheh touched his shoulder and they began to walk down the path to the back gate. After a couple of steps, Marheh turned quickly back to find Lorac just catching them up.

"I'll do gate duty," she said lightly, before anyone had the chance to question her presence.

Together they continued along the path to the gate.

"Bolt it after us," Marheh said to Lorac as Tep drew the bolts to open it. "I'll drop this over the gate when we come back."

She showed Lorac her handkerchief, once white, but now marked with clayey fingers from her afternoon in the studio. Lorac gave a little giggle and Marheh grinned at her.

"I'll bet yours is just the same," she said and followed Tep through the gate.

Outside they stood for a moment against the wall, but there was no indication anyone had found the narrow path that led from the road. They slipped across the path and into the woodland beyond. Here they had a degree of cover and made their way cautiously, moving silently from tree to tree, until they approached the road.

The noise of the chanting covered any sound they might have made, but equally hid from them any evidence of pursuit. When they reached the road they turned away from the attackers, hoping to be able to cross the road unseen. The unknown individual who was directing the attack had positioned himself close to the wall in front of the pottery and so was in heavy shadow and well protected from any observer in the house.

They chose a spot about fifty paces away, where two trees on either side of the road almost met overhead, casting deeper shade and providing a degree of cover. One at a time they crossed the road, moving quickly and quietly from one tree to the other. Then they began to make their way back towards the attackers. A ditch and a hedged field lined this side of the road, with a few scattered trees. Marheh was hoping to find a gap in the hedge so that they could approach unobserved. Even a small gap might be enough to allow them to push through. It was no time to worry about the possibility of a few scratches. They moved slowly and cautiously, keeping low and walking in the ditch, which was soft and full of weeds, but not actually wet.

They had not gone far when the hedge seemed to thin a bit on either side of a large tree. Marheh climbed cautiously out of the ditch and stood pressed against the tree trunk. Tep crouched in the ditch beside her. They were still too far away to be able to recognise any of the attackers, but stones were still flying at intervals and the chant of "Out, out, out" came and went.

Marheh kept her eyes on the shadowy figure of the controller. He was the one who might see them approach, the rest of the gang were facing the other way. She waited until the blur that was his face seemed to be turned away, then squeezed herself around the tree trunk and into the field behind the hedge. A few moments later Tep had followed. They grinned at each other in the moonlight, then began following the hedge towards the attackers.

The going was easier here for the field had not been planted right to the hedge and there was a narrow space between the hedge and the newly sprouting crop. They needed to keep low and move steadily, but it was good cover and they were soon opposite the pottery and peering through the hedge at the row of backs, still chanting and throwing. It was not so easy to see across the road and into the shadows by the wall and though they could make out a shadowy figure, it was too dark to see, even whether the controller was male or female.

Marheh put her hand in her pocket and showed Tep a small handful of pebbles.

"Do you think one of them might miss?" she said with a grin.

A slow smile spread over Tep's face.

"It's just possible," he said, taking one of the stones.

Choosing a moment when the chant was at its loudest and the attackers' arms raised to throw, Tep took careful aim. Then, at the word of command, he lobbed his pebble over the hedge. It fell short, just beside the controller's feet. He jumped back and shouted something, then stepped forward angrily. The chanting had stopped and now they heard him shout "Careful of your aim."

Tep looked at Marheh and whispered his discovery. The combination of voice and movement and the momentary step out of the shadow, revealed him to be the Club Treasurer.

The chant began again, and this time Tep lobbed his stone at the furthest end of the row of attackers. The man was standing a little forward of the two on either side of him. They saw him clutch at his upper arm and turn accusingly from one side to the other. Tep took another stone.

"Careful," Marheh whispered. "We don't want them to guess."

Tep smiled.

"This is one thing I'm good at," he said. "They won't guess."

He threw again and the stone found its mark on the same large, slow moving attacker. He lunged angrily at the man on his left, who held up both hands and backed away. Immediately the ordered ranks disintegrated. The Club Treasurer shouted, but seemed to have lost his effectiveness.

There was more yelling and then a push, closely followed by a punch.

Marheh and Tep looked at each other and grinned.

"We might as well leave them to it," Marheh whispered and led the way back along the hedge.

Marheh's handkerchief provided them entry as planned. Lorac was eager to hear what had happened but recognised the sense in waiting until they were inside with the others. Fali gave them each a hug as they came in the door.

"They've gone for the moment," Tep said. "We were hiding behind the hedge when they marched in the other direction, over the hump and into the village."

He turned to grin at Marheh.

"It was quite like the old days, Marheh the Great and her sidekick against the enemy."

Marheh laughed briefly.

"I remember, but then battle ceased at teatime, not now."

She looked at the others.

"It was the Club Treasurer telling the men what to do. They were just men from the village. I recognised Kevin amongst them. It's hard to know whether they were persuaded, bribed or controlled, perhaps a bit of each."

"I hate them."

Nicken, in pyjamas and dressing gown, came and snuggled up to Marheh.

"Why are they doing it to us?"

"I don't think they know really," Marheh said. "Most of them are just ordinary men from the village, but the people who run YRTHA think it would be good if they had the pottery, so they have persuaded some people to help them hurt us."

"Well we won't let them," Nicken said firmly.

"No," said Marheh. "We won't let them, but we might have a hard time for a while."

She gave Nicken a hug and looked over her head at Fali.

"Perhaps a warm drink would make us feel better. Then we could go to sleep. I expect they will come and gloat in the morning, so it would be good to get up early and get things cleared up."

Tith and Lorac went to prepare the drinks and Fali brought out the biscuit tin.

"I think we all need a bit of a treat tonight," she said.

Broken Pot

CHAPTER FIFTEEN

Gelis' shift had begun with peeling, potatoes first, some for mash but others for what she thought of as potato slush. Then there were carrots and onions for the steak and kidney and finally a bucket of peas to shell. At about eight o'clock she was sent off for her own meal at the little table in the cloak room and when she went back both Madam and Karl were in the kitchen and the real work of the evening had begun.

It was the first time she had seen Madam cooking and she was reluctantly impressed by what almost seemed like sleight of hand as she assembled neat platefuls for the waiter who whisked in and out. The menu was hardly cordon bleu but each plate went out looking and smelling appetising.

Every time the doors opened for the waiter the sound of riotous celebration floated down the lift well. She could not help wondering just what kind of party it was.

The last half dozen meals were put on a trolley and Madam told Gelis to take it up in the lift and wait for the empty plates from the starter. She was to go up one floor only, to the restaurant, this time. The waiter went with her, carrying a couple of extra plates. Gelis offered him a tentative smile during their short journey.

The lift opened into a small kitchen with a serving hatch, similar to that beside the private dining room. The hatch was open and through it Gelis could see an assembly of men in various stages of inebriation. The waiter took his plates through a side door and Gelis put the others carefully on the serving hatch for him to collect. The restaurant had been arranged so the tables were together in a long row, which gave the waiter plenty of room to move around.

He needed every inch. The diners were extremely exuberant and boisterous, thrusting their chairs back suddenly to stand up, punching the air to emphasis a point and almost climbing on the table to reach some desired condiment. Just over half had been served with food and a cheer went up from the others as the waiter appeared. He moved swiftly to place the three full plates he carried. Gelis admired his deft movements and smiled at him as he returned to the serving hatch. He winked and grimaced as he picked up another three plates and went quickly to off load them. He was the first normally behaving YRTHA employee Gelis had met.

He returned for the last three plates, two helpings of steak and kidney pie and one of sausages and mash. He was just putting down the last plate when a loud shout came from the second last man he had served. It seemed he felt he had been given the wrong meal, or perhaps had made the wrong choice. Gelis could not quite grasp what he was saying, but the angry bull's bellow filled the room.

The waiter slipped quickly back into the small room where Gelis waited.

"Lot of yobs," he muttered. "I don't know what's got into them."

Gelis shook her head.

"They are certainly excitable," she said carefully, knowing it was an understatement, but not quite sure of her listener.

He gave a short, rather bitter laugh.

"You could say that," he said. "I'm supposed to bring you the empty dishes from the starter, but I'm not going back in there until they have calmed down a bit."

"I don't blame you," Gelis said sympathetically. "They are appallingly badly behaved."

The waiter stood beside her and together they looked through the open serving hatch.

"I know some of these chaps from the village," he said. "I don't know what has got into them. Some of them drink too much and get silly, but this is absurd."

They all seemed to be wolfing down the meals so he slipped back into the restaurant and began to bring Gelis the dirty dishes. She took them from him and loaded them onto her trolley, listening as she did so, in an attempt to catch some of the conversation.

The waiter was bringing what must have been the last load, carrying a pile of small plates, some cutlery and a couple of empty bread baskets, when one of the diners shot his chair back suddenly. The waiter made a valiant attempt to avoid him, but he was too close. He teetered for a moment then fell, plates and cutlery crashed to the floor and a solitary bread roll turned over and over across the polished boards before coming to rest against the wall.

There was a stunned silence for a moment, then a couple of the men began to cheer and shout and soon the room was filled with noise again. The waiter scrambled to his feet and walked quietly back to where Gelis waited.

"Louts," he said bitterly.

Bits of food had stuck to his uniform and blood dripped from a cut on his hand. Gelis closed the serving hatch and turned on the tap over the sink.

"Here," she said. "Put your hand under the tap."

She grabbed some paper towel and gave it to him.

"I'll go and clear up," she said.

There was a broom standing in one corner of the kitchen and she picked it up and pushed through the swinging door and into the restaurant.

Immediately there was a loud wolf whistle, then another and more cheering. Gelis did her best to ignore this and took her broom to where the mess of food scraps and shattered plates was thickest. She tried to sweep everything away from the diners, but they were not helping and she found herself the centre of attention as well as the target for lewd suggestions and one or two attempts to grab her as she passed.

The pile of rubbish was becoming more contained and she was beginning to sweep it towards the kitchen when one large, red-faced diner got up from his seat and came up behind her. She whisked around, the broom in front of her.

"Give us a kiss," the man said, seizing the broom.

Gelis held on, trying to snatch it away. Then she realised she was not going to succeed. She let go suddenly and the man staggered back, giving her enough time to make a run for the kitchen. The noise and jeering increased, but she was safe behind the door. The waiter helped her to push the bolts that stopped the doors from swinging then she leaned against them, breathing hard.

"Thanks," she said, smiling at him. "That was a bit scary."

She pushed herself away from the door and went to her loaded trolley. As she pushed it towards the lift she thought back to the big man with the beery breath who had accosted her and the two rows of red, shouting faces. That had been bad enough, but what really frightened her was the cold satisfaction on the face of the one man who was not red-faced and shouting, the quiet, pale person at the head of the long table.

● * * *

Marheh had found it difficult to settle despite the warm drink and the biscuits. It was quite late by the time she made her way down to *Day Bringer*. She was very tired, drained by the weight of the two souls she carried but also by the weight of expectation. The family were confident that she could help them and she knew their problems were bound up with her own, but she was struggling to find the way ahead.

"When in doubt, sing," she told herself, but it didn't help much when she felt so tired and helpless.

Even the everyday tasks of undressing and putting herself to bed seemed impossibly hard. She had done her best to put on a positive, confident face for the family, but now she was alone she recognised the lie. She needed to think of Gelis too, especially during the time when she was working at the club, and she had failed her apprentice today.

For a few minutes she stood in the saloon, unable to push herself to act. The warm darkness was comfort of a sort however and, at length, she moved to light a candle and sit with it in front of her. A couple of long, slow breaths and before she knew it she was singing, carried now by her two guests.

Their songs wrapped and lifted her providing the harmonic ground that let her song climb higher and extend further. They seemed to sense her weariness and gently restrained her when she tried to push into the darkness. This song was for her, they seemed to be saying.

She let herself be held and soothed by the music and hardly recognised the moment when she left them to slide into sleep.

● * * *

Gelis and the waiter, whose name, she discovered, was Peter, went back to the main kitchen together feeling shaken and indignant. Perhaps neither would have complained on their own behalf, but each was prepared to speak for the other and soon Madam had the whole story. Almost the whole story, Gelis thought, for Peter had not mentioned the pale, quiet man and neither did she.

Madam was not exactly dismissive of their tale, but neither was she particularly sympathetic. She told Gelis that she would need to stay late in order to clear up after the party and informed her that she had sent Ved away with this news. Gelis could think of nothing to say and obediently followed her as Madam led the way up the stairs to the club foyer and handed her over to the Odd Messenger she had encountered on her first visit. He was to show her to the room she could use for the night.

"You came back then." The high voice and the child's body contrasted with the old, old face. "They'll have you yet."

Gelis smiled politely, not knowing how else to respond. The Odd Messenger led the way across the foyer and up the stairs. The metallic sculpture on the landing still cast its strange dark shadows, but she had no time to stop and look now. Up she went, then up again, following the little man, who was almost running. The speed seemed effortless to him and his voice came back to her, clear and unhurried.

"Come along, hurry up."

She climbed faster, puffing a little.

Three floors the stairs rose. The first two floors were obviously for guests, or people more important than she was, for to this point the stairs were wide and gracious with concealed lighting and carefully placed pictures on the landings. There was a broad expanse of polished floor at the top of the first flight and a small, comfortably furnished foyer at the top of the second flight, but the third flight was narrow and dark and led only to a short corridor with four doors along one side.

The messenger stopped in front of the first one and waited until Gelis was standing beside him before turning the handle and pushing open the door.

"Here you are," he said. "Fine, well-appointed accommodation for the lady."

Gelis laughed.

The room was small and neat, empty except for a single bed. It was made up and a folded towel lay on the end of it. A door led to a tiny bathroom with a shower and toilet. Here there were a wrapped piece of soap and a small toothbrush, also wrapped.

It was a matter of moments to look around.

"Thank you for showing me," Gelis said. "I had better be getting back now. Is there a key?"

No key it seemed.

"What's to steal?" the messenger said.

Gelis smiled and said nothing. She could hardly tell him it was her own safety she was worried about. There was no chain on the door and not even a chair in the room to use as a barrier. She let him go ahead of her then shut the door. There was a keyhole, she noticed as she turned to go.

The Odd Messenger scooted off ahead of her and she followed more slowly, no longer needing his guidance. It was very quiet and felt empty, untenanted. Only when she reached the ground floor again was there any sense of other people about and she realised that the noise she could hear then was the roistering in the restaurant. She hurried across the space of the foyer and down the stairs to the kitchen again, where mountains of clearing up awaited her.

* * *

Marheh did not sleep long and woke feeling much more positive. The candle she had lit was about half burned, and that, as well as the deep silence, suggested the very early morning. She stretched and stood up, taking the candle with her to the bathroom to wash and anoint with antiseptic the couple of scratches she had discovered. Then she dressed in her nightclothes but settled again in the armchair instead of going to bed. Gelis was on her mind. The need to support her kept nagging at her.

Painstakingly she began to build a mental picture of her, setting herself to bridge the space between them. Gelis was tired and alone. There was a worried frown on her face. Marheh continued to work, stretching her mind to her. Gradually the frown smoothed out and her habitual look of quiet contentment was revealed. It was enough.

She blew out her candle, closed down the fire and went to bed.

* * * *

Gelis bent down to put away the last pile of plates she had taken from the dishwasher, then straightened and leant wearily against the bench. She thought it was probably past midnight. The men in the restaurant had been taken away, still yelling and unruly. Madam said they were to be driven to their homes. Once they had gone she had given Gelis her orders and disappeared, but Karl was around somewhere, she knew, and Peter had been in and out clearing tables and setting up for tomorrow.

Just now she appeared to be alone. She thought perhaps she had better look for Karl or Madam before going off to her room, at least that would be her excuse for looking around. There was no one in the big cold room, though it seemed extremely well stocked with provisions. She opened the door of the freezer, but knew as she did so that it was unlikely to be tenanted by anything living. In the pantry she was surprised to see the two big pots of potato slush she had prepared earlier, but there was no sign of Karl or Madam.

There had been something odd about the whole evening. The diners had been excited and noisy when they arrived and no one had tried to calm them. The meal itself had begun late and the menu, though well prepared, had been not only very limited, but also rather pedestrian compared with some of the food she had seen cooked there. She decided to take the lift to the restaurant and see if Karl or Madam were there. Of course the menu was very appropriate for the type of diners they were, she thought, as she pressed the button to call the lift.

The big lift was cold and bright. Gelis huddled in the corner near the buttons wishing she could just be transported back to *Day Bringer* and Marheh and the peace and serenity she found there. The doors opened silently and she stepped out into the small service kitchen. It was empty and cleaned, ready for use. The serving hatch was closed and the door to the restaurant bolted. There was no sound. She looked at the door. It would not be difficult to unbolt it and look through. She only wanted to say goodnight, and to make sure it was alright for her to finish.

Quietly she slid the bolts and opened the door, but the big room was empty. The tables had been returned to their normal places and all was tidy. The food and broken china had been cleared away and there was no sign of the earlier hooliganism. Sighing a little she closed and bolted the door and took the lift back down to the kitchen. She was so tired and she felt as if she had discovered nothing, made no real use of what opportunities she had had.

She was just entering the kitchen again, stepping quietly out of the quiet lift, when she saw Karl and the Odd Messenger heading towards the scullery and the kitchen exit. She was just about to call out when she realised Karl was carrying one of the pots of potato slush. She had just time to register this and wonder when the door swung closed behind him. She ran lightly across the floor and stood by the door, listening. There was no sound so she pushed through into the scullery. It was empty and dark.

Cautiously she went to the outer door, opened it a crack and peeped out. The steep steps went up ahead of her, dark and shadowy. She could see nothing, but she thought she heard footsteps crunching on the gravel path.

Without stopping to think, she slipped through the door, pulling it to behind her. Quickly and quietly she climbed the steps. Her eyes began to be accustomed to the night and she realised that it was not really dark. The sky was clear and the moon shone. Not far ahead of her two figures were silhouetted by the light they carried as they moved steadily away.

She watched for a few moments as they went purposefully onwards. Her fear and tiredness had lifted for the moment and she was only waiting to follow them from a bit further away. This must have been the light in the night, she thought, smiling to herself at the involuntary rhyme.

At the top of the stairs she waited, then stepped carefully off into the grass, remembering the sound of footsteps on gravel. The dot of light was heading down hill, flickering a bit as they passed between trees. She tried to picture the drive and how it lay in relation to where she stood. There was a small path leading to the kitchen door, but she could not think of any other. Carefully she began to follow the light, not moving steadily as they were, but slipping from tree to tree.

At first she was going downhill towards the drive and soon she found it in front of her, a river of gravel, paler than the grass. There was no sound now and she knew she must cross it without alerting them. Carefully she placed each foot, allowing her weight to change slowly from one to the other. It was very nerve wracking and she breathed a sigh of relief when she was safely across. The flickering light was further away now and she began to hurry. She seemed to be cutting across the hillside and felt very exposed as she darted from one bit of cover to the next.

The light had stopped moving now and she was getting closer to it when suddenly it disappeared. She froze. Had they become aware of being followed, or had they perhaps reached their destination? Carefully she continued in the direction she had last seen it. The trees were thicker here and the moonlight did not reach the ground. It was difficult to keep focused on the place the light had disappeared when shadowed tree roots caused her to stumble and small bushes seemed to spring from nowhere across her path.

At last she reached the place she thought must have been their destination, a wooden door in a small hut that appeared to be built against the hillside. Trees and bushes grew thickly around it and she could not see where it ended or what it was made of, but it seemed secret and somehow clandestine. Cautiously she approached, listening hard. She could hear nothing, even when she put her ear to the door, and no crack of light escaped to indicate that there was anyone inside. Putting her hand on the door knob, she took a deep breath then let it out slowly. Having gathered her courage, she tried to turn it gently, carefully applying pressure, but the door would not budge though the handle moved around obediently. Stepping back a bit she studied the door, but in the darkness there was no sign of any weakness. She turned away. If she could not get in now, she must make sure she got back to the kitchen undiscovered then perhaps she could try again when she was better prepared.

The return journey seemed quick and easy without the anxiety of following unseen. She let herself into the scullery and closed the door, then collected her coat before going through to the kitchen. Madam stood surveying her domain, her back to Gelis. For a moment Gelis froze then she managed to shut the kitchen door naturally and to speak as Madam turned towards the sound.

"Is it alright if I go to bed now?" she asked, allowing her weariness to show in the words.

Madam looked at her sharply.

"Where have you been?"

Wordlessly Gelis held out her clothes. Madam continued to look at her for a moment, but Gelis resisted the temptation to say anything, just stood, clutching her things and emptying her mind.

"Yes, go," Madam said impatiently, and watched as Gelis crossed the kitchen and began to climb the stairs leading to the foyer.

It seemed a long way to her room, and when she got there she still could not rest, realising again her lack of security. There was nothing moveable in the room, even the bed was fixed. In the end she went down to the lounge foyer on the floor below and took a small coffee table. It would not stop anyone determined, but at least it would give her warning if anyone tried to come in, she thought as she carried it up to her room.

She wedged it in the corner where the door opened, took off her uniform and fell into bed. In the last moment before she slept she saw Marheh smile at her.

* * * *

They were all up early at the pottery and as soon as it was light the whole family were outside in the yard, surveying the damage. Marheh came up from *Day Bringer* when she saw them there.

"It could have been worse," Tep said, his gloomy tone belying the optimism in his words.

"Much worse," said Fali firmly. "There are no windows broken and it's not raining so the slates can wait."

Nicken and Lorac picked up the biggest pieces of slate while Tith and Kina took a yard broom each and began sweeping up those stones that had fallen over the roof.

"What about the front?" Marheh asked.

"That's next," Tep said. "I expect it will be worse there."

He, Fali and Marheh went through the side gate. The house was quite close to the road, with a small garden and a high wall of mellow, weathered brick. Fali enjoyed the little garden, which was a sheltered, sunny spot, and she and Kina often worked there together or sat chatting when work was done. Now the pretty peaceful place was a shambles. Rock, stone, bits of slate littered the grass and broken, dying plants lay sadly, their bright colours fading. Two of Fali's big pots were broken and soil spilled over the paved area where they stood. There were even some bricks knocked from the top of the wall.

For a moment they were silent, then Fali drew a deep breath.

"We'd better get started," she said.

Marheh gave her a quick hug.

"You take care of your plants. Tep and I will tidy up the rubbish."

It was not long before they were all hard at work. Then the others came through from the back and soon the little garden was looking respectably tidy if not quite as usual. Tith even mixed up a bit of mortar and re-seated the bricks in the top of the wall. The bits of stone were not easily disposed of, but Lorac brought a wheelbarrow round and she and Tith took them away and piled them in a hidden corner. It was still early when they decided their work was done and went in for a well earned breakfast.

The meal was finished, Nicken had gone to school with Kina and Tith and Lorac were at work, but still Tep, Fali and Marheh sat over their sperit discussing the damage, the slates that needed repairing, the pots to be replaced and the possibility of a further attack.

"I'm just wondering about putting a big tarpaulin over the roof, rather than replacing the slates straight way," Tep said.

"That might be a bit of protection for the roof too," Fali agreed. "Do you think they will try again?" she added, turning to Marheh.

"I'm afraid so," Marheh said. "Though perhaps not in the same way."

Fali was just gathering up their empty mugs when the front door bell rang. They looked at each other.

"It has to be them," Fali said.

Marheh nodded.

"Do you mind if I stay with you?" she asked. "I think it is time I showed myself."

Tep's reply was drowned by the door bell pressed long and loud, followed by the sound of knocking, but Marheh understood that he was supporting her suggestion.

Together they stood up and went through to the front hall. Marheh and Fali stood back as Tep went to the door. He opened it quickly and surprised a large man preparing to knock again. It was one of the Club Treasurer's men in suits and the Club Treasurer and the other suit stood behind him.

"No need for all that noise," Tep said mildly. "What can I do for you?"

The suit lowered his hand and snarled. Tep looked from him to the Club Treasurer and the other suit, an expression of polite enquiry on his face.

"I understand you had a little trouble last night," the Club Treasurer said smoothly.

"Trouble?" said Tep. "Just a minute while I ask my wife and my sister."

He turned to Fali and Marheh and winked.

"Did we have any trouble last night?" he asked them, imitating the Club Treasurer's smooth and condescending tone.

Fali went forward, then Marheh.

The Club Treasurer did not actually hiss when he saw Marheh, but his feelings would not have been expressed more clearly if he had. Fali nodded and smiled politely at him, but he paid her no attention. Marheh remained grave and contained, saying nothing.

"It's between us then," the Club Treasurer said at last.

Marheh remained silent, continuing her steady gaze, while the Club Treasurer turned and went out the gate, followed by his two, rather surprised looking companions.

"What did you do?" Fali asked, while Tep went to close the garden gate behind them.

"Nothing," Marheh said. "But because I'm here he knows that you are not on your own. The kind of tactics they tried last night won't work."

"But they'll keep trying?" Fali said. "That was what he meant, wasn't it?"

Marheh nodded.

"Yes," she said. "They'll keep trying, but next time it won't be just a matter of a few bits of rock."

* * * *

Gelis was up early too despite her late and tiring day. She had slept soundly, soothed by the feeling that Marheh was watching over her, but at dawn she woke and could not get back to sleep again. It was too early to return to her lodgings, even though she had a key, but not too early to explore a little.

A quick shower and yesterday's clothes and she was out, grabbing her uniform to put with the kitchen laundry as she went. She did make the bed before she left, assuming that she might well return to this room if she had to stay late again.

Quietly she made her way down stairs, replacing the little coffee table as she passed through the lounge foyer. She had a look around while she was there, but there was no sign of recent occupancy, everything was clean, neat and precisely arranged. The corridor leading to the rooms was dimly lit and quiet. She went a little way along and carefully tried the handle of the first door. It was not locked and opened into a room very different to the one she had slept in. It was more than twice the size and very luxuriously appointed – and empty.

There were ten rooms on this floor and Gelis looked in each one. All were similar to the first and all were empty.

She went down one floor. Here the broad empty expanse of foyer allowed access to the private dining room as well as to a corridor with more doors. Again she carefully tried the handle of the first door, but this one was locked. The next was not and she cautiously opened the door a few inches then froze as she realised the room was occupied. Reflected in a mirror hanging over a small table, she could see part of the bed and the top of a head on the pillow. With infinite care she backed away, closing the door behind her.

Looking along the corridor she considered her options. There were ten doors on this floor also and obviously one, or more were occupied. It was early and probably most people were asleep, but perhaps it would be better to take a closer look at the private dining room than to risk discovery by opening the wrong door.

She crossed the foyer quietly, glad to be wearing her kitchen slippers. There were three doors on this side, the centre one wider and panelled. All were locked. More decisions, she thought, remembering the lift and the service kitchen. She hurried down to the ground floor foyer then down the stairs to the kitchen. This was legitimate, she had reason to be here. She decided to make herself a hot drink.

As she put the kettle on she glanced at the kitchen clock and saw that it was still only six o'clock. She would have time to explore the first floor, or to retrace her steps on the previous evening, probably not both. Which would be most useful, provide most knowledge?

She sipped her drink, wishing it was sperit, wishing she was drinking on *Day Bringer* with Marheh to advise her. She had followed the potato slush, seen where it went and come against a locked door. The locked door would still be an obstacle she was unlikely to be able to overcome. The private dining room was locked, but she knew the lift stopped behind it. She remembered the other doors off the lift foyer and made her decision.

Quickly she finished her drink and washed up the cup. Then she made for the lift, depositing her yesterday's uniform in the laundry basket as she went. It seemed to take forever for the lift to open, though on other occasions she had been impressed by its speed. She stepped in and pressed the button for the floor she wanted. Silently the doors slid shut and she felt herself carried upwards. All too quickly the doors opened again and she had to leave the illusion of safety it provided.

The small foyer was as she remembered it, empty, with a door ahead of her and one to either side. She went towards the centre door, the one she knew led to the service kitchen and the private dining room. It was not locked, nor was the door between the kitchen and the dining room. That was bolted, but the bolts were on her side. She drew them quickly and, opening the door, stepped through into the small, beautifully decorated room.

It was like the dining room of a small country house. The ceiling was decorated with carved and gilded fruit and flowers, the walls were wood panelled and shone softly. Light came from two high, narrow windows in one wall. There was a long table of polished wood in the centre of the room with six chairs on either side. A sideboard stood against each of the long walls. Three candelabra decorated the table and a piece of fine china was displayed on each sideboard.

Gelis stood for a moment, forgetting her purpose in admiring the gracious, elegance of the room, then she walked towards the right hand sideboard. It was beautifully crafted of simple design, with three drawers side by side beneath the polished top and two cupboards beneath the drawers.

Carefully she tried the drawers. Each one slid open smoothly to reveal sets of cutlery, polished silver, gently gleaming in the soft light. The cupboards beneath contained the fine china Gelis had washed a couple of days ago. She walked around the table to the other sideboard. Its design matched the first, but the drawers and cupboards were filled with stationary, paper, pens and pencils, everything needed for a business meeting.

Gelis sighed and looked around the room again, thinking she must have missed something. There was a door in one of the long walls, fairly well camouflaged in the panelled walls. She tried it cautiously and found herself in a spacious office. All the drawers and cupboards were empty or locked and the large desk held only an empty tray, but beside the desk she did discover a waste paper bin with a couple of spoiled sheets of paper. She put them in her pocket with stopping to examine them. Perhaps they might tell her something.

There was another door out of the office. Gelis went out through it and found herself again in the lift foyer. The third door led, she remembered, to the small lecture theatre. It did not seem a very likely source of enlightenment, but she pushed open the door and looked in just in case anything had been left about. The chairs were still stacked against the wall and the speaker's lectern was in place and empty, but behind the lectern was a big board on an easel and on the board was a map of the village.

Gelis studied it for a moment. It was not just any map because it showed the water road, and there, by the tunnel mouth, was the pottery with a red circle around it. It was another indication of their intentions toward the pottery, Gelis thought, though not really specific enough to be helpful for defence. She spent a moment longer examining it, but it did not yield any particular secrets and she turned away and went back to the lift.

It was when she was choosing the floor that she noticed again that the lift accessed a level below the kitchen. She looked at it thoughtfully then pressed the button decisively. It was still early and this might be her only chance. She half expected lights to flash and sirens to ring, but all that happened was the lift doors closing and the lift smoothly and silently obeying her direction.

Moments later the doors opened again onto what seemed like a huge, dark cave. The light spilled from the lift, but scarcely illuminated the space beyond. Gelis stood in the doorway, trying to orient herself, wondering whether she would be able to get back if she allowed the lift doors to close. As her eyes became accustomed to the dim light it seemed almost as if she was seeing reflections. The lift door tried to close and she reached in to press the Door Open button. What she wanted was something to wedge the door.

Without thinking too much about possible consequences, she took the lift back up to the kitchen and grabbed the trolley. It would make a solid wedge and perhaps even provide her with an excuse, should she need one. She wheeled it into the lift and went down again. This time when the doors opened, she pulled the trolley behind her and left it half way across the gap.

Again it took a few moments for her eyes to adjust to the dim light, but gradually as she moved away from the lift, she began to make out shapes. There was a fine edge of light away in the opposite wall, but no windows she could see.

She took a few more cautious steps forward, wondering. The shapes seemed somehow familiar, then suddenly she realised. The darkness and the chill, the hint of reflections came from water that lay almost at her feet. The dark shapes were boats, boats like *Day Bringer*. There must have been more than a dozen filling the space.

Still, chill
Something haunts the darkness
Nothing, something
Shapes edged into consciousness
Through a dark veil they showed themselves
Helpless, all brightness dimmed.
Familiar, unfamiliar
Lost, not found
Lost.

Gelis

CHAPTER SIXTEEN

"Silberay boats," Gelis whispered, creeping closer to the water's edge.

She was standing on what was virtually a wharf, with a boat close beside her. Carefully she reached out to touch it. Instead of the smooth, shiny surface she was used to on *Day Bringer*, this boat felt rough and seemed to have no name or decoration. It was hard to tell in the dim light, but she thought it was just matt grey all over.

She walked the length of it as best she could, but found nothing to identify it. The lit cave of the lift reminded her of the possibility of discovery. It was time she went before someone called the lift from another floor. She needed to get word to Marheh too, somehow they would have to meet.

She pushed the trolley back into the lift and followed it in, then pressed the button for the kitchen. The doors slid closed behind her and moments later she was wheeling the trolley back into its place. Then she let herself out through the scullery and headed for home, at least for her temporary home, trying not to look anxious or hurried, but feeling both.

She reached her lodgings just as Ved was leaving for work.

"Ved!"

She hurried towards him.

"David," she said, seeing the front door still open. "I'm so sorry you had a wasted journey last night."

"That's no trouble, I enjoyed the walk."

He came towards her.

When he was very close, passing her on the short path to the front gate, she said quietly, "I must see Marheh."

He nodded.

"You go in and have breakfast. I'll see to that."

She smiled gratefully.

"Thanks again David," she said for Evelyn's ears and waved as he went out the gate and away.

Evelyn appeared in the doorway, apron on. Gelis smiled at her.

"I'm sorry I couldn't let you know, sorry David had a trip for nothing."

"He didn't mind," Evelyn said. "And it shows they were looking after you."

Gelis smiled politely, wondering whether the lonely, sterile little room could be described as being looked after.

"Have you had breakfast?"

Gelis shook her head and followed Evelyn gratefully inside.

●   * * *

Marheh woke knowing Gelis was in need of her, so she was not surprised to see Lorac running down to *Day Bringer* from the house and she had had time to consider possibilities. They had not thought to plan a meeting place before Gelis went off to YRTHA, but Marheh felt she could depend on Beytha for help, and so it was arranged, with Lorac hurrying to visit Mrs Entally and Ved popping back home to deliver the message to Gelis. Evelyn was not best pleased to see him and he had to make the excuse that he had forgotten something, but he managed to pass a note to Gelis as he whisked in and out.

She finished her breakfast and told Evelyn she felt like a walk, asked if Evelyn needed anything from the shop, grabbed her coat and went out. It only took her a few minutes to find the address she had been given. The small cottage opened straight onto the street and she was about to knock on the door when it opened suddenly and a smiling woman welcomed her inside.

Gelis smiled back shyly.

"I'm Gelis," she said.

"Of course you are," Beytha said. "I've been watching for you."

She closed the front door and opened another that revealed a small

223

sitting room.

"I'm Beytha. Marheh is not here yet, but she'll be along shortly."

She ushered Gelis inside and invited her to sit down.

"Marheh and I went to school together. We've been friends a long time."

Gelis sat down, grateful for the gentle flow of talk that eased the meeting.

"I'm her apprentice," she said. "I haven't known her long at all, but I think she is a special person."

Beytha smiled.

"She is indeed."

She was standing, half hidden by the curtain, looking out.

"I don't want her to have to wait in the street," she explained. "So you only have half my attention."

Gelis smiled.

"Of course," she said, studying her hostess.

She was not much like Marheh, quite short, a little plump and showing her seventy years, but she had a look of determination and a kind smile.

"You wouldn't think Marheh and I are the same age," she said now, the smile again in evidence.

Gelis reddened a little at this reading of her thoughts.

"Marheh is ageless," she said.

"She is indeed," Beytha said, continuing to study the street. "And here she is."

She whisked out into the little hall and opened the front door.

"This is good of you Beytha," Gelis heard Marheh say.

"Not at all," Beytha responded. "Gelis is here already. I've been enjoying talking with her.

Gelis stood up as the two women entered. She felt close to tears as she saw Marheh looking just as usual.

"I'll go and put the kettle on," Beytha said. "Let you two have some time to talk."

She smiled at Gelis.

"You come and get me when you're ready for sperit."

She went out, closing the door behind her.

Marheh crossed the room to Gelis.

"Are you alright?" she asked, putting her hands on Gelis' shoulders and looking at her intently.

Gelis nodded.

"Yes, truly. Tired, scared sometimes, but fine really."

Marheh smiled.

"And you've discovered something important?"

"I think so."

She began her story, first the night time adventure following the potato slush, and then the morning. She tried to give Marheh an understanding of the extent of the YRTHA premises and the way she had felt that morning as she explored. Finally she told her about the underground wharf and the grey boats.

Marheh was silent for several minutes after she finished her story. At last she said quietly.

"And they seemed to you like Silberay boats?"

Gelis nodded.

"They were the same shape, only not bright and shiny, no names, just drab grey."

Marheh sighed.

"How did we let them get so powerful?" she said.

Gelis knew it was not a question for her. Marheh seemed lost in thought. Gelis waited quietly, glad to have unburdened herself.

"I think it is time for sperit," Marheh said at last. "And I want you to tell Beytha something of what you've told me."

She sat down as Gelis went to the door.

A minute or two later she came back with Beytha carrying a steaming mug and a plate of biscuits, while Beytha carried two more mugs. She passed the things she carried to Marheh and then received a mug from Beytha.

She sighed.

"I've longed for sperit," she said. "And I dare not even mention it to Evelyn or to Madam."

When they were all seated comfortably with biscuit and mug, she began her story again. Beytha and Marheh listened intently, Marheh interrupting occasionally to ask a question. When she had finished, she reached into her pocket and drew out the pieces of paper she had found in the waste bin in the office.

"I forgot about these," she said, explaining where they come from. "I haven't looked at them so I don't know whether there is anything useful."

She unfolded the first paper. It had writing on it, hand writing, a name written over and over. She passed it to Marheh.

"James Corcoran," she read aloud.

"That's the Mayor's name!" Beytha exclaimed.

Marheh passed her the paper and she studied it for a moment.

"That looks like his signature," she said at last. "Someone at YRTHA is trying to forge his signature."

"That is what it looks like," Marheh nodded. "I don't know him. Is he a good Mayor?"

"He is a good man," Beytha said thoughtfully. "I'm not sure whether he is a good Mayor. I think perhaps he is a bit too trusting."

"But he would not go along with something unjust?" Marheh asked. "Like this?"

She held out the second paper. It was a typed sheet headed Compulsory Acquisition Order and seemed to be a draft of an official document. A couple of words had been scribbled out and others written in. There was a space for the Planning Officer and a space for the Mayor to sign. It referred to the pottery.

Beytha took the paper.

"What right do they have?" she said angrily. "No, James wouldn't sign anything like this."

"What about the Planning Officer?" Marheh asked.

"Oh he would," Beytha said bitterly. "He and the Club Treasurer are best mates."

She handed the paper back to Marheh.

"I don't really understand what is going on, but I know I don't like it."

"I think," Marheh said slowly. "That they are trying to build a base where they can hide and grow strong. Already they have influenced a group of villagers in different ways and they seem to be trying to draw in anyone of any standing in the village."

She looked at each of them.

"I think the boats Gelis saw are Silberay boats. They have managed to draw them in as *Day Bringer* was nearly drawn in."

She did not speak of the souls she carried with her own, but asked Gelis whether perhaps the potato slush could have been intended to feed prisoners.

Gelis nodded slowly.

"The Silberay from the boats," she said. "They might be behind that door in the hill."

"What can we do?" Beytha asked. "You feel so helpless."

Marheh shook her head.

"The Yareblis are clever and insidious and they abuse people's natural desire to trust each other. For the moment what you can do is continue the way you are."

She smiled.

"And watch out for Gelis."

She turned to Gelis.

"Will you go back?" she asked. "Do you think you will be safe there a bit longer?"

Gelis nodded.

"I'm pretty sure no one was about this morning. I'll be careful and obedient and that should satisfy them."

Marheh nodded.

"The arrangement with Ved is a good one. They know you are not alone, that someone knows where you are."

She stood up and went to her.

"Be very careful, be watchful and don't take any risks. Perhaps you could take a morning walk past here each day so we have another means of communicating."

She turned to Beytha.

"Is that alright?"

"Of course," Beytha smiled. "I'd love to invite you in each day, but we don't want you tarred with my ideas."

"Your ideas are the ones I want to be tarred with," Gelis said firmly. "But not publicly, not yet."

She stood up.

"I'd better go, hadn't I?" she asked Marheh rather wistfully.

Marheh hugged her.

"I'm afraid so. Be careful," she said again.

Beytha stood up and gave Gelis a hug too.

"We'll be friends and allies," she said. "Thank you on behalf of Deerford."

Gelis blushed.

"Thank you," she said, following her to the front door.

When she had gone and Beytha was sitting down again, Marheh turned to her.

"You will look out for her?" she asked. "Now, and especially if anything happens to me."

Beytha looked at her sharply.

"What are you planning?"

Marheh shook her head.

"I'm not sure really," she said, and Beytha knew she would say no more.

* * * *

After she had delivered her message to Beytha, Lorac thought she would make the most of the opportunity and take a walk around the village. She had been so involved in her masterwork, and in Ved, she acknowledged to herself, that it was ages since she had even been to the shop. Marheh had only needed a response to her request if Beytha was unable to help, so there was no need to rush back and she was feeling as if she had done very little to help the family struggle.

She wandered along to the gates of the club and looked up at the club premises. Of course she could not do what Gelis was doing, she was known in the village, but she would have liked to be able to. It was very quiet. Everyone at work, she thought, feeling a little guilty that she was not. She knew that her role in keeping the pottery going was important, but it felt very ordinary compared to what Gelis was doing, or even Ved.

She turned away from the club and walked slowly back towards the village centre. Reaching the ironmongers, she stopped to study the bits and pieces displayed on the pavement. It was a funny little shop and she had been fascinated by it as a child, enjoying the odd shapes of things in the window and expecting to find treasure in the bins and baskets lining the entrance.

She and her friends had usually walked this way home from school and for them, the now departed sweet shop had been the main attraction. Perhaps it had for her also, she thought, trying to be honest with herself, but the ironmongers still drew her. It was well over a year since she had been anywhere near, she realised, wondering at herself. Somehow the display looked a bit tired, rather dusty, which it never had before. She wondered whether the shopkeeper was still the man she remembered who had encouraged her interest and found her some special tools when she began her apprenticeship.

She peered into the dim interior then stepped inside. The smell was different, she thought immediately. It used to be oil and polish, now it was dust and a hint of damp. There was no one in the shop, but she could hear voices from the back, one loud and hectoring, the other just a mutter. A bell had rung somewhere when she entered and now the voices stopped and a man came through to stand at the counter.

She had to look twice to recognise the shopkeeper as the man she had known. He was of average height with nothing particular about him except his enthusiasm for the goods he sold and his bright interested eyes. Now he even seemed to have shrunk in height, his movements were slow and his eyes sad and tired.

"What's the matter?" Lorac said, shocked to see him.

He looked at her then and Lorac knew he had recognised her.

"Go away," he said, and there was an unexpected edge to his voice. "Go now. Go!"

Behind him loomed the tall, bulky silhouette of another man. Lorac looked up at the menacing shape then back to the shopkeeper. In his tired eyes she seemed to see a flash of warning.

"Just looking," she said, nearly gabbling in her confusion. "Thank you."

She backed away from the counter.

"Thank you," she said again and turned and almost ran out of the shop.

Once on the pavement she did run, up the hill and as far as the market square, before slowing to a walk and heading for home. It had been a strange encounter and frightening in a way. She thought she would tell Marheh about it.

●   * * *

Marheh left Beytha's house shortly after Gelis and walked thoughtfully back to the pottery and *Day Bringer*. The streets were quiet and she met no one. She needed to spend some time with her guest souls and try to share with them something of what she had learned.

The pottery was quiet also. Tep, Lorac and Tith were busy working, Kina was out with the van making deliveries, Nicken was at school and Fali was in the garden, planting some new pots.

Marheh sat on the grass beside her. Fali looked up, smiled and continued to settle her young plants carefully into the soil. Marheh felt herself relax in the quiet peace.

"You saw Gelis?" Fali asked at last.

Marheh nodded.

"She has found some Silberay boats hidden at the club."

She lay back on the grass and gazed at the sky.

"There are indications that they have prisoners too."

Soft clouds passed slowly across the blue. She breathed slow and deep.

Fali looked at her sympathetically.

"What will you do?" she asked.

"I think I know what I ought to do," Marheh said slowly, closing her eyes and enjoying the sun on her face, the bright darkness behind her lids. "But I'm afraid I will not be strong enough."

"Then perhaps it is not time yet," Fali said. "You will be strong when the time comes."

She stopped work for a moment and laid one hand over Marheh's.

"You are not alone."

Marheh smiled, squeezed Fali's hand and sat up.

"Yes, I know that. Thank you."

She stood up slowly. She was not alone. As well as the warmth of Fali's affection she had felt another reassurance, a reminder of the two souls she sheltered. They would add their strength to hers.

"I'll be on *Day Bringer* for a bit," she told Fali, knowing she needed to allow space for communication with them.

As she stepped on board she caressed the shining paintwork and gave thanks for the comfort, peace and security she felt there. She walked through the boat, drawing strength from its strength and reliability, then sat down in the saloon and began to compose herself. If the souls were to be able to give her strength for any coming confrontation their communication needed to be total and not dependent on her spending time meditating in order to reach them.

She stood and stretched and tried to turn inward. Her life had been spent in strengthening her spirit, her soul against evil, but she had felt the power of the Yareblis before in her life and understood that somehow they had been able to confine Silberay souls. What had happened to body and mind she did not know, but sensed that physical death might liberate the soul to continue the struggle on a different plane. As she thought and wondered she felt the soul song build in her. There were no words, words belonged to the mind and stood in the way of the song, nevertheless she began to understand that which the song expressed. The harmonies they built together would strengthen and defend all their souls, but she would need her own strength of mind and body, since she must contain the struggle.

For some time she sat, allowing the song to rise and fall within her, beginning to feel confident in the harmonies they made together, understanding where and how they supported each other. At last she stood up, allowing the song to sink into the background, deep within yet still present. She walked slowly back to the pottery, ready to test herself, to interact with those around without losing touch with the harmony beneath. The effort of concentration seemed enormous, yet the balance seemed to involve an undoing, a negation of effort, so that she felt as if she walked a knife edge that she could perceive as a broad path.

As she passed the entrance to the pottery Lorac came running out.

"Did you see Gelis?" she asked.

Marheh smiled.

"Yes, she's fine. Thanks for taking the message."

"I wish I could do more."

She hesitated.

"Have you got a minute?"

"Of course. Do you want to come down to *Day Bringer*?"

Lorac shook her head.

"It's just something unsettling that I saw in Deerford."

She kicked at one of the cobbles then looked back to Marheh.

"I haven't been there for ages, so I thought I'd walk around a bit after I'd seen Mrs Entally."

She grinned at Marheh.

"I wasn't really skiving, just stretching the walk."

Marheh laughed.

"You work hard enough."

"I went past the ironmongers," Lorac continued. "I used to love that shop and Mr Beddis was always friendly and helpful, so I went in, just for a quick look."

She paused and Marheh saw her face change as she remembered.

"Mr Beddis looked terrible, old and ill and he told me to go. Then another man came from behind. I ran."

She stopped suddenly, then went on.

"I suppose it was nothing really, but I was frightened."

"And you are not frightened of nothing," Marheh said, giving her a quick hug. "I'm glad you told me. It all helps to give me a picture of what is happening in Deerford."

Lorac returned the hug and ran back to her wheel, leaving Marheh to continue on her way to the house.

She found Fali still in the garden with her pots. Fali gave her a long look.

"Are you alright?" she asked at last.

Marheh nodded.

"Yes, I'm fine," she said.

Fali continued to look at her.

"Take care," she said at last. "You look more translucent than usual, as if the light within is brighter."

"It probably is," Marheh said. "I hadn't realised there would be a visible change though."

"Not very visible," said Fali, returning to her plants.

"I'm just going back to the village," Marheh said. "To visit the ironmonger."

Fali looked a question.

"Lorac told me an interesting story about what she saw there this morning. It worried me. Jul is another villager I've known since schooldays and it sounded as if he was under pressure."

"Take care then," Fali said.

Marheh nodded, touched Fali's hand and continued out of the garden and into the street. Rather weary, she set off into the village, trying to forget her seventy years and concentrate on the prospect ahead.

Jul had been a class or two behind Marheh, but the school was small and it was easy to know all the students. She remembered him chiefly for his enthusiasms. He had been a passionate collector of all kinds of things from stamps and matchboxes to caterpillars and insects. He had been too tender-hearted to keep the living creatures for long, but made fine, precise drawings of them before returning them to a bush or a leaf. He had gone to work for the ironmonger when he left school and Marheh had seen his collections change to reflect his job, although he had not stopped making fine, precise drawings. She had gone away then and taken up her life as Silberay, but there had been occasions when she needed a tool, or a fastening and had visited the shop, which had become his when his employer had retired.

As she walked she tried to place these memories where her soul's companions could reach them, tried too, to allow them to feel her concern, maintaining the balance she had discovered. She hoped she was also sharing with them the bird song, the wildflowers and the feel of the sun and wind on her skin. These were things of the senses and they would be missing them. She wondered whether mind and body were imprisoned behind the door Gelis had found and tried not to think of how the Yareblis might be trying to exploit them.

Steady walking soon brought her into the centre of the village and she paused to look around before continuing down the lane to the ironmongers. The pub was just opening before lunch and a man was busy placing sun umbrellas at the few outdoor tables on the square. There were cars parked and people coming and going from these to the shop, but not many and none who greeted each other.

She walked on, feeling a kind of nostalgia for the place where she had grown up. Not all were friendly faces even then, but there was life in the square and a sense of community. A few minutes more and she had reached the ironmongers. She stopped outside and gazed at the window display, more to give herself time than for any other reason. Then she stepped resolutely into the shop.

The bell rang somewhere ahead of her and she paused to allow her eyes to become accustomed to the dim light. For several minutes she waited quietly beside the counter, looking about her, noting the sad, tired look of the place, then she picked up the small hand bell beside the till and rang it gently. The pretty, tinkling sound seemed incongruous in the gloom, but it made her smile. A few moments later a figure emerged from the back. There was no smile and no hint of recognition in the blank grey eyes.

"Hello Jul," Marheh said gently, trying not to show her dismay.

For a moment there was a flicker of life before blankness returned. Marheh looked at him, trying to meet his eyes.

"Hello Jul," she said again, calling his soul name with all her strength.

A spasm passed across his face and a single tear squeezed from the corner of each eye, hung suspended for a moment then rolled slowly down the blank, expressionless face.

Marheh reached out to him, mind and soul as well as the hand that clasped his.

"Jul," she said again, continuing to look at him.

He groaned and shuddered and Marheh seemed to see his mind struggling within the grip of a huge fist. Her own mind flew to his aid, struggling to pull away the fingers and break the grip. She stood still and quiet, yet shook with the effort of the struggle.

Gradually she seemed to see first one finger, then another release its hold. The captive seemed to gain new strength from this and suddenly the fist fell apart and disappeared. Marheh stood again opposite Jul and now his face showed weariness, but there was light in his eyes as he responded to her greeting.

"Marheh," he said, with the beginnings of a smile. "How can I help you?"

"By telling me what has been happening," she said. "How you came to be in that state?"

"State?" he said warily. "What state?"

"Think Jul, something had hold of your mind and was squeezing it to death. That state."

He drew a long breath.

"Is that what was happening? And you and some others released me, I think I understood that."

"You must have struggled alone first."

Marheh shook her head.

"I'm sorry Jul, you must be exhausted and I'm pestering you with questions."

"I do feel rather tired, but part of me seems to understand what you are asking."

"Will you come with me to a safe place where you can sleep?" Marheh said gravely. "Then we can talk."

Together they closed up the shop and walked slowly back to the pottery and *Day Bringer*. They did not speak much and they met nobody until they reached the pottery, where Fali was still in her garden. She smiled and greeted them as they passed on the way to the mooring.

"Where are you taking me?" Jul asked at last. "Where is safety?"

"Probably nowhere in the end," Marheh said. "But for now my boat, *Day Bringer*, will shelter us both."

"I'm to enter a Silberay boat. I'm honoured."

"No more than I am," Marheh said, stopping at the side of the boat. "Do you see her?"

"I see something, a coloured shadow over the grass."

Marheh reached out one hand to him and placed the other on *Day Bringer*'s roof.

"Close your eyes and come with me, she said, stepping carefully on board, still holding his hand and murmuring directions.

He followed her carefully. When she invited him to open his eyes she saw his face light as he began to perceive the boat. She led him slowly through into the saloon, where he could sit while she made sperit. She longed to question him, but knew he needed space to recover, so she passed him the mug of sperit in silence and sat beside him with pad and pencil making little sketches, leaving it to him to tell his story when he was ready.

"I think you came just in time," he said at last. "Was it your young niece who alerted you?"

"My great niece." Marheh smiled. "Fancy being a great aunt!"

Jul nodded.

"Very aging," he said, and there was the hint of a twinkle as he spoke. Then he sighed. "We are all getting older, even you. It makes one vulnerable."

Marheh nodded.

"Have you no one, an assistant perhaps?"

He shook his head.

"There is very little custom these days, barely enough to support myself. That's why it seemed so strange when the treasurer from the YRTHA came and offered me a good price for the business."

He sipped at his sperit and looked at Marheh.

"I'd forgotten about sperit. Nobody offers it any more."

Marheh smiled at him, seeing the beginnings of colour coming into his face.

"It always seems specially good when you're weary."

He nodded.

"I don't think I've ever felt so tired. Not just tired, empty, dragged down."

He paused, gazing into his mug, deep in thought.

Marheh waited a few moments then said softly "What happened?"

"I'm not sure that I know," Jul said at last. "I wasn't averse to selling, but I didn't want to rush into it. I told them that I needed to think about it and they seemed to be agreeable to that. Then I told them I didn't want to leave my home over the shop, even if I sold the business. That seemed to be all right too.

"The treasurer started dropping in most days, just for a chat. Then he began bringing someone with him, My Strong Right Arm, he called him." Jul paused in his recitation and looked at Marheh.

"You know I never did learn their names, either of them, though they were very free with mine."

Marheh nodded.

"They use names for power," she said.

"It seemed at first as if they were just being friendly and coming to learn the business should I decide to sell."

He shrugged.

"I think in a way their visits prolonged my decision. There seemed no hurry whilst they kept in touch and I knew I would sell eventually."

He paused, frowning thoughtfully.

"In a way it was a kind of game, but then Club Treasurer stopped coming and Strong Right Arm came more often and stayed longer, until he sat all day in the office behind the shop – sat there and swelled."

"Swelled?"

"Not literally, but it got so that I felt squeezed into a shrinking corner."

He looked at Marheh.

"Why would they do that?" he said. "Why me?"

"It seems as if the YRTHA people want to possess Deerford," Marheh said. "And your shop got in the way."

"My shop!" Jul sounded sceptical. "How could my shop get in the way?"

"It has a real, caring human being in it," Marheh said, smiling at him.

She stood up.

"I'm going to make us a sandwich," she said. "Then we'll go and talk to Fali. The YRTHA people are threatening the pottery too, so perhaps you can help each other."

They had just about finished eating when they heard running feet coming down the garden and a voice calling for Marheh. She hurried out onto the deck, then stepped off onto the wharf when she realised that Kina could not see her.

"You are there!"

Kina was obviously trying to control her anxiety.

"You don't have Nicken on board by any chance?"

"No, I haven't seen her today." Marheh spoke slowly. "I thought she had gone to school."

Kina nodded.

"I dropped her off on my way out with the deliveries. It seemed like a good idea not to let her go wandering about. I went back to get her just now and she wasn't there. I was a little bit late, but she knew I was coming."

"I'm sure you've tried her friends," Marheh said. "And followed the route she might have walked?"

"I spoke to one of her friends. It seems she started walking, but she should be home by now."

Kina's face twisted with the effort of containing her feelings.

"Normally I wouldn't worry, but with what's happening just now…"

She looked at Marheh.

"I just hoped she might have been with you."

Marheh touched her arm lightly.

"I wish she was. Why don't we take a wander back along her route? She's probably been side-tracked by something."

Kina nodded and tried to speak lightly.

"Little monkey, she'll probably come home with an abandoned puppy or an injured sparrow and wonder what all the fuss is about."

"Just let me hand Jul over to Fali and we'll be on our way."

"Jul looked tired?" Kina said as they went out the gate.

Marheh nodded.

"YRTHA have been after him too," she said. "He needs a bit of support."

They turned into the road and walked across the tunnel. The day was bright and warm, but clouds were visible to the north and the wind was strengthening. There was no one about. Kina wanted to hurry, but Marheh held her back.

"We are just taking a stroll," she said. "Look around, see if you can see anything that might have attracted her attention."

They walked on into the village. There was a group of three young girls laughing and talking together outside the shop. Marheh looked at Kina.

"Do you know any of them?"

Kina shook her head.

"They look a bit older than Nicken."

"They might know her though," Marheh suggested.

Kina nodded.

"It's worth asking."

The children watched as they approached and one tall girl giggled suddenly. Kina took a deep breath to calm herself before asking whether they knew Nicken.

A small, pert twelve year old constituted herself spokesperson.

"Nicola Carron?" she repeated. "Do we know Nicola Carron?"

The tall girl giggled again and the girl who had answered smirked and continued.

"Are you her mother?"

Kina was past recognising the mocking tone, but Marheh heard it and looked sharply at the girl as Kina answered. The girl did not notice, but continued to watch Kina.

"We call her Nutty Nicola," she said.

The three girls ran away then, the sound of their giggles dribbling behind them.

Kina stood stunned for a moment then turned to Marheh speechlessly.

"Oh yes," Marheh said grimly. "It's everywhere. Unkindness spreads like the plague once it takes hold."

"But they're children," Kina protested.

"Children who have parents who might have stoned the pottery the other night."

Kina still stood staring after them. Marheh touched her lightly.

"Come on. They don't know anything. We should keep walking."

Automatically Kina stepped forward a couple of paces then stopped again and turned to Marheh

"But Nicken likes school. I'm sure she does."

"I'm sure too," Marheh reassured her. "She has friends there, just not those three."

"We're not going to find her this way, are we?" Kina demanded. "Something has happened to her."

"I still think we should continue to the school," Marheh said gently. "Then we will go home and who knows, if we don't find her, she might be there waiting for us."

The two women continued through the village and into the school grounds. There were still one or two teachers about, politely sympathetic to Kina's anxious queries, but they learned nothing new. They walked back to the pottery almost in silence, each of them turning over anxious thoughts.

●   * * *

Gelis got herself ready reluctantly and set off to walk to work. She was not afraid exactly, for she did not think she had been observed during any of her explorations, but she was uneasy and aware that she could accidentally reveal her knowledge or her allegiance at any time if she was not careful enough. It still seemed odd to be setting off to work in the late afternoon, but at least it meant time to herself in the mornings. The fine warm day had become almost hot and rather sultry as if a storm was brewing. She noticed a bank of cloud building on the horizon and wondered whether she should have brought rain protection.

Everything was quiet when she reached the club. She walked up the hill as slowly as she dared looking around her for evidence of her previous night's discoveries though trying to disguise her interest by pretending to greater weariness than she actually felt. She saw some signs of repeated traffic where the grass looked more tired, though it could hardly be called a path.

The kitchen seemed much as she had left it in the morning and she wondered again at the purpose of such a huge and under-used facility. There was no one about when she arrived and even after she had changed into her uniform and made herself a cup of tea she still seemed to be alone. Putting her drink on the bench she began to empty the dishwasher and put away the small amount of crockery it contained.

It was nearly an hour before Madam arrived, sweeping in from the lift and looking at Gelis as if she were one of an army of worker ants. Gelis found it hard to suppress a half hysterical giggle at the absurdity of it, but she managed to look dumbly respectful instead as she received her instructions for the evening. Karl apparently was having his day off, so she would be assisting Madam herself.

Madam was not very specific, but Gelis began to understand that there was to be a large number of overnight guests, a convention of some kind it seemed, and since they would all require evening meals and breakfasts, she, Gelis, would be expected to give her all. Her heart sank at the thought of another night in the tiny room she had been allocated, but she set to work on the vegetables with apparent docility. Madam worked ferociously along side her, scooping up vegetables as she cut them, sending her for ingredients from the cool room and filling the kitchen with appetising smells. Gelis could not help but feel a degree of respect for her skill.

There was no conversation, only orders and the occasional admonition. What ever it was, this convention was causing the only real flurry of activity that Gelis had seen. Peter, the young waiter she had met before, appeared and re-appeared with trays of dirty coffee cups for her to put through the dishwasher. The Odd Messenger was in and out for this and that and even the woman from reception, who had been her first YRTHA encounter, came gliding through the kitchen to the cool room, reappeared with a large tin of ground coffee and clicked back upstairs with it.

It seemed odd that Karl should be having his day off, just when he might be really needed, but perhaps he had commitments he could not change. Several hours went past at top speed before there was a brief lull and Gelis was given her meal. She had barely time to eat before she was sent with the trolley to the small kitchen behind the restaurant. The serving hatch was partly opened so that Peter could put the dirty dishes through for her to collect.

Curiously she looked out. The room was attractive, with flowers on the tables and bright sparkling glass and silverware. There were perhaps thirty people sitting at tables of four or six, men and women elegantly dressed and carefully groomed, but there seemed to be almost no interaction between them. The room was as silent as if there were no more than three or four diners.

Peter came towards her laden with dishes. He gave her a grin and said under his breath "A bit different to last time!"

Gelis smiled at him and began loading the trolley.

"Who are they?" she asked quietly.

He shrugged and shook his head then went back for more dishes. Gelis admired the way he moved, neatly and quickly, but without appearing hurried. Her trolley was soon full and he helped her guide it towards the lift.

"Funny lot, these," he said to her. "All dressed up to party, but never crack a smile."

Gelis laughed.

"You seem to be the only real person here."

Together they stepped into the lift.

Peter made a face and spoke with an exaggerated tremor in his voice.

"All the rest are aliens!" he said, and grinned.

Not exactly aliens, Gelis thought, but the next thing to it. She grinned at Peter, gripped the trolley and pushed it into the kitchen.

* * * *

At the pottery there was still no sign of Nicken. All work had stopped. Tith and Kina had been out in the van, driving the streets of Deerford calling on all Nicken's friends. Lorac and Tep had taken forgotten footpaths and visited the wood alongside the water road. Marheh and Fali sat in the kitchen. For a time they sat in silence, Marheh struggling with what she must do.

Finally she looked at Fali.

"I shall move on in *Day Bringer*," she said. "And allow myself to be taken by their current."

An unexpected task,
Watching a sleeping child.
Not a job for the kitchen hand
One would think.
Not a job for the kitchen hand.
Her job is to wash dishes
And peel potatoes,
And peel
Potatoes
And
Peel.

Gelis

CHAPTER SEVENTEEN

The dishes seemed never-ending. Gelis wondered that thirty people could eat so much, but the work was more interesting when it was busy and there were things happening around her. She enjoyed the occasional word with Peter too. He was cheerful, communicative and had a quirky sense of humour that lightened the long, hard night. The meal was eaten with dispatch and the diners disappeared. Gelis was sent to help Peter get the restaurant ready for breakfast.

"Where are they?" she asked him. "Do you know?"

"Having a lecture upstairs," he said. "I've got to take them coffee when it's over."

"I wish I knew who they are," she said.

"Better not to ask," Peter said. "They don't like you to be too curious around here. Just get on with the job and take the money."

Gelis nodded.

"I can't help wondering though."

They stood together and looked around the room.

"I think we've finished," Peter said. "But no doubt Madam will want to inspect. They think because we are young we are stupid."

He pushed open the door and held it for Gelis.

"They only gave me a job because they want to get on the right side of my father – at least that is what I think."

243

Gelis walked through with the trolley and went towards the lift.

"The whole set-up seems odd to me," she said. "But as you say, it's a job."

She wanted to ask him who his father was. She wondered whether she could confide in him, but decided she was safer not to.

She was just taking the last load out of the dishwasher and putting it away when she became aware that Madam was engaged in some kind of argument, or perhaps energetic discussion, with the Odd Messenger and the Slick Receptionist. Moreover, judging by the direction of their glances, they could be talking about her. She felt herself go cold. Had they somehow discovered where she came from, who she was? She forced herself to continue calmly placing crockery on appropriate shelves. A few minutes later she found herself directed to go with the Odd Messenger. Dutifully she followed him up the stairs to the foyer outside the private dining room. He turned down the corridor to the bedrooms, beckoning her to follow. Outside the furthest room they stopped. He put his finger to his lips and waited until she had nodded her understanding then he took a key from his pocket and unlocked the door. Slowly he turned the door knob and quietly pushed the door open.

At first Gelis could see little in the dimly lit room. Clearly it was a bedroom, but the curtains were closed and the Odd Messenger standing in her line of sight. He moved aside and she realized that there was a figure in the bed. Then he switched on the bedside lamp. The figure in the bed turned and muttered and Gelis realised it was Nicken.

She was glad the Odd Messenger was not looking at her, sure that something of her surprise must have been reflected on her face. She managed to turn her little gasp into a whispered question.

"Who is it?" she asked again, when the Odd Messenger made no reply.

He switched the lamp off and drew Gelis out of the room again.

"She's the daughter of one of the conference delegates," he told her. "She has been ill and her mother is anxious about her. She wanted us to find someone to watch over her, keep her quietly in bed, make sure her sleep is not disturbed."

"Me?" Gelis asked. "You want me to baby sit?"

"Madam agrees. The mother will pay."

Gelis hesitated, knowing she must agree to the job, but also that she must get a message to the pottery.

"Not a difficult job," the Odd Messenger said.

"I will, of course," Gelis said slowly. "But I feel bad about my landlady. David is coming to meet me at 10 o'clock. Could I ask him to give her a message?"

"What sort of message?" The Odd Messenger looked doubtful. "The child shouldn't be left."

"Perhaps a note, just letting her know I won't be back tonight. She was anxious the last time I stayed."

He nodded and indicated the room.

"There is pen and paper in the room and a dim light won't disturb the child. I'll be back for the note in five minutes."

He opened the door again and let Gelis pass into the room.

"Five minutes," he whispered again.

Gelis nodded and went across to the small table where she could see the pen and paper. The Odd Messenger closed the door quietly behind her and she heard a key turn.

She felt a sudden rush of panic at being locked in, but forced herself to ignore it and focus on composing a note. She knew there was no possibility of it being sealed. Whatever she wrote would have to contain a hidden message. At first she could think of nothing that would not be too general to communicate anything, then she sat down, picked up the pen and began to write.

Needed here. I am caring for a Child. Keen to do well Even if it means staying up all Night.

She signed it, folded it once and wrote on the outside

David please give this to my landlady and apologise for me.

She signed it again, sighed and sat back. Surely Marheh would understand. They must be anxious about Nicken already and Ved, surely he would take anything from her to Marheh.

A moment later she heard the key turn in the lock and the Odd Messenger reappeared. Gelis stood up as she saw him.

"You locked me in," she said indignantly. "What if I need help through the night? What if the child becomes worse?"

The Odd Messenger put his finger to his lips then held out his hand for

Gelis' note. She shook her head, picked it up from the table and began to walk towards the door. The Odd Messenger backed out as she approached and she felt an inward satisfaction that she had asserted herself. She stepped through the door after him and stopped.

"If you want the door locked," she said. "Then let me lock it and keep the key."

They looked at each other for a long moment, each assessing the other.

Gelis smiled kindly.

"You must realise that I'm no use at all if I can't communicate with you."

He continued to look at her. She let her gaze fall and fiddled with her note, but did not otherwise move.

"I'll leave the door unlocked then," the Odd Messenger said and held out his hand again for her note.

Gelis stood her ground.

"Better if I have the key though, because then I could lock the door if I did need to leave the child and go for help."

She thought for a minute he was going to refuse, but she concentrated on looking harmless and stubborn and after a moment he thrust the key at her. She thanked him politely and gave him her note.

"Tell the mother I'll look after her as carefully as I can," she said. "I really will."

It was nothing but the truth and carried conviction. The Odd Messenger nodded and turned away. Gelis stood and watched as he moved down the corridor, covering the ground more quickly than she would have thought possible though without seeming to hurry. When he had gone she went back into the room, closing and locking the door behind her. She put the key in her pocket and went quietly across the floor to look at Nicken. "Now what?" she wondered.

* * * *

After she had made her announcement, Marheh stood up.

"It's the only way," she added.

Fali came to take both her hands.

"Are you sure?" she asked.

Marheh nodded.

"Yes, I've known for a while really, but I needed to think it through and I was afraid."

Fali looked at her.

"And you are not now?" she asked.

Marheh gave a little laugh.

"Of course I am, but that doesn't seem important any more."

She gave Fali a hug then stood back.

"I'll need help though. I'm not planning to set off tonight. If they have taken Nicken as we fear then we need to go carefully."

Fali sat down heavily.

"Would they do that?" she asked, without hope of any good answer.

Marheh nodded.

"Perhaps the others will find her, but something has prevented her from coming home. She would not stay away willingly. She knows we will be anxious about her."

Fali covered her face with both hands while Marheh stood silently beside her, staring into some private inner space.

They were still in the same position, each with their own, painful thoughts, when the door opened and Tep and Lorac came into the kitchen. Marheh and Fali looked up hopefully, but they shook their heads and came to sit wearily beside Fali. Both were damp and dishevelled and let in the noise of the rising wind as they entered. Another few minutes passed and they heard the sound of the van returning, but one glance at Tith and Kina revealed their lack of success. They stood in the doorway, white and exhausted. Kina's face was wet with tears.

There was a long silence then Marheh realised that everyone was looking at her. She went to the door and drew Tith and Kina into the kitchen to sit with the others, then she sat down herself.

"We are afraid YRTHA have taken her," she said, making it clear for them.

Kina gasped and shook her head, but it was not a real protest.

Fali took her hand.

"Marheh has a plan," she said. "But we will all need to help."

"Marheh has a plan," Tith repeated bitterly. "Marheh has a plan. What good is a plan?"

Marheh reached out to touch him.

"Perhaps not much good, but I'll tell you about it."

She met his eyes and saw the pain in them.

"We will get her back, we must."

"Marheh is going to let herself be taken with *Day Bringer*," Fali said. "Gelis has learnt that they have Silberay boats hidden under the clubhouse. Marheh thinks they have Silberay prisoners too."

"So what good will it do for you to be a prisoner as well?" Tith said. "Or do you think you can take them on by yourself?"

Marheh shook her head.

"Not by myself, but I will know what I'm up against and where my support is. Gelis told me of something she learned that suggests where prisoners might be held. I'm hoping to have her lead you there at the same time as I am arriving."

She was beginning to elaborate on her ideas when they heard footsteps and a knock on the kitchen door. Before they could respond, Ved called out. Lorac hurried to the door.

"What has blown you in?" Tep asked. "This is a late visit."

"It's a note from Gelis," he said. "I thought I'd better bring it straight away. She's staying at YRTHA overnight."

He held it out to Marheh.

"It says it's for her landlady, but I think that's you."

"Thanks Ved."

Marheh took the note, unfolded it and read it through. Then she smiled and laid it on the table.

"Nicken is there and Gelis is with her," she said.

Kina snatched the note and read it aloud.

"Caring for a child," she repeated. "That doesn't have to be Nicken."

"Look at the capital letters," Marheh said. "Gelis would not normally write that way. She has done it for a reason."

Kina studied the note in silence for a moment then handed it to Tith.

"Nicken," she said. "The capital letters spell Nicken."

There was indrawn breath and silence as the note was passed around.

"Gelis is with her, caring for her," Kina said hopefully.

Marheh nodded.

"Which gives us a little time to plan our offensive."

Ved looked puzzled.

"What offensive? What has Nicken got to do with it?" he asked.

There was a babble of talk as they realised that Ved did not understand the magnitude of the news he had brought. Then Kina hugged him and the others fell silent as she explained.

Ved nodded.

"They didn't let me speak to Gelis, just handed over the note," he said. "Obviously she had to be very careful how she communicated."

"Both of them are still in danger," Marheh said. "But Gelis won't leave Nicken if she can help it and it means we have knowledge they don't know we have."

There was a new optimism around the table, a sense of common purpose directed towards the rescue of Nicken and the defeat of YRTHA.

Tith looked towards Marheh.

"You'd best rally the troops and get us organised before you go and do the hard stuff."

Marheh smiled at him, understanding his apology and moments later they were deep in discussion, pouring over a sketch map of the club grounds that Ved drew up and Marheh added to from her meeting with Gelis.

At midnight they were still sitting round the table, weary and anxious, but not wanting to leave the support and companionship. They heard a clock strike twelve then moments later the front door shook under a series of loud blows. Tep and Tith were first on their feet and Tith ran to open the door. He was just in time to see the front gate closing, but at his feet was a white envelope. He snatched it up before the wind could take it and turned to the others who had all followed him.

"Open it," Kina said urgently. "Open it! What does it say?"

Slowly, his hands not quite steady, Tith lifted the flap of the envelope and drew out a folded paper. The others stood silently around watching him unfold it.

"Child for pottery," he read. "Fair exchange."

Marheh drew in a deep breath. Her greatest fear was that YRTHA might discover that Nicken could see the water road, but they had not done so yet it seemed. She said nothing to the others, knowing they were anxious enough already. The Yareblis would try all manner of coercion to recruit Nicken if they knew her ability. Marheh hoped that Gelis would encourage her to hide it from them.

The letter was passed from one to the other.

"It is meant to intimidate," Marheh said. "They won't harm her while they think they can bargain. Obviously they have no idea about Gelis either or they would not have put her to watch over Nicken."

She looked at them all, Lorac and Kina, white-faced with dark shadowed eyes, Fali and Tep grey with fatigue, Tith, a red spot on each cheek and sweat on his forehead and upper lip, Ved, anxious and willing.

"I know it is hard," she said. "But I think we should try and rest for a couple of hours. We will need to have our wits about us."

Fali nodded.

"Ved, you must go," she said. "Evelyn will be anxious."

He looked at Marheh questioningly.

She nodded.

"You know the plan. Go now."

He said goodbye and slipped away as the others began to make their way upstairs to bed. Marheh watched them go then walked slowly to *Day Bringer*. She had her own preparations to make before morning.

* * * *

It was quiet, even restful watching over the sleeping Nicken. At first Gelis' mind had raced anxiously through possibilities, but as the night wore on she began to reach for the soul song as Marheh had taught her. It brought calm and readiness to act when Nicken awoke. Twice the Odd Messenger had popped in and Gelis knew he was keeping an eye on her. Obviously he had another key to the room, or a master key of some kind. Each time he had beckoned Gelis out into the corridor and kept up the fiction of the conference delegate mother. Each time Gelis had sent a message of reassurance.

Now, as she sat watching, she realised that Marheh must soon take action. The capture of Nicken would force her and the others to respond.

She hoped her message had been received and understood, for that would give them some respite from the anxiety they must be feeling. It had been quite some time since the Odd Messenger's last visit, but Gelis did not dare to hope he would leave them alone for much longer. She reached out and gently touched Nicken's cheek, lifted a strand of hair and moved it off her face. Quietly she breathed her name. It was not the first time she had tried and received no response. Nicken lay, breathing slowly and deeply, and otherwise completely still.

She had barely sat back again when she heard the Odd Messenger's key in the lock. As before, he opened the door and beckoned to her.

"The child seems to be sleeping comfortably," she said, pre-empting his question. "I don't think her mother need worry too much."

She looked innocently at him.

"Surely the conference meetings must be over by now. Won't her mother want to see her?"

The Odd Messenger shook his head.

"She has too much important business. She just needs to be assured of her comfort."

Gelis shook her head over the mythical mother's preoccupation with business, but reiterated her belief that the child was sleeping easily. The Odd Messenger handed her a tall glass filled with what he said was orange juice and instructed Gelis to give it to Nicken should she wake. Then he departed again and she returned to her post.

Once again she reached out to Nicken, touched her gently, spoke her name softly in her ear. This time there was a response. Nicken did not wake, but stirred and muttered in her sleep. Gelis waited a few minutes then tried again.

"Nicken," she said quietly. "Nicken, wake up."

Again she stirred and Gelis saw her eyelids flutter as she struggled to emerge from whatever it was that held her in sleep. Gelis watched her carefully, holding one of Nicken's hands in hers, leaning over so she would know her. There was a moment when she thought Nicken had wakened enough to recognise her and she felt the small hand grasp hers, then she sank back into sleep. Gelis sighed, pulled her chair closer to the bed and allowed herself to relax and try again to practise her song.

* * * *

Marheh stepped onto *Day Bringer* and stood for a moment, breathing deeply. Through the stresses of the night she had been trying to maintain the balance she had achieved with her two guest souls, but it had not been easy and at times she knew she had lost them. Now she must try to be sure they understood her plan. She would need their help when it came time to battle for her own soul. It was a battle they must win, not only for Deerford, but for all the imprisoned Silberay souls and for the future of the water road. *Day Bringer* moved uneasily in the gusting wind but the noise and tumult only heightened the sense of safety she provided.

As she moved through the boat she touched it gently, thinking of all the women it had sheltered before her, wondering whether any of them had needed to put *Day Bringer* at risk for the sake of their calling. In the saloon she sat down heavily and stared about her. She was weary and afraid yet she knew she must put these feelings away from her. However inadequate she felt herself, this seemed to be her task.

"Eat, sleep, sing and go," she said to herself, trying to be sensible and positive.

The familiar actions involved in boiling the kettle, cutting bread and buttering it, were calming and the simple food refreshed her. She washed up her cup and plate and went to lie down, lighting a candle beside her for company and comfort. She thought perhaps she would not sleep, but closed her eyes and tried to quieten her mind. As consciousness slipped away she understood her guest souls were there, holding her, and she relaxed and smiled in her sleep.

About two hours later she woke feeling surprisingly alert and refreshed. It was easy now to stretch herself to include her guest souls and to slip into the soul song where she could communicate with them and renew her spiritual strength. The space where the three souls danced together and wove harmonies of sound was timeless and seemed both a moment and an age. Scarcely an hour had passed of ordinary time, Marheh decided, when the song ended at first light. The huge winds of the night had passed, but there were still strong gusts buffeting *Day Bringer*. Marheh felt her strain against her moorings.

Quietly she performed the engine checks that were so much part of her daily life. Then she put on her boots and her outdoor clothes and went outside.

A light shone from the upper floor of the house and she was tempted to go and say goodbye, but she thought of the distraction of people and voices and knew it would be better to hold to the silence and the song. Briefly she acknowledged each family member in her mind, wrapping them in love. Then she threw her warmth around Nicken and Gelis for a few moments before turning her attention to *Day Bringer.*

Carefully she started the engine and listened to its deep throbbing. Then she went to untie her mooring ropes, front first, then the back. Just before she stepped back on board she looked again towards the house and waved in case anyone was watching. *Day Bringer* moved uneasily as the wind gusted and a gap appeared between boat and bank.

Marheh looked around at the familiar shapes of the pottery, just beginning to be defined in the dim light. She looked at the sky showing faintly pink in the east, with grey blotches of cloud moving fast over lighter, slower cotton wool masses. Then she gripped the tiller, pushed the throttle forward to engage the gears and moved slowly forward towards the Yareblis' trap.

* * * *

Gelis too was conscious of the faint emergence of dawn. She went to the window and looked out, curious to see the extent of the club. She found she was looking over the terraced bank she had ascended on her first visit, and down the hill to the gate, but way to her right, only just visible before the corner of the building cut off her view, she glimpsed the basin and the white boats, ghostly in the dim light.

She turned back to the bed to find Nicken with her eyes wide open struggling to sit up. Quickly she returned to the bedside, leaping forward to prevent Nicken's glad cry of recognition. She gave her a quick hug and pushed her gently down again.

"Best if you can pretend to be asleep if anyone comes," she told her.

"Where am I?" Nicken asked. "Why are you here?"

Gelis grinned at her.

"I work here," she said quietly. "I'm supposed to be looking after you."

Nicken lay back and looked at her.

"You work at that club," she said. "Is that where I am?"

Gelis nodded.

"We have to be really careful," she said. "I hope I've got a message to the pottery to say where you are, but we mustn't let them know that we know each other and especially we mustn't let them know we can see the boats and the water road."

Nicken nodded.

"That's why it's best if I'm asleep," she said thoughtfully.

253

She lay silent for a minute, eyes looking inward.

"Am I kidnapped?" she asked Gelis at last.

"Yes," Gelis said after a moment. "I suppose you are."

Nicken yawned, curled onto her side and reached for Gelis' hand.

"Lucky you're here then," she said, and sank back into sleep.

After a few minutes Gelis gently disengaged her hand and went back to the window. If Nicken had been able to wake earlier it might have been worth attempting to leave, but already it was too late, she thought. She wondered what might happen as people began to wake. Would they let her stay with Nicken once she woke to protest her imprisonment, as they must realise she would.

Through the window she watched the light increase soft, faintly pink. Much of the grounds were still in deep shadow, but she could see the trees respond to the gusting wind and an occasional light from the village beyond. The village seemed impossibly remote from where she stood and her sense of isolation grew. There seemed little chance now that Gillian, kitchen hand, could return to being Gelis, Silberay. She sighed and turned back to her chair by the bed. She had no plan, no clever stratagem, only the conviction that she must stay with Nicken if it was humanly possible and that they must both keep their talent not just secret, but as if it had never been.

* * * *

Tep turned away from the window and looked to Fali who watched him from their bed.

"She's gone," he said. "Just now. She waved, though I don't think she could see me."

"She would," Fali said. "Just in case."

"It's a lonely life," Tep said, remembering how he had seen her."

"Solitary, I think," Fali said. "It's what she chose."

Tep nodded and yawned. They had not slept much although they had been tired when they went to bed. He sat on the bed beside Fali looking rumpled, his blue pyjamas creased, his hair standing on end.

"I feel as if I need to be up and doing," he said. "Although Marheh doesn't want us to go in until she has been away a couple of hours."

"We should let the others have another hour of sleep," Fali said. "After that will be time enough to wake them."

Tep nodded and got back under the covers.

Fali snuggled close to him.

"I keep thinking of Nicken and Gelis."

Tep put his arm around her.

"I do too," he said. "Especially Gelis. She is only a young woman, but she has chosen never to have this kind of warmth. She reminds me of Marheh as a girl."

He stopped and thought for a few moments then grinned at Fali.

"Except she was not really like Gelis at all."

Fali smiled.

"They must have something that makes them alike."

She sighed a little and put her head on his shoulder.

"I wonder about Nicken, part of me doesn't want her to make the same choice, but part of me will be very proud if she does."

They fell silent, each with their own thoughts, each enjoying the comfort and warmth of their closeness.

At last Fali moved and stretched.

"Time to get up," she said.

Tep drew her close for a minute then sat up, swinging his legs out from under the covers. Fali got up too and they dressed almost in silence and went down stairs to start the breakfast.

Soon everyone was gathered in the kitchen. Tith and Kina looked white and tired and obviously had had little sleep. Lorac's eyes were set in dark smudges. There was little to say. Lorac and Fali hugged Kina wordlessly then Fali hugged Tith too and pushed him into a chair at the table. Kina sat next to him and the others found their places while Lorac made mugs of sperit for them all.

"I still don't think you should be here on your own," Tep said to Fali, continuing an argument they had begun last night as they discussed their plan of action.

"Someone needs to be here, and I'm the best one," Fali said. "It would be foolish for anyone else to stay to look after me. There is risk in everything."

Tep looked unconvinced. Fali took his hand.

"Do you want to stay with me?" she asked.

He looked surprised.

"I thought perhaps Lorac," he said.

"Of course Lorac can stay if she wishes," Fali said. "But I don't think she does, anymore than you do."

Lorac put his mug on the table in front of him.

"It's your instinct to look after the women and children, isn't it Grandfather dearest? But the women and children don't want looking after all the time."

Tep smiled at her and squeezed Fali's hand.

"Understood."

He picked up his sperit and looked around the table.

"Here's to our success this day," he said.

The others drank and the mood around the table lifted a little.

"Is it time?" Kina asked.

"Soon," Fali said. "Try to eat something."

Lorac put a piece of buttered toast in front of her. Tith slid the jar of marmalade to where she could reach it.

"What if they've hurt her? What if we misunderstood Gelis' message?"

"There are lots of what ifs."

Tith put his arm around her.

"But we can only act in one way, and that is the way we have planned."

He reached across and cut up her toast.

"Try to eat," he said coaxingly.

Kina sipped her sperit and nibbled her toast and looked blankly at nothing. No one had much to say and no one was hungry though they all went through the motions and dutifully consumed some of the porridge and toast Fali had provided. At last Tep looked around the table.

"Ready?" he asked. "Is everyone clear about what they are doing?"

There were nods and mutters of assent and a couple of last minute visits to the bathroom, but very quickly they were assembled again, coats on and ready to leave.

Fali stood and hugged each one as they filed past her and out into the yard, then she waited, framed in the doorway, while they piled into the van, Tith and Kina, respectable in the front, Tep and Lorac, illegal and hidden in the back. She waved as they backed and turned and drove out of the yard.

* * * *

Marheh stood at the tiller. *Day Bringer* was moving at her slowest speed through the quiet water, going closer and closer to the place where the current had tried to draw her off course. On either side, the trees moved uneasily as the wind gusted. The tops of the trees were beginning to be dusted with light, but below they were still dark and mysterious. Marheh recognised the narrow place with the overhanging trees, where she had lost her chimney.

"Not far now," she thought and deliberately relaxed her tight grip on the tiller.

Carefully she edged *Day Bringer* through the bushes, ducking down herself to avoid being scratched. Then she felt it, the powerful draw of the current. At the speed she was going she could not pull out of it even if she had wanted to. Ahead she saw the white gates swing open, saw the fleet of white boats in the wide pool.

She breathed slowly and deeply and reached out to her guest souls as *Day Bringer* was sucked through the white gates to the still waters beyond. Glancing back she saw the gates swing closed behind her.

An indrawn breath, a stare.
Awe and wonder and then the awakening.
In the stillness, a living death.
Who, what how, why?
This prison, these prisoners
Where was their hope?
Who was their hope?
A woman, remote, strong, disciplined,
An almost woman, learning, striving,
And love that reached out,
And conquered.

Gelis

CHAPTER EIGHTEEN

Gelis sat watching Nicken sleep and the morning gradually awake. She realised she had forgotten to offer Nicken the orange juice, but it didn't seem to matter. She stood up to get it and put it by the bed where she would see it next time Nicken woke. She was anxious that she might be summoned to the kitchen and turned over possibilities for helping Nicken escape while things were still fairly quiet.

After a short time she woke Nicken, who seemed much more alert. She sat up, looked around and smiled at Gelis.

"Is there a toilet?" she asked, and then, as she pushed back the covers. "Are my clothes somewhere? I'm only wearing my undies."

She sounded faintly scandalised at this and Gelis smiled as she answered her.

"You nip into the bathroom and I'll have a look for your clothes," she said. "And then we'll plan our escape."

"Yes!" said Nicken, leaping out of bed and making for the bathroom.

Gelis opened the wardrobe and searched the few drawers, but there was no sign of any clothes and she was trying to decide whether she could spare any of her own garments when Nicken emerged from the bathroom fully dressed.

"I found them," she said, grinning at Gelis. "Let's go."

Gelis shook her head.

"Not quite so fast. We want to delay discovery for as long as possible. Do you think you could hop back into bed with your clothes on?"

Nicken made a face.

"If you want." She giggled. "I've never been to bed with shoes on before."

Gelis looked at the glass of juice.

"They brought this for you," she said picking it up and taking the cover off. "Do you want it?"

Nicken shook her head.

"It's probably poisoned," she said dramatically.

"I don't expect so." Gelis sniffed at it. "But I suppose it might have something in it to make you go to sleep again."

"I don't want it anyway," Nicken said. "Let's pour it down the sink, then they'll think I drank it."

"Good idea," said Gelis.

She tasted a tiny sip and shook her head.

"It tastes alright. Are you sure you don't want it?"

"Pour it out," Nicken said. "I want you to pour it out."

So Gelis carried it to the bathroom and washed it down the sink, running the tap until there were no traces left.

Nicken pulled back the covers and sat on the edge of the bed looking expectantly at Gelis.

"Get right in and pretend to be asleep," Gelis said. "I'm just going to look outside."

She thought for a moment, unlocked the door to the passage and handed Nicken the key.

"I want you to lock the door behind me then hop back into bed. If I want to get in I'll tap a little rhythm." She reached out to the bedside table. "one, two," she said, tapping lightly. "One, two, three... one, two. Okay?"

Nicken echoed the rhythm back to her.

"Good. Unless you hear that you must be asleep. I might have someone with me when I come back."

Nicken nodded solemnly. Gelis bent and gave her a quick hug.

"I won't be long."

She went quietly to the door and let herself out, waited until she heard the key turn, then set off along the corridor towards the foyer and the stairs. Looking to right and left and listening hard, she crossed to the door of the private dining room and tried the handle. It turned and she opened it a crack. There was no sound from inside so she peeped in. The table was bare and there was no sign that breakfast would be served there.

Carefully she closed the door again and went to the head of the stairs. Peering over the banisters, she strained to see down, then she took a step or two, before turning back to cross the foyer and look up towards the floor above. She mounted the first couple of steps and paused, wondering where the Odd Messenger might be. If she could encourage him to visit Nicken now it would give them a little extra time perhaps, but she did not know where he would normally be found. If she was truly worried about Nicken she would go looking in the entrance foyer, she decided, and set off down the stairs, hoping her story would hold up and that she had a suitably anxious expression.

She did not reach the foyer, but met the Odd Messenger on the first landing and began to talk.

"The child is still asleep, and I might be needed in the kitchen soon," she said. "I don't think she has a fever or anything, but surely she should not still be asleep. Perhaps it is a coma."

"I doubt it." The Odd Messenger continued past her and up the steps. "Has she woken at all? Did you give her the orange juice?"

Gelis trailed behind him as he reached the foyer and headed down the corridor towards Nicken's room.

"Yes, she had that," she answered, glad she had washed the sink carefully.

"Then it is not a coma," the Odd Messenger said firmly. "Just a healing sleep."

Gelis was still a couple of steps behind him when he reached the door. He pulled out his key and put it in the lock, turned it and waited for Gelis to come closer before opening the door and standing back to let her enter. She looked quickly at Nicken, who lay on her side, breathing evenly, the blankets pulled up to her chin. The Odd Messenger walked across and stood looking down at her. Gelis held her breath, praying Nicken would be able to maintain her pretence.

"Do you think she is alright?" she asked softly.

The Odd Messenger turned to look at her.

"Of course she is," he said. "You are worried about nothing."

He began to walk toward the exit door.

"And the kitchen will just have to do without you. You are needed here."

She followed him, pausing in the doorway.

"Are you sure?" she asked. "Madam might need me."

He looked at her sharply.

"Karl is away on leave," she added apologetically. "Madam told me."

"Nothing for you to worry about."

The Odd Messenger spoke patronisingly and headed away along the corridor without a backward glance.

Gelis watched from the doorway until she saw him turn to go down the stairs then she shut the door and went quickly back to Nicken, who still lay feigning sleep. Gelis touched her lightly.

"Well done," she said. "That was perfect."

Nicken's eyes opened. She looked bright and alert. Gelis grinned at her.

"This is what we are going to do," she said, sitting on the edge of the bed. "Are you ready?"

She explained her plan and a few minutes later they were putting it into action.

Gelis went first, looking cautiously out into the corridor then walking along to the foyer whilst Nicken waited beside the door, where she could see Gelis and respond quickly to any signal. She held the key ready in her hand, and when Gelis beckoned her forward she quickly locked the door and ran towards her. Gelis held the door of the private dining room open and together they slipped inside. They grinned at each other, sharing the excitement. Then Gelis led the way to the service area and out to the lift foyer. The lift arrived in its usual swift and obliging fashion and they got in and went down to the kitchen level. There was nowhere to hide so it seemed best to walk openly and trust to luck and the early hour. A search for some breakfast might provide some kind of justification should she need one.

At first she thought the kitchen was empty, but as she took another couple of steps forward she saw that Peter was there, preparing the trolley with cups and saucers and pots of tea and coffee, ready to take early morning drinks to the bedrooms. The thought crossed her mind that this would have been her job if she had not been sent off to mind Nicken.

A moment later Peter had seen them. He smiled.

"I thought you were not coming in this morning."

He looked from Gelis to Nicken and smiled again.

"You're a bit young for a kitchen hand aren't you?" he joked.

Nicken giggled and Gelis smiled at him.

"I'm supposed to be looking after her," she said. "We're just going out for some air, but I don't think we're supposed to, so could you forget you have seen us?"

"Seen who?" he said. "I'm talking to myself here. It passes the time and at least I get an intelligent response."

Nicken giggled again, then looked solemn.

"I have to go home," she told him. "My Mum and Dad will be worried."

"Off you go then," Peter said, looking a question at Gelis.

"Later," she said. "Thanks."

She took Nicken's hand and led her across the kitchen. As they went through the door to the scullery she looked back at Peter, who gave her a reassuring thumbs-up. She smiled briefly at him then continued on, guiding Nicken towards the outer door. Soon they were creeping up the steps, Gelis first with Nicken crouching behind. As soon as she could see into the grounds Gelis stopped and studied the view. It was almost fully light now with very little cover apart from the few trees. She crouched down to Nicken.

"We have to pretend everything is normal," she whispered. "We are just going for a walk, but if I tell you to run, run down hill as fast as you can, okay?"

Nicken nodded, her eyes enormous.

"What about you?" she whispered.

"I'll be helping," Gelis said. "Come on – very natural, not too fast."

Together they took the last few steps and walked out over the grass.

* * * *

Marheh stood poised and erect on *Day Bringer*'s back deck. Fear was there, but placed resolutely to one side so she could maintain the connection with her guest souls and focus on understanding what was happening around her. As the gates closed behind her the current that had drawn her seemed to ease and die. She throttled back then put the engine into reverse to stop the movement forward. In a few moments *Day Bringer* was no longer travelling in any direction, but drifting, nearly stationary, in the middle of the broad pond. Around her was the fleet of white boats and above them the grand, shining façade of the club building. The early morning sun cast long dark shadows in sharp contrast to the white boats and their white reflections. There was tautness, a tension in the atmosphere like something feral waiting to spring.

Alert, holding herself ready for what might follow, she watched and waited. She sensed the supporting presence of her guest souls and their fear and knew they had already experienced this place, this tension. *Day Bringer*'s engine was still pulsing gently, but without any forward movement the rudder was useless. Carefully Marheh eased the throttle into gear and turned her slightly. It would not be useful to drift into one of the white boats, but there was not a great deal of room to manoeuvre. She wondered what would happen if she reversed to the gates and tied up there. Then at least she could give her whole mind to consideration of what was before her.

The difficulty was that she had no idea what to expect and nothing seemed to be happening. Was that part of their strategy, or had her presence not yet been noticed? She imagined herself challenging them, "Here I am, come and get me!" and smiled inwardly at the melodramatic possibility. Perhaps she should move in a bit closer and see if there was a place she could moor. Perhaps that was what they were waiting for. Physically she would be more vulnerable once *Day Bringer* was suitably tied up. She put the engine into gear and crept forward.

* * * *

Tith drove the little van carefully, mindful of his passengers in the back with nothing but an old rug to sit on and needing to brace themselves each time he swung round a corner. Beside him in the front Kina sat, silent and anxious. He reached out a hand to her briefly, spared momentarily from the needs of gears and steering wheel.

It did not take long to reach the village, travelling the same route Marheh had walked a day earlier. It was very quiet. The door of the store was open but there did not appear to be any customers. It was early of course, Tith thought, heading towards the little lane by the ironmongers. Down the hill and around the corner and they were in sight of the gate. Kina drew in a deep, shuddering breath. Tith touched her hand again before climbing out to release his passengers.

263

Ved emerged from a shadowed corner of a nearby wall and gave a hand as Tep and Lorac scrambled out. A quiet greeting, a few muttered words and Tith was back in the van, driving up to the gate, hoping it would open. Behind Ved, Tep and Lorac moved quickly and quietly, planning to slip in as the van entered.

It seemed to Tith that the gates would never open. He had time to wonder about using the van as a battering ram, but in fact it was only a few moments before a gap appeared and they swung back to admit them. He revved the engine impatiently. In his side mirror he saw the other three, now standing beside and a little behind him, ready to move when he did. He revved the engine again and began to move forward. They kept pace with him and together they entered the grounds, after which he accelerated noisily away leaving the three pedestrians to slip sideways onto the grass and make for the cover of the trees.

Now Tith could let his anger show and the little van protested noisily as he forced it up the hill towards the clubhouse. Kina sat forward gazing hungrily at the high white façade as if she might see right through the walls to where she believed Nicken was held captive. The drive curved as it climbed the hill, then swung round to level out in front of the terraces leading up to the front entrance. Tith swung the van round in the wide forecourt then pulled up with a jerk.

"Best to be facing the exit," he said, pulling on the handbrake and switching off the engine.

Kina sat slumped in her corner.

"What are we doing here?" she said. "They're not going to tell us anything."

Tith took her hand.

"We are going to be angry and noisy and maybe we will find out something useful and maybe all we will do is provide distraction."

He began to climb out of the van.

"We know Gelis is looking after her."

He walked around to open the door for her, but still she sat, sunk in gloom.

"Do we?" she asked. "Do you really believe that?"

"I don't know what I believe," Tith said fiercely. "Except that they have Nicken somewhere here and I'm going to create the biggest fuss they have ever seen."

He leaned into the van to look into her face.

"Come on. We have to."

Slowly Kina swung her legs around until she could climb down, Tith helping her. She stood for a moment looking up at the brilliant façade, the climbing terraces.

"Come on." Tith's voice sounded beside her. "Be angry, don't give in to them."

Abruptly she started for the steps. Tith went after her and together they strode up towards the entrance. The four darkened glass doorways gave them back their own reflection. For a moment Kina started away from the sight of two angry figures coming towards them. Tith pushed at the doors, scarcely breaking his stride when the first failed to open. The next swung inwards and they came suddenly into the spacious foyer with its baffling shadows and pools of mellow light. The stillness and silence seemed to hold menace. There was no welcome for them here.

They stopped for a moment, suddenly confused. Then Tith gave an angry bellow. Kina thought his words were "Where are you?" but understood that words were immaterial and his cry was more the explosion of his fear and frustration. They walked forward into the space. Still no one took any notice of them. The pools of light illuminated empty chairs and meaningless images, the surrounding darkness seemed empty of life.

"Where is everyone?" Kina whispered. "Surely they must know we are here by now?"

"They will know in a minute." Tith spoke a little louder than his normal voice as if to combat the silence. Then he made for the foot of the stairs.

"Nicken," he called at the top of his voice. "Nicken, where are you?"

Kina hurried after him and they had just begun to climb when the Odd Messenger appeared on the first landing and the Slick Receptionist materialised behind them. The Odd Messenger said nothing and made no move towards them, but they stopped involuntarily, looking up at him. Tith knew he wanted to climb higher, to stand on a level with the figure above him, to interrogate him with all the energy and anger he contained so precariously, but he could not move his foot to the next step, try as he would.

The cold, clear voice of the Slick Receptionist asked politely if she could help them. Together they turned to her. Kina put a restraining hand on Tith's arm.

"We are looking for our young daughter," she said. "We heard she was

265

here."

The Slick Receptionist assumed a sympathetic mask.

"A child?" she asked.

Kina nodded.

"Our child. She's missing."

"I'm sorry." The words were appropriate, the tone just slightly out of tune. "There are no children here."

"How do you know? You haven't looked." Tith turned back to the stairs. "I want to look for her."

He put his hand to the banisters and tried again to move upwards.

"I assure you sir, there are no children here." The Slick Receptionist continued, cold and sweet. "This is a conference centre and an association for adults."

Tith did not even look at her, he was still struggling against whatever held him on the bottom step. Gripping the banister with all his strength he hauled himself forward, but though his body leaned in until he was almost kneeling on a step above, his feet would not leave the floor. Kina looked at him in alarm.

"What are you doing? She isn't here."

Tith shook her off angrily, still fighting the stairs.

"Yes she is, I know she is."

He called her name again and again. Kina tried to apologise for him, begged him to be quiet, to leave with her. The Slick Receptionist and the Odd Messenger stood cold and silent watching his struggles. At last he slumped against the banister and allowed Kina to take his hand. She led him back past the Slick Receptionist, between the pools of light towards the dark doorways.

The Slick Receptionist followed several paces behind them. The Odd Messenger descended from his vantage point to hover at the foot of the stairs, but Tith and Kina were unaware of this. They were aware only of defeat. Tith, in particular knew there had been a struggle which he had lost, though he was unclear as to the nature of it. Kina hardly realised that she had been disarmed before her fight began. Once through the door they stood on the top terrace looking out. Tith half turned to go back and renew the struggle now that the force that had thrust him down seemed to have released its grasp. Kina took his arm, shaking her head.

266

"It's no good," she said. "Maybe she isn't here after all."

"She is here," Tith said. "But they are too strong for us."

He gazed out to where he guessed the water road might be.

"We can keep them occupied though, so Marheh has less to deal with."

* * * *

Gelis and Nicken began their walk to the gates. Had they left five minutes earlier they might have encountered the pottery van with its hidden passengers, but as it was they saw no one and reached the gates unchallenged. The gates swung open as they always did when Gelis left work each day and together they stepped out onto the streets of Deerford. Gelis gave a sigh of relief. That was the worst part over. Nicken gave a jump and punched the air.

"Yes!" she cried. "Can't catch me!"

Gelis grabbed her hand.

"We're not safe yet," she told her, moving away from the gates and stepping out briskly. Nicken skipped along beside her.

"Are we going home? Mum and Dad will be worried."

Gelis did not reply immediately. She felt she needed to return to her job and she did not want to be away too long. Neither did she want to let Nicken go alone.

"Beytha," she said, pleased to have found a solution. "I'm taking you to Beytha. You will be safe there."

A couple of minutes later they were standing in Beytha's small sitting room while Gelis explained rapidly.

"Of course I will look after Nicken," she said, smiling at her. "I expect you would like some breakfast too."

Nicken nodded.

"And then can I go home?"

"We need to make sure it is safe first," Gelis said seriously. "I have to go back there before they find you gone."

"But I want Mummy and Daddy."

It was the first sign of a release of tension and she seemed surprised at the tears that accompanied her words. Gelis gave her a hug.

"Of course you do, but you'll be safe with Beytha and they will come and get you as soon as they can." She held her at arm's length and looked her in the eye. "Okay?"

Nicken nodded.

"Good. I'll see you soon."

Releasing her, she said goodbye to Beytha and let herself out into the street again.

Going back was risky, she knew. If they had discovered Nicken's escape she would be in danger of retribution. As she hurried along she tried to work out how she would respond to any accusation and decided that righteous indignation would be her best approach.

If Nicken had woken and explained she was a prisoner that would have been her reaction. "You lied to me!" she heard herself saying. No one liked being lied to. She guessed it had taken about half an hour to get Nicken to safety, perhaps it would be as long as an hour by the time she got back to the room on the first floor and discovered Nicken's departure. She could hardly expect to be unobserved as long as that, although the Odd Messenger had left them alone for longer periods overnight. At the gates she hesitated, tired, fearful, half wishing she could retreat to the comparative safety of her room at Evelyn's house, but the gates opened at her approach and she entered as she knew she must and began the long trudge up the hill.

* * * *

In the grounds, Ved, Tep and Lorac were trying to find the hidden door in the hillside. Ved had a general idea of the direction as Gelis had pointed it out the evening he met her, but now in the daylight it all looked different and they were hampered by the need for caution. Communication was difficult. They could hardly shout, so they needed to be in sight of each other, but neither could they stand out in the open making signals. Progress was slow and frustrating, indeed it seemed non existent, as they felt they had no more idea of the location than they had when the search started.

"But we do," Ved said, as they crouched together taking stock, out of sight of the club house. "We know where it isn't."

"Do we?" Lorac asked. "Maybe it is like the water road and you need a different kind of sight."

"Gelis didn't say that," Ved protested.

"She wouldn't know."

There was a dispirited silence.

"Perhaps I should go up to the kitchen and call for Gelis," Ved suggested. "They know I do that."

He and Lorac looked at Tep for guidance.

"It can't hurt," he said at last. "Even if they still want her to work you might be able to talk to her."

Ved nodded.

"You stay here," he said, setting off for the road. "I'll be as quick as I can."

His timing was impeccable. He met Gelis as she walked up the drive way. Happily she went with him to meet the others, sat with them on the hillside and exchanged news and realised she could abandon all idea of returning to her job. This was where she was needed now.

"I can't help feeling someone will challenge us for trespassing," Lorac said. "This is the strangest place. I feel as if I am doing something wrong just by being here."

Gelis nodded.

"I felt that too, the first time when I came to ask for a job, but I've been thinking about it," she paused and scrambled to her feet. "And I think that is what they want you to feel."

"You mean they actually create a hostile atmosphere?"

Tep stood up too and held out his hand to Lorac.

"It sounds weird, I know." Gelis was apologetic. "But it means they keep casual callers out without much effort."

"I suppose so." Ved sounded sceptical. "What ever it is I certainly felt like an intruder the times I've called for you."

Where they stood, below the brow of the hill, only the top floor of the Club House was visible, but as soon as they begin to climb higher, towards the door they were looking for, they would be more exposed to the a casual observer. There was not much cover, certainly nothing that would hide a group of them. Gelis studied the ground around, trying to work out exactly where she should lead them.

"Best to go in twos," she said, thinking aloud. "We need to be casual, not hurry. Keep out of sight if we can."

Tep nodded.

"What if I came with you and the other two follow?"

"We won't move until you signal," Ved said.

Gelis looked from one to the other, seeking reassurance. Tep reached out to touch her.

"Let's go," he said.

She smiled at him briefly and together they set out across the turf.

* * * *

Marheh edged her way through the flotilla of white boats. They all looked the same, high and proud, with sleek lines, very different to the sturdy simplicity of *Day Bringer*'s long, low shape. None had names that she could see, just a neat blue number painted on the cabin sides. Most had curtains drawn over their windows but she saw into one smart white galley and caught a glimpse of puffy white cushions in another. There was only just room for *Day Bringer* to squeeze between and Marheh needed all her skill to keep on course. The white façade of the clubhouse was closer now and seemed to tower over her. Then she caught a glimpse of colour and saw the pottery van struggling up the hill and felt warmed by the knowledge that she was not alone.

There seemed to be no space to moor and no alternative but to reverse out of the narrow channel. Marheh began to wonder about what she was doing. This did not seem like the route to rescuing Nicken or the imprisoned Silberay, only the frustration of inaction and the patience and attention needed to keep *Day Bringer* on her slow course. She looked back, preparing to reverse, but where there had been a narrow channel, now there was none. "So they had noticed her presence," she thought, almost pleased to have obtained a reaction. *Day Bringer* was barely moving, but now there was no possibility of stopping. Ahead a deep shadow was cast by the drive as it spanned the narrow channel and beyond she could see only darkness. "This," she thought and the fear broke free for a moment as the shadow covered *Day Bringer*'s prow and she was carried towards it.

"Only a bridge," she told herself, striving for the commonplace, but there was no light on the other side and she could barely see half a boat length, then a quarter, then nothing as she was engulfed. Automatically she reached for the tunnel light, switched it on, but its narrow beam illuminated little but the cabin top and seemed to be swallowed by the thick darkness that surrounded her. Behind her, she heard a loud creak and swung around to see the square of light that had been her route disappearing rapidly.

This was the place Gelis had spoken of, she realised, full of grey Silberay boats. Abruptly she cut the engine and switched off the tunnel light. Better to be able to hear, and for her eyes to grow accustomed to the darkness.

The sudden silence aroused the fear again for a moment until she heard the water still gently lapping around *Day Bringer* and the sound of her own breathing. She sensed *Day Bringer* was still moving slowly forward, but Silberay boats, if that was what was here, would forgive a gentle bump, and she waited for it, hoping to be able to tie alongside and perhaps even scramble across the raft of boats to reach the edge. The possibility of action sharpened her senses, her focus, and then the battering began.

The first blow, though not to her physical being, almost knocked her off the boat as she reeled from its power. She clung to the cabin top and tried to build a shield. Occasionally she managed to deflect a blow and in the moment of respite to spin her own power around herself, but the attack seemed endless and the attackers beyond number. Her physical self shook with the strength of the battle within. In a moment of detachment she knew that she would gain a measure of protection if she could get inside *Day Bringer*. This was her aim when she could manage coherent thought.

Keep the shield, move the foot, suffer the blow, move the hand, the shield, the foot, the blow, the shield, the foot, the pain and then the thread of song as her guest souls responded to her anguish.

This was how it happened, she saw, stumbling into the back cabin as the song beckoned. With no help and no warning of danger the soul fled from the pain and was lost. Her pain eased and the song swelled into warmth and harmony, but she knew this moment of respite would not last. She reached Gelis' bed and fell onto it. Now her physical self was taken care of and she could give herself entirely to the struggle. It was the song that was the key, she must weave the harmonies and endure.

* * * *

In the grounds, Gelis and Tep moved purposefully from tree to tree, the others following at their signal. As the shrubbery became denser and the hill rose more steeply before them, Gelis knew they were approaching their goal. Here they were less exposed, hidden from secret eyes watching from the clubhouse. They came closer together until at last Gelis stopped and beckoned Ved and Lorac to join them. How different the place looked in the morning light, a simple door, a bit over grown, a bit neglected, just a seldom used garden store.

"Here," she said. "This is where they came that night." She reached out to the door handle. "It was locked, and it is now."

The others gathered around. Ved tried the door.

"It doesn't look like much," he said. "You couldn't keep people shut up in here."

"This is where they came with the saucepans," Gelis said. "I'm quite sure. I think maybe it is bigger than it looks."

Tep was prowling round trying to see through the jungle of foliage.

"You thought it might go back into the hillside didn't you?" he asked. "I think you're right. Certainly I can't see any way to get behind it."

"So what do we do?" Lorac asked. "Can we break the lock? The door doesn't look very strong."

Ved leaned his shoulder into the door and pushed.

"Strong enough," he said, standing back again.

Tep was studying what he could see of the structure around the door. He lifted up a trailing curtain of shrubbery and poked at the cladding beneath.

"It wouldn't take much to get a bit of this timber off under here. It's half rotten with all the stuff growing over it."

They looked at each other.

"It seems a bit destructive," Lorac said, sounding apologetic.

Tep grinned suddenly

"If we find nothing but gardening tools in here, I'll personally come back and repair the hole."

Gelis gave a little laugh then fell silent. They looked at the place Tep indicated. Ved knelt down to examine the place, pushed at the timber and looked back at Tep.

"I think so," he said. "Once we get the first bit off it will be easy."

Gelis held back the shrubbery, Lorac kept watch and the two men attacked the shed. It seemed as if they could not get any leverage to make the first break, but Tep had his bunch of keys in his pocket and the big old key for the workshop made a useful tool once he remembered them. Soon they had a hand hole and after that it was easy. The rotting wood broke as they tugged and a dark space appeared.

"I could get through there," Gelis said, as they leaned back to examine their handiwork.

"But I couldn't," Tep replied, turning to look at her.

"I thought perhaps the door could be opened from the inside," she said.

"If the door is bolted inside, there must be someone in there to have done it," Tep said. "Best we all go this way."

It did not take much longer and there was a hole big enough for the largest of them. Tep sat back on his heels.

"Once we let the shrubbery down it won't be very obvious – especially if they only come here in the dark."

He poked his head through the hole then drew it out again.

"It's pretty dark in there. I can't see much. Might as well get going."

Soon his head and shoulders were out of sight and the rest of him was flat on the ground, wriggling forward. There were a few grunts and a sigh as he disappeared from view, then it was Gelis' turn. Being smaller than the men, she and Lorac scrambled through without much difficulty. Ved had a little more trouble as he had no one to hold back the shrubbery for him, however it was not long before they all stood together in the small, shadowy space.

At first glance it seemed as if their exertions had been for nothing. The interior housed an old post, a wheelbarrow with a flat tire and a broken handle and a variety of other old and broken bits and pieces of doubtful use. It was very dirty and cobwebby, which discouraged exploration, and too dark to see much. However, they persisted and it was Ved who discovered, behind the wheelbarrow and a couple of old planks, another door opposite the first. This door was a much more serious affair than the last. Dark and impervious, it seemed to be made of some kind of metal. It looked new and solid, but the bolts, heavy and ominous, were thrust home on their side. Solemnly they gathered beside Ved and studied it thoughtfully.

"We should open it," Gelis said softly. "There are prisoners, I'm sure."

She reached for the top bolt, but Tep stopped her.

"We don't know what is behind there. We need to go carefully." He leaned against the door. "You and Lorac move the bolts – very slowly and quietly. Ved and I will keep the door closed in case."

The bolts moved easily as if they were well oiled and in regular use. In a moment they were drawn and the door ready to open, but still Tep leaned against it.

"Move away," he said. "Separate. We don't know what is behind here."

Quietly they spread to the corners of the little space and slowly and carefully Tep opened the door. Behind was a dark tunnel, apparently cut into the hillside. Gelis drew in a quick breath and moved towards it. Tep blocked her way.

"Someone needs to stay here," he said. "We can't risk all being locked inside."

"I have to go in," Gelis said, as if there could be no argument.

Tep nodded then looked at Ved and Lorac.

"You two stay. I will go in with Gelis."

Together they stepped through into the tunnel and began to walk carefully forward towards the darkness.

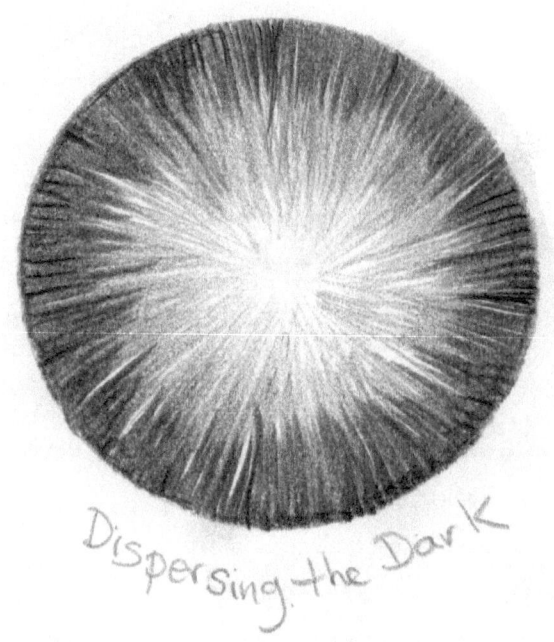

Dispersing the Dark

CHAPTER NINETEEN

Tith and Kina remained for some minutes staring out over the valley below the club house. They were not high enough to see where Gelis and the others moved around the grounds on their way to finding the door in the hill, nor could they see the water road and the white fleet of Yareblis' boats that lay before them, although a gleam of rather scummy water that had been the village pond caught their eye and suggested the possibility of that other dimension. Neither wanted to leave the place where they believed Nicken to be held, but they were not sure of how to proceed.

"There must be another way in," Kina said at last. "I'm sure Ved said something about meeting Gelis at the kitchen door."

Tith nodded.

"We'll go quietly this time, see if we can get under their guard."

Kina clung to his arm.

"We will find her, won't we?"

"Gelis is looking after her, I'm sure of that and if she's here we'll find her."

Tith sounded more confident than he felt.

"Come on, we'll walk all the way round the building and look for another entrance," he added.

Together they made their way back down the steps to the road then followed the high, blank wall that rose beside them. Stopping to gaze upward they could see windows perhaps twenty feet above, but there was no entrance visible anywhere along this face. Walking as close to the wall as they could, heedless of the small shrubs and bits of garden that were attempting to grow in the shadowed ground, they soon came to the next corner. The long wall ahead of them seemed at first glance to be as blank and uninviting as the one they had just left, but as they looked more closely and began to move along it they saw the steps dug into the hillside.

Kina clutched Tith's arm.

"There!" she whispered excitedly. "Look!"

Tith nodded and covered her hand with his.

"Looks promising," he said. "Come on."

They hurried towards the steps, crept down them and pushed cautiously at the door. It swung silently inwards to reveal the scullery with its big sink and store of vases and the hooks for outdoor clothes. A zippered fleecy jacket hung there above a pair of scruffy trainers. Quietly they looked around, observed the two doors, one straight ahead, one to their right.

"One of them must be the kitchen," Kina said.

"My guess is the one straight ahead," Tith said and went towards it.

Like the entrance door, it was not locked and opened smoothly as Tith pushed it. A moment later they were gazing around the vast, white, empty kitchen. Rather tentatively they stepped inside. There was steam issuing from a kettle and a smell of coffee brewing, but no other indication of occupation.

"This is absurd."

Tith spoke forcefully, pushing away his apprehension. Kina held his arm tightly and said nothing. For a moment they stood, trying to take it in, to see where they might go in order to push further into the clubhouse. Then they heard footsteps and the rattle of crockery.

"Hello."

Peter was pushing a trolley full of dirty cups. He had completed his morning tea delivery and was about to stack the dishwasher.

"Can I help you?" he asked them.

He began to unload his trolley.

"Are you here to see Madam?"

Kina went towards him.

"Let me help," she said, gathering up tea spoons.

"I don't know where she is," he said, passing the cutlery container. "Everyone is behaving even more strangely than usual this morning."

"You're not one of them," Tith said slowly. "You're from the village."

Peter nodded.

"That's right. I work here sometimes when they are busy."

He accepted a pile of saucers from Kina and stacked them neatly into the dishwasher.

"Were you looking for a job?"

"No," Kina said. "For our daughter."

Peter stopped his work and looked at her.

"Little dark girl?" he asked. "About so high?"

Kina caught her breath. Tith leapt forward and grabbed him by the arm.

"Where is she?"

"Steady on!"

Peter pulled from his grasp.

"Please," Kina said. "You've seen her. Is she alright?"

Peter looked from one to the other.

"What's going on?" he said slowly, then again. "What's going on?"

They both opened their mouths to tell him when suddenly the sound of a siren wailed through the building drowning their voices with its clamour.

* * * *

Lorac and Ved heard the siren as they stood together in the dirty little hut keeping guard. Gelis and Tep heard it too, but its high panicked call was muffled where they stood beside yet another door in the hill. The short

277

tunnel, though rather dark, had not been difficult. Whoever had built it had laid an even path, faintly illuminated by softly glowing blocks of some translucent material inset at intervals along the edges. As far as they could tell, the walls and arched ceiling were smooth and impervious although slightly damp with condensation in places. Although not very long, there was a smooth curve that soon hid the end where they had entered.

This third door was much the same as the second, bolted top and bottom on their side. Gelis looked at Tep and reached out to unfasten the top bolt. Tep bent to the lower one then stood ready as Gelis pushed the door. It swung smoothly inwards to reveal a broad cavern. Like the tunnel, this was dimly lit and so still that at first they thought it was empty. Part of it had been a natural cave and stalactites hung in long festoons from sections above while strange twisted pillars grew from the floor and palely gleaming shapes lay over rocks or formed clumps in corners. They stood and gazed, trying to make sense of the scene before them. Gelis took a step forward, then another, then froze.

Some of these shapes had eyes and although they were so still, she recognised the gentle rise and fall of their breathing. Then she saw that some were dressed in the traditional Silberay uniform that Marheh wore and realised the magnitude of their discovery.

What had been done to them to make them immobile? What could she do for them? She looked at Tep and saw that he too, had recognised the prisoners. More than that, it seemed that he had recognised one particular prisoner. He crossed to a man, seated on a rock, quite close to where they stood and touched his arm.

"Kel," he said quietly. "Kel."

At first there was no response, but then signs of struggle appeared. His eyes moved, his face twisted and at last he spoke in a voice rusty with disuse.

"What did you call me?"

"You're Kel," Tep said gently. "Marheh's friend. I'm her brother Tep. You remember me."

"Marheh," the man said and her name seemed to help his struggle.

He sat straighter, attempted to stand then turned his head towards a younger man sitting on the ground at his feet.

"Loc," he said. "My apprentice. I failed him."

Gelis had edged closer during this exchange. She shook her head.

"I'm sure you didn't," she said. "How can we help?"

"You gave me a name," the man said to Tep. "But it doesn't belong to me."

"Yes it does," Tep said. "It's your name, your soul name."

"My soul is somewhere else."

Again he attempted to stand and this time he succeeded.

"Loc," he said and touched the younger man's shoulder.

This prompted the same kind of struggle they had awakened in Kel and before long he too was standing, looking around rather blankly at his prison and his fellow prisoners.

"Controlled, all controlled."

Kel's words were a lament.

"Saying your name seemed to waken you," Gelis said. "Perhaps that would waken the others."

They tried. Kel and Loc identified people, Gelis and Tep moved to touch them and speak the name, but without success. Kel and Loc were becoming increasingly agitated as if something was drawing them away and only a habit of polite thoughtfulness was keeping them from leaving.

"I think we need Marheh," Gelis said. "She will know what to do."

"Marheh is here?" Kel asked.

"She was on her way here in *Day Bringer* to try to engage the enemy," Tep said.

Gelis looked at him, surprised by this news.

"She will let herself be taken?"

Tep nodded.

"She said it was the only way."

Kel and Loc were already moving towards the door of their prison. Gelis and Tep hurried after them, wondering a little. What was calling them? Was it something positive or would they lose themselves again?

A brief exchange with Lorac and Ved was enough to encourage them to remain keeping watch although they both would have liked to follow the others.

Even that short conversation was long enough to allow Kel and Loc to get quite a way ahead. Gelis and Tep ran after them as they hurried towards the road. By the time they reached Kel, Loc had left him to scramble down the bank to where the channel of water went under it. The blaring siren was still raising its panic stricken cry and the noise was deafening.

"You can't go that way," Gelis shouted, wondering what he was trying to do.

The young man looked back at her then returned to his exploration. Gelis turned to Kel.

"He has to come back. What does he want?"

Kel made no answer, but Gelis remembered the boats beneath the kitchen.

"I'll take you," she called. "Come with me. I know the way."

She waited for the young man to take in her words then held out her hand to help him up the steep bank.

"This way," she said, keeping hold of him until she knew he was following.

She led them around the corner to the back steps and in through the scullery to the kitchen. The siren seemed even louder echoing in the empty room. There was clearly no point in trying to be quiet and invisible so she hurried across to the lift and pressed the call button. It was coming down from above and took a moment to arrive. Kel and Loc seemed hardly able to endure the short delay but Tep's quiet assurance was steadying. Then the door slid open to reveal Peter with Tith and Kina.

Kel and Loc were first in, even before the others had time to register surprise.

"Nicken," Kina demanded urgently.

"Safe with Beytha," Gelis said.

It was all they had time for before the lift door opened again and its passengers stepped out into the underground boathouse.

* * * *

Marheh knew none of this. All that she was, all the learning of her disciplined, solitary life, the very essence of herself, was engaged with the enemy. Her skill with the discipline of the mind, so carefully honed, struggled to keep the invading minds at bay. On other occasions she had learned she could fight illusion with illusion, but there was no illusion now, instead agony and darkness as many minds fought to break her. Somehow she held on, enduring the pain, pushing beyond it to sing with her guest souls. Only the music had the power to free those other souls imprisoned, only the music could spin light and warmth in the dark places, only the music could hold her outside the battering of the enemy.

Once out of the lift, Gelis and Tep, Tith, Kina and Peter stood to stare at the scene before them. The space was not dark as it had been when Gelis first saw it but dimly lit with an ugly greenish glow. All along the edge of the wharf stood the still, concentrating figures of the Yareblis. Gelis recognised Madam, the Slick Receptionist and the Odd Messenger, Tep saw the Club Treasurer, but there were others, focusing so intently on something on the water that they seemed unaware of the new arrivals.

Silberay boats, over-painted with a dull grey, lined the edges, about twenty of them, two or three deep in places, but in the centre, her colours still glowing, her brass bright, was *Day Bringer*, quietly floating. She seemed to exist in a different light, a clear soft sunshine, like a spring morning. Gelis felt a pang of longing when she saw her. Then she realised that Kel and Loc had not stopped to stare with the rest of them, but were scrambling over the moored boats, heading for *Day Bringer*. Impulsively she followed them. Marheh would be on board. She might need her.

Tep could see the boats and how the members of YRTHA seemed to be drilling into *Day Bringer* with the power of their combined concentration, but for the others it was all confusion. They saw Gelis disappear after the two Silberay. They saw the standing figures of the Yareblis. Sometimes, from the side of his vision, Tith would catch the gleam of water or the shape of Gelis moving. Kina caught a glimpse of *Day Bringer* as if she were painted on glass. Peter, however, saw nothing but the gloomy basement and the still, concentrating figures of his employers.

Catching sight of Madam, he began to make his way towards her.

"What's going on?" he asked loudly when he reached her.

She took no notice of him, seemed not even to know he was there, so he moved to stand in the line of her gaze.

"Are you alright?" he asked, placing one hand on her arm.

A tremor ran through her and she blinked.

At that moment, on *Day Bringer*, Marheh felt the cold ease a little, felt her song spread out and the harmonies grow. A thread of hope began to wind itself into the music. If only she could bear her guest souls until they found the key to open the prison of souls. The thread that linked her voyaging soul to mind and body was very thin now, but her guest souls moved lightly and though their presence strained the link their song strengthened hers.

In the boathouse Tep saw that Peter's action had disconcerted the members of YRTHA and realised that the light surrounding *Day Bringer* had spread outwards. He made his way to the Club Treasurer and tried to break his concentration and for a moment succeeded. The light around *Day Bringer* pulsed outward again, then the Club Treasurer hit out at Tep catching him unexpectedly on the side of the head. He fell to his knees, clutching at the Club Treasurer as he went. Tith was with him in a moment, ready to defend him. This was something he could see and understand.

Gelis and the two Silberay had reached the edge of the boat closest to *Day Bringer*. There was still a fair gap over the water however and the light had not quite reached them. The younger of the two Silberay supported the older as he stretched, far off balance, over the water. As the tip of his fingers entered the field of light surrounding *Day Bringer* it was as if some magnetic force drew them together. *Day Bringer* rocked a little in the still water, the older Silberay touched her, drew her in close enough to put a foot on the gunnel. The younger Silberay made a leap and they were aboard. Gelis reached out to them. This was her boat, they couldn't leave her behind.

The older man was already half way through the cabin door, but the younger seemed to recognise Gelis' right to join them. He hesitated, stretched out his hand. She made a great, trusting leap out to him and found herself clinging like a monkey to *Day Bringer*'s side. The young Silberay was already following his companion into the back cabin. Gelis scrabbled with her feet until she was balanced on the gunnel then went in after them.

What she saw as she entered was something she knew she would never forget. Marheh lay still on her bed. The older Silberay had reached across her to take the hand that rested next to the wall, the younger had taken her other hand and was about to complete the triangle by joining hands with his companion. As he did so a cry escaped Marheh and her body twitched once and again was still. The two Silberay seemed to go into themselves and Gelis knew they were with Marheh. Quietly she sat down on the back step and tried to give them her own song as she had practiced.

Marheh felt the flare of anguish as her guest souls left her and for a moment the song faltered. The thread spun between body and soul stretched almost to breaking point, but then the music began again, stronger than before, as the souls of the two Silberay sped to support her. Now there was a surge of power, the music poured into the darkness, triumphant and joyous. Only moments passed before they were pushing against the impervious darkness that imprisoned the other Silberay souls, but now their song was full and rich enough to spread over the surface and enclose the dark place. When it was wrapped in light and music the darkness began to crumble. From within, a hint of dolorous sound reached, touched, and began to harmonise, drawing in ever more voices until the darkness was completely dispelled.

That was the moment when Lorac and Ved, waiting anxiously in the entrance to the tunnel, heard a murmur of sound from the place beyond. They looked at each other uncertainly. Ved put an arm around Lorac as the sound grew, but it did not feel threatening. Rather, there was a sense of purpose and soon, a rustling, as of quiet movement.

Not long after a couple of figures appeared in the tunnel, then a couple more. They moved stiffly and looked dazed and uncertain. Lorac recognised that one wore Silberay uniform. She smiled at him tentatively and he stopped to greet her.

"You are not our gaoler," he said.

She shook her head.

More figures emerged from the tunnel and gathered around them. All had the same look as if they were just waking from sleep.

"We should go," Ved said. "Better to be away from here."

"But we need to be sure there is no one left behind," Lorac said.

"We are the last."

Two women, the younger supporting the older, stood at the back of the group. It was the older who had spoken, her voice rusty with disuse.

"This way then," Ved said, pushing his way through the hole they had made in the shed and holding back the shrubbery for the others.

One by one they stepped out into the sunlight and set off towards the road and the clubhouse as if drawn, Ved and Lorac following.

* * * *

Marheh continued to sing although the harmony began to dissolve as, one by one, the other souls found their proper dwelling and withdrew. At last she was dancing in the light with only those two souls who had been her guests. Then they too withdrew and she began the journey back into herself.

Gelis, earnestly offering her fledgling song to Marheh, heard a moment of melody as her gift was recognised then eased back to awareness to see Marheh stretch, open her eyes and smile at her and the other two Silberay.

She looked drained and exhausted once the brief smile left her.

Kel drew her into his arms and Gelis heard her speak his name, but she looked away from them then, not wanting to intrude on this reunion.

The young man, Loc, smiled at her and gestured towards the back deck. Together they climbed the steps and went to stand looking out over the grey boats to the wharf where Tep and the others stood alone now. There was no sign of the Yareblis.

"Have they gone?" Gelis wondered aloud.

"Just for the moment," Loc said. "They'll be back unless we disable them."

Gelis was about to ask what he meant when Kel arrived beside them.

"We'll let Marheh sleep for a bit," he said. "Let's see if we can find the way out of here."

He looked at Gelis.

"Will you allow me to take over?"

He looked tired too, but kind and reliable. Gelis nodded. She knew her skills were not developed enough to manoeuvre in this confined space.

"What about them?" she asked, looking towards the wharf.

There were just the four of them. She thought Kina was urging them to leave and of course she would want to reassure herself that Nicken was safe and well. Tep reached out to her then pointed towards *Day Bringer*.

"We'll take them on board," Kel said. "There's room enough."

He reached for the ignition and a moment later *Day Bringer* came to life. Loc seemed to know what he was thinking and scrambled along the gunnel, pushing aside the other boats. Gelis tried to copy him on the opposite side and it was only a minute or two before *Day Bringer*'s prow was nudging the wharf and she could step off.

Tep, Tith and Kina had all experienced the step into the water dimension and it was easy for Loc to guide them. It was different for Peter, but Gelis persuaded him to trust her, and with Loc prompting, she talked him through the blind step that would bring him on board.

When he was safely in the saloon with the others she turned to grin at him.

"That was the first time I've done that, and here you are!"

"I can't quite believe it," he said, looking around.

Day Bringer was already moving back from the wharf and Loc was outside again fending off. They needed to leave, if they could find the trigger to open the way.

* * * *

Outside, Lorac and Ved had followed the Silberay across the grass and watched, puzzled, as they seemed to be looking for something under the road. They were obviously gaining in strength and confidence, especially the younger ones. A couple of the older ones just stood soaking up the sunshine. The old woman who had been the last to leave seemed to be remonstrating with her younger companion.

"Don't be silly Beuda. I'm perfectly capable of standing here by myself while you go and look with the others."

"But Bixa…"

"Excuse me," Lorac interrupted. "But what are you looking for? Can I help?"

The two women spoke at once then stopped and looked at each other fondly.

"You've helped already," the older woman said. "But you're not Silberay, are you? How did you find us?"

"It was Gelis really," Lorac said. "Marheh's apprentice, she…"

"Marheh's apprentice!"

The older woman's face lit up.

"It was Marheh's song, of course it was. Where is she?"

"She's here somewhere," Lorac said. "She was going to let herself be taken, but I don't see the water so I don't know where."

Bixa reached out to touch Lorac, responding to the wistful note in her voice. She might have spoken, but at that moment *Day Bringer*'s prow appeared in the tunnel under the road and there was a great cheer from the Silberay.

"What is it?" Ved demanded, taking Lorac's hand.

"It's *Day Bringer*," Bixa said softly.

The other Silberay had moved together towards something neither Ved nor Lorac could see, but Bixa remained with them.

"There is a channel of water passing under the road," she said. "It seems to lead beneath the building. Marheh's boat is just emerging. There are

285

people standing in the well deck. One of them is Loc, Kel's apprentice, but I don't know the others."

Lorac sighed.

"I wish I could see."

Ved put his arm around her.

"You see enough for me."

"*Day Bringer* is out in the sun now, but it isn't Marheh at the tiller." Her voice held a touch of anxiety. "It's Kel."

She paused for a moment then continued.

"You can see where the Silberay are moving now. They are following beside *Day Bringer* going towards a pond, an empty harbour really, with jetties. Now Kel is preparing to moor. A girl with brown curls is gathering up the front line."

"That must be Gelis," Lorac said. Then, a moment later, "It is!"

She called out to her and Gelis looked up and waved before continuing with her task. The Silberay were crowding around *Day Bringer* now and for a few moments Gelis was lost to view, then she pushed through the crowd and hurried up to where Lorac and Ved and their companions stood watching.

"They've all woken up," she said happily. "And the Yareblis' boats have all gone. I think Marheh did it."

"I expect she did," Bixa said. "But not without help."

She smiled at Gelis.

"Are you perhaps Marheh's apprentice?"

Gelis smiled and nodded, studying the woman who stood with them. She was obviously very old, but she stood tall in her Silberay uniform and her eyes were bright and interested.

"My name is Gelis," she said.

Down by the jetty Silberay were disappearing onto *Day Bringer*. Tep, Tith, Kina and Peter had alighted and were coming towards them. Tep nodded politely to Bixa but spoke to Lorac and Ved.

"Tith and Kina are anxious to go to Nicken," Tep said. "Do you want to go with them?"

They looked at each other then Lorac shook her head.

"We'd rather stay. We want to know what is happening."

"Kel and his apprentice are taking as many as they can, back in to look for their boats," Tep said.

"Is Marheh alright?" Bixa asked.

Tep nodded.

"Kel seems to think so. She's just sleeping."

He smiled at Bixa.

"You've all had quite an ordeal."

"Which has ended thanks to you and your friends. We're very grateful."

She paused a moment then continued.

"You obviously know the Silberay and Marheh…"

It was not quite a question, but Tep was happy to explain.

"I'm Marheh's brother," he said. "We're her family."

Introductions followed before Tith and Kina hurried away.

Day Bringer returned without her passengers. Marheh was at the tiller. Gelis spun around ready to start down to help her moor, but there were other Silberay already there.

Was Marheh really alright? There had been pain and struggle in what she had been doing.

She moved from foot to foot indecisively then saw Marheh look up, over the heads of her helpers and felt rather than saw the smile that thanked her for her concern.

"Wait," Bixa said gently. "She's coming up to us."

And then she was there, weary but seemingly at peace.

Hugs were given and received, Tep and Bixa, Lorac and Ved and last, but longest, Gelis.

"My apprentice," Marheh said affectionately. She held her at arm's length, studying her and smiling. "A fine representative of the Silberay."

ABOUT THE AUTHOR

Rosalind, like many Australians, loves to travel. She fell in love with the canals of England during her first visit there and this has remained a life-long passion. She spent nearly three years living and traveling aboard a 37ft narrowboat and this experience has informed her writing so that although the stories are fantasy the boating experience is authentic.

When not writing she enjoys walking her dog, practicing her violin, painting watercolours, choral singing, reading and of course traveling.

Marheh can be contacted at Marheh@gmail.com

Or keep up to date with Rosalind's writing at https://rosalindkentwell.net/

www.ingramcontent.com/pod-product-compliance
Lightning Source LLC
Chambersburg PA
CBHW031255170626
46807CB00001B/158